Certain Justice

A Marc Kadella Legal Mystery

by

Dennis L. Carstens

Marc Kadella Legal Mysteries Also Available on Amazon

The Key to Justice

Desperate Justice

Media Justice

Personal Justice

Delayed Justice

Political Justice

Insider Justice

Exquisite Justice

Copyright © 2015 by Dennis L Carstens

Email me at: dcarstens514@gmail.com

"Those who abjure violence can only do so by others committing violence on their behalf."
George Orwell

ONE

Thirteen Years Ago

The two men sat silently staring through the windshield of the dark blue Chevy sedan. The passenger, whom the driver called Big, had his window open an inch while he smoked. Big was flicking the ashes out the window and staining the outside of it with gray, wet, cigarette ash. It was a cold, rainy, windy, miserable night, especially for mid-September. While Big stared silently into the night, the driver whom Big referred to as Little, fidgeted anxiously in his seat and occasionally coughed lightly due to his partner's smoking. Even though Little was a smoker himself, in the enclosed space of the car's interior the smoke annoyed him.

Big crushed out his cigarette in the car's ash tray, careful not to toss it out the window and possibly leave DNA evidence for the cops. When he did this, Little broke the silence by saying, "Roll your damn window down and let some air in."

Without turning his head, Big replied, "Roll yours down. It's raining out there."

A gust of wind came across Lake of the Isles shaking the oak tree they were under on Parker Street. The sudden burst of wind shook the big tree causing a small torrent of rain water to splatter down on the car. A second, less powerful wind burst broke off a tiny, leafy branch from the tree that landed on the windshield directly in front of Little. The sudden appearance of the oak leaves and the noise it made caused Little to jump in his seat, bring his hand to his heart and say, "Jesus Christ!" Big, who rarely smiled and almost never laughed, cracked a brief grin at his partner's discomfort.

"Time?" Big asked.

Little checked the digital read on his watch and said, "At least five more minutes."

Big's real name was Howie Traynor. At twenty-seven he was already a career criminal and no stranger to jail cells. He was a first-rate burglar because his nerves were almost non-existent. Nothing ever seemed to faze him.

At a very early age his parents began to notice that Howie was a little off. He seemed to be a little too quiet and unhappy. When he started school, his teachers didn't tell his parents he didn't play well with the other kids. He didn't play with them at all. He showed no interest in making friends, rarely participated in kids' activities and basically kept to himself. By the time he entered high school he had become a bit of a bully who scared just about everyone, including his teachers, and was someone to avoid.

During his junior year his parents took him to a psychologist who somewhat reluctantly told them that Howie appeared to be a pure sociopath; a person without empathy or any real feelings for or a connection with other people. A Minnesota Multiphasic Personality Inventory was administered, and Howie's results revealed a 49 profile. He was quite intelligent but had a marked disregard for social norms, mores and standards. He was essentially someone with little or no conscience or regard for anyone else.

The oddity was that people exhibiting these traits normally come from economically depressed, fractured environments. Howie was the anomaly. John Traynor, his father, was a dentist with a very successful practice. His mother, Monica was a surgical nurse. Between them, they made an excellent living and provided well for Howie, his brother Martin who was three years older and a sister Alison, two years younger. The family had an upper-middle class home life in an upscale neighborhood of a Minneapolis suburb. The family was caring, loving, nurturing and almost exactly what any child should have. His brother and sister showed none of the antisocial traits of Howie and both had become normal, self-supporting, law-abiding adults. Howie was simply not wired right.

His criminal life began while still in high school. There was nothing too serious at first. He was joy riding in stolen cars with a couple of other boys with behavioral issues, shoplifting items he didn't really need and one arrest for burglarizing a house. Howie's behavior in school steadily worsened as the years went by. None of it was very serious just antisocial to the point that everyone in the building breathed a sigh of relief when he dropped out of school two months before graduation. He gave no explanation why. One day he simply walked into the principal's office and announced he was leaving. No one, not even his parents, bothered to try to talk him out of it.

From that day until tonight, his family having given up on him years ago, Howie was unburdened with human ties or responsibilities. He bounced around from one loser job to another, his adult life spent in and out of trouble, jail and the workhouse without a care in the world. Howie was a criminal. He knew he was a criminal and simply accepted it as a fact.

Howie made most of his money from home invasion burglaries. With his total lack of conscience, he justified it by simply believing it was what he was meant to do and that was that. The only legitimate job he had that he liked was as a nightclub bouncer.

He was big only in comparison to the man in the front seat next to him. Howie was a touch over six feet and one hundred eighty rock solid pounds. While not at work, Howie could be found at a boxing school in North Minneapolis training and working out.

When he first started working as a bouncer, his actual size rarely intimidated the average drunken idiot, until the drunken idiot crossed the line with Howie. One night, a well-known and very large Viking football player tried to show off to his entourage. Howie politely asked the man and his friends to settle down, but the football player thought he would have some fun with the smaller Howie. One punch from Howie and the fool's eyes rolled back in his head, his knees buckled and the table they were seated at shattered when he fell on it. No one messed with Howie after that story got around.

Howie's burglary partner was a man named Jimmy Oliver. Eight years older than Howie, Jimmy was Little to Howie being Big because he was barely five foot six and rail thin. Howie hooked up with him because Jimmy was a first-rate safe cracker and knew all of the best places in the Cities to fence stolen property. Jimmy kept it well hidden but in reality he was scared to death of Howie who reeked of menace. Jimmy had witnessed Howie scaring cops with little more than a nasty look.

It was Jimmy who had scoped out the job they were on tonight. He had taken a job using a false identification and forged documents with a home cleaning service. This would be the second job he had come up with while cleaning homes with this company and he figured the cops would find the connection after one more. The third one would be it and then he would have to move on.

The house they were going to hit was a sixteen-room beauty overlooking Lake of the Isles surrounded by a six-foot-high, spike-topped, wrought iron fence. Jimmy had been inside with a weekly cleaning crew three times. The third time the home's owner, a seventy-eight-year-old widow, was arguing with her daughter about selling the place. The daughter was adamant that it wasn't safe for her mother to live there alone and the place was simply too much for her. The daughter also let it slip that they would be out of town and the place would be empty for several days, including the night Big and Little now found themselves sitting patiently across the street.

The two men were parked in between two other cars on a side street in this very upscale Minneapolis neighborhood. They were less than one hundred feet from the corner where Parker Street and Lake of the Isles Boulevard met. Despite the lateness of the hour, almost 11:00 P.M., the darkness and the storm, they could clearly see the lake barely a hundred yards in front of them by the ambient light reflecting off of the water. Lake of the Isles is one of the chain of lakes that gave the City of Minneapolis, and the Los Angeles Lakers, its nickname; The City of Lakes. Surrounded by beautiful, expensive homes, many dating back to the turn of the nineteenth century, the area would be a crown jewel in just about any city in the world.

"Time?" Big asked again a few minutes later.

"Any minute now," Little replied.

Despite the weather, they watched as a man in tights marked with reflective tape jogged past the corner on the path surrounding the lake. When Big saw the jogger he muttered, "Asshole" just as lights from a car on Lake of the Isles Boulevard illuminated the man and a moment later a police patrol car passed by the corner.

"Right on time," Little said. "Every eighteen to twenty-four minutes." Little had done a thorough recon of the house and neighborhood and had spent several nights timing the cops patrolling around the lakes.

"Let's go," Big said as he opened his car door. Having removed the single bulb from the interior light, the car remained in darkness as the two men got out. Hunched over against the wind and light rain, they quickly ran across Parker Street to the back door of the house.

Next to an alley that ran behind the building was a small, unattached one car garage facing Parker Street. It was constructed of the same brick material as the house from over eighty years ago and looked tiny, almost ridiculous, next to the seven thousand square foot home. Above the door was an old-style exterior light to illuminate the small, barely ten-foot driveway. Little had previously loosened the bulb of the light above the garage door and the area in front of the garage was quite dark. Between the missing garage light, the weather and the all black clothing the men wore, the two of them were practically invisible.

The corner of the house met the corner of the garage at this point and there was an entryway door into the house. The lock on the door looked as if it had last been replaced in the '50s. It took Big less than a minute, even in the dark, to pick the lock and the two of them were in.

They both carried a flashlight with the lens taped over leaving a hole for the light to come through about the size of a pencil's eraser. Once inside, they turned the flashlights on and Little went up the single flight of stairs and into the kitchen. With Big casually following him, Little went through the kitchen and into a hallway closet. Inside the closet, while Big shined his flashlight on it, Little removed the cover to the alarm box and quickly attached a bypass hookup to the alarm before the alarm company could be notified of their intrusion.

Little turned around and said, "Okay, we're good to go."

"You're sure there's no one here?" Big asked for at least the fifth time that evening.

"They're out of town," Little replied. "Six minutes. No more."

"I know the drill, asshole," Big snarled causing Little to flinch. "You go do the safe. I'll check things out upstairs."

Little hurried toward the far end of the first floor where the study was. Having already discovered and photographed the safe, he was extremely confident he would have it open in under two minutes.

While Little went toward the study, Big started up the carpeted open stairway to the upstairs bedrooms. Little had told him the bulk of the items worth taking, the solid silver utensils, candlesticks and other items, many of which were expensive antiques, were on the main floor. While working with the cleaning crew, Little was able to scout the upstairs and told Big to take no more than one minute to go through the master bedroom only. There wasn't anything in the other rooms worth the time and effort.

Big almost carelessly opened the door to the master bedroom which caused it to bang slightly against an antique armoire behind it. The noise it made, while not very loud, made a significant impact on the silence of the room.

Big ignored the noise and while standing in the doorway began to play the flashlight around the room. In the middle of the bedroom, directly in front of the door was a king size, four poster bed, complete with a canopy above it. He slowly moved the light over the bed then heard the obviously frightened and shaky voice of an old woman say, "Who are you and what do you want?"

Big didn't hesitate for an instant. He didn't think about what to do or take a moment to consider it. He simply reacted. In barely a second he leapt over the bed's baseboard, flew across the length of the large bed and came down directly on top of her. He heard the air rush out of her lungs as he clamped his left hand down on her mouth and with his right hand he grabbed a pillow, roughly pushed it down to cover her face and used both of his powerful hands to hold the pillow in place.

The elderly woman tried her best to fight back. She kicked her legs, thrashed about back and forth and tried to claw at his arm with her hands. The poor woman never had a chance. Less than thirty seconds after it started her back arched, her eyelids fluttered, and her body went completely lax.

Big held the pillow over her face for another minute to be sure she was dead. He got off of her body, found his flashlight and surveyed what he had done. Then he did something even he could not have explained. Big pulled the blankets down, took the woman's hands, gently folded them together and placed them on her stomach. He then covered her up to her chin with the blankets, put the pillow he used to kill her back where it was and fluffed the pillow under her head. Despite the sudden and violent attack, she looked quite peaceful and serene. Apparently satisfied, he returned to his task.

Big opened the door to the study and found his partner seated at a desk with the contents of the safe spread out on its surface.

"Hey," Little began when he saw his partner. "We did okay. Looks to be about seven or eight grand in cash and if the jewelry is real, and it looks like it, should be another hundred here easy. Everything okay upstairs?"

"Yeah, everything's fine," Big lied. "Why?"

"What do you have there?" Little asked indicating the black cloth sack Big carried.

"Silver," he answered.

Little looked at his watch and said, "Times up, we need to get out of here before the cop comes around again."

TWO

"I know you told the other officer what happened, Carlotta, but I need you to tell me," Detective Tony Carvelli patiently said to the obviously distraught Latina woman.

Carvelli and his young partner, Antwone Spenser, a recently promoted detective with the Minneapolis Police Department, were seated in matching, obviously expensive cloth covered wing backed chairs. The two men were facing two women, both of whom appeared to be the same approximate age. The women were seated together on a sofa and the four of them were in the main living room of the house on Parker and Lake of the Isles.

Carlotta took a deep breath, squeezed the hand of the woman next to her and said, with barely a trace of an accent, "I got here at eight just like every day. As soon as I came into this room, I noticed some things missing. I looked around for a few minutes and could tell that a lot of the silver things were gone. Then I realized Mrs. Benson wasn't downstairs. She's almost always here when I get here," she explained. "So, I hurried upstairs and went into her bedroom. She was still in bed and not moving."

Carlotta stopped and wiped a couple of tears away, looked at the woman seated next to her and said, "I guess I knew right away she was dead. Her eyes were closed, she wasn't moving, and her face was really pale." She sniffled and said to the woman, "I'm so sorry Miss Janet."

"It's all right Carlotta," the woman said rubbing the back and shoulders of the upset housekeeper.

Carlotta turned back to the two detectives and continued. "I checked to see if she was breathing, which she wasn't, then I came downstairs and called Miss Janet from the kitchen."

"I called 911 then drove here as quickly as I could. There was a police car already here when I arrived," Janet Benson Milliken, the victim's daughter said. "I came inside and before they could stop me, hurried upstairs to Mom's bedroom.

"I came back down, and we talked to your officer, the tall black man. And we both told him what happened. He had us sit down here and told us not to move around or touch anything. More police and other people started arriving and we've just been waiting. Do you think my mother was murdered by burglars?"

"It's too soon to tell," Carvelli softly replied.

"It's all my fault," the daughter said fighting back a sob. "We were supposed to be at my cousin's cabin, but something came up at my job and I decided to stay for a couple more days."

"Wait, wait, wait," Carvelli soothingly said looking into the daughter's eyes. "This is not your fault. If this was done by the guy who did the burglary, he's the one to blame. Don't do that to yourself. Don't start second guessing things. It won't bring your mother back and it isn't true. We'll get this guy and put him away."

"Sarge," Carvelli heard a voice say coming from the living room's entryway. It was the same officer the two women had first talked to. "Sergeant Waschke just pulled up," the man said referring to the arrival of a homicide detective.

"Thanks, Jefferson," Carvelli replied looking up at the man. He turned back to his partner and asked, "Did you get everything?"

"Yeah, I did, Sarge," the much younger man answered.

Carvelli looked at the women and said, "We should clear out of here and let the crime scene people do their job. You'll get me a list of the missing items?" he asked the victim's daughter.

"Yes, as soon as I can. The insurance company will have an inventory of everything. I made sure of that. There are also photos."

"That's smart. Good job," Carvelli said.

Leaving Jefferson at the door, the four of them went out through the front door. Carvelli nodded his head at the beefy man coming through the front gate. They all waited at the bottom of the step as the man approached.

Carvelli and Waschke shook hands and Carvelli introduced the homicide detective to the two women.

"I'm sorry for your loss," Waschke sincerely told Janet. "I should go take a look," he said to Carvelli.

Carvelli indicated to his partner to stay with the women while he and Waschke started up the front steps to go inside. Jefferson was at the door with a clipboard making a record of everyone who entered the crime scene. He took down Waschke's name and badge number. As the two men were walking up the stairs, Waschke said to Carvelli, "Keep an eye on him. He's sharp as a razor and will make a damn fine detective and soon."

"Where's Collins?" Carvelli asked referring to Waschke's current partner.

"He's got his old lady knocked up again and they had some doctor's appointment this morning."

"Another kid?" Carvelli asked. "What's that, five or six?"

"Yeah, something like that. I'm not even sure he can keep track."

"Maybe you ought to have a little talk with him about how to avoid it."

"I've tried. He won't listen," Waschke growled as he walked into the bedroom.

He greeted the two people from the medical examiner's office who moved away from the body to allow Waschke to look over the elderly woman.

Waschke looked over the woman's face for a moment then asked the tech standing next to him, "What's this on her cheek?"

The tech leaned over next to Waschke and with a pen, pointed at a very lightly discolored area along the right jawline. "That right here?"

"Yeah."

"It could be bruising. Look at this." He picked up a pillow lying next to the woman and pointed to a very light stain on it.

"What is it?"

"Can't say for sure," the tech said. "But it could be a bit of lipstick. Even if a woman washes it off before bed she wouldn't get all of it. We'll know more when the CSU guys run some tests. Could be trace saliva on it too."

"He held a pillow over her face," Waschke said as he straightened up.

"Maybe, we'll know more in a day or two."

"Put a rush on it, will you Paul? I got a call from the chief this morning who got a call from the mayor about this. I guess this is a pretty prominent family."

"Sure, Jake. Will be a lot of political heat on you for this one. Sucks to be you."

"Thanks for the reminder," Waschke sarcastically answered.

The two detectives had just stepped through the doorway leading to the front yard when a small Cadillac limousine pulled up and double parked in front of the house. They stopped and watched as a very attractive woman in her early fifties exited the back seat of the car. When she did this, the victim's daughter walked quickly to the gate in the wrought iron fence. The two women gave each other an affectionate, consoling hug then walked up the sidewalk toward the house.

"Who is she?" Carvelli asked.

"I do believe that is Vivian Donahue, top dog of the Corwin family. You know them?" Waschke answered his friend.

"I know of them. Since this looks like a homicide and I'm in burglary, I'll let you deal with her," Carvelli said. He then turned and went back into the house.

Waschke walked up to the women as the older one was consoling the housekeeper. Waschke gave a slight jerk of his head at Carvelli's partner to indicate he could leave which the young detective did as quickly as seemed polite. Janet introduced him to Vivian Donahue and explained that her mother was Vivian's aunt. Janet had called her earlier after calling 911. Waschke immediately realized this explained the call from the mayor to the chief of police and the subsequent call to him.

"May I see my aunt?" Vivian politely asked.

"I believe they're about ready to move her," Waschke replied. "Plus, it's a crime scene and the fewer people that go in there right now, the better."

"There's nothing much to see," Janet said to her cousin. "Mom looked like she was peacefully asleep."

"You're sure there was a burglary?" Vivian asked Jake.

"Yes, absolutely," Janet answered before Jake could respond.

"Is her death a homicide? She had a bad heart..." Vivian began to say.

"As long as she took her meds she was fine. I made sure each week her pill box was filled for each day. I checked the one for yesterday and she had taken her pills," Janet interjected.

"We don't know," Waschke said to Vivian.

"She'll have to have an autopsy?"

"I'm afraid so," Waschke shrugged.

"Oh, God, how ghastly," Vivian said. "But, I suppose we have to know." She handed Waschke a personal card with her name and private number on it. "Please keep me informed as much as you can, Sergeant. I don't mean to interfere but..."

"I understand," Jake replied. "I'll do what I can," he continued while thinking, *if you can't use the kind of clout she has what's the point of having it?*

Jake handed one of his cards to each of the three women and told them if they thought of anything to call him.

Vivian Donohue slipped her left arm through Waschke's right arm and led him several steps away from the daughter and housekeeper.

"I won't hold you to it but tell me what you think," she quietly said when she let go of his arm and looked up at him. Waschke was a large, veteran cop who knew how to intimidate people with just a look. Rarely did he ever experience the uneasiness he felt because of the look this woman was giving him.

"It's probably a burglary gone bad. Likely he found her and smothered her with a pillow."

"Will you catch him?"

Jake took a deep breath, scratched his chin and thought about his answer. "I'll be honest, the odds are not good. If we can recover some of the stolen property..."

"Which isn't likely," Vivian said.

"Usually not," he agreed. "We have our best people on it. We'll do our best. I promise you that."

THREE

Jimmy "Little" Oliver, having called in sick at his job with the cleaning company, was on the living room floor of his North Minneapolis apartment. Jimmy made a point of living modestly. Having spent all of the time in prison he cared to spend, he was determined to keep a low profile, avoid the cops and move on to a warmer climate next year. He had laid out the loot from the night before and was trying to decide the best way to dispose of it. The two of them had divided up the cash, almost three grand each. Not as much as Jimmy thought there would be in the safe but not bad either. It was at least enough to last for a couple of weeks until he moved the silver and jewelry.

The television in the corner was on and turned to a local station. It was mid-morning and Jimmy had it on looking for news of the burglary. So far not a word was mentioned, which was always a good thing. He picked up his phone to call a guy he knew to fence the goods when a news alert flashed across the TV screen. Still kneeling on the floor in front of his second-hand Goodwill couch, he found the TV's remote and turned up the volume.

Jimmy stared in stunned disbelief while the female reporter told the audience what the police had found. She was standing in front of the house on Parker Street and Lake of the Isles Boulevard reporting the previous night's event. Jimmy barely listened wondering how they discovered it so quickly with the homeowners supposedly out of town for another couple of days. At first he was not too concerned; it would be reported to the cops sooner or later. Later, of course, would have been better, especially if he could have moved the goods first.

The attractive young blonde woman said something about the body being found in her bedroom. It didn't register right away with Jimmy what she meant. The camera panned to the front door of the house and two men wheeled a gurney down the front steps with a black body bag lying on it. He focused on what the woman was saying, and her words made sweat break out on his forehead and his hands start to shake.

Jimmy stood up, sat down on the couch and stared silently at the screen listening to the newscast. By the time it was finished he had calmed himself, turned off the TV and said out loud to himself, "You crazy, sick sonofabitch. What the fuck did you do?"

Jimmy walked into the dimly lit bar on Franklin Avenue and stood in the doorway waiting for his eyes to adjust from the bright sunshine. It was almost two o'clock in the afternoon and he had spent most of the day cruising dive bars around town searching for Howie Traynor. Jimmy looked toward the back where the pool tables were located and saw the back of Howie's head with its close cropped, quarter inch haircut.

"We need to talk," Jimmy quietly said to him as Howie casually chalked his cue.

"Yeah, what about?" Howie laconically asked.

Jimmy stared at the younger man for several seconds, a look of disbelief on his face, then finally raised his eyebrows and quietly said, "About last night. About what happened when you went upstairs. About that, remember? Let's go outside for a minute."

The two men walked the ten feet to the bar's back door and went into the parking lot. When they got about thirty feet from the door, Jimmy said, "What the hell happened upstairs?"

Howie shrugged and simply said, "The old bag was home. She was in bed. She sat up and saw me so, I did her. No big deal. What was I supposed to do?" Howie then described exactly what happened and how he murdered Lucille Benson.

"This is bad, dude," Jimmy said as he began to pace about in a small circle. Howie folded his arms across his chest, leaned against the trunk of a parked car, listened to Jimmy and watched him nervously pace.

"This is really fucking big time bad," Jimmy kept repeating over and over.

"What's the big deal? We keep our mouths shut and the cops can't prove dick."

Jimmy stopped pacing, looked at Howie and said, "You don't get it. The chick on TV said the woman is a member of a rich, powerful, politically connected family. They won't just let this slide. They'll want to nail somebody for it."

At that precise moment, Jimmy Oliver realized exactly what he had to do. Otherwise he was a dead man and he knew it. Based on some little things Howie had said in the past, Jimmy suspected Howie had killed before, in fact, probably two or three times. People often believed Howie's attitude was caused by a lack of intelligence, but Jimmy knew better. Howie was, in fact, a really bright guy.

"So, move the shit, get me my money and we'll cool it for a while," Howie said. "Think about it. What evidence do they have? Nothing," Howie said.

Jimmy pretended to think it over then slightly nodded his head a few times as if agreeing with the sociopath, then said, "Yeah, you're right. I was never in there without gloves and a hairnet. They won't find anything. We should be okay. I guess I just got a little rattled, you know, when I saw it on TV."

"No problem," Howie said as he stepped forward. He patted Jimmy on the cheek and asked, "How long do you think it will take to get the cash?" Howie took a pack of cigarettes from his shirt pocket, removed one, took a lighter from his pocket and lit it.

"I'm going to see a guy tonight. I'll know more then. Cool lighter. Where did you get it?"

Howie held up the gold, engraved lighter and said, "Off the old lady's dresser last night. I know, I need to get rid of it," Howie said. "I will in a couple of days. It's nice though," he continued as he rolled it over in his fingers. "Maybe I should come with you tonight."

This was something Howie had never done before. For some reason Jimmy had never quite figured out, Howie always trusted Jimmy to fence the stolen property, get a good price and give him his share. Thinking quickly, Jimmy said, "No, this guy don't take well to strangers. He knows me. I'll handle it."

Howie stared into Jimmy's eyes which caused a slight shudder in him. "Okay, I'll call you tomorrow. We'll get together."

When Jimmy had driven his old Chevy a couple of blocks, he stopped and parked. He took a business card from his wallet, called and spoke with a man he knew quite well. The man assured him he could come to see him right away. Ten minutes later, Jimmy took a seat in one of the client chairs in the office of his lawyer, Charles Ferguson.

For the next half hour, Jimmy told Ferguson what he had done the night before and exactly what he had in mind to do now. When Jimmy finished his story, the lawyer asked, "Are you sure about this? Once we go down this path, there'll be no turning back."

"I know," Jimmy agreed. "This psycho asshole will kill me once he gets his money. I could read it in his face. He scares the shit out of me."

"Okay," Ferguson said. "I'll make the call."

FOUR

Jimmy Oliver, accompanied by his lawyer, exited the elevator on the twentieth floor on the court side of the Hennepin County Government Center. Ferguson had called a friend of his in the county attorney's office, a woman who Ferguson had tried several cases against named Rhea Watson and set up this meeting.

Watson came out to the reception area of the county attorney's offices and greeted Ferguson and his client. She then led them back to a conference room where three men were seated on one end of a long, well used, government issued conference table.

"Hey Tony," Jimmy said to Tony Carvelli who was sitting to the left of the county attorney himself, Gary Mitchell. To Carvelli's right, also facing the door was a man Jimmy did not know who was obviously a cop, Jake Waschke. Watson took the chair to her boss' right. Ferguson and Oliver took chairs on that same side several spaces away.

"Jimmy, good to see you again," Carvelli answered. "You going to tell us what you've been up to lately?"

Carvelli had been a detective in the burglary department for almost three years. He knew Jimmy Oliver and suspected him of a number of burglaries. No one in the room was happier than Tony Carvelli.

"We need to set some ground rules…" Ferguson tried to begin.

"Bullshit," Waschke interrupted staring at Jimmy. "Your client is scared shitless of his psycho buddy and he needs our protection. He'll give us Howie Traynor and hope we're in a generous mood. How am I doing, Jimmy?"

"Not bad," Jimmy quietly agreed.

"Jake let's hear what he has to say," the county attorney said. He then looked at Ferguson and asked, "What are you looking for, Charlie?"

"Witness protection…"

"Won't happen," Mitchell answered. "This isn't a mob case. This is a couple of low-life criminals turning on each other. You're just going to have to trust me, Charlie. I'm prepared to be lenient depending on what he has to say. You know me, Charlie. We've known each other quite a while and you know I keep my word."

"Yeah, Gary, okay," Ferguson said. "I had to try." He turned to his client and said, "Go ahead, tell them."

When Jimmy finished his confession, giving as few details as he believed he had to, Jake Waschke was the first to speak up. "That's it?

That's the bullshit you expect us to believe? According to you, Howie practically forced you to help him rob the woman."

"It's true, he's the scariest dude I've ever met," Jimmy said practically pleading.

Waschke, who could play the bad cop role with the best of them, leaned forward in his chair. He placed his arms on the table and glared directly at Jimmy. "I say we throw this lying little asshole in a cell, go pick up his partner and see if he'll be more cooperative. See if he wants to make a deal."

This little act Waschke was performing had been agreed to and set up before Jimmy and his lawyer arrived. Unfortunately for those people seated at the head of the table, Jimmy knew Howie Traynor a lot better than they did. Instead of being intimidated, Jimmy burst into genuine laughter.

"Go ahead," he said while he held up a hand to stop Ferguson from speaking. "Pick him up and see what you get. I know this psycho. You can beat on him for a week and he'll spit in your eye. He's hard as a rock."

"Cut the bullshit, Jimmy," Tony Carvelli interjected. "We've known each other a while now so cut out this babe in the woods act."

"Rhea," the county attorney said, "would you show Charlie and his client to your office? Charlie, give us a few minutes, please," he said to the defense lawyer.

"Sure Gary. I need to talk to him anyway," Ferguson said sending a clear message that he would convince his client to be more cooperative.

After they left, Matthews asked the two detectives, "Well, what do you think?"

"He's holding back," Waschke calmly said.

"Of course, he is," Carvelli agreed nodding at his friend. "But you know this asshole Traynor," he said to Jake then looked at Matthews. "He is a bad dude. We suspect him of a lot of burglaries, car thefts, you name it and a couple of home invasion homicides. You remember Jake," he continued, "last year, that couple in Edina."

"Yeah, I remember," Waschke agreed.

Rhea Watson returned and took her seat next to Matthews and said, "I remember that case. We liked this Traynor guy for them but didn't have enough for an arrest, let alone a conviction."

"Uncorroborated accomplice testimony is not enough for a conviction. We'll need more than Charlie's client," Matthews reminded them.

"The M.E. says there's enough skin and hair under a couple of the victim's fingernails for a DNA test. If our little asshole here is telling the truth, it should be Traynor's," Waschke said.

"That would do it," Rhea said. "I say we have enough probable cause for an arrest and a DNA swab."

"I agree," Matthews said. "Rhea, go tell them to come back in. Then you do up an affidavit and get a warrant and DNA request signed."

"Give me fifteen minutes and I'll have them both," Watson said looking at the detectives.

"We'll wait in here or come to your office," Carvelli told her.

Matthews asked the two men, "Do we give this guy a walk?"

"No," Carvelli emphatically said. "He needs to do some time. A couple of years in Lino Lakes is fine, but he doesn't walk completely from a felony murder without something." Lino Lakes is a minimum-security prison in a suburb of St. Paul. "And," he continued, "I want a written confession of every burglary he's done and who his fence is. We might as well clear some cases."

"Jake?" Matthews asked Waschke.

"Yeah, I'm okay with that. I know this Traynor. He's a bad boy that we need to get off the streets."

There was a light knock on the door before Jimmy and his lawyer came back into the room. They sat down in the same chairs, Ferguson removed a legal pad from his leather satchel and looked at Matthews.

"Okay, here's what we'll offer," Matthews began. "I'll recommend ten years in prison…"

"What?" Jimmy practically yelled.

Ferguson placed his right hand gently on Jimmy's left arm and calmly said, "Let him finish."

"I'll recommend ten years in prison and ask the judge to stay eight years of it. You'll do two years in Lino Lakes, sixteen months actually, then ten years of supervised probation. You'll have the remaining eight years of jail time hanging over your head. You will fully cooperate in the prosecution of your partner, including testifying if necessary. You will be absolutely truthful, and you will not withhold anything. Any lying and the deal's off and we prosecute you for burglary and felony murder. Do you understand?"

All eyes turned to Jimmy who sighed heavily, swallowed hard and said, "I hate the thought of going back to prison."

"It's Lino Lakes," Ferguson reminded him.

"Or, we can kick your ass loose and you can deal with Howie Traynor on your own," Waschke said.

Ferguson glared at the homicide detective and sternly said, "These kinds of threats aren't necessary, Jake."

"Just a friendly reminder Charlie," Waschke replied.

"And one other thing," Carvelli said. "You will write down, in detail, everything about this case and every job you've done since you got out of Stillwater three years ago. And," he continued pointing his right index finger at him, "just because we haven't been able to bust you for them, doesn't mean I don't know about them. If you lie or leave anything out, I'll know."

FIVE

"Okay, any questions? Everybody know what to do?" Jake Waschke asked the five men and two women. The eight police officers had gathered behind a Taco Bell on Twenty Eighth Avenue and Franklin in Minneapolis. They were less than a block away and across Franklin from their objective, the *East End* bar.

Jimmy Oliver had suggested they try to find Traynor in this bar. It was where Jimmy had confronted him earlier that afternoon. Waschke had sent in an undercover cop he knew to check the place out. He had reported back that Traynor was there still shooting pool. The undercover officer was also still in the bar keeping an eye on him.

The eight cops gathered at the Taco Bell to conduct the arrest were Waschke and his partner, Carvelli and his partner and two plain clothes from burglary. Carvelli had also rounded up two uniformed cops. The two women were one of the plainclothes from burglary and one of the uniforms.

The plan was for Waschke, Carvelli, the two plain clothes and the two uniforms to go in the front. Waschke's and Carvelli's partners would come in through the back.

Jimmy assured them Traynor would not have a gun but could not say he would not have a different weapon. He also assured them it was unlikely Traynor would go peacefully and quietly. Waschke made sure everyone had on a vest and the two plain clothes cops would carry Tasers.

Everything went exactly as planned until they approached Howie Traynor. While the two uniforms blocked the front door and the two detectives came in through the back, Waschke walked up to Traynor holding the arrest warrant.

"Howard Traynor," Waschke began while his three compatriots spread out to form a semi-circle around him. The other two detectives remained blocking the back door.

Traynor, his backside to the group, was bent over the pool table lining up a shot. After taking the shot he stood up, turned to Waschke and casually asked, "Who wants to know?"

"I have a warrant for your arrest for the murder of Lucille Benson," Waschke announced.

When he did this, the dozen or so people at and around the pool tables went completely silent. The ones closest to the table Traynor was leaning against quietly moved away. The *East End* was a tough bar in a tough neighborhood. Its patrons were not strangers to the police. But even these guys knew a murder warrant was not something in which any of them wanted to become embroiled.

Traynor looked over the four cops with an indifferent expression while shifting the pool cue to turn it into a club. He looked at Waschke and said, "I'm not done with my game." This comment drew some mild laughter from the spectators and a sinister smile from Tony Carvelli.

"Howie, you're coming with us and you know it. Put the cue down and let's make this easy," Carvelli said.

"Tell you what," Traynor said to Carvelli, "you take it away from me and then I'll come nice and easy."

When he heard this, Waschke looked at the male plain clothes cop who had come in with them and nodded his head to him. Without hesitating, the man aimed the Taser he was holding behind his back and fired it at Traynor. The leads hit him in the mid-abdomen and fifty thousand volts began to course through his body.

Howie's knees began to buckle, he dropped the pool cue, let out a large groan and then did something amazing. He grabbed the Taser's wires, jerked the leads out of his body and threw them at the cop who fired them. Before anyone could move, he charged the cop who shot him and drilled him with a wicked right-hand punch that lifted the cop completely off of his feet and flat on his back.

Waschke, for a big man, could move quick as a cat when he needed to. He swiftly jumped behind Traynor and as he did so, he flicked his wrist and expanded the twenty-one-inch, steel, telescoping baton he was holding. He laid the weapon behind Traynor's right knee immediately collapsing it sending him downward. He also hit him with the palm of his open left hand in the back of the head. As Traynor fell face first toward the floor, the woman plainclothes cop fired her Taser and hit him in the back. This time, the weapon did its job.

The two police sergeants, Waschke and Carvelli, immediately went into action taking control of the situation. The woman who tased Howie, Helen Barkey, cuffed Howie then knelt next to the unconscious policeman. Waschke quickly walked away from the pool tables toward the front door. He walked through the curious crowd in the bar and told the senior patrolman, Owen Jefferson, what he wanted. No one was to leave without giving the cops their identification. While Waschke did this in the bar area, Carvelli told his partner and Waschke's partner at the back door, the same thing. Get everyone's name and no one leaves.

Waschke came back, grabbed a chair and he and Carvelli, none too gently slammed the now hand cuffed Howie Traynor into it.

Barkey stood up and said to the two sergeants, "Conlin's hurt pretty bad. Maybe a busted jaw." She then pulled her radio out and called for backup and an ambulance. Within ten minutes there were a dozen more cops in the place and two EMT's were working on the assaulted policeman.

While all of this was taking place, Traynor was yelling and cursing at the cops claiming police brutality and a broken leg. Waschke leaned over him until his face was three inches in front of him. Traynor finally shut his mouth with the big cop glaring at him.

"Helen, come here," Waschke said without looking away from Traynor. "You got your Taser and is it ready to go again?"

Barkey checked the weapon then said, "Good to go, Sarge."

"Fine. If this asshole doesn't shut up or if he even flinches, tase him in the balls. You got it?"

"My pleasure, Sarge," the policewoman said and from three feet away, aimed the weapon right at Traynor's crotch. "Please give me a reason," she said to him.

A few minutes later a uniformed police captain arrived. Both Waschke and Carvelli knew the man personally and were confident in his ability to take charge of the situation. Carvelli gave the captain a brief report on what happened. At the same time Waschke found two large uniformed officers. They gathered up Traynor and half-dragged and half carried him through the back door where Carvelli's young partner had parked their car.

The two beefy patrolmen strapped Traynor into the back seat with the seat belt, his arms still cuffed behind him.

Carvelli was driving with Waschke in the front passenger seat. "Have you ever seen anybody do that, pull those taser leads out of themselves like that?" Carvelli quietly asked Waschke.

"I've heard of it but never seen it myself."

They were going west on Franklin toward downtown Minneapolis and the Old City Hall which housed the police department. They had traveled barely two blocks when Traynor said, "You two idiots really fucked up. I'm gonna walk from this. You forgot to read me my rights." He laughed heartily at this as if he had pulled something over on them.

Carvelli simply smiled and Waschke turned to look at Traynor and said, "Holy shit. What a screw-up. I didn't know you were a lawyer. Where did you go to law school, Harvard? I got some disappointing news for you, dickhead. We haven't asked any questions so, technically, we don't have to read you your rights yet. But as long as you brought it up, I'll do it now." Waschke recited them to him, smiled and said, "Now I want you to invoke your right to remain silent and shut your mouth for a while until we do ask you something."

"I want a lawyer," Traynor sullenly said.

"We'll get you one. Now be quiet for a while."

The detectives each held one of Traynor arms as they led him limping to the booking window. While Waschke removed the handcuffs, the sergeant in charge of booking said to Carvelli, "We heard about this. Great job for you guys. Excellent work."

"Thanks, Frank," Carvelli said. "Empty your pockets," he told Traynor.

Traynor began removing the contents of his pants' pockets while the booking sergeant began filling out an inventory envelope to record the contents. He pulled out a pack of Camel filters and a lighter and set them on the counter. Carvelli instantly recognized the lighter.

"Whoa! What have we here?" Carvelli said. He pulled a handkerchief from his back pocket and used it to carefully pick up the lighter. He rolled it around in his hand, careful not to let it touch his skin, then turned his head to look at Traynor.

"I found that," Traynor said.

"Sure, you did. And I know right where you found it. It was on the dresser in the bedroom of Lucille Benson. I saw a picture of it this morning. Her daughter brought it in to help us identify the shit you two assholes stole after you killed her mother. It's an antique lighter that's been in the family for almost a hundred years"

"I don't know nothin' about any of that. I found that lighter this morning," Traynor replied showing nervousness for the first time.

"Good defense strategy," Waschke chimed in. "I'd stick with that if I were you."

The booking sergeant held open a clear plastic evidence bag and Carvelli dropped the lighter in it. He then held it in front of Traynor's face and said "What we have here is corroboration, proof that you were there. Then when the DNA comes back as a match, well, you're gone, tough guy."

"What DNA? You're lying."

"The hair and skin found under the victim's fingernails. There's enough to test," Waschke said.

"It's yours, moron. Bye bye," Carvelli said.

Defiantly, Traynor glared at them and said, "I'll be there to piss on both of your graves."

SIX

Marc Kadella wearily sat on a padded bench in the hallway outside courtroom 1523 in the Hennepin County Government Center. The pain in his lower back was finally gone. The stress of doing his first homicide trial had tightened up his lower back muscles for the duration of the trial. Four days and no relief. The case had been given to the jury only two hours ago and the pain was already gone.

Marc leaned back against the hallway wall and vacantly stared across the empty space at the government side of the big building. He found himself taking simple pleasure watching through the windows as the county employees worked at their desks or busily scurried about. It felt good to have his mind in neutral; not thinking about the trial or what he should be doing to prepare for it. It was over. He had given it his best shot and there was nothing more he could do.

Marc thought about his client, Howie Traynor. He was accused of first- and second-degree murder in the death of an elderly woman during the commission of a burglary. Going into the trial, Marc believed he could beat the first-degree charge but probably not the second degree. His client was likely looking at three serious felony convictions, including assault on a police officer. If convicted of everything but the first-degree murder charge, he was looking at thirty years, minimum.

It had been eight months since the crime was committed. Fall and winter had come and gone, and a lot had happened during that time. The murder of a member of a well-known, respected, politically prominent family had generated a lot of publicity and media attention. Being a novice at dealing with the press, Marc could only hope he didn't come across as too much of an inexperienced fool. For a solid hour after the case went to the jury, Marc, and the lead prosecutor, Rhea Watson, had both given multiple impromptu interviews here in the hallway. While replaying it in his mind, Marc appreciated the quiet and solitude even more.

Marc began to go over the trial in his head. He knew it was a bad idea to do this. It would lead to second guessing himself and thinking of new things he should have done. But he couldn't help himself.

The first thing he mentally replayed was his cross examination of the medical examiner who had conducted the autopsy. During the man's direct exam, he testified that there were microscopic cotton fibers found in the victim's mouth and nose. These fibers, he testified, were an exact match with the pillow found next to the body. A lab tech had previously testified that there were traces of lipstick that matched the lipstick worn by the deceased. Also, DNA analysis showed saliva from the same spot on the pillow as the lipstick. This allowed the ME to testify that, in his medical opinion, someone held that pillow over the face of the victim and was the proximate cause of the heart attack that killed her.

Replaying the cross exam, Marc was satisfied he had done as good a job as anyone could trying to find reasonable doubt about the cause of death. He was able to get the doctor to admit the lipstick and saliva on the pillow could have happened simply by the deceased rolling on her side or putting her mouth on it while she slept. And this could have caused the small cotton particles to enter her nose and mouth.

The problem he had was the bruising on the jawline. There was simply no reasonable explanation for how that could have happened except by someone holding the pillow over her fragile face. Between that and the DNA evidence from the hair and skin found under the victim's fingernails, a 99% match, Howie's goose was cooked. Howie Traynor was going down for the murder of Lucille Benson, second degree felony murder. Marc believed he was not going to get first degree premeditated murder. Howie did not go up those stairs intending to kill anyone. According to the state's star witness, Jimmy Oliver, they believed no one was home, so how could anyone have gone into that bedroom planning to kill someone who wasn't supposed to be there? Clearly the prosecution had overcharged.

Marc thought it over for another fifteen or twenty minutes then satisfied himself that he had done a good job. Not only that but, being honest with himself, he wasn't the least bit upset that Howie was going to prison for a long time. The simple truth was even if Howie did not admit it, he was guilty as hell. And, like just about everyone else who came in contact with him, Howie Traynor scared the hell out of Marc Kadella.

"Replaying the case? Second guessing yourself?" Marc heard the voice of his counterpart; Rhea Watson say to him. He had been so lost in thought he didn't notice her walk up next to him.

Marc looked up at her, smiled and said, "Hey, Rhea."

"Mind if I join you?" she asked.

"No, not at all. Have a seat," Marc replied as he picked up the briefcase he had set on the seat next to him and put it on the floor.

"Yeah, I was thinking it over," Marc agreed as the lawyer sat down, crossed her legs and pulled her skirt down to her knees.

"Don't," she said. "You did a good job. Old Mickey would have been proud of you. He may have been a bit of a drunk and notorious womanizer, but he was a damn fine trail lawyer. I bet you learned a lot from him."

"Yeah, I did," he agreed. "Learned a lot the hard way the past few days."

"That's probably the best way. You beat us on the first-degree charge. I think we got you on everything else. I'll make you a new offer. He pleads to second degree, we recommend thirty years. Peterson will go along with it," she said referring to the judge. "Otherwise, we're going to ask for an upward departure on the homicide and consecutive sentencing on everything else. He'll get forty for sure. This guy scares everybody, including the judge."

The thirty-year offer was ten years more than the original offer they had made six months ago.

"I'll go across the street and tell him but don't hold your breath," Marc said as he stood and retrieved his briefcase.

"Tell him it's good for another hour only. I'll be upstairs for a couple more hours. If he says okay, call me and we'll see Peterson yet today."

"You think the jury will be back today?" Marc asked as the two of them walked toward the elevators.

"Doubtful. They have way too much to go through with all of the charges on your guy."

"Please don't call him my guy," Marc protested as he pushed both the up and down buttons at the elevator bank. "I'll call you one way or the other after I talk to him," Marc said as he stepped onto the elevator that arrived to take him down stairs.

"Will the defendant please rise," Judge Ross Peterson intoned.

Marc arose from his chair immediately, but his client stood up as if this was little more than an annoyance.

The jury had come back with a verdict before noon on the day after the trial concluded. It was now two hours later after allowing for lunch and to get all of the parties, including the media, together. In the back row, a serious looking man in a charcoal suit and stylish tie sat patiently waiting for the verdict to be read. He was the current head of the security for Vivian Corwin Donahue. He was to call her as soon as he had the news. Vivian was not a woman who liked to be kept waiting.

The jury foreman, a man named Elliot Sanders, held up the paper with the verdicts written out. He cleared his throat and read the charges and the verdict for each.

Marc had guessed correctly. The first one the foreman read was the murder one charge and the finding of not guilty. Every other charge, the felony murder second degree; assault on a police officer; resisting arrest; multiple breaking and entering and burglary charges were all guilty verdicts.

While each was being read, Marc was thinking that with the not guilty of first-degree murder, Traynor could not be sentenced to life without parole. Later that day, he would find himself wondering if that was a good or bad thing.

When the foreman finished, Peterson ordered a presentence investigation report and set the date for sentencing thirty days out. He thanked and dismissed the jury and adjourned.

Before Traynor could be led away, he turned to Marc and sarcastically snarled, "Nice job rookie. I won't forget it."

On the day of his sentencing, Marc and his client stood silently and patiently while Judge Peterson went over the list of reasons he was sentencing Howie to forty years in prison. This was a significant upward departure than what the sentencing guidelines called for and the judge was obligated to make a record of his reasons for it. In the event of an appeal, which Marc was extremely grateful he would not have to handle, the appeals court would have to know why the longer than normal sentence was given.

The judge finished, looked at Howie and asked, "Do you have anything to say?"

Howie opened his mouth as if to say something causing Marc to cringe at the thought of what might come out, then Traynor simply said, about as politely as he was capable of, "No, I guess not, your Honor."

Marc got off the elevator on the second floor of the building. He had his cell phone in hand and before he had walked twenty feet, he could hear the phone he dialed already ringing.

"Hey Karen, its Marc," he said.

"What did he get?"

"Forty years total. It's all yours now," Marc told the lawyer with the Minnesota State Public Defenders office. They would be handling Howie's appeal and Marc was delighted to wash his hands of it. "And good luck."

"Thanks," she responded a touch sarcastically. "I'll have someone get started on it. Do you want us to keep you informed?"

"Not really," Marc replied. He had arrived at the elevators in the corner of the building to go down into the underground parking area. He pushed the button and said, "I've seen all of Howie Traynor I care to."

SEVEN

Present Day

Douglas Dylan stifled a cough then held his breath hoping the urge to cough again would dissipate. His body went rigid and he gripped the arms of the chair he sat on as tightly as his weak, frail body could. Douglas lost his mini-battle and a hard cough came out of his lungs. He groaned and bent forward in an effort to alleviate the pain that wracked his rib cage and swept up to his shoulders and down into his groin. Two more coughs escaped and this time the pain almost caused a short blackout.

Still bent at the waist, he wrapped his arms around his chest, closed his eyes and forced himself to calmly breathe. Thirty or forty seconds later the pain was gone, and he was able to relax and sit upright in the chair. Douglas took several deep breaths and thought, "Getting better. Not as bad as it used to be."

Two minutes later he pushed himself up and out of the chair and stepped over to the window. Looking down from the sixth floor of the Southdale Medical Center building, he could see the roof of the parking ramp next door and the cars on the Crosstown Highway spraying the rain as they hurried past.

A single tear trickled down his cheek and he emitted a slight sob while watching the rain come down. Douglas wondered how much longer he would be able to see such mundane, everyday sights; the traffic hurrying by, a cloudy sky, a rainy day? It had been three weeks since his last chemo treatment and two weeks since the most recent PET scan. His oncologist had the results of the scan and in his heart of hearts, Douglas knew that he was waiting in this exam room for bad news.

There was a light knock on the door and he turned to see the doctor, Gail Fedder come in. She was carrying his inch-thick file, smiled at him and said, "Good morning, Doug. How are you feeling?"

Douglas sat down in his chair before answering. "Better. A little more energy and I'm sleeping a bit better. Coughing doesn't hurt as much."

The doctor took the chair at the room's work station, set the file on top of the table and turned on the computer. She called up his file and took a minute to pretend to read it over. She knew what was in it. Once again she had to perform the worst part of being a cancer doctor. The doctor looked at her patient and said, "Doug, I've always been completely honest and up front with you and I'm not going to stop now. We got the results of the PET scan back and…"

"They're not good," Doug said.

Gail hesitated then said, "No, they're not."

"How long?" he quietly asked the question anyone in his position would ask.

"I can't say for sure. Over the last month or so, it has spread quite a bit. I'd say a month, maybe two."

He lowered his head and quietly sobbed while he cried. Douglas knew this was what he would be told today yet there was always a sliver of hope. That word, hope, had become enormously important since his diagnosis almost two years ago. Now it seemed even that word was no longer available to him.

The doctor reached over and took his hand in hers. At the same time, she handed him a box of Kleenex. He took it and used three or four to blow his nose and wipe his eyes.

"Do I need to go into a hospice?"

"Not if you don't want to. We can set up a bed and nurse you at home if you prefer," she answered. "I want you to come in once a week, sooner, if you need to." She hesitated a moment then said, "What are you thinking?"

He sat silently for a half a minute then said, "I'm just disappointed. I mean, you know, so damn disappointed. I'm not even angry anymore. Just disappointed and, of course, a little sad. I'm thirty-seven. I've never smoked or spent much time around smokers. I've led a pretty healthy life and I get lung cancer. I don't know. I don't know what to say."

The two of them sat silently for another minute or so, Douglas staring blankly at the far wall while the doctor patiently waited, holding his hand.

"Doug, you should go see your priest, Father Paul. Talk to him. You need him now."

Douglas nodded his head, looked at his doctor and weakly smiled. "Yes, I was just thinking that. I'll call him when I get home."

Douglas opened the door to his parents' home in west Bloomington and let Father Paul come in. Because of his illness and the difficulty, he had caring for himself, he had given up his apartment several months ago. The priest was carrying a plastic bag which contained two boxes of combo meals from Kentucky Fried Chicken. Douglas had discovered early on in his fight against cancer that KFC meals were quick, inexpensive and tasted fairly good. Chemotherapy didn't make food taste bad, that was caused mostly from radiation therapy. The problem with food and chemo was that the patient was almost never hungry. One simply did not feel much like eating.

The two men sat silently at the kitchen table eating the lunches the priest had brought for them. Father Paul was a parish priest at St. Edward's in Bloomington. He was a decade older than Douglas and had known the younger man since Douglas was in high school. Although Douglas was mostly a C and E Catholic, Christmas and Easter, they had maintained a sort of loose friendship over the years.

Father Paul finished eating before the younger man then set his empty box aside and patiently waited for Douglas. A few minutes later Douglas also finished, and Father Paul suggested that Douglas wait in the living room while the priest cleaned up.

Expecting the news to be bad, Father Paul took a chair facing the couch where Douglas was seated.

"Do you want to talk about what the doctor told you?" Father Paul asked, looking across the glass-topped coffee table between them.

"Nothing good," Douglas replied with a weak smile. "The treatments aren't working, and the cancer has spread. It's in my bones and brain. They can give me more chemo and radiation for the brain tumors but I'm not sure I want to."

"What did Dr. Fedder say about that?"

"She said at best it might give me another few weeks," he shrugged. His eyes watered up and he heavily sobbed. He took several deep breaths, wanly smiled and continued by saying, "It just really sucks. I am so disappointed about this. I'm too young. I wanted marriage, children, the whole deal and now…"

"I understand and…." Father Paul began.

"Don't give me any of that 'God's plan' bullshit! There's no plan going on here. God is not micromanaging us. This is just, well… shit happens I guess."

"Yes, you're right. Shit happens," The priest agreed.

The two of them had been down this path several times before with the same, basic result. Douglas pulled his slender legs up on the couch and silently stared at the table top between them. The priest waited for him to speak. After a full three minutes had passed between them, Douglas finally looked at his friend.

"There's something else, Father Paul. Something that has been eating at me off and on ever since this started."

Father Paul leaned forward, his elbows on his knees and said, "I know. Or, I've suspected it. Let's have it. It's time you got it out."

Douglas looked directly in the priest's eyes, nodded his head three or four times and said, "Will you hear my confession, Father?"

"Of course, my son," the priest replied. He stood and walked around to the couch and sat down next to Douglas.

Douglas sat up, put his feet on the carpeted floor, turned to the priest and held out his hands for Father Paul to hold.

"Bless me Father, for I have sinned a terrible sin that I cannot take to the grave," he began.

When he finished, the priest, still holding his hands, said, "This is not something that can be remedied with a Hail Mary or two, Douglas. You will have to make this right. I will bless you and give you God's forgiveness, but you must inform the authorities and do what you can to fix this."

"I want to Father," Douglas sincerely said. "I don't know how. I don't know who to go to. I'm afraid if I go to the police, they'll sweep it under the rug and do nothing. Who do I go to?"

"I know someone, a lawyer. A man I grew up with and still see and play golf with. I'll call him now. He can help us."

Less than half an hour later, the priest and his penitent took the client chairs in front of the desk of Father Paul's friend. The lawyer's name was Michael Becker and he was a partner in a midsize firm of twenty-seven lawyers in Minneapolis. The priest had told him a little of the story over the phone. Becker sat back in his big, leather executive chair while Douglas told him the story in detail. When he finished, the lawyer had him go over it again, this time Becker took detailed notes.

When Douglas finished, the lawyer put down his pen, removed his cheaters and said, "Jesus Christ..."

"Mike..." the priest began to admonish him.

"Give me a break, Paul," he smiled at his friend. He turned back to Douglas and continued. "I can't even begin to count the number of felonies you've committed. Fortunately, the statute of limitations has run out on all of them I'm sure."

Not having thought of this, Father Paul, with a little panic in his voice said, "Do you think they'll want to prosecute him?"

"No. Time's up. Plus, the cancer's terminal?" he asked Douglas.

Douglas nodded and said, "A couple of months."

"I'm sorry," the lawyer said. "What do you want to do about this?" he continued holding up the legal pad with his notes on it.

"I want to come clean. I want to make it right. At least as much as I can."

"Okay. I have a friend in the attorney general's office. I'll call him right now and set up a meeting. Maybe even today."

"Mikey," Father Paul said, "he doesn't have much money..."

Becker waved a hand at his friend and said, "Don't worry about it. I'll take this pro bono. This may sound a bit mercenary given the circumstances but the publicity this shit storm is going to raise will make it worth while. Besides," he continued as he looked for a card in his rolodex, "I try to be a good Christian even if my job won't always let me."

The three of them met with Becker's friend, a man named Luis Aguilar and told Aguilar the story. By the end of the hour, Douglas had told it three more times including once to the AG herself and another in front of a camera.

Aguilar and Becker treated the filmed confession as a deposition. Aguilar conducted the questioning and Becker represented Douglas. All of the lawyers were satisfied he was telling the truth.

"Douglas is getting a little tired," Father Paul said when they were done taking the deposition.

"You okay?" Becker asked him as the film tech and court reporter were leaving the conference room while Aguilar looked on.

"Yeah," Douglas said. "I am pretty tired. It's the cancer and chemo. But, I feel a lot better. It feels good to get that off my chest. Now what?" he asked looking at the AG's lawyer. "What's going to happen to me?"

Aguilar looked at him, uncertain about what he meant. He finally said, "You mean are we going to prosecute you?"

"Yeah."

"No, Douglas. It's too late. The statute of limitations has run out. Plus, can you imagine the political fallout if we prosecuted a terminal cancer patient?" This last comment was aimed at Becker.

"We might get a new AG," Becker said. "One that's a little more even handed. One that doesn't see her job as being everyone's do-gooder mommy."

"Ssshhh," Aguilar said smiling as he put his finger to his lips. "The room might be bugged. Now," he continued again looking at Douglas, "we start pulling case files and contacting lawyers. I'll get you a copy of the tape and the transcript and keep you informed," he said to Becker.

EIGHT

Marc Kadella finished proof reading the divorce settlement he had prepared for a client he represented. Satisfied that it contained all of the terms the wife's lawyer, Marc and their clients had agreed to, he signed the last page. Marc slipped it into the large envelope Carolyn had provided to mail the document to the other lawyer. This case had been a bit of a headache proving, once again, hell hath no fury as a woman scorned.

Marc was a lawyer in private practice and as a sole practitioner rented space in a suite of offices shared by other lawyers. His landlord, Connie Mickelson, a crusty, older woman, working on her sixth marriage, did mostly family law and personal injury work. The others were Barry Cline, a man about Marc's age, who was becoming modestly successful at criminal defense and business litigation. The fourth lawyer was Chris Grafton, a small business, corporate lawyer with a thriving practice who was a few years older than Marc and Barry.

Marc was a sandy-haired, blue-eyed man of Scandinavian and Welsh ancestry. He was a little over six feet tall, in his mid-forties and the recently divorced father of two mostly grown children, his son, Eric age nineteen and a daughter, Jessica, age eighteen.

Marc placed the envelope on a corner of his desk then swiveled his chair around. His office, with the door closed, was getting a little stuffy so he opened a window overlooking Charles and Lake Street. The intercom on his phone buzzed, he swiveled back around and picked up the handle of the phone.

"What?" he asked.

"Marc, there's a man out here, a walk-in, who says he's your Uncle Larry. He says he has a serious problem and he needs to see you right away."

"Larry's here? Okay, I'll be right out."

Wondering what his seventy-five-year-old uncle who probably never had so much as a speeding ticket in his life needed to see him about, Marc stood and went through his office door. He immediately saw his mother's brother seated in one of the waiting room chairs. Once again Marc noticed Larry's full head of hair and flat stomach and hoped those genes had been passed on to him.

"Hey Uncle," Marc said as he walked over to the older man.

Larry almost jumped out of his chair, rushed up to Marc and threw his arms around his nephew. Marc stiffened up as if this was an awkward moment and when Larry released him said, "You're hugging me? I don't think you've hugged me since I turned five. This must be serious."

"It's a great case for you. The publicity will make your practice," the older man replied while holding Marc's shoulders at arm's length. "You'll see."

"Larry, I've had all of the publicity I need for a while," Marc replied while thinking: *Why do I doubt this?*

Marc turned to lead Larry back to his office and saw everyone staring at him. "C'mon back," he said as he walked to his door ignoring the inquisitive looks.

Thirty-five minutes later, Marc and his uncle emerged. Marc walked Larry to the exit door where they shook hands as Marc said, "I'll look into it. We'll take it one step at a time."

Larry looked at his nephew and said, "Okay but, let's go and you know what I want to do so, show them who's in charge."

"Larry...." He began to sternly reply then thought better of it. "I'll get back to you. Okay?"

With that, Marc opened the door and politely ushered the older man out. Marc closed the door, turned to face the wall and while everyone in the office waited to hear about this meeting, leaned forward and lightly thumped his forehead several times on the wall.

Connie Mickelson came out of her office laughing while he did this then said, "What was that about?"

Marc turned to face her. Drew a deep breath, shook his head and said, "You can choose your friends but not your family."

Marc sat down in one of the waiting area chairs to face all of his officemates who were now quite curious to find out what this was about. He looked up at the ceiling, laughed an ironic laugh, looked at his friends and said, "First of all, Larry's wife passed away about three years ago. Ellen. Nice lady. I liked her a lot and Larry was hit pretty hard. Anyway, he's been alone ever since."

"Oh, oh," Connie said correctly guessing where this was headed.

"Larry," Marc paused before continuing, "got arrested yesterday for soliciting a prostitute. He got caught up in a sting downtown..." he tried to continue amid the laughter.

"Good for him," Chris Grafton said.

"What's the big deal?" Connie added. "The cops should've let him slide on it."

"Actually, that's what I thought when he told me," Marc agreed with a big smile. "But," he continued, "that's not the problem. Larry says he won't plead. He says he wants a trial. And, he wants the TV and newspaper people to cover it."

"What?" Carolyn said as the others burst into another round of laughter.

"Yeah, he, ah, wants the publicity. See Larry lives in a senior apartment complex..."

"Oh no," Connie said covering her mouth to stifle more laughter.

"Exactly," Marc said looking at Connie. "He wants it to get out to all of the single women living there that he still has, as he put it, plenty of lead in the pencil."

This revelation brought another roar from the small crowd that could be heard in the hallway. Even Marc couldn't help himself and joined in.

"Actually," Marc continued when the laughter died down, "the best part, for me at least, is he wants me to make sure his sister, my mother, doesn't find out about it. How I'm supposed to get this on TV and not let my mother see it? He didn't have that part figured out."

"And, of course, he's not paying you," Barry Cline asked.

"No, of course not," Marc said as he stood up.

"What are you going to do?" Connie asked.

"I don't know," Marc sighed. "I'm not going to trial, that's for sure."

A short while later Marc was out of his chair and putting on his suit coat to go to lunch with Barry and Chris when the intercom buzzed.

"Chuck McReady's on the phone," he heard Sandy say when he answered it. "He says it's important."

"Really? Okay, put him through," Marc said. McReady was the number two lawyer at the State Public Defender's office. They handled appeals for indigent defendants and McReady had recently handled one successfully for a client of Marc. Before McReady came on the line. Marc searched his memory for any current cases but came up blank.

"Do you want the bad news first or the bad news first?" McReady asked him.

"Please, by all means, give me the bad news first. I hardly ever get any bad news doing criminal defense work," Marc sarcastically replied while he sat down again.

"That's a good point," McReady replied. "Criminal defense is all feel good, peaches and cream. Anyway, I hope you're sitting down. Do you remember a client of yours by the name of Howard Traynor?"

"Sure, he was my first homicide trial. The case, and my client, both scared the hell out of me. Why, what's up?" Marc said.

"Have you seen today's paper?"

"No, come to think of it, I haven't," Marc said.

"You got the Star Tribune there?"

"Yeah, why?"

"Go get it, the Metro section. I'll wait," McReady said.

Marc went out into the common area to find Barry and Chris waiting for him. "Ready?" Barry asked.

"No," Marc said as he picked up the paper from a table of magazines. "I'm on a call and I may be a while," he said looking over the front page of the "B" section. He looked at Barry and said, "You guys go ahead. I'll catch up if I can but don't wait for me."

Marc returned to his desk, sat down and picked up the receiver. "Okay, what am I looking for?"

"Below the fold on page one, the one with the headline about tainted evidence," McReady said.

"Okay, found it," Marc quietly said while he started to read the story.

"Take a minute to read it," McReady said.

Half-way through the article, Marc said into the phone, "Holy shit! Is this true?"

We got a call from the AG's office yesterday afternoon. They've known about it for about a week but kept it quiet while they checked up on it. They called us because we handled the appeal for all six of them and the AG wanted to give us a heads up. Then they released the statement to the media. We're calling all of the trial lawyers."

"Okay, now what?" Marc asked.

"I've been assigned your guy's case. I'm going to schedule a motion to have him released as soon as possible. You should be there. I'll put your name on the pleadings and you'll have to sign off."

Without realizing it, sweat broke out along Marc's hairline. "The appeal was based on ineffective assistance of counsel because I didn't get an independent DNA test done. I'm going to get disbarred," Marc said.

"Stop it," McReady said. "It wasn't your fault. I read the case file. Judge Peterson denied your request for money to have the test done. You're not obliged to pay for it out of your own pocket on a public defender assignment case."

Feeling a little better, a little relieved, Marc said, "So, they're going to let Howie Traynor out. I have to tell you, Chuck that does not give me a warm, fuzzy glow. In all my years of practice, I've never met a guy quite like him and I've represented some bad dudes."

"All of these guys are serious assholes," McReady said. "Except for a couple of them who were, past tense, serious assholes."

"Two of them are dead?"

"Yeah, both died in prison."

"Well, that's something," Marc replied.

"As defense lawyers, aren't we supposed to be glad that we're getting these people released?" McReady asked.

"I've heard that somewhere," Marc answered. "Normally, I would be but, Howie Traynor..."

"I'll let you know when the hearing is and send the pleadings over when they're done, probably later today."

Mark took out his personal phone and pressed a button to dial a friend. The man he was calling answered on the second ring.

"Hey, counselor," he heard the gruff voice of his private investigator friend, Tony Carvelli. "What's up?"

"What are you doing for lunch?" Marc asked.

"I'd planned on letting you buy me lunch today," Carvelli answered.

"Well, I'm glad I called. See you in a little bit," Marc replied.

Tony Carvelli was a Minneapolis police detective who retired from the force about ten years before. He started his own P.I. business and had thrived. He did mostly corporate security, background checks and investigations. Tony also did the occasional investigation for criminal defense lawyers which is how he met Marc. The two of them, kind of an odd couple in reality, had become good friends.

While Marc was still on the office phone with Chuck McReady, he remembered that Carvelli had been one of the arresting officers in the Traynor case. Knowing this, Marc decided he better give his friend a heads up that Traynor was likely to be released soon.

"How the hell did this happen?" Carvelli angrily asked Marc after the waitress took their lunch orders and left. The two men were seated in the back booth of a small Italian restaurant in the Uptown area of Minneapolis; a place where the two men met with some regularity.

"The story in the paper has it that this guy, Douglas Dylan, was a tech in the lab at the BCA in St. Paul when he was in college. He claims the cops let him know on a few occasions with certain suspects, that a positive DNA test result would put away some very bad people. He claims they never put pressure on him, just let him know which ones. So, he made sure the test results came back the way they wanted.

"He's now terminally ill with cancer and doesn't want to die without coming clean about it. They are all cases where the defense didn't request an independent test, or he claimed the sample was too small for a second test. He says if anyone requested a second test he would always say the sample was too small and had been destroyed during the original test."

"And Howie Traynor was one of them," Carvelli said, a statement not a question.

"I thought you should know. After he was sentenced he made some statements about getting even with some people," Marc replied.

"Most of these assholes say shit like that," the P.I. said waving a hand in dismissal. "Though I have to admit, Howie was one of the few guys who scared just about everyone, including Jake Waschke."

"Is he still in…"

"Yeah, but I hear he's getting out soon," Carvelli replied.

"Good," Marc said. "I was always sorry about what happened to him."

"I forgot that you were Traynor's lawyer. How'd that happen?"

"I was a couple of years out of law school and working for Mickey O'Herlihy. Remember him?"

"Sure, everyone remembers the Mick."

"O'Herlihy got the judge to assign the case to him. Lots of publicity…"

"Which Mickey was never shy about."

"Right. Anyway, I was kind of assisting him, my first homicide, and learning from him. Then two months before the trial, Mickey has a heart attack and dies on me."

"Is it true he was in the sack with a high-class hooker client?"

"Yep, he sure was," Marc replied. "He dies, I have no experience, so I go to the judge to withdraw and have someone else assigned. The judge looks at me and says, 'Too bad, you're up.' So, I had to try it. I got him off on the first-degree charge, but he went down for everything else. Judge Peterson came down on him like a ton of bricks."

Marc then gave Tony the names of the other five convicts, including the two who were now deceased. Tony recognized most of them, but he still wrote their names down in a notebook anyway and said he would check on the four who were still alive.

"Tell your friends at the MPD, they're about to let this psycho out," Marc said.

"And a couple others," Tony added as he held up the small notebook.

NINE

Marc entered the courtroom where the hearing was being held and looked around the room. To his left, seated in the gallery's first three rows closest to the bar railing were at least a dozen members of the media. Several of them turned to look at him while he stood in the doorway. Gabriella Shriqui, a reporter Marc knew well, smiled and wiggled her fingers at him. Marc made a mental note to ask her how she found out about today's event.

Seated at a table in front of the railing, also to his left were three men. One he recognized was the lawyer from the state public defender's office, Chuck McReady. The one seated in the middle with his back to Marc, must be Howie Traynor Marc assumed. The third man, seated to Howie's left, startled Marc and caused him to stare. He was an older man, probably mid-fifties, wearing the coat and collar of a Christian cleric. Marc was unsure if the man was a Protestant minister or a Catholic priest. Just seeing him with Howie Traynor was enough of a shock.

While he stared at the man, the door behind him opened and the attorneys from the county attorney's office and state AG's office came in.

"Hey," Marc quietly said to the lawyer from the county, Steve Gondeck.

The two men shook hands and Gondeck introduced Marc to the woman from the AG's office, Alicia Carlson. Marc and Gondeck had known each other for many years, having tried several cases against each other. The two men were at least friendly, if not friends.

Marc noticed McReady turn to look at the three lawyers in the doorway and then Marc gestured to McReady to join them. McReady stood and walked back to the doorway and the foursome of lawyers all went out into the empty hallway. Marc introduced McReady to Gondeck and Carlson then asked them, "What's your position here today?"

Gondeck gave Marc a puzzled look then said, "We filed pleadings. Didn't you get them?"

"No, I didn't," Marc answered.

"Did you?" Gondeck asked McReady.

"Yeah, I saw them," McReady answered.

"Sorry, Marc," Gondeck shrugged. "You must've been overlooked."

"We're totally opposed to release," Carlson interjected.

"And, we believe there was enough additional evidence to sustain a conviction," Gondeck added.

"Okay," Marc said. "I guess we'll see."

Marc followed McReady through the gate and as he did so, Traynor and the cleric stood to greet him. Marc noticed Howie looked basically the same, a little older for sure but, except for his hair being three or four inches long, he was the same man.

When Howie saw Marc, he extended his hand and with a genuine smile, pleasantly said, "Mr. Kadella, it's great to see you again. You're looking well."

A startled Marc shook hands with Howie then Howie said, "I'd like you to meet my good friend, Father John Brinkley. Father John," he continued turning to the priest, "this is Marc Kadella, the lawyer who handled my trial."

The two men shook hands, exchanged a brief pleasantry then Howie stepped up to Marc and quietly said, "You might not believe this, Marc, but I'm a changed man and Father John is totally responsible for it."

"That's great Howie," Marc said looking directly into his eyes. "Maybe we can get you released, and you can salvage your life."

"Bless you Marc," Howie sincerely said. "That would be a gift from God."

"All rise," the sheriff's deputy said as Judge Whitney Hogan came through the door and onto the bench. She quickly ordered everyone to be seated. The court clerk read the case number and file number into the record. The judge then took a few minutes to say a few words to the audience about court decorum.

Judge Hogan looked over both tables and said, "Starting with the Petitioner, let's have the lawyers enter their appearance."

McReady went first then each of the four lawyers stood and announced their name to the court reporter and whom they represented.

Hogan looked at the priest and politely asked, "Is it Father or Reverend?"

The priest arose from his chair and said, "Father John Brinkley, your Honor."
Hogan looked at the court reporter and said, "Let the record reflect the Petitioner is accompanied by his priest, Father John Brinkley. Okay," she continued looking at McReady, "you may proceed."

For the better part of an hour each side in turn argued about whether or not the tainted DNA was sufficient to overturn the second-degree murder conviction. Since both sides had already submitted lengthy legal briefs detailing their respective arguments, complete with legal authority, the oral arguments were not all that necessary. Both sides essentially restated what was already in the pleadings and affidavits previously filed with the court. Marc sat quietly during the entire exchange, as did Alicia Carlson, and allowed McReady and Gondeck to do all of the talking.

When both lawyers had exhausted their argument, Hogan said, "Bearing in mind, I've read the pleadings, briefs and affidavits, do you have anything else?"

None of the lawyers had anything further and after a moment of silence, Judge Hogan looked at Gondeck and Carlson and said, "From what I can see, without the DNA evidence, the prosecution has no way of linking anyone to the death of Lucille Benson. She died of a heart attack and without the DNA you can't prove beyond a reasonable doubt that she wasn't already dead before Mr. Traynor entered her bedroom.

"The lipstick and saliva on the pillow are hardly enough and even the bruising on her jawline does not point to Mr. Traynor without the DNA. Do you have any other evidence to link Mr. Traynor to the deceased to prove causation?"

"No, your Honor," Gondeck reluctantly replied.

The judge looked at Howie and said, "Do you have anything you wish to say to the court?"

Howie stood up and when he did, Father John also stood causing Marc and McReady to stand as well. "Yes, your Honor," Howie began. "I admit I was a bad man. A criminal with no concern for anyone or anything. Then, in prison, I met Father John and through his help and the love of our Lord and savior, Jesus Christ, I changed my life around.

"I believe God is giving me this second chance and, if you agree and overturn my conviction, I won't let you down."

Impassively, having heard this same claim or close variations of it dozens, if not hundreds of times, Hogan said to the priest "Would you like to add anything Father?"

"Nothing except to confirm what Howard told you, your Honor. He is a changed man," the priest said.

Hogan looked at Marc and McReady and asked, "Gentlemen, anything else?"

"No, your Honor," they said in turn.

"All right," Judge Hogan began, "the Petitioner's conviction for second degree murder and manslaughter are hereby overturned and will be expunged from his record. All other convictions will stand. Petitioner will be credited for time served on those convictions and I order his immediate release. Mr. Traynor, you're free to go and sin no more…"

With that Hogan dropped her gavel down once and left the bench. While the subdued crowd was leaving Marc noticed his friend, Tony Carvelli looking at him from the gallery. Tony held his hand up by his ear in the universal symbol of a phone then joined the crowd squeezing through the exit.

Marc congratulated Howie, then the deputy escorted Howie and the priest out the back to process Howie's release.

"Do you believe him?" Marc heard Steve Gondeck's voice behind him.

Marc turned, shook hands with his friendly adversary and said, "Don't be so cynical. It happens. He might've turned his life around."

"Yeah, I guess," Gondeck replied.

TEN

Marc went out the courtroom's exit door and ran headfirst into a wall of reporters. Since the story first broke, the media was all over it. Marc managed to make his way through the small crowd leaving Chuck McReady to get a little publicity. He turned left when he reached the elevators and almost ran into Gabriella Shriqui. She was waiting with her cameraman, Kyle Bronson, to get Marc alone.

"Hey, Gabriella, how's my favorite TV person? That's not much of a compliment, by the way," Marc added.

"Hi, Marc," she replied ignoring the mild insult. "Do you have a minute for me?" she asked intentionally personalizing the request. Gabriella was stop traffic gorgeous. The product of Moroccan Christian parents who immigrated to America when her mother was pregnant with her older brother. Gabriella had silky black hair six inches below her shoulders, light caramel colored skin that looked like a perpetual tan and dark, almost black, slightly almond shaped eyes. She was also quite adept at using her looks to help her get a story, especially with the males of the species.

Marc had first met her while he defended a corrupt judge accused of murdering his wife. Despite the fact that he was well aware of her game of using her sensuality, looking into her eyes once again caused him to cave in and talk to her.

Marc spent a few minutes answering her questions about Howie Traynor's case. Mostly what he had to say amounted to little more than innocuous statements such as, "Justice has finally prevailed."

When his elevator arrived, as he held the door open he said to her, "Seen Maddy lately?"

"Sure, we get together once in a while. She's a good friend."

"I should take her to lunch. Maybe both of you. If you talk to her, tell her to call me."

"I will and thanks Marc."

Marc ascended to the seventeenth floor and quickly walked down the hallway to courtroom 1745. This was the courtroom of his much better half, Judge Margaret Tennant. They had made a date for lunch as they normally did whenever Marc was downtown.

When he reached her courtroom door, it banged open and Marc was almost knocked down by three angry insurance defense lawyers and one smiling plaintiff's lawyer. Marc stepped aside to let them pass then went into the courtroom. Expecting to find Margaret still on the bench he was mildly surprised to see she was already gone. Still at her desk next to the bench and writing in a file was the judge's clerk, Lois.

"Hi, Lois," Marc said as he passed through the gate in the bar. "Is her Highness available?"

"Hey Marc, let me check," she said picking up her phone. A couple of seconds later Marc heard her say, "There's a smartass man out here who wants to know, and I quote, if her Highness is available."

Lois listened for a moment, then said, "I don't know. I'll find out," she covered the mouthpiece with her hand and said to Marc. "She wants to know if the smartass man has a cute butt. Turn around and let me take a look."

Marc's shoulders slumped. He closed his eyes, shook his head and with a half-smile, half-laugh said, "I am not going to turn around and let you take a look."

Lois said into the phone, "He won't cooperate." She listened, for a moment then said, "Uh huh, yeah, I'll tell him," and then looked back at Marc.

"She told me to tell you that you'd better have a cute butt, or she'll throw your non-cute butt in jail for contempt."

"Tell her if she's not careful it could be a while before I let her get another look at my cute butt," Marc said doing his best not to laugh.

Lois repeated this, barely containing her own laughter. She listened for a moment, hung up the phone and said, "She says she's really sorry, she doesn't want you to withhold butt viewing privileges and you're to go right back."

While Lois laughed, Marc thanked her and went through the door to the judge's chambers. As he walked passed her desk, Lois couldn't resist saying, "You do have a pretty cute butt."

"And they talk about us..." Marc muttered as he entered the back hallway.

The waitress finished taking their order, a salad for Margaret and a cheeseburger and fries for Marc, then left to place the order. They were in a booth in a restaurant named *Peterson's* across Fourth Avenue from the government center. Margaret caught Marc watching the teenage girl walk away.

"A little young, don't you think?" she said.

"I was just thinking that," Marc smiled. "How young they're getting to be."

"They're not getting younger," Margaret started to say.

"I know you don't need to remind me."

"Well, tell me about the hearing. How did it go?" she asked.

"Interesting," Marc said after thinking it over for a moment. Marc spent the next ten minutes briefly describing the arguments made and the judge's decision.

"So, she kicked him loose, huh? I'm not surprised. I probably would have also. Even with the other evidence the tainted DNA test makes the murder conviction impossible to uphold."

"She let stand the convictions for everything else. The B & E, the burglary, assault on a cop, resisting arrest, all of it. Even without the DNA there's enough to uphold those convictions. She let him off with time served.

"Let me tell you about Howie Traynor. Remember how scary I told you he was? The attitude and dead eyes?"

"Yeah," she answered as the waitress returned with their meals.

When the pretty blonde left, Marc continued. "It seems Howie found Jesus in prison. He even had a priest there on his behalf. He sat at the table with us. Howie greeted me like we were old friends."

"It happens," Margaret said pausing with a forkful of salad on its way to her mouth.

Marc had wolfed down his burger and was now working on the fries. He paused between bites and said, "Yeah, but it's usually right before they throw the switch on Old Sparky. He seems genuine but..."

"What?" she asked.

"You didn't know him back when. Did I tell you Tony was one of the arresting officers?"

"No, really?"

"Yeah I didn't know him then. I talked to him a couple days ago and he was in court this morning, probably checking on things for Vivian Donahue."

"Why would Vivian Donahue care about this case?"

"The victim was her aunt," Marc replied.

"Really? Small world," Margaret said.

"Anyway, Tony remembered Howie and said he even scared the shit out of the cops who had to deal with him. He said when they went to arrest him one of the guys hit him in the chest with a Taser and Howie jerked the Taser leads out, threw them at the cop then busted the guy's jaw with one punch. It took four cops to put him down."

"Do you think he'll sue for wrongful imprisonment?" Margaret asked.

"I don't know. What do you think? You think he has a case? What are his damages? The time he served could easily be for the other convictions."

"He could probably get something. The City of Minneapolis and Hennepin County would write him a big check just for the asking. You know what they're like," Margaret said.

"I'm a little worried about him suing me or filing a complaint with the Office of Professional Responsibility for my representation," Marc said.

"Why?"

"For not having the DNA sample independently tested."

"Did the technician who rigged the tests say that he ran the tests and they all came back negative and he doctored the results?" Margaret asked.

"No," Marc said after he thought for a moment. "In fact, he said he never tested the material at all. Just phonied up the results and if anyone asked to get the sample for an independent test he claimed there wasn't enough left, or it had been destroyed. He covered it up."

"So, even if you had requested a test, who's to say it would have been done. Why didn't you?"

"It was a public defender appointment. Mickey O'Herlihy, my boss at the time, got it. He loved these long shot cases. I was going to second chair the case and then Mickey has a heart attack screwing a hooker client. I asked to be allowed to withdraw and the judge, Ross Peterson, refused. Then when I asked for funds to do an independent DNA test, he turned me down. He said it was a waste of the taxpayer's money. I didn't have the money to pay for it myself, so..."

"What did the court of appeals have to say?"

"They ruled two to one, that it was not judicial error to turn me down. The dissent wrote I should have paid for it myself under the doctrine of zealous representation."

"That's a crock," Margaret said as she handed her empty salad bowl to the waitress. "No one says a lawyer has an obligation to bankrupt himself."

Marc's phone went off, he pulled it from his coat pocket, looked at the ID and answered it.

"Hey, paisan, we were just talking about you."

Marc listened for a moment then said, "I'm with Margaret at *Peterson's*, the place across Fourth from the government center," he said in answer to the caller's question.

"Tony says hello," Marc said to Margaret. "What?" he said into the phone. "Sorry", he said to Margaret. "Tony says hello beautiful." He went back to the phone and said, "Sucking up to her won't help. The next time you get arrested there's no guarantee she'll be your judge."

Margaret reached across the table, pulled Marc's hand that was holding the phone toward herself then loudly said, "Yes, I will. I'll see to it."

Marc listened again then said to Margaret, "He says you should dump me."

Margaret took the phone from him, then speaking into it said, "I would but he's got such a cute butt. I can't let it go," and started laughing.

Marc took the phone back, shook his head and said to Carvelli, "So, what's up?"

He listened for a moment then said, "No, she has to go back to work, but I can stay for a while."

He listened again then said, "Okay, I'll see you in a few minutes."

ELEVEN

Ten minutes later, Carvelli entered the restaurant through the skyway entrance. Marc saw him first and waved him over to their booth. Walking through the restaurant, he looked to be half cop, half Italian Wiseguy. He was just under six feet, broad shoulders and in his early fifties. He still had a full head of mostly black hair and wore his standard, thin, brown leather jacket and white silk shirt, two buttons undone.

When he reached the table, Margaret slid out and said, "I have to go. I'll let you two boys talk," and offered her cheek for Tony to kiss.

Carvelli gestured to their waitress to bring him a cup of coffee. He then slid onto the bench seat opposite Marc and placed a manila envelope he was carrying onto the table.

After the waitress delivered Tony's coffee, Marc asked, "What's this?" referring to the contents of the envelope.

While pouring some cream into his coffee, Tony said "For starters, our boy Howie's prison record."

"How did you get that so quickly?" Marc asked as he removed the documents from the envelope. "I thought I'd have to get Madeline to use her charms on somebody to get this." He leafed through the papers and said, "What's it say?"

"He was a pretty bad boy the first two years or so. They suspected him of several assaults. My cop pals talked to a couple of ex-cons who knew him and did time with him. They claim he got his ass kicked by gang bangers a couple of times. Then one-by-one, he caught up with the guys who did it. He put several of them in the hospital. After a while even, the bad asses left him alone.

"About that time, he started acting as an enforcer for a white Aryan gang suspected of smuggling drugs in. Two or three years ago he started getting counseling from that priest, what's-his-name?"

"Brinkley?"

"Yeah, that's him. According to his psyche evaluation, the prison officials were a little skeptical at first. But now they think he may have found Jesus and straightened out."

"Interesting," Marc said. "What do you think?"

"I've been around a while and I know I'm a bit cynical…" Tony began.

"Cops and lawyers," Marc interjected.

"Right," Tony agreed. "It will take more than a report from a priest and a shrink to convince me. It's not like they can't be fooled.

"This guy Traynor was a first-class psycho asshole back in the day. He killed Vivian's aunt that night and we believe he did at least two others and probably a third one in prison. There are reports in there," Tony continued tapping the documents on the table in front of Marc, "about the other five guys whose DNA tests were faked. Three of them are out or getting out and the other two are dead. Both died in prison. One died from cancer and the other one from an accident. At least that was the official finding. The corrections officers and my pals with the MPD I talked to suspect it was Traynor's Aryan buddies and likely Traynor himself who caused the guy to 'accidentally' fall from the top tier and break his neck and crush his skull."

"What about the other three?" Marc asked.

From memory, Tony told Marc who the other three were. The first was a now thirty-six-year-old Hispanic-American, Angelo Suarez, convicted in Ramsey County of rape. He was suspected of at least six others and many more. Originally from the Dallas area, he had moved several times throughout the Midwest leaving a trail of unsolved sexual assaults in his wake. Considered extremely intelligent he had left no DNA at the others before the one he was convicted of in St. Paul. He was released several days ago.

"Great," Marc said. "We've got a serial rapist on the loose."

The second was a thirty-nine-year-old member of a biker gang by the name of Eugene Parlow, convicted of second-degree murder and drug dealing. He was also suspected of being in the Aryan prison gang with Traynor.

"Wait a minute," Marc said. "The prison authorities believe Howie was in an Aryan prison gang then quit when he found Jesus? Do these gangs allow something like that?"

"I wondered if you would catch that," Tony said with a sly smile. "Good question. The answer is normally, no. Once you're in, you're in for good. That's a question the cops will be asking this douche bag Parlow once they catch up with him."

"The cops have already lost track of him?"

"He's around. They'll find him but until he does something he's not a high priority. All of these guys need to have an eye kept on them, but they can't be harassed either.

"The last one is a man named Aaron Forsberg, now age forty-seven. He was convicted in Hennepin County of murdering his wife. He always insisted he was innocent. He was a very well-off investment banker."

"I remember that case," Marc said. "Rumor was his defense cost a couple million bucks. He had a team of lawyers headed up by Julian Segal, now Judge Segal over in Ramsey County."

"Yeah, that's right," Tony said snapping his fingers. "I knew I heard that name before."

"It was really high profile and all over the news for months," Marc said. "Why wouldn't Segal do a second DNA test?" Marc wondered.

"In the report," Tony said referring again to documents in front of Marc, "the test material was not enough to do a second test and the judge let it in anyway."

"Who was the judge?" Marc rhetorically asked as he leafed through the papers to find the one he wanted. "Ross Peterson," he quietly said when he found it. "The same judge I had with Howie and he ruled the same way. Interesting." He looked at Tony and said, "I'll read these over when I get home tonight. How did Vivian take the news about Howie getting kicked loose?" Marc asked.

"She wasn't pleased," Tony said. "More disappointed than angry."

Tony slid out of the booth as did Marc and handed Marc his check for the coffee. He took two dollars from his pocket and dropped them on the table.

"I'll talk to you later. I'm working today. See ya," Tony said.

TWELVE

Carvelli was walking through the skyway over Sixth Street back to the ramp where he parked his car when his phone went off. He removed it from the inside pocket of his leather jacket and checked the screen. The call was coming from a phone at the Minneapolis Police Department. Hopefully it was the call he was expecting.

"Carvelli," he said as he stepped to the window of the skyway and looked east up Sixth.

"It's Owen, Tony," he heard a man say. "What's up?"

"Hey, Owen, thanks for calling back. You in the office?"

"Yeah, I'll be here for a while."

"Mind if I stop by for a few minutes? I need to talk to you about something."

"Sure, no problem. When?"

"I'm only a block away," Tony said. "I'll see you in a few minutes."

Carvelli continued across the skyway to the parking ramp, hurried down a flight of stairs and exited the building on Sixth. He walked the short distance to Fourth Avenue, then turned north to go to the Old City Hall.

A half a block away he jaywalked across Fourth and waved at a cop he knew who was cruising by. The cop stopped his squad car next to Tony and pushed the button to open the passenger window. The cop leaned across the seat and yelled, "Hey, numbnuts, you want a ticket for jaywalking?"

Tony leaned into the window and with a big grin said, "Yeah, Belton. Give me a ticket for jaywalking. It would be the most work you've done for a month. And, I'll take you to court just to be a pain in the ass."

"You don't have to take me to court to be a pain in the ass you dago troublemaker. How you doing Tony? What are you up to?"

"I'm heading to see Owen Jefferson about something, Paul. Good to see you again."

"Stay out of trouble," the cop said as he pulled away.

Carvelli continued his journey toward the Old City Hall. He looked up at the ugly granite structure with the Big Ben style clock in the tower. Opened in 1909, the building was an anachronistic reminder of a time gone by. These days, it looked totally out of place, but Tony still liked the old building a lot. To him, it had been home for over two decades while he worked as a cop and it had twice as much character as any of the glass, chrome and concrete sterile monstrosities being built now.

He strolled across Fifth Street against a red light crossing the light rail tracks barely twenty feet ahead of an oncoming train. Tony entered through the back entry on Fifth and walked to the detective's squadroom where Jefferson had a desk. On the way he said hello to almost a dozen policemen and women he knew.

Carvelli was supposed to check in with security and receive a visitor's badge. Ignoring this rule gave Tony an almost school boy mischievous sense of satisfaction. Besides, virtually everyone in the department knew who he was anyway.

"What's up?" Jefferson asked him as Tony approached the detective's desk. Owen Jefferson was a lean, bald, six-foot four-inch black man with a tiny gold stud in his left ear. He had been a homicide detective for over four years and his case closure rate was the best in the department. It was rumored that his boss was about to be promoted to captain and kicked upstairs and every detective in the department expected and wanted Jefferson to succeed her.

Carvelli nodded and waved a greeting at several of the detectives who looked up from their desks. He dropped into the uncomfortable, padded gray government issued chair next to Jefferson's desk and looked around the room while the detective patiently waited for him to speak.

"You know," Carvelli began while still looking around the room. "I don't think this place has changed a bit; probably not since the turn of the last century."

"So, that's why you wanted to stop by, to critique the décor? You going into the interior decorating business?"

"You'd have to redecorate this place with a flamethrower."

"Please stop. You're offending my sensitive side," Jefferson sarcastically said.

"Howie Traynor," Carvelli said turning his head to look directly at the detective.

"Yeah, isn't that interesting?"

"Have you seen his prison record and psych eval?" Tony asked.

"Yeah, read it yesterday."

"What do you think?"

"I think it's bullshit," Jefferson answered. "You remember this guy. He was ice cold back in the day. You think he's found Jesus and all of a sudden he's touchy feely friendly?"

"No, but you and I are cynical cops."

"So," Jefferson continued, "what do you have in mind? He hasn't done anything, and I can't watch him."

"After the trial, he made a shitload of threats when he was taken away. I heard from jail guards he said he'd get even with everyone."

"A lot of these assholes say that," Jefferson shrugged as he opened a desk drawer and put his feet on the drawer and his hands locked together behind his head. "Again Tony, there's not much I can do until he does something."

Carvelli thought for a moment then leaned in across the desk and quietly said, "I'm just giving you a heads up. I don't believe this guy's bullshit for a minute and I'll quietly keep an eye on him."

The tall detective shrugged his shoulders, dropped his feet to the floor, placed his forearms on the desk and in a whisper said, "Do it. Just be careful and keep me informed of anything you find."

"Will do," Tony said as he patted his friend on the arm and stood to leave.

Carvelli went out the same door he came in, went down the building's concrete stairs and onto the light rail platform. He looked across Fifth at the fountain on the plaza in front of the government center and took in all of the people around it. It was a beautiful late August day and seeing the young women strolling about made him a touch nostalgic for his youth.

Coming back to reality he removed his phone and pressed a very familiar number. Barely a second before the call went to voice mail a woman answered.

"Hello, Anthony," Vivian Donahue said.

Vivian Corwin Donahue was the matriarch of a very well-known family that was one of the most socially prominent, politically connected and old-money wealthy in Minnesota. In her mid-sixties, she was still a very attractive woman and she could proudly boast, with the only exception being her hair color, it was all natural.

The Corwin lineage could be traced back to the 1840's when the family patriarch, Edward Corwin, immigrated to the mostly empty prairie that was Minnesota at the time. Edward started farming and began building an agricultural empire that was worth billions today. The family itself was no longer involved in Corwin Agricultural but Vivian, as the current head of the family, could still move political mountains and when she called a governor, senator, congressman or mayor, that person had better sit up and pay attention.

"Are you home right now?" Tony asked his sometime lover.

"Yes, come right over," she replied.

Twenty minutes later Carvelli parked his shiny, black Camaro next to a candy-apple red Bentley. He was in the circular driveway of the Corwin family mansion on fifteen acres of very expensive lakeshore property. The sixteen room mini-palace had been in the family since the early twentieth century. Even though Vivian often referred to it as a mausoleum, she would never part with it. It was the one place the entire Corwin clan, over one hundred of them, could gather.

Tony reached for the doorbell but before he could press it, the door swung open and a very pretty young woman smiled, wrapped her arms around his neck and kissed his cheek.

"Hello, you gorgeous stud," Vivian's barely twenty-year-old granddaughter, Adrienne greeted him.

"Hello, sweetheart," Tony replied.

"Grandma's out by the pool," she said as she put her arm through his.

"How are you?" Tony asked the young girl as the two of them walked through the big house toward the patio door. "Ready to go back to school?"

"Oh, yes and no," she said. "I like it here but I'm finding out you can't stay a young dilettante forever. Especially with the Dragon Lady around," Adrienne giggled.

Tony looked at her and said, "I'll tell her you mentioned her."

"Don't you dare! Besides, you know how much I love her."

They reached the double French patio doors leading to the pool and patio. Adrienne opened the door for him, patted him on the back and let him go through the door alone.

Vivian was sitting in a padded patio chair next to a round table with a large umbrella in its middle. Tony walked over to her, bent down and kissed her cheek.

"Hello, Anthony," she said with a genuine smile. Vivian was the only person, other than his mother when she was mad at him, who called him Anthony. For some reason that he could not quite explain, it seemed right coming from her.

Tony removed a copy of the prison record of Howie Traynor from his coat pocket and placed it on the table before her. He took off his jacket, hung it on the back of the chair next to her and sat down.

"Is this the prison record?" she asked.

"Yeah," Tony replied.

"Give me the Cliff's Notes version. I'll read it all later."

Tony poured a glass of lemonade from the pitcher on the table and refilled Vivian's as well. They sipped their drinks while he gave her a brief overview of the report he had just handed her.

"Do you believe this miraculous transformation Mr. Traynor made from homicidal sociopath to devout Catholic?" she asked when he finished.

"Not for an instant," Tony emphatically said. "When I was in burglary, everyone knew who this guy was. Homicide knew him too. I knew a couple cops who were on the street undercover at the time who told me most of the dirt bags in the Cities knew Howie Traynor. He scared the hell out of everyone, including the cops. It was as if he had no feelings at all. Didn't care about anyone or anything, including himself. Now he goes from that to a choir boy? I don't think so."

"Can the police do anything about him?"

"Not really. They don't have the manpower to follow him even if they could. They pretty much have to wait until he does something."

"Do you think he will?"

"I don't know. He made a lot of threats when he was convicted, even to his own lawyer, Marc Kadella."

"Marc was his lawyer then?" Vivian asked with genuine surprise. She knew Marc and was genuinely fond of him and respected him as a lawyer and a person. She also knew Marc's love, Margaret Tennant.

"Yes, he was," Tony nodded. "It was his first homicide trial. Long story how he got stuck with it. Anyway," he continued, "from what I remember and what others said, Marc did a good job for him, but Howie didn't see it that way.

"Then at his hearing to get him released, Marc told me Howie acted like they were best friends. Marc said it made his skin crawl."

For the next several minutes they sat in silence while Vivian looked across the beautifully manicured lawn at the sailboats gliding by on Lake Minnetonka. Tony finished his lemonade and refilled their glasses.

"I want to hire you to keep an eye on him," Vivian finally said. "At least for a while until we're sure one way or another."

"Vivian," Tony said sternly looking at her. "This is not your responsibility. In fact, I would advise you to stay out of it."

"Anthony, this man murdered my aunt and gave it no more thought than if he had swatted a fly. That makes it my business. Plus, at this point, we both believe he will kill again, and the police are helpless to prevent it. All I'm asking is to hire you to do what you do and watch him until we're sure."

Knowing the futility of trying to dissuade this headstrong, remarkable woman, Tony looked at her, shrugged his shoulders and said, "Okay, I'll do it. Better me than someone else. But, I do have other clients and…"

"I know that," Vivian said.

"…I'll call Maddy Rivers and…"

"I was going to suggest that you do. Send me your bill, pad it all you want, I don't care. Talk to Madeline and bring her to see me. She's so gorgeous even I like looking at her."

"I was going to say, Maddy Rivers and some other guys I know, retired cops, to help me."

"Bring in whomever you need."

THIRTEEN

While Tony was driving away from the mansion he took out his phone and pressed a speed dial button. It barely finished ringing once when it was answered.

"Hey, Carvelli," he heard a P.I. friend of his, Madeline Rivers say.

Madeline Rivers was an ex-cop from the Chicago Police department in her early thirties. In her three-inch heeled suede half boots she liked to wear she was over six feet tall. She had a full-head of thick dark hair with auburn highlights that fell down over her shoulders, a model gorgeous face and a body worthy of Playboy. In fact, foolishly posing for that magazine was what led her to quit the Chicago PD.

Maddy, as she was called by her friends, had moved to Minneapolis after quitting the Chicago cops following her Playboy spread. At the same time, she also went through an ugly breakup when she found out the doctor she had fallen for was married. After arriving in Minnesota, she got a private investigator's license. Maddy was befriended by Tony Carvelli and she was now doing quite well herself.

"You busy?" Tony asked her.

"You mean right this minute?"

"Yeah, we need to meet. I got a project and I'm going to need another body."

"Okay, where and when?" she asked.

Tony gave her the name of a place in downtown Minneapolis; a British style pub and restaurant on the Nicollet Mall.

"Yeah, I know it," she said. "I'll see you there in about twenty minutes."

"I'll meet you upstairs in the patio area. I'll be there in a few minutes and get us a table."

"Okay, see you then."

Maddy entered the pub through the door on Nicollet. She removed her sunglasses and stood at the entrance for ten seconds to allow her eyes to adjust to the darkness. Satisfied she could see, she told the young hostess she was going upstairs to the patio. Despite the fact that it was mid-afternoon of a work day, the pub was more than half full of customers. While Maddy walked toward the stairway, almost every male head and most of the females turned to watch her. Dressed in designer jeans, a white sleeveless silk blouse, her usual three inch heeled half boots and the sunglasses on her head, she looked like a model strolling through the dining room.

Ignoring the gawkers, she went up the stairs into the bright sunlight and looked over the crowd until she saw Tony wave at her. When she reached his table, she offered her cheek for a quick kiss then took a seat.

"So, what's up?" she asked.

"Have you been reading the papers? Watching the news about those guys released from prison because of bad DNA tests?"

"No, not really. I've been in Chicago to see my parents. I just got back yesterday," Maddy replied.

"How's your Dad?"

The waitress came to their table and took their orders.

"He's good," she smiled. "The cancer is in remission and his strength is back and he's doing pretty well, thank God. I never realized how much I would miss him until he got sick. So, tell me..."

Tony saw the waitress returning with their drinks and waited for her to set them on the table and leave. For the next fifteen minutes he told her the entire story and brought her up to date.

"This guy murdered Vivian's aunt. That can't make her happy and that's one lady I wouldn't want to have displeased with me," Maddy said.

"Oh, I forgot," Tony said. "Guess who this Traynor had for a lawyer?"

"Marc?"

"Yep. His first homicide and Traynor threatened him too."

"What can we do? What can the cops do?"

"The cops can't do anything. If they even go near him they could get slapped with a harassment suit. The two of us, though," Tony continued, "can do loose surveillance and I know some retired cops we can get to help. Vivian insists on paying us. What I'd like to do is spend at least a couple of weeks watching him. See where he goes, who he talks to, stuff like that. See if we can find out if he really found Jesus or if it's an act."

"Where do you want to start?"

"This is for you," Tony said as he handed her a photo of Howie Traynor. "It's a little old but it still looks like him. He's pushing forty now and his hair is a little longer, but you'll recognize him.

"First thing I have to do is find him. He's not on parole or in a halfway house so we don't know where he is. I know a few places to check out. If he's still here, I'll find him."

"What about the priest that was in court with him?" Maddy asked still staring at Traynor's picture.

"He's on the list. I'll see him if I have to."

"Dead eyes," Maddy muttered. "If you look in his eyes..."

"Oh, I had the opportunity, up close and personal and there's nothing behind them. When I saw him there wasn't a spark of human emotion. But don't let that fool you. The shrinks say he has a 130 IQ. He's no dummy."

"Get me a copy of everything you have, please."

"Yeah, sorry. I should have and didn't think of it. I will," Tony apologized. "I'm going to take off and see if I can get a line on him."

"You want me to check out some places?"

"No," he shook his head as they both stood to leave. Tony dropped a twenty-dollar bill on the table and said, "You'd stick out like a sore thumb in these dives. Plus, it will be better if you stay in the background for now. I'll call you later."

Tony parked the Camaro at the back of the bar's parking lot away from any other cars. Most of the patrons of the *East End* on East Franklin Avenue were not likely to be too concerned about banging their car door against another car. This was the fourth place he had been and so far, no luck.

When he got inside, he took a seat at the bar close to the door and ordered a glass of beer. While he sipped his drink he casually looked over the crowd, several of whom were also checking him out. Tony could see into the back where the pool tables were which reminded him of the night they had dragged Howie Traynor out of here. After a few minutes he saw a disheveled, long-haired, heavily tattooed man come out of the men's room and join the pool players. He was dressed in old jeans, a black T-shirt with the Rolling Stones' tongue logo on the front, battered sneakers and a denim vest.

About two minutes after leaving the men's room he made eye contact with Tony. Carvelli quickly finished his beer and set the empty glass on the bar. As inconspicuously as possible, he stood and strolled out the door to wait in his car. Fifteen minutes after leaving the bar, Tony saw the man he was waiting for leave the bar and start walking west on Franklin. Carvelli patiently waited another three minutes to be sure no one followed the man then drove out of the lot looking for him.

Two blocks down Franklin, he pulled to the curb, buzzed down the passenger side window and said, "Eddie, got a minute?"

The best undercover cop in Minneapolis stuck his head in the window, smiled and said, "Hey, Tony. How the hell are you?"

"Get in Eddie, I need to talk."

Eddie Davis got in the passenger side and, as Tony punched the gas and the powerful car jumped forward, Eddie said, "God I love this car. How are you doing, dude?"

Tony looked him over and said, "Jesus Christ, Eddie, you need to get off undercover. Aren't you tired of looking like this?"

"Hey, I save more lives busting dope dealing assholes and help put away more scumbags than any of you desk jockey detectives."

Tony thought about it and said, "You know, you're probably right. When you retire, the city should put up a statue."

"Damn straight," Eddie said laughing.

Tony took a minute to tell Eddie who he was looking for and gave Eddie a brief description. As soon as Tony described him, Eddie stopped him.

"You got a picture?"

"Yeah, here," Carvelli said pulling a copy of Traynor's photo from his pocket.

Eddie looked it over then said, "He was at the *East End* earlier today. He's older and hair a little longer?"

"Yeah," Tony said.

"That's him. He was in asking about a safe cracker named Jimmy Oliver."

"You know Oliver?"

"Sure, I know Jimmy. He's supposed to be straight. Tends bar up Northeast," he continued referring to a district of Minneapolis. "*Tooley's* I think. I'm pretty sure."

With one hand on the wheel Tony slipped the picture back in his coat pocket. "If you see Traynor again, call Owen Jefferson and tell him to call me."

"Okay, will do," Eddie said.

"I'll run up to *Tooley's*. Where do you want me to drop you?"

"Anyplace along here is fine," Eddie answered.

Tony pulled the car to the curb and more completely explained to the detective what he was up to and why. "If you come across anything, let me know. You can always call Jefferson and he'll get in touch with me."

"Will do. Good to see you again, man," Eddie said. The two men shook hands, Eddie got out and Tony drove off.

Fifteen minutes later Tony found a parking space on the street between two cars fifty yards down from the front door of *Tooley's*. *Tooley's* was a neighborhood saloon in a working-class part of Northeast Minneapolis. It had been here for over seventy years and the bar and its clientele had barely changed a bit during the entire time.

Tony put the transmission in park and unbuckled the shoulder harness to leave the car. As he was about to open his door he looked at the bar's front door and saw Howie Traynor turn the corner and go inside the bar.

"Well there you are," Tony muttered to himself.

Instead of getting out of the car and afraid he would be recognized, Carvelli slid down in the seat and waited. It was almost a half hour before Traynor came out. When he did, he looked around then walked back from where he came.

Tony waited about a minute then started the Camaro to pursue him. As he was pulling away from the curb, Traynor drove around the corner right in front of him. He was driving a ten-year-old gray Buick and he turned right to head straight away from Tony.

Keeping his distance while following Traynor on Central Avenue toward downtown, Tony easily followed him right to his front door. A half mile north of downtown on Sixteenth Street, he turned east off Central. Three blocks later, Traynor pulled to the curb and parked his sedan on the street. Tony pulled over, took a small pair of binoculars from the Camaro's console and watched Traynor enter an apartment building.

The building was one of four identical brick three story apartment buildings sitting side-by-side on Sixteenth Street and Clark Avenue NE. Built before the war, each building housed twelve apartments, four on each floor. The basement of each building was used for a laundry room and storage space. Each apartment was assigned one of the small rooms for storage.

Carvelli decided to stake the place out and waited until after eleven to see if Traynor would go anywhere. While he waited he made two calls. The first was to Maddy Rivers to let her know he had found Traynor. The second was to Owen Jefferson to give him the same news. He also got Jefferson to agree to go to *Tooley's* and question Jimmy Oliver about his visit from Howie.

Traynor's apartment was on the third floor of the second building from the corner. It was a small, one bedroom with a kitchen, bathroom and a living room. The living room was up front facing the street and had two windows side by side. Howie was able to afford the apartment because of the lawyer he retained to sue the city. She had contacted him before he was released from prison and promised to get him big bucks in the wrongful incarceration lawsuit. Generally considered unethical, she had loaned him money for the apartment, the car and living expenses to be repaid from any settlement money. Shortly after eleven, looking out through the blinds of the window on the left, he saw the dark colored Camaro pull away from the curb and drive past his building. Howie had spotted the car on the street at *Tooley's* and had deliberately allowed the man, whom Howie assumed was a cop, to follow him home.

While Tony sat in his car down the street from Traynor's apartment, Marc was enjoying a quiet evening at Margaret's Edina home. After dinner, Marc flopped on the couch while Margaret worked on several case files she had brought home. Shortly before nine she stopped and joined him on the couch to watch one of their favorite shows. It was about a cowboy Deputy US Marshall and the Hillbilly Mafia in Kentucky.

During the 10:00 newscast they watched a one-minute story of a press conference held by an infamous lawyer from California. A high-profile self-promoter named Glenda Albright was railing about the egregious injustice done to her clients. She had been retained to represent the victims of the intentionally altered DNA tests of the men recently released from prison. She named all four of the men who she claimed to represent including Howie Traynor.

"So, the Wicked Witch of the West has arrived on her jet powered broom to teach us ignorant folks out here in fly-over country about justice," Margaret irreverently said.

"Looks like," Marc agreed. "Except I'm not sure she has much of a case, at least with Traynor."

"You know Minneapolis," Margaret added. "They are probably already writing the checks."

Maddy Rivers parked her car in the only spot available on Howie's street close enough to watch both his apartment and his car. She was in the shade of a large Elm tree to her right on the street's boulevard. She thought about the tree and having spent twenty-five dollars for a thorough car wash the day before, hoped the tree was not full of birds.

It was just past noon on a sunny, warm Saturday and Howie Traynor had been at church until noon. He had a job at St. Andrews Catholic Church helping with custodial duties. St. Andrews was in Northeast Minneapolis, a couple of miles from Howie's apartment. It was also the parish of Howie's priest, Father John Brinkley, the one who had appeared in court with him.

Maddy had discreetly followed him home from a safe distance and was taking another turn at a stakeout of him. She had seen him get a parking spot in front of his building then watched as he went inside.

She settled in for what was likely to be a dull afternoon, until another of Carvelli's friends took over later. He would stay until 10:00

or 11:00 that evening if Howie didn't go out and Maddy would be back in the morning.

The team of P.I.s and ex-cops had been doing a rotation surveillance of Traynor for a couple of weeks. So far, there was nothing to report. Spending Vivian's money to pay everyone, Tony wanted to give it at least another week or two. It was boring work but paid well and Maddy liked and admired Vivian Donahue enough so that she would likely do it without pay.

Maddy picked up a hard cover book from the passenger seat and opened it to the page marked with a bookmark. As long as she had to sit here, she would indulge herself in her secret passion; a steamy romance novel.

While Madeline was enjoying her book, Howie Traynor used the index and middle finger of his right hand to slightly part the vertical blinds of a window in the front room of his apartment. He peaked through the opening and watched the beautiful brunette sitting in the front seat of her black late model Audi sedan. He watched for almost a full minute then turned and walked into his bedroom.

At 5:15 that afternoon, Maddy's phone went off. She checked the screen, pressed the talk button and said, "Hey, Dan, don't tell me you can't make it."

"No, no, sweetheart. I'm on my way. I'll be there in about ten minutes. Anything going on?" asked Dan Sorenson, a retired cop who was Maddy's relief.

"Nope. He hasn't moved all day. The street is pretty crowded. I'll watch for you and pull out as you're coming up the street, so you can have my parking spot. And Dan," she continued, "hurry up. I gotta pee. Bad."

Sorenson laughed and said, "On the way."

FOURTEEN

The two old friends cruised across Balm Lake in Northern Minnesota heading toward a favorite fishing spot. The sun was just about down and the men, long time neighbors on the relatively small lake, were going to get in some night walleye fishing.

Sitting in the stern and steering the twenty-year-old Alumacraft was Robert Smith, a retired judge of the Minnesota Court of Appeals. The judge's fishing partner, probably the best friend he ever had, was seated in the bow silently acting as the guide to their spot. He too was retired from a medical practice in Bemidji, Minnesota. His name was Jay Patterson and the two men had been friends for almost twenty-five years, ever since Bob Smith and his wife Gloria had purchased forty acres adjacent to the doctor's lake home. The Smiths had built a nice four-bedroom two-story a quarter mile from the Pattersons. Over the years the two men and their wives had become the best of friends.

Three years ago, upon reaching the mandatory retirement age of seventy, Smith retired with the intention of living at the lake home full-time. Unknown to the Pattersons, this had been a source of contention between Bob and Gloria. Two days after his official retirement date, Gloria filed for divorce.

Once the initial shock wore off, the judge realized he didn't really care. The divorce was amicable; the property and monetary settlement was reasonable, and the couple parted but remained, if not friends, at least friendly.

"This is it," Patterson said.

"No, not quite," the judge disagreed. "A little farther."

The little disagreement was a normal routine part of their friendship. If one said up the other would automatically say down. Despite this petty little quirk, the two men made the friendship work.

The judge throttled down the twenty horse Johnson outboard and the eighteen-foot aluminum fishing boat slowed and stopped.

"You went too far," the doctor said as he dropped the anchor into twenty feet of water.

"I know," the judge smiled to himself. "I just wanted to annoy you."

That day had been sunny and warmer than usual for mid-September. The two friends had played eighteen holes at a course near Black Duck. Now, with the sun down and out in the open water on the lake, the air temperature was rapidly cooling. Because of the coolness of the evening, both men decided to use lures rather than leeches to catch the fish they were after. They each attached a Rattlin' Rapala and began casting for walleyes. An hour into their fishing, the entire time having passed in silence between them, the wind began to pick up a bit.

"Getting a little cool," Patterson said as he put down his rod and reel and pulled a pair of gloves from his coat pocket.

"Not bad yet," the judge muttered. "It's getting there though."

Another hour went by and the fishing had not been good. They each landed a couple of walleyes and several crappies, none worth keeping. Shortly after nine p.m. the two men decided to call it a night. They packed up their gear and ten minutes later the judge throttled down the motor and the boat gently bumped into the Patterson's dock.

The doctor gathered up his fishing equipment and stepped onto the dock. He stood under the light on the dock's end, looked at his old friend and said, "Good night, you old fart. See you in the morning."

"We're going to the Bemidji Country Club first thing in the morning, aren't we?" the judge asked.

"You bet. So I can kick your ass in golf again."

"That'll be the day," the judge grumbled. "Good night, Jay. Pick me up about seven," he said as he fired up the boat's motor to pull away from the dock.

"Good night, Bob," the doctor said then turned around to walk to his house.

After docking his boat, the judge trudged the two hundred feet up from the lake to his house. He entered through the back door and stepped into the mud room. He flicked the light switch, removed his coat and boots, propped his fishing pole in the corner and set his tackle box on the floor. Feeling a little hungry, he decided a snack would be a good idea. He went up the half-flight of stairs, through the living room and turned into the kitchen. He flicked on the light and heard a man say, "Hello, Judge Smith. I'm delighted to finally meet you."

"Who are..." the judge started to say but stopped when the fifty thousand volts hit him in the chest and he dropped straight to the floor.

The next morning, Jay Patterson was having a second cup of coffee while Sharon, his wife of over forty years finished clearing the table. The television was on and tuned to a cable news channel. Sharon returned to the table, poured herself more coffee, looked out through the large, plate glass kitchen and said, "What was that?"

It was barely past six and still fairly dark. For a brief moment Sharon had seen something moving through the trees.

Her husband turned in his chair to look through the same window and said, "What was what?"

"I thought I saw an animal moving through the trees heading toward Bob's place," she said quietly while she sipped her coffee. "There!" she exclaimed pointing.

"A wolf," Jay said having seen the predator himself. "Wait, no, there's another one. No, two more…"

"Three more," Sharon said.

"What the hell are they up to?" Jay rhetorically asked.

There were wolves throughout northern Minnesota. Seeing one occasionally was no longer as rare as it had been when the animals first began making a comeback. Seeing several of them in a pack this close to the house was extremely unusual.

"There's another one…" they both said almost simultaneously as they stood in front of the window to watch.

"They're headed toward Bob's," Sharon repeated. "You think they might have a deer there?"

"I don't know," her husband replied. "I don't like it though."

He set his coffee cup on the table and went to the gun case. He opened the glass door and looked over the weapons deciding what to take.

"Jay, what are you thinking?" Sharon sternly asked as she walked up behind him. "You're not going out there with five wolves…"

"Something's wrong over at Bob's," he said as he removed the AR-15 from the case. He leaned over, opened a drawer on the case and removed two twenty shot magazines filled with 5.56mm cartridges. He also strapped a belt around his waist with a .44 caliber Ruger Blackhawk in the holster.

"Get your coat please, and the flashlight off the refrigerator. I want you to come with me."

"Shouldn't you take the Remington 700 for more power?" she asked. Being a northern Minnesota girl, Sharon knew as much about guns as most men. "That AR-15 is a toy compared to the 700."

"True but I just want to scare them off not blow a hole through them. Besides, if I miss the bullets won't travel far. With the 700 they could go across the lake and go through someone's cabin."

The two of them put on coats and boots then Sharon went back to the gun case. She took out the double barrel Citori, loaded it with double ought buckshot and the two of them went out.

They walked past their garage and the motion light on a pole alongside the gravel driveway lit up. Something in the back of the doctor's mind told him there was a serious problem at his friend's home. When he reached the road that serviced the houses and cabins on this side of the lake, his pace quickened until he was almost jogging. The doctor's seventy-year-old wife was struggling to keep up while carrying the shotgun and flashlight and repeatedly whispered at him to slow down.

The couple reached the driveway of the judge's property when there was a low, ominous, unmistakable growl coming from the woods to their right. Jay stopped to allow Sharon to catch up. It was a mostly cloudy morning and the sunrise was just beginning.

"Did you hear that?" the doctor whispered.

"Hear what?" Sharon said, standing so close to her husband, their shoulders were touching. She was pointing the flashlight at their feet while they looked into the trees. Suddenly they heard it again.

"Shine the light at that spot," he said, pointing the rifle at where the noise came from.

Sharon held the light in her left hand pointed into the trees and the beam of light hit two pairs of eyes glowing menacingly back at them. She slowly moved her hand back and forth looking for more of them. As she did this, the doctor took one step forward as he raised the AR-15 to his shoulder.

Aiming at the ground directly in front of the sinister looking eyes, he quickly pulled the trigger five times. The five shots sounded like a cannon going off in the stillness of the morning. The bullets hit in front of the wolf pack leader who yelped, turned and ran off.

"Something's wrong," Jay said to his wife. "Wolves aren't normally that brave to get so close to humans."

Alarmed now at the brazenness of the wolves, the two of them turned and ran up the driveway. As they passed the equipment shed on their right, the motion light above the shed came on illuminating the yard and driveway.

Her husband continued to hurry toward the house but something out of the ordinary caught the corner of Sharon's eye. She turned to her right, shined the light alongside the shed and audibly gasped and yelled, "Jay!" when she saw him. Twenty feet away, the judge was sitting on the ground between two birch trees, each hand nailed to a tree, his head slumped forward, and his shirt covered in blood.

The doctor turned to the sound of his wife's voice and immediately saw the light shining on his friend. "Oh my God," he muttered as he hurried back to his wife.

"Give me the light," he said as he took the flashlight from her. "Go in the house and call 911," he continued while still holding the light on the body. "Call 911 and tell them there's been a homicide."

Sharon had been staring, her eyes unblinking as he said this. Realizing what her husband had said, she snapped to and as she turned to go to the house, she simply said, "Yes," and ran toward the building.

Jay's instinct as a physician was to examine the body to be sure his friend was dead. During the years of his practice, the doctor also acted as a county coroner. The position rotated among himself and six other physicians, each doing the job for two years then passing it along. Because of this, Jay Patterson had been at a few murder scenes; enough to know the protocol and to be careful not to contaminate it. He could clearly see Smith was dead, so he stayed back where he was. He also kept one eye open for the wolves realizing the scent of his friend's blood had been the source of their interest.

Balm Lake is located twenty-eight miles northwest of Bemidji, the Beltrami county seat. In less than half an hour of receiving Sharon's 911 call, the judge's property was literally crawling with Bemidji police and Beltrami County Sheriff's deputies.

Sheriff Ed Newton, who was called at home, arrived forty-five minutes after the 911 call. A long-time veteran of law enforcement, the sheriff immediately took charge. It was now past sunrise and the sheriff already had teams of officers carefully combing through the woods looking for evidence. On the way to the crime scene, the sheriff had called the local office of the state Bureau of Criminal Apprehension to request their assistance.

"What's that on his head?" Newton rhetorically asked the medical examiner as he bent to look at the body. "Jesus Christ," Newton said when he realized what it was. The killer or killers had placed a double-strand of barbed wire that had been twisted together and made into a crown, on the judge's head.

"Is this some kind of sick, religious thing?" Newton asked.

"Don't know," the ME answered. "I'll know more when I get him back to town but, he was tortured too. Look," he continued as he pointed his pen at the dead man's hands. "All of his fingers and toes have been crushed by something. Probably a pair of pliers."

"Jesus Christ," the sheriff softly said again. "Look Doc, keep the details, especially the broken fingers and toes to yourself. Keep that out of the media and the public for now."

"You got it, Sheriff."

By the next morning the news had reached the Twin Cities. A murdered Minnesota Appeals Court judge, even a retired one, merited at least some attention. The killer saw the Channel 8 report which took up about five minutes of air time just before a commercial break. The report was short on details and since it took place two hundred miles from the metro area, didn't create much of a stir. Within forty-eight hours, it was completely forgotten by the population, including the cops of the Cities.

FIFTEEN

Aaron Forsberg parked the Ford mini-van he had borrowed from his uncle in the garage of his uncle's home in Golden Valley, a suburb west of Minneapolis. He shut off the engine and exited the vehicle. It had been a long night and Aaron was dead tired and in no mood to discuss his whereabouts, even with the only person he knew who had stood by him and still did.

Aaron had been convicted of murdering his wife a little more than eleven years ago. At the time, it had been a sensational trial with infidelity, jealousy and of course, money all thrown into the mix. Aaron had been a very successful investment banker earning seven figures in salary and bonuses. The problem was he had to work ninety to a hundred hours per week to do it. This, of course, made for a very lonely home life for his wife and three children. Not surprisingly his wife Sarah, a still attractive woman in her mid-thirties, struck up an affair.

One late Friday night while all three children were at friend's homes or their grandma's, Aaron came home late to find Sarah lying on the kitchen floor in a pool of blood. Her skull had been cracked like an egg with a claw hammer the cops found in the garage. The hammer had traces of Sarah's blood and hair and Aaron's fingerprints. Aaron's DNA was discovered on the body in the form of saliva found on Sarah's face. Aaron claimed it was from him leaning over the body, sobbing and probably drooling a little because he was so distraught. Once his wife's affair and the one Aaron was carrying on with a co-worker came to light, no one bought his story.

A year later, Aaron was sentenced to two thirty-year prison terms to run consecutively. One of the factors Judge Ross Peterson used to depart from the sentencing guidelines and make the terms consecutive was Aaron's refusal to accept responsibility. Aaron insisted he was innocent and steadfastly maintained that position and still did for the murder. Aaron believed it must have been his wife's lover, but the man had an air tight alibi.

While in prison, Aaron lost everything. His children hated him, his friends and relatives abandoned him, and all of his money was gone. The money went to legal fees or into a court ordered trust fund for his children. The only one who believed him and stood by him was the uncle with whom he now resided, John Forsberg, his deceased father's younger brother.

For his own protection, Aaron had been sent to a prison in Michigan to do his time. As angry and bitter as he was after the trial, prison life also took its toll on his personality. Never one who could be described as warm and cuddly, prison had instilled a sharp, edgy hardness in him.

Aaron entered the house from the attached garage through the kitchen door. He passed through it and found his uncle seated at the small, round, wooden dining room table directly in front of him facing the garage door. The morning paper was scattered about the table top and the TV was on in the living room.

"Where were you all night?" John politely asked him.

"Out," Aaron tersely replied lightly placing his hands on the back of a table chair while looking down at his uncle.

"It would be nice if you would let me know if you're going to do that. You've been gone since yesterday afternoon."

"Sorry," he replied without inflection.

"Your lawyer called."

"What did she want?"

"Didn't say. She asked me to tell you to call her."

"On Sunday morning? That's a little odd," Aaron said. "I'm tired. I'll call her later."

John hesitated for a moment and looked directly at Aaron's face before saying, "One of the judges who turned down your appeal was murdered last night." Uncle John couldn't swear to it, but he thought he saw a flicker of something from Aaron's eyes and face.

"No shit, huh. Well, the bastard had it coming."

"You wouldn't know anything about that, would you?" John asked still looking for a reaction from his nephew.

Aaron hesitated a brief moment then said, "Why would you think that?" Aaron released his grip on the chair, stepped back and indignantly said, "I'm going to bed." Without another word, he walked through the living room toward the guest bedroom.

He looked at the TV just as the young woman announcer told the viewers about the murder of a retired state appeals court judge. She gave his name and said the body was found at his cabin near Bemidji. No further details were available. Unseen by his uncle, Aaron slyly smiled and went into his bedroom.

While he watched his nephew walk away, John couldn't help wondering about Aaron's reaction. He had not asked a single question about the murder of the judge. Who was it? Where did it happen? How did John find out? Nothing. Not a single inquiry. And John couldn't help noticing that, although Aaron admitted nothing, he didn't deny anything either.

As the morning sun was making its way from east to west, a single ray beamed through the bedroom window and hit Eugene Parlow in the eyes. Still in bed after a long day and longer night, he was in no hurry to get up. Parlow was the second of the four men released from prison because of tainted DNA. Because the DNA test results were the only solid, physical evidence against him, his lawyer had opted for a trial to the bench without a jury. Her reasoning being a judge would be less likely to convict on DNA evidence only. Parlow was convicted of second-degree murder in the stabbing death of a Minneapolis street prostitute.

He was released a few days before Howie Traynor and wasted no time reacquainting himself with old friends. In just a few weeks he had already been involved in one armed robbery and three burglaries. Parlow's total share of all of the felonies was barely three thousand dollars, most of which he spent on booze and prostitutes. The rest of the money, Parlow like to joke, he just wasted.

Parlow spent several minutes covering his eyes from the sun while thinking of the previous night's events. He rolled his head to his right and saw that it was almost noon. Having arrived home and to bed around five a.m., he contemplated going back to sleep. With the sunlight now streaming through the window he realized that was probably futile.

Parlow tossed the blankets aside and by the time his feet hit the floor he had reached for his cigarettes and lighter from beside the clock. Putting a cigarette in his mouth as he stood, he lit it with one hand while scratching his crotch through his boxers with the other.

He relieved himself in the toilet then shuffled out of the bathroom to the living room of his tiny apartment. Parlow thought about the lawyer, the Albright woman, who had loaned him some money and guaranteed him a huge settlement for being falsely convicted and sent to prison.

Parlow plopped down on the ratty looking, second hand couch, picked up the TV remote and pressed the power button. The TV, a 42-inch flat screen, was the only decent item in the tiny apartment. Purchased with money from the lawyer, it was the nicest thing Parlow had ever owned.

When the screen lit up, a male anchor with perfect hair and perfect teeth was reading the news. The lead story was about the judge found murdered at his cabin in northern Minnesota. Parlow watched and listened with great interest but the details, other than the man's name were very limited.

SIXTEEN

Tony Carvelli walked through the door of the detectives' squad room and headed toward Owen Jefferson's desk. On the way he said hello or waved a brief greeting to several cop friends including Jefferson's boss, Lt. Selena Kane who smiled and waved back from her glass enclosed private office.

Sensing the disturbance of the ambient atmosphere of the room created by Carvelli's arrival, Jefferson looked up from the file he was reading. He closed the file and placed it on the desktop then swiveled in his chair, leaned back, crossed his right leg over his left and laced his fingers behind his head.

Carvelli grabbed one of the cheap padded metal government chairs from another desk, placed it alongside Jefferson's and sat down.

"I didn't know you knew Selena," Jefferson commented.

"Yeah, I've known her for a while. She made detective just before I retired. Word is she's about to get kicked upstairs and you'll get her job," Carvelli said.

"Huh," Jefferson almost snorted. "I'll believe that when it happens."

"You want her job?"

Jefferson removed his hands from behind his head and thought for a moment before answering. "That's another question but, yeah, I think I do. Why not? More money less street hassle."

"Whatever I can do to help, let me know," Carvelli sincerely offered.

"With your reputation upstairs?" Jefferson said raising his eyebrows. "Please, don't help me."

"That's insensitive," Carvelli said feigning hurt feelings. "I'm a very sensitive guy."

"Uh huh. About as sensitive as a biker gang," Jefferson said with a wry grin. "So, what's up with our boy? Come up with anything?"

Carvelli went over in detail the surveillance he had out on Howie Traynor. For the past two weeks they had been on him from the time he left his apartment until he got home. A typical day would see him leave around 8:00 a.m. He would drive directly to the church where he worked and head home, usually between 3:00 and 4:00. Sometimes he would leave a little earlier, sometimes a little later. Traynor would normally drive straight back to his apartment maybe stopping at a grocery store on his way home. He would have dinner early then four or five times a week go to a gym and workout. After that, straight home and in for the evening. The surveillance would stay with him until around 10:30 or 11:00 when the TV and lights in his apartment would go out. So far, he had no guests stop by and did not leave the apartment at all except to go to the gym. The only thing out of the ordinary he had done was to make a couple of trips to see his lawyer, Glenda Albright, at an office she was using in downtown Minneapolis.

"Did your guys interview Jimmy Oliver about the little chat he had with Howie?" Carvelli asked.

"Yeah, I did personally. He claims Howie told him he forgives him. Said he wanted to let Jimmy know he had nothing to fear from him."

"Did Oliver buy it?"

"He's not sure. He remembers the Howie Traynor from back in the day. He told me when he saw Howie standing at the bar he almost passed out. But Howie assured him it was all good. Maybe this conversion to Jesus is legitimate," Jefferson said.

"Maybe," Tony shrugged. "But my cynical cop intuition tells me it's bullshit. I can't explain why but I can't shake it either."

"Hmmm. Cynical cop intuition is a good thing and it's been my experience that it's often right. How long will you stay on him?"

"I don't know," Tony said. "At least another week, maybe two. The guys don't mind. It gives them something to do and the money's good."

"Vivian Donahue's money. She must have some."

"This is nothing for her plus she's pissed this guy got cut loose. If you ever get the chance to cross her, don't. This lady is not someone you want as an enemy."

"I'll keep that in mind the next time I run for governor," Jefferson said. He spun around in his chair, picked up the file he was looking over when Carvelli arrived, handed it to him and said, "Take a look at this. Ever see or hear of anything like it?"

Tony took the thin file and quickly read through its slim contents. It consisted of a police report and preliminary autopsy. When he finished it, he handed it back to Jefferson.

"This that judge that was killed up North Saturday night?" Carvelli asked.

"Yeah, Robert Smith. Retired judge of the state appeals court. Somebody didn't like one of his opinions," Jefferson half-joked.

"I've heard of victims being posed but nothing like this," Carvelli said. "Must've been a helluva site for the neighbors to find. They're lucky the wolves didn't get to him first."

"Beltrami County is looking for help," Jefferson said. "They're sending this," he continued as he tapped the file, "all over the upper Midwest and to the Feebs to see if anyone has come across anything similar."

"They'll probably come up with something. At least something similar," Tony said as he stood to leave. "I'll check around. If I come up with anything I'll let you know. I'll keep in touch about our boy Howie too."

Jefferson stood, the two men shook hands and Tony turned to leave.

While Carvelli was meeting with Owen Jefferson, Marc Kadella was across Fifth Street in the government center. He was attending a pretrial conference in a courtroom on the fifteenth floor. It was the pretrial conference for his uncle's solicitation case. Normally the pretrial conference is an opportunity for the defense to talk to the prosecutor about the case. To check out the strengths and weaknesses and, in all likelihood, make a plea arrangement, especially for first-time misdemeanor defendants.

Marc had patiently waited in the gallery seated next to Uncle Larry for the better part of an hour. The judge was not on the bench and whenever a deal was made, one of the lawyers from the city attorney's office, the defense lawyer and the defendant would go back to the judge's chambers. There the judge would hear them out and decide if he would accept the plea arrangement. Since the cases being considered were all misdemeanors, it would be extremely rare for the judge to turn it down. Normally there would be a fine, maybe a little jail time and some typically unsupervised probation. The judge would have his clerk and stenographer come in and they would make a formal record. Once that was finished, the case was completed.

One of the city attorneys, a balding, heavyset man dressed in a cheap suit in his early fifties, Earl Bicknell, looked over his shoulder at Marc and motioned him forward. Marc told Larry to wait, went through the gate and took a seat at the table with Bicknell.

"Hey, Marc," Bicknell said. "Haven't seen much of you lately since you became such a hot shot celebrity."

Marc leaned forward and whispered, "Fuck you, Earl," to which both men laughed.

Bicknell opened the file and said, "Larry Jensen. First time solicitation. I'm feeling generous today. Three hundred dollar fine plus costs."

"Sorry, Earl," Marc said. "No."

Bicknell looked at him to see if he was joking, then said, "What do you mean, no? I sent you a copy of the recording. It was loud and clear. He offered an undercover policewoman fifty bucks for a blow job. Your guy's seventy-five years old. What the hell...."

"I know," Marc sighed looking up at the ceiling. "He says he wants a trial. Won't plead."

Bicknell stared at Marc for several seconds then said, "What the hell are you doing? Talk some sense into him."

"I've tried Earl. Believe me it's just, well…." Marc answered.

"Well?" Earl said wondering what was coming.

Marc grimaced then confessed, "He's my uncle and…"

"Seriously?" the prosecutor said with a laugh.

"Yeah, I'm afraid so. He wants a trial, so he can look like a stud at the retirement home where he lives. He wants me to get the media at the trial, so it will be on TV and impress the geezer chicks."

With that, Bicknell could barely contain himself from laughing out loud. Marc started to speak but the lawyer held up his hand to stop him. After a good thirty seconds, Bicknell was able to calmly breathe again. He looked at Marc and said, "Let me guess. He gets the pro bono family discount?"

"No," Marc quietly said. "In fact, I quoted him a fee that I thought would make him come to his senses. Instead, he wrote me a check, which is still in my desk drawer."

"Tell you what, two hundred and we skip the costs and fees. Tell him, if we go to trial, I'll ask for jail time."

"Ah, that's an empty threat and we both know it. No judge will waste jail space on a horny seventy-five-year-old widower for this. But, I'll tell him."

Marc went back to where he had left Larry and told him about the offer. He barely got the words out before Larry vehemently turned him down.

Marc went back to his chair at the table and said to Bicknell, "Sorry, no deal. He wants a Rasmussen hearing. Go ahead and schedule it and I'll see you then."

"Okay, see you then."

Marc turned to leave, and Bicknell reached out and grabbed the sleeve of his suit coat. Marc turned to look back and Bicknell quietly said, "The two hundred bucks is on the table until the Rasmussen hearing."

"I'll keep it in mind and see what I can do. Hell, I'll pay the fine for him myself if I have to."

Marc and Uncle Larry parted company on the north side of the government center across Fifth Street from the Old City Hall. Larry walked toward the train platform on Fifth Street to catch a train and Marc started across the government center plaza to his car. A few feet from the fountain his phone began to vibrate in his coat pocket. He checked the caller ID and answered it by saying, "Hey paisan, what's up?"

"I'm just leaving the police department downtown, I want to talk to you. Can we meet for lunch?" Tony Carvelli said as he walked across Fifth at the corner of Fourth Avenue. "Where are you?"

Marc was looking east across the plaza on the north side of the government center. "I'm about a hundred feet away looking right at you. Look to your right."

Carvelli stopped in the middle of the sidewalk, looked toward the fountain in the plaza and saw his friend wave at him. While Tony waited on the sidewalk, Marc walked over to him.

The two men shook hands as Marc said, "Let's walk over to *Peterson's*," indicating the restaurant across the street a block away on Sixth.

The waitress walked away after taking their order and Marc asked Tony, "So, what is it you want to talk about?"

Carvelli gave him a quick summary of the surveillance of Howie Traynor and what Howie was up to.

"During his trial, you got to know him at least a bit. What do you think? You buying his 'I found Jesus' act?" Tony asked Marc.

Marc thought it over while the waitress placed their meals in front of them. He waited until she finished then said, "I don't know. I remember back then being scared of him. Thinking this guy had no empathy, no feelings for anybody, probably including himself."

"A pure sociopath," Carvelli said while chewing a bite of his burger.

"Yeah," Marc nodded, "pretty much. He just didn't seem to give a damn about anything or anyone. I know his prison record says he changed but..."

"Can someone like that ever change? Or is it genetic or some organic quirk, some physical attribute that makes somebody that way?" Carvelli said.

"I remember back then talking to his parents. They wanted nothing to do with him. Both said he was a bad seed and always had been. His sister wasn't much help because she was several years younger and didn't know him very well. But his older brother believed it was something he was born with. People can change," Marc said with a shrug. "You going to keep an eye on him?"

"Yeah," Tony nodded while swallowing. "At least another week, probably two."

"I remember when he was found guilty, or maybe at his sentencing, I can't remember which, he said something threatening to me. Something like, 'I won't forget this'. It sent a shiver down my spine. I've had unhappy clients, but none scared me like this guy."

SEVENTEEN

Rhea Watson waited until her date turned the corner of the short hallway leading to the restaurant's restrooms. As soon as he disappeared, she tossed a twenty-dollar bill on the table and wrote a short note. The gist of the note was Rhea didn't think it would work out between them. She put the note on the twenty-dollar bill, grabbed her purse and almost ran for the exit.

Hurrying to her car, a new Mercedes C-Class, Rhea muttered to herself, "Why do I keep doing this to myself?" She was referring to the first date she was fleeing from that she had set up through an online dating service, the most popular one on the net.

This was now at least the tenth first and only date she had set up through that service and she was getting discouraged. Were there no honest men out there? This one was at least three inches shorter, thirty pounds heavier and a lot less hair than was on his profile or indicated by his picture. The picture was at least ten years old and, on top of it, he actually admitted he was still living with his wife, although he tried to claim they were separated in spirit and preparing for a divorce. Rhea decided she wasn't going to stick around for any more bad news.

She drove out of the small parking lot of the trendy, little restaurant on Lyndale and headed south toward home. The four thousand square foot Tudor style house in the upscale Minneapolis neighborhood of Kenwood was her prize from the divorce. Rhea had just turned forty-seven, although her dating profile had her age at forty-two, and it was time to move on. After more than twenty years of marriage, she had forgotten how hideous dating could be.

After graduating cum laude from the University of Minnesota law school, Rhea had spent ten years in the Hennepin County Attorney's office. It was a great place to hone trial skills and putting criminals in prison was richly rewarding. Eight years ago, the third largest law firm in Minnesota dangled a great job offer in front of her and she jumped.

Rhea was initially hired to work in the firm's white-collar crime department. Firms of this size did not handle run of the mill "criminals". Their clients didn't steal hundreds of dollars with a gun. Theirs was a much better class of crooks who stole millions with computers and bogus contracts.

Rhea had been promised the chance to move into the high-end world of corporate litigation. It became obvious to her several years ago, just before she was made partner, that promise was not going to be kept. Still, the money was more than she had dreamed of and she was driving one of the perks. And now that her son, an only child was attending Northwestern she was relishing her independence.

Rhea waited for the garage door to finish rising then drove her car in and parked it on the double door side of the attached three car garage. She pressed the button of the remote in the Benz to put the door down. She entered the house through the kitchen, shut off the alarm, and dropped her purse and keys on the countertop.

While walking through the dining room she glanced at a wall clock and noticed it was barely past 9:00. Rhea stopped at the open stairway leading up to the bedrooms, leaned on the railing and took off her shoes. A few seconds later she reached her destination, the liquor cabinet in the living room.

At the liquor cabinet, she half filled a large brandy snifter with an expensive Courvoisier she was a little too fond of and swallowed a large gulp. Rhea would not admit it but over the last three years or so, she had developed a bit of a drinking problem. In her mind it was her cheating husband that caused the divorce and not her drinking and indifference to him that contributed to the cheating. She took another large swallow of the smooth cognac, refilled the glass and headed upstairs.

Rhea took a quick shower and with a large bath towel wrapped around her torso, strolled back into her bedroom. She picked up her glass from the vanity, took another swallow then went to her large, walk-in-closet. She opened the door to expose a full-length mirror, loosened the towel and allowed it to drop to the floor.

Rhea took another swallow from the goblet and finished off the drink. Standing naked in front of the mirror she gave herself a reasonably objective review. She was certainly not bad for a forty-seven-year-old woman. Her breasts were still fairly firm but, like most women her age, her butt and hips were spreading just a bit. All in all, not bad, she thought.

She bent down to pick up the towel off the thick carpeting. Facing to her left away from the mirror she began to wrap the towel around herself to go back downstairs to the liquor cabinet. Out of the corner of her eye something in the mirror caught her attention. She turned her head to look at the mirror again and that's when she saw him, a strange man standing in her bedroom doorway.

Rhea turned and bolstered by the courage supplied by the alcohol, angrily said, "Who the hell are you and what do you think you're doing in my house?"

The man merely smiled a sinister smile then said, "I'm hurt that you don't remember me, counselor."

When he said that, the light of recognition came on in Rhea's mind and she immediately realized she was in serious trouble.

The intruder started slowly walking toward her, still wryly smiling at her. He was dressed totally in black including a tight Spandex skull cap and a slick, nylon windbreaker. His right hand was in the pocket of the light jacket, obviously concealing something.

Rhea took a step back to get away from him and backed into the mirror. She turned to her right and started to run but he was too quick. He jumped toward her, grabbed her left arm with his left hand and spun her around to face him. She started to scream but was abruptly cut off when he jammed the Taser into her left side and floored her with fifty thousand volts.

When Rhea came to, she was tied to a wooden armchair in her unfinished basement. Naked, her wrists were tied to the chair's arms and her ankles to the chair's legs. Still a little foggy, it took her a moment to realize where she was and remember what had happened. Seated on a similar chair, barely three feet in front of her was her obviously psychotic antagonist.

"I was only doing my job," she shakily said when she again realized who he was. "Please don't hurt me," she sobbed.

He stood up and as he looked down at her she said, "Please, take anything you want, I promise I won't report it. You don't have to rape me, I'll help you…"

"Sssshhhh," he softly said as he leaned forward and covered her mouth with a strip of duct tape. Still leaning down, his nose barely three inches from hers, he quietly said, "I'm not going to rape you. That's not my thing. But, before I'm done, you'll wish that was all I wanted."

He sat down in his chair, leaned forward again, his forearms on his thighs, he continued by saying, "You see Rhea, you don't mind if I call you Rhea do you?" he said to the horror-stricken woman. "You claim you were just doing your job but, that's not really true," he calmly continued. "If you had really done your job I wouldn't have spent all those years rotting in prison. Your job should not have included using doctored DNA evidence."

By now Rhea was sitting up as stiff as a board. She was trying to yell or scream, make at least some noise through the tape covering her mouth. Nothing but weak, muffled sounds could be heard as her wide-open, terror filled eyes darted about the cold room.

Her tormentor pulled his chair closer to her so that their knees almost touched. She watched as he removed a metal object from his back pocket and held it in front of her face. This was when she first noticed he was wearing surgical gloves and recognizing the metal object she tried to scream "no" several times. As she did he grabbed the index finger of her left hand and clamped the pliers on it and squeezed it, breaking the skin and crushing the bone. He smiled at the crunching sound the bone made as the pliers shattered it like an egg shell. Rhea tried to scream but it was muffled by the tape.

He waited for her to calm down then looked directly into her eyes and said, "That's just the first one. Soon you'll start passing out from the pain but don't worry, I'll wake you. I don't want you to miss a second of this."

Tricia Dunlop knocked softly on the door of the seventeenth floor corner office of Frawley, Markowitz and Kent. As she turned the door's handle to enter a voice from within politely said, "Come in."

Tricia walked into the well-appointed senior partner's office and said to the woman behind the glass-topped desk, "Jackie, I'm getting worried. Rhea hasn't come in or called yet and she's scheduled for a settlement conference in court now. I just got a call from Judge Halladay's clerk that she hasn't shown up yet."

Jacqueline Neeley, Rhea Watson's friend and immediate superior took off her glasses and let them hang from the chain around her neck. A seriously worried expression came over her face and she said, "Have you called her?" Neeley immediately realized what a foolish question that was knowing how responsible and efficient Tricia was.

"Of course, several times. I have a key to her house and the code for her alarm. Do you think I should go check for her?"

"Yes, but wait a minute." Neeley picked up her office phone and dialed 411. She asked for the non-emergency number for the MPD and had the call connected to them. A woman answered and Neeley took a minute to explain who she was and why she was calling.

"I don't know that it's an emergency, but we have a key to her house and myself and Ms. Watson's assistant are going to check. Could we have a patrol car meet us there?"

She listened for a moment then said, "Fifteen minutes. That would be great. Just a moment…"

She held the phone handle out toward Tricia and said, "Address."

Tricia took the phone and told the woman Watson's address.

Twenty minutes later the two women pulled up to Watson's house. Neeley parked her Mercedes in the driveway and they both got out as a middle-age patrol officer with the three stripes of a sergeant on his uniform sleeve, Norm Anderson, walked toward them. His patrol car was parked in the street and he was ringing the front door bell when the women arrived.

He introduced himself to them and said, "I walked around the outside and looked through the windows. I didn't see anything out of the ordinary. You have a key and permission to enter?"

"Yes," Tricia said handing the officer the front door key. "There's an alarm system too. I have the code," she continued holding up a small slip of paper.

They went through the front door and Tricia checked the alarm box and said, "It's not on. Maybe she forgot."

Anderson gently took both women by an arm and as he guided them back to the front door politely said, "I want you both to wait outside. I'll do a walk through and check the place out."

"But…" Tricia started to say.

"There may be something in here you don't want to see."

"Oh, God," Tricia said biting a knuckle.

"And if there is," Neeley continued the thought, "this could be a crime scene."

"Let's hope not," Anderson said reassuringly. "Let me check first."

He closed the front door and walked into the large foyer. When they had first entered the house, the veteran cop had noticed a very slight, coppery odor in the air. Understanding immediately what it came from was why he had hustled the two women out.

Anderson pulled his pistol from his holster, pointed it at the ceiling and started up the staircase. He quickly went through the four bedrooms and three baths. The only thing out of the ordinary he found was a damp bath towel on the floor of the master bedroom. Anderson also noticed the odor he detected was now gone. Back downstairs he moved methodically through the rooms. As he got closer to the kitchen the smell became a little stronger. Finally, he stood in the open doorway leading to the basement and knew for sure where it was coming from and what he was likely to find.

Owen Jefferson glanced at the crowd gathering across the street as he got out of his car. He then walked quickly across the large well-kept front yard of Rhea Watson's home. He looked to his right and saw an ambulance from the medical examiner's office parked in the driveway where Jackie Neeley's Mercedes was before she moved it. He noticed the two women being interviewed by a female homicide detective and saw Norm Anderson standing near them. The detective, a young woman recently assigned to homicide, introduced the women to Jefferson.

"I'm sorry for your loss," Jefferson said to the women. "Marcie," he said to the detective, "when you're done here you can let them go."

He turned back to the obviously distraught women and said, "We'll be in touch. If you think of anything give Detective Sterling a call."

"If there's anything we can do, please let us know," the older woman said.

Jefferson slightly nodded his head then turned to Anderson. "Hey Norm, tell me what's up," Jefferson said as the two men stepped away from the women.

Anderson went over everything for the lead detective. When he finished he said, "Owen, its Rhea Watson. Remember her?"

"The lawyer from the County Attorney's office?"

"Yeah, that's what her friends told me. At least she used to be with Slocum's office. She went into private practice a few years back," Anderson said.

Jefferson turned to look at the front door, silently thought for a moment then muttered, "No shit, huh? That's interesting." He turned back to Anderson and quietly said, "Keep this to yourself for now. I'll go take a look."

"Marston's down there now," Anderson said referring to Clyde Marston, a doctor with the medical examiner's office.

The cop at the door took down his name and badge number then he entered the house and pulled out a pair of surgical gloves. There were already four CSU cops going through the house. One in the living room as Jefferson passed through. Jefferson went down the basement stairs and found the ME kneeling in front of the body. The instant he saw her the light in his head came on as he recognized the scene. He quickly walked over to her and stood staring at her for several seconds.

Seated on the bare, concrete floor of the unfinished basement was the naked body of Rhea Watson. Her legs were extended before her, her back against the bare cinderblock wall and her arms stretched out to her sides, the hands having been nailed into the wall. The nails in her hands had been driven into the cinderblock and on her head she wore a double strand of barbed wire as a crown. Her chest and stomach were covered in her own blood and her head was tilted forward, her chin covering the gash across her throat.

"I need to talk to you," Jefferson said to Marston. "And you two guys also," he told the CSU techs working the basement. "Come here a minute, please."

"Have you ever seen this before?" Marston asked him.

"Listen," he said to all three of them ignoring the question. "Not a word of this leaks out to anybody." He pointed at the body and continued. "We need to put a lid on this. No details to the media, other cops, your wife, girlfriend or mom. You got it?"

"It's going to get out, Owen," one of the CSU guys said.

"I know Rick. But we need to keep it quiet as long as we can. At least a couple days to give me a chance to check into some things."

"Okay," they all said.

Jefferson spent a few minutes walking around the basement. He examined the chairs where she had been tied up and her killer sat. He then turned back to the M.E. and asked to speak with him.

"Tell me about the fingers and the toes," Jefferson said.

"How did you know...?"

"Just tell me."

"They're all broken, probably with a pair of pliers of some kind. Owen, he tortured her. From the look of the coagulation of the blood on her fingers, I'd say he took at least a couple of hours. Sadistic bastard. She probably passed out a few times then he would wake her to do some more. Look at this," Marston continued pointing a gloved finger at two marks on the left-hand side of the body. "Taser burns. That's how he took her down."

"Okay," Jefferson said while staring at the spots. "For now, this is a burglary gone bad. You got a time of death?"

"I'd guess the TOD was between ten and two last night. I can nail it down a little better when I get her back to the lab."

"Okay. Give me a call when you know more."

Jefferson hurried up the stairs and back outside. He found Norm Anderson again and gestured for him to come to him.

"Norm, have you told anyone anything about this? The body or what you found or didn't find in the house?"

"No, Owen. I told you before; I called it in as a homicide but no details. Why, what's up?"

"For now, this is a burglary gone bad, okay? You keep the condition and posture of the body to yourself. Nothing to the media or anyone else."

"Sure," a puzzled Anderson said, "whatever you want."

The woman detective who had interviewed the two women approached the two men.

"We'll start canvassing the neighborhood. Do you have a time frame?" she asked Jefferson.

"Last night. Probably between eight and two," he shrugged. "Listen Marcie, I want you to do something. You go gather up the guys to start the canvass and as you do it, casually make a call to Stan Abramson in burglary. You know Stan?"

"Yeah, sure," she answered.

"Tell Stan we have a burglary gone bad homicide here. Make sure the uniforms hear you."

"Okay," she said with a puzzled look.

"I want one of them to leak that to the media. I don't know which one will and I don't care. I just want that story to get out through the back door. Tell Stan I'll call him later."

"You're the boss," Marcie said then turned to carry out her instructions.

Jefferson shook hands with Norm Anderson and walked back across the lawn to his car. When he got there, just before he got in, he took a quick look over the crowd of seventy or eighty people who had gathered across the street. Among the many faces he glanced at one that he should have noticed was out of place in this upscale neighborhood. Looking back at the detective through large aviator sunglasses and wearing a decent disguise was the brutal man who spent the previous evening being entertained by Rhea Watson's fear, pain and death.

EIGHTEEN

"What do you think?" Selena Kane asked her subordinate, Owen Jefferson as he lowered his long frame onto the seat in front of her desk. It was three days after the murder of Rhea Watson. Due to scheduling conflicts, this was the first chance the two of them had to discuss the case. "You think we have a serial on our hands?"

"Too soon to tell," Jefferson answered her. "Watson and Judge Smith were almost certainly killed by the same person or persons. The crime scenes and the way the bodies were staged are exact. The only difference being, Watson was naked, and Smith was fully clothed."

"No evidence of sexual assault?"

"No. There was a damp towel on the floor of Watson's bedroom suggesting he caught her coming out of the shower. We're looking for a connection between the two victims. So far it doesn't look like they even knew each other."

"What about a professional connection. He was a judge, she was a lawyer?"

"Yeah," Jefferson continued nodding his head a few times. "We're looking into that too. But he was on the court of appeals and was never on the trial bench. Rhea Watson did trials but never handled appeals. As far as we can tell, they never even met each other."

"What about appeals that he handled of cases she tried? Guilty verdicts that were appealed and he was the judge that upheld the verdict?" Kane asked.

"Shit," Jefferson quietly said as he sat up thinking about what his boss had suggested. "I hadn't thought of that."

"Have Jeff Miller, the department's computer whiz, see what he can find."

"There could be a ton of them," Jefferson said. "But it's a place to start. Good catch, Boss."

"Did you look at her ex-husband?" Kane asked.

"Sure. He was the first one on the list. I took Bob Hagan with me," Jefferson answered referring to another detective. "The husband was pretty shocked and upset. He seemed genuine. We talked to her co-workers, especially her secretary. They all agreed, as did the ex that the divorce was amicable. Plus, he's remarried."

"What about money? Who inherits?"

"The son and he was in school at Northwestern in Chicago. Chicago cops verified it for us. He's alibied.

"When the story and her picture hit the news, we started getting calls from men who had met her recently through a dating site. We've interviewed all of them and they all said the same thing. They met her for one date, they didn't hit it off and that was that. No hard feelings. Plus, none of them even knew her last name. The only way they communicated was online by email. She was out on such a date the night she was killed."

"Oh," Kane said, her eyes opening wider as she leaned forward on her desk.

"Forget it," Jefferson said seeing her reaction. "He came forward too. I got his name and information, but we checked it out. They were at a restaurant for about an hour. He went to the john and she left when he did."

"That's kind of cold. Didn't it make him mad?"

"You would've run out on this guy too. Besides, the bartender verified the guy stayed until midnight," Jefferson replied.

"How do you know you got all of the men she met through this dating site?"

"We brought in her computer from home and went through all of the emails and anything having to do with it. We're pretty confident that we matched up the men with the one's she was communicating with online. Looks like she was just shopping a bit."

"What about her work computer?"

"The law firm wouldn't let us have it without a court order. Her secretary and supervisor went through all of her emails and they assured us there was nothing in them about dating or anything that might point to someone," Jefferson answered.

"You believe them?"

Jefferson shrugged and said, "We have no reason not to. They've all been very cooperative except when it comes to privileged client information."

"Anybody else we should look at?" Kane asked.

"Not so far. We'll keep checking but most of the people she knew were lawyers and judges. Not exactly murder suspect types. I still think our best bet is to find a link between her and the judge."

Jefferson started to get up from his chair, but Kane held up a hand to stop him.

"There's something else, Owen," she said. "I want you to do me a favor. I want you to take Marcie Sterling under your wing and work with you on this."

"Okay, no problem," Jefferson said. "But, it will probably take more than the two of us if this is what we think it might be. We'll see."

Later that afternoon, Jefferson sat watching the newly minted detective, Marcie Sterling. He was sitting at his desk, his left elbow on the desktop, his left hand covering his mouth and hiding the smile.

Marcie had personally spent most of the day the body was found walking the neighborhood where Rhea Watson had lived. She had been promoted to detective less than six months ago and had been assigned to homicide for only two weeks. Unknown to her, Selena Kane had specifically requested the assignment in an effort to get more women moving up the department's ladder.

Marcie was a single woman, no children, who had decided on a career in law enforcement at age sixteen. She had graduated from Hamline University in St. Paul with a B.A from their Criminal Justice Program and was immediately hired by the Minneapolis Police Department.

Like any other cop, she had paid her dues riding patrol through bad neighborhoods nights and weekends. Barely three months on the job, Marcie and three other cops had answered a bar fight call in South Minneapolis. While breaking up the fight one of the drunks had punched her squarely in the forehead. Before the other three cops, all men, could react, Marcie had used her kick boxing training to put her much larger assailant face down on the sidewalk. Marcie Sterling had taken a huge leap toward earning the respect of every cop in the MPD.

Jefferson continued watching with amusement as she struggled to move her personal belongings to the desk adjacent to his. Fifteen minutes ago, he had told her she was assigned to him and the Watson investigation. She tried to hide it, but her excitement was obvious.

While Marcie was finishing putting her things in and on the desk butting up against Jefferson's, a slight figure in short-sleeve shirt buttoned to the throat entered the room. He was carrying a six-inch-high stack of papers and went straight to Jefferson's desk. When he reached the detective's desk he dropped the pile of paper in front of Jefferson. It hit the desktop with a loud thud.

"What's this?" Jefferson asked. Ignoring the sergeant's question, Jeff Miller, the department's number one computer geek, turned to Marcie, smiled and said hello to her.

"Jeff," Jefferson said. "What's this?"

"You wanted all the cases Judge Smith handled on appeal that Rhea Watson tried and won. Here they are. There are seventy-four," Miller answered. He picked up a few pages from the top of the pile, handed them to Jefferson and said, "This is a list of the names. Case names and numbers; names of defendants and all of the lawyers and judges. That includes all of the judges involved in the appeal and the trial judge. The rest of the pile are copies of the decisions. I thought you'd want those too."

"I didn't think there would be this many," Jefferson slowly, quietly said while looking over the stack of papers.

"Jeff," Marcie interjected, "can you go back and run a query to find out how many of those people are still alive? The judges, lawyers, defendants, everybody?" She looked across the desks at Jefferson and said, "Maybe we can narrow it down." She looked at Miller again and added, "Can you check to see how many of the crooks are still in jail?" Turning back to Jefferson she said, "I assume we're thinking about dirt bags with a score to settle."

"Good point," Jefferson said. "We'll start on this," Jefferson continued as he held up the papers he was holding. "Let us know about the dead and still incarcerated ones as soon as you can."

"You got it, Sarge," Jeff said but he was looking at Marcie. "I'll get right on it."

Miller left, and Jefferson handed half of the list of names across his desk to Marcie. He set the pile of court case decisions aside and said, "We might as well get started."

"Okay," Marcie replied. "Where do you want to start?"

"Look for violent crimes first. Look for guys who were convicted of serious crimes. Then check them out on our data base," he continued referring to the desktop computer with arrest and conviction records. "Let's see if we can find some with a history."

The two of them started going down their separate lists checking each individual's conviction and then his background. After an hour of this Jefferson stood up to stretch, looked across the cheap government issued desks at his new partner and said, "How are you doing?"

Sterling sighed and moved her head back and forth a few times to work out the kink in her neck from staring at the screen. She looked up at the tall black man and said, "I'm not really eliminating anyone. Even guys convicted of drug crimes. You check their record and there are arrests and convictions for other things, including violent acts."

"Yeah, I know," Jefferson agreed as he sat down again. He stared across the desks at Marcie for several seconds without speaking, obviously in thought. "Burglars," he quietly said as if speaking to himself. "He got past Watson's alarm…"

"Assuming it was on," Sterling said.

"Still we should be looking at guys with a history of burglary first then expand as we need to."

"Okay," Sterling agreed. "I had a couple of them," she continued as she leafed through the pages she had completed. She looked back at Jefferson and said, "Although, any of these people could learn about committing a burglary while locked up in a criminal academy."

"True," Jefferson agreed. "But it's still a place to start."

At that moment Jefferson had a thought about a specific name he wanted to check. Using his right index finger on the pages of names, he quickly scanned down the list.

"Holy shit," he quietly said when he found what he was looking for. "Here he is, Howard Traynor."

"Who's Howard Traynor?" Marcie asked.

Before answering, Jefferson picked up his phone and quickly skimmed through his call list, found the number he wanted and dialed it. While it rang he looked at Marcie and held up his index finger in a gesture requesting that she wait a moment.

"Hey, Owen," Tony Carvelli said. "What's up?"

"Are you still on Howie Traynor?"

"Yeah, we are. But, I'm about to give it up, why?"

"You heard about Rhea Watson?"

"Sure, but if you're thinking it was Howie, forget it. I already checked. We put him to bed just before eleven that night."

"Shit," a dejected Jefferson said into the phone. "You're sure?"

"Yeah, Tommy Evans was on him that night. He waited until the lights and TV went off. This guy is so boring I don't think we can justify spending Vivian's money on this much longer."

"Do you have your surveillance records with you?"

"Yeah, you want me to check one?"

"Yes, the night that judge was killed up in Bemidji," Jefferson said. He gave Carvelli the date and time of death from the autopsy report and waited while Carvelli checked.

"Found it," Carvelli said. "Same thing. He got home that day about noon and never left. And Sorenson was on him until midnight. Next day, Maddy Rivers picked him up when he left for church at nine."

"Okay," Jefferson said. "I guess that takes care of Howie."

"You thinking somebody is out for revenge?" Carvelli asked.

"It's a place to start," Jefferson answered. "If you think of anyone…"

"…I'll let you know," Carvelli finished the thought.

NINETEEN

Madeline Rivers waited for the red light to change on Seventh Street and Second Avenue in downtown Minneapolis. She was on Seventh, a one-way heading west, watching Howie Traynor drive into a parking ramp past the intersection a half-block ahead of her on the left side of Seventh. Maddy was in the left-hand lane and there were two cars ahead of her waiting for the light.

Maddy had been on station at Howie's apartment before seven a.m. that morning. Never one to be an early bird, the effort to get out of bed early enough to be there was almost painful. The night before Tony Carvelli and she had met with Vivian Donahue to discuss the surveillance of Traynor. Vivian had been adamant that it continue to the point where she actually threatened to hire someone else if need be. Tony had mentioned the call he received from Owen Jefferson concerning Rhea Watson and the murder of Judge Smith outside Bemidji. With that news Vivian was even more certain to continue following Howie.

At eight o'clock, Howie came out of the apartment dressed for work at the church carrying a thermos and a bag lunch. Maddy decided to take a chance that he was going to the church. Instead of following him, she took a different route and got there ahead of him. She found a spot on the street, parked and within seconds Traynor arrived and parked in the church's parking lot.

During that day Maddy and two of Tony's retired cop friends switched off watching the church. Shortly after 1:00 pm Maddy was back on stakeout. At 1:30 Howie came out and drove off. Within a few blocks, having followed him downtown twice before on the same route, she knew exactly where he was going.

The light up ahead turned green and a driver to her right honked his horn. "Relax, pal," she whispered to herself. "This is Minneapolis not New York."

Maddy drove through the intersection, pulled to the curb in a no parking zone and stopped. In less than a minute she saw Traynor emerge from the parking ramp. He looked to his right for traffic then jogged across Seventh to the office building he was going to in mid-block between Second and LaSalle. She waited two minutes to be sure he wasn't coming out then picked up her phone from the passenger seat and speed dialed a number.

Maddy reported in with Carvelli who told her to give it five more minutes then go. He would send one of the other guys, a new guy by the name of Franklin Washington, to pick up the tail of Howie.

When Howie Traynor came though the door of the parking ramp onto the sidewalk on Seventh, he looked to his right to check traffic. As he did this, he saw the brunette in the black Audi parked at the curb. He trotted across Seventh with a small, barely discernible smile on his face.

He entered the art deco office building. The building was the old Raines Building named after a long-deceased railroad Baron. Built in the 1920s, the artwork of stylish marble and granite flooring and walls still attracted art, design and architecture students from all over the country. Of course, this was totally lost on Howie Traynor.

Ignoring the looks his somewhat shabby appearance generated, he went immediately to the bank of elevators. The after-lunch crowd was still returning to work and the elevator he rode to the sixth floor was practically elbow-to-elbow.

Disembarking, Traynor quickly went to the tastefully decorated offices of Adams & McBride an all female law firm. The firm normally and almost exclusively catered to women clients dealing with women's issues. They were not "man-haters". In fact, all seven lawyers were happily married. The two founding partners simply decided to concentrate their business on women. Glenda Albright liked to portray herself as a hard-core feminist in public. In private she was a pragmatic, self-promoting, publicity hound and money chaser. She was renting space in the office to handle the wrongful imprisonment suit for her tainted DNA clients.

Howie looked around the familiar reception area and saw two men seated in client chairs. One of them, Gene Parlow, he knew from prison. The other, Aaron Forsberg, was not someone he recognized.

Howie checked in with the receptionist who pleasantly informed him that Glenda would be out soon. He stepped over to the two men as Parlow arose from his chair. Howie and Parlow exchanged a prison yard handshake and awkward man hug.

"Hey, dude," Parlow said. "Good to see you again."

"Yeah, you too Gene," Howie answered him. Traynor turned to the third man, extended his hand and said, "Howie Traynor."

Forsberg hesitated for a moment, looked up at Howie then almost reluctantly took the proffered hand and slightly shook it while saying, "Aaron Forsberg."

Howie sat down on Parlow's left and asked, "You both here to see Glenda Albright?"

"Yes."

"Yeah."

"What's up? Did she tell you anything?" he asked looking back and forth at them.

Parlow shrugged his shoulders and said, "No."

Forsberg said nothing, just shaking his head slightly.

The door to the offices opened and Glenda came out to collect her clients. The woman was in her late sixties but could easily pass for mid-forties. Of course, living in Southern California gave her access to some of the finest plastic surgeons in the country. She also knew how to dress, especially for the cameras.

Albright quickly shook hands with the men who stood up when she came through the door. They followed her back to a glass-enclosed conference room with a great view of South Minneapolis. They all took a chair at the long conference table. With Glenda at the head, she started to explain the purpose of the meeting.

"Okay," she began. "We've had a settlement offer from the City of Minneapolis and Hennepin County with the backing of the State of Minnesota."

"How much?" Parlow quickly asked with obvious lust in his eyes. Traynor and Forsberg sat quietly assuming she would get to it.

"They all want to settle as quickly as possible. They don't want to drag this out for three or four years."

"Three or four years?" Parlow asked. "It could take that long?"

"If we have to go to trial, it will easily take that long," Albright answered him.

"I thought there were four of us," Forsberg said. "Where's the other guy, the Mexican?"

"I don't know," Albright said. "I haven't been able to get a hold of him. Don't worry about it. The offer is quite a bit more than I thought it would be. I was looking for between one point two and one point six million."

"How much?" an anxious Parlow asked again.

"Two point eight million," Glenda finally answered him. "After fees you will each receive…"

"Four hundred sixty-nine thousand," said Forsberg, the former investment banker who was able to run the numbers in his head. "And you'll get nine hundred twenty-four thousand which is bullshit, Glenda."

"Four hundred grand!" Parlow said. "When do I get it?"

"Wait, Aaron," Albright said. "I know all of you agreed to the standard fees of one third. But because I've been able to scare them into a big early settlement without going to trial, I'll cut that down to twenty per cent."

"That's five hundred sixty grand each, including you," Forsberg said. "I'm not taking it, Glenda. It's more than enough for these guys. They're career criminals, street thugs…"

"Who the fuck you think you are, asshole?" an angry Parlow asked glaring at Forsberg.

"I was an investment banker. A very successful one making seven figures every year," he said glaring back at Parlow. "That's twice as much as this every year." With that he slammed his fist down on the table, stood up and angrily stormed out of the room.

While all of this was taking place, Howie pushed his chair away from the table about two feet. He leaned back, crossed his legs, folded his hands in his lap and quietly listened.

After Forsberg slammed the door behind him, Albright looked at the other two men. "There's more," she began. "You wouldn't get the money all at once. It would be structured over ten years."

"What does that mean?" Parlow asked. "I wouldn't get it for ten years…"

"No, you'd get it in equal payments paid monthly for ten years," Albright said She looked at a legal pad she had placed on the table in front of herself. It was filled with notes and figures. When she found the one she was looking for, she continued by saying, "Four thousand six hundred sixty-six dollars per month."

Being told he wouldn't get the money up front, Gene Parlow slumped back in his chair.

"What if we say yes and he still says no?" Howie asked pointing a thumb at Forsberg's now empty chair.

"I don't know," Albright said. "I don't think they would go for that, but I can ask. Look," she continued, "You don't have to decide anything this minute. I obviously need to let him cool down," she continued referring to the departed Forsberg. "I'll talk to him in a couple days. Give it a few days and we'll meet again."

Howie Traynor parked his car in the small lot behind the Reardon Building on Lake Street and Charles. He was facing the south side of the building and turned his head slightly to his left. Howie was looking for the black man in the Chevy sedan who had followed him from his lawyer's office. He saw the man drive by and the man was looking into the lot for Howie as he continued down Charles. Howie got out of his car and walked toward the back door.

Howie had never before been to Marc Kadella's office. He looked him up in the yellow pages and decided it was time to pay him a visit. Plus, he genuinely wanted a second opinion about the settlement offer. As he went up the long flight of stairs to the second floor he again thought about not calling ahead for an appointment and simply ignored the thought. He found Marc's name listed by the door along with the other lawyers, lightly knocked and went in.

Marc was at his desk working on a divorce case when the intercom sounded. He picked up the phone and heard Carolyn say, "Marc there's a man here who says he's an old client, Howie Traynor. He'd like a few minutes if you can spare it."

The instant he heard Howe's name announced Marc's immediate reaction was to wonder: *Oh, God, now what?*

"Um, yeah, okay," he stuttered. "I'll be out in a minute."

Two minutes later he was again seated at his desk, the door closed and Howie Traynor in one of the client chairs.

"I really appreciate you taking the time to see me," Howie said for the second time.

"It's all right," Marc answered a lot more casually than he felt. "What can I do for you?"

"I, ah, just came from my lawyers and I'm, well," he nervously began. "I was wondering if I could get your opinion about a settlement offer we got."

Traynor went on to give Marc a complete account of the entire meeting. Who was there, who was missing, who liked the deal and who didn't. He made sure to tell him about Forsberg stomping out and that Parlow was ready to accept it up until Albright told them about the settlement being structured for a ten-year payout.

When he finished he leaned back, looked at Marc and said, "Well, what do you think?"

After hesitating for a moment as if thinking it over, Marc replied, "Howie, I can't really say if it's good or bad. I don't do these types of cases. I have no idea if it's good or bad. Let me ask you this: What do you think of the offer?"

"The more I think about it. The better it sounds. It wouldn't make me rich, but it would be a nice, steady check coming in every month. I don't think the other guys will take it, though. Forsberg was really pissed. What an asshole he is thinking he's worth more than the rest of us."

"I can see his point," Marc softly said. "These things are normally based on how much earning power someone has. How much income he made before it happened. He was making a lot of money, according to the news reports. What about the fourth guy, what's his name?"

"Suarez," Howie said. "I don't know him. He wasn't there. I did meet him once, but I have no idea what he would do. I was thinking I'll tell her I'll take it. I don't want to screw around for another two or three years. What do you think?"

"I think Howie, to be honest, I'm a little surprised you would want my opinion," Marc said.

"Really? Why?" Howie asked.

"Well, the first time we met your case didn't exactly go too well and…"

"Oh, that wasn't your fault. That was some guy at some lab who screwed me and the other guys."

"Did you know he died?" Marc asked.

"Seriously? He died? How?"

"Cancer. It was in yesterday's paper. He had terminal cancer and that's why he came clean or, so I heard. He didn't want to die with that on his conscience."

With a mildly surprised look on his face, Howie said, "Well, I guess I'm glad he confessed to what he done."

Howie stood up, extended his hand to Marc as Marc arose from his chair and Howie said, "Listen, thanks for seeing me, Mr. Kadella. I think I'll take the deal, if I can."

TWENTY

After leaving the meeting with Glenda Albright and her other two clients, Aaron Forsberg began driving out of downtown in an easterly direction. He was still steaming mad because of the paltry settlement he was offered. As he drove east on Eighth Street Forsberg mentally kicked himself for signing on with Albright in the first place. He should have known better than to attach himself to a self-promoting gasbag lawyer and the other three scumbags she represented.

When he reached Eleventh Avenue, satisfied he was past the construction for the new stadium, he turned left on Eleventh to go the two blocks north to Sixth Street. At sixth he turned right and punched the gas to take the freeway ramp onto I-94 east to St. Paul.

On his way to St. Paul Forsberg reflected on his current mental and emotional well-being. Before his wife's murder and his subsequent trial, he had been a relatively well adjusted man; at least he would have said so. About the only anomaly to which he would admit was an overly driven need to succeed.

Forsberg had graduated in three and a half years from Notre Dame with a degree in Business Administration. He then obtained a master's degree in Finance from the Carlson School of Business at the University of Minnesota. While working on his MBA, he had gone to work for a large investment bank, Landon & Fletcher in their Minneapolis office. By the time he was thirty, he was married, a second child was on the way and his salary and bonuses would top a million dollars. Aaron Forsberg worked hard, put in a lot of hours and had a gift for sales and market analysis. His clients made money, his firm made money and he made money. Life was good.

The only glitch was the more he made and the better he did, it never seemed to be enough. Aaron Forsberg was addicted to the opiate of greed and success. And because of that, he worked ninety to one hundred hours per week. Many nights he would simply sleep in his office. It was the best way to stay on top of foreign markets and the global economy.

Between the ages of thirty and thirty-five, he took a grand total of three short vacations with his family lasting barely one week each. Even then his phone and at least two laptops came with him. And yet he was shocked to find out his wife was having an affair.

Prison life had taken a serious toll on Forsberg. Before prison, even though he was consumed by a drive to succeed, he was always a fairly affable man. His colleagues, the only friends he had, genuinely liked him and he got along well with them. During this time, he even had a couple of harmless affairs. At least he believed they were harmless. After all, he was killing himself at work to provide a lavish lifestyle for his wife and children. He deserved a little fling or two. Then it all came crashing down like an avalanche the night he found his murdered wife.

Driving east toward downtown St. Paul he replayed it again. The arrest, trial and conviction for something he didn't do; the years in prison and the loss of his family and his life. Now that he was free he looked back upon all of it as if it were a surreal bad dream. Except it wasn't.

Prison had hardened him as it does many people. Aaron had an edge, a cynicism and mistrust that were not there before.

When he first arrived at the state prison in Michigan City, Indiana, the terror of where he was, took two weeks to dissipate. He expected to be beaten, raped and sold for a pack of cigarettes at any minute. Once he realized that wasn't going to happen, he calmed down and settled in. That is when he noticed it in other inmates; the convict attitude. Don't let anyone get too close, don't make friends and be very careful whom you trusted.

Aaron Forsberg needed help and he knew it. He should be in counseling and probably drug therapy. Unfortunately, Aaron wasn't interested. He liked being in the mental and emotional state that he was in and the edge he felt it gave him. Perhaps when everything was over he would seek treatment but, not yet.

Forsberg exited I-94 at the Marion Street exit and drove the van straight ahead to pick up Kellogg Boulevard. He traveled on Kellogg into downtown and found a metered parking space on Kellogg just before St. Peter Street. Not bothering with the semaphores on the corner, Aaron ran across Kellogg and then St. Peter to get to his destination. He entered the Ramsey County Courthouse through the Kellogg entrance.

This was Forsberg's first time in the art deco style building and he walked past the elevators and into the ground floor hall. Not all of his education and appreciation for life had been knocked out of him by prison. He could still enjoy the architecture and design of the twenty-story limestone building built during the Great Depression. He took a quick tour of the ground floor, admiring the old-style workmanship and the building's centerpiece, the thirty-eight-foot, white onyx statue of the Indian God of Peace.

Remembering why he came, he checked the directory and found the destination he wanted. A couple of minutes later he quietly opened the door for courtroom 1230 and slipped unobtrusively onto a bench in the back.

A trial of some kind was taking place with a witness on the stand giving testimony to the judge. There was no jury and only a few spectators in the gallery. Forsberg sat silently watching the trial and the surroundings of the mahogany paneled room.

Ignoring the participants, he finally turned his attention to the judge. The man's hair was thinner and completely white, and the face was more lined. His former lawyer, Julian Segal, was not aging particularly well. Forsberg guessed his age to be about sixty and he looked at least seventy. But there he sat up high on his throne. The longer Forsberg stared at him, the higher his blood pressure went. There sat the one man who could have kept him from prison if he had done his job. If he had been more forceful, more demanding and fought the admission of the DNA test harder, Forsberg would have been acquitted. Or so he believed.

Before twenty minutes was up Forsberg decided he couldn't take another minute of the judge and the last thing he needed was to draw attention to himself. He quietly stood up and left the courtroom.

Forsberg turned off Kellogg on his way back to the freeway and onto Summit Avenue. Summit was old money Minnesota. It was lined block after block with very large, old, multi-room homes stretching from the St. Paul Cathedral several miles to the bluff of the Mississippi River. Forsberg had found Segal's address and curiosity got the better of him. About two miles down Summit he found the house he wanted and pulled over to the curb. He sat across the street from it, a brick two-story sporting four fireplace chimneys. He stared for ten minutes then put the van in drive and slowly drove off.

Gene Parlow casually strolled through the crowd of his favorite bar, *Whiskey World*. It was mostly a biker bar located off the West Bank of the University of Minnesota campus on the downtown side.

There was a minimally talented country band on stage doing their best Lynyrd Skynyrd interpretation. On the dance floor was a decent sized crowd doing a group line dance that Parlow didn't recognize.

Parlow got a shot and a bottle of Pabst at the back bar then took a seat by the pool table. He tossed down the shot of Jack then worked on his beer while watching his brother, Troy, shoot pool. Troy was not a particularly good pool player although he thought he was. A couple of minutes after Gene sat down the game ended. Troy opened the large, brown leather pouch he had chained to himself, removed a twenty-dollar bill and paid his opponent. The next player was racking the balls while Troy took the chair next to Gene. The meth business being what it was, the twenty he just lost wasn't a big deal to Troy.

It was obvious the two men were brothers. Except for Gene's citizen haircut, they looked alike and were dressed basically the same. T-shirt, leather vest and motorcycle boots which made them indistinguishable from the other one per centers in the bar.

"Hey, bro," Troy began after a fist bump with Gene. "I think I found a bike for you. A Harley that's a little warm but should be ready in a day or two."

"What about a job? Am I in or not?" Gene asked referring to the meth business.

"I'm working on it. Relax. It'll happen. You check out your old lawyer?"

"Yeah," Parlow answered his younger brother. "She's still around."

"Well?" Troy asked.

"Well what?"

"No bitch would ever get away with fuckin' me up the way she did you," Troy said.

Gene turned his head away from the pool players and looked directly at his brother. "Don't worry about it and keep your goddamn mouth shut," he whispered. "You hear about what happened to that lawyer the other day?"

"Yeah, I did. Did you know her?"

"She was the prosecutor that sent me away," Gene continued still looking directly at Troy and speaking very quietly. "She got what she had coming."

"Did you do…"

"Shut up, dummy. Don't ask questions I ain't gonna answer."

Chloe Winters got off the elevator on the sixth floor. She was in the same parking ramp in downtown St. Paul where she parked every day. She walked quickly toward her car on the almost empty floor, the only sound coming from the clicking her shoes made on the concrete surface. It was almost ten o'clock at night and she was tired, hungry and in a hurry to get home after another long day. Trial preparation could be exhausting.

As she approached her two-year-old Camry, she was a little surprised to see a beat-up Ford van parked next to it. The van wasn't there when she had arrived in the morning. For a sparsely populated downtown parking ramp, it looked decidedly out of place.

She hit the unlock button on her key fob to unlock the car. As she was opening the driver's door, the side door of the van flew open and before she could move, he was on her.

Instead of panicking, Chloe knew exactly what to do. Her assailant had her in a choke hold and was starting to squeeze when she hammered the heel of her right shoe down on the instep of his foot. She then reached back with her right hand and grabbed and squeezed his testicles as hard as she could.

He let out a sharp, short scream and eased up on his choke hold. Chloe hammered the back of her head into his face and drilled him squarely on the nose. She pushed him back hard and slammed him into the van. He released her, and she spun around to face him. With both hands she gave him a hard shove just as his fist struck her on the side of her face.

Chloe went down onto the concrete floor between the two vehicles. Her shove was enough to make her attacker fall backwards, trip and go down himself. After years of prison food and weight lifting, the man was small and wiry but also quick and strong. He was back on his feet and coming at her again in less than a second.

When Chloe hit the ground, she was still clutching her purse in her left hand. She quickly reached into it as the Hispanic looking monster stood up and started toward her. The first bullet hit him in the stomach, the second in the chest and the third squarely in the forehead. He flew backwards, and his head made a sharp cracking noise as it hit the concrete floor and this time he wasn't getting up.

Chloe's oldest sister, Ann, had been brutally attacked and raped almost fifteen years ago. The man who did it had never been caught. This had happened when Chloe was a teenager living in Kansas City with her parents. From that moment on, Chloe became determined to never let anything like that happen to her. She worked so hard at self defense she eventually became an instructor for other women. When she moved to Minnesota for work one of the first things she did was obtain a conceal-carry permit for a handgun. She always made sure if she had to work late, her 9mm automatic was in her purse. And as her assailant would testify to if he could, she was a very good shot.

A few days later the St. Paul police told her the man she killed, by an amazing coincidence, was the man the Kansas City cops believed had raped her sister and was suspected of at least a dozen more. That night Chloe and Ann shed a lot of tears of joy on the phone and a dark cloud was dispersed from over their family.

Angelo Suarez, the fourth client of Glenda Albright in her tampered DNA case, was not going to rape another woman ever again.

TWENTY-ONE

The morning after his meetings with Glenda Albright and Marc Kadella, Howie Traynor left St. Andrews at 10:00. One of Tony's retired cop pals, Tommy Evans, was on duty and he followed Howie south on Central Avenue. On Twenty Second, Howie turned into the lot for the Northeast branch of the Hennepin County Library. Evans pulled over to the curb on Central and watched as Howie went into the library building.

A half hour went by and Howie had not come back out. Realizing this was an unusual event, Evans called Carvelli on his cell to report in. He quickly filled him in about why he called.

"He's at the library? What the hell could he be up to at the library?"

"Maybe taking out books?" Evans wise cracked.

"You see this guy as a big bookworm do you? Give him another half hour then slide in there and see what he's up to," Tony replied.

"You got it," Evans said.

The first thing Howie did when he went inside the building was to go to the help desk and apply for a library card. The older woman behind the desk pleasantly helped him fill out the form and used Howie's driver's license to confirm his address. Ten minutes later he had a temporary card to use until the permanent one was mailed to him.

He found an open computer and spent the next forty-five minutes online researching the trial of Aaron Forsberg. Never having met the man and knowing nothing about the case, Howie wanted to learn what happened to him. Halfway through the reporting he found it did jog his memory. Even though he was in prison at the time, Forsberg's case had generated quite a bit of interest, at least locally. When he finished and knowing there was someone following him, he went over to the library's fiction section.

Howie spent three- or four-minutes roaming through the aisles more or less randomly selecting books. He found a few authors he had actually heard of and when he had gathered four books, he checked them out and left.

Less than five minutes before he was going to go in looking for him, Evans saw Howie leave the building. He noticed Howie was carrying several books then watched him get in his car. Evans ducked down in his seat to let Howie go by after he exited the parking lot. Howie was headed north on Central, probably on his way back to the church. Evans watched him in his side mirror until Howie had gone a full block. After a few seconds, the traffic cleared, and Evans did a U turn in the middle of the block. Barely five minutes later, Howie was back in the church's parking lot. Tommy Evans parked his car and called Carvelli again to bring him up to date.

"You're getting to be a regular around here, Carvelli. People are starting to talk about you and Jefferson," an MPD detective by the name of Clark Fields smart mouthed Tony.

Carvelli was back in the detective's squad room again to talk to Owen Jefferson. He heard the comment, turned toward its source and saw Fields leaning back in his chair, a big grin on his face.

Clark Fields was treading water on the job to hang on long enough to get a thirty-year pension. He was wearing his standard polyester slacks, black shoes, a white shirt and rayon tie. Tony had known him for almost twenty years and basically despised him. The reason being Fields started treading water toward retirement ever since he made detective.

"Did you think that up all by yourself, Fields? I've been wrong all these years. I always thought you were both lazy and stupid. Now I see you're really very clever. I'll be sure to laugh at your rapier wit later," Tony said staring down at the seriously overweight cop.

Tony's comment elicited a good bit of laughter from the half dozen or so other detectives in the room.

"Fuck you, Carvelli," an obviously embarrassed Fields said.

"Clear a case asshole, then you can talk to me," Tony said then turned his back to the man and walked away.

"Was that fun?" Jefferson asked Tony after he had taken the chair next to the detective's desk.

"He's a clown and he should know better than to run his mouth to me," an annoyed Carvelli said.

Tony brought Jefferson up to date on the surveillance of Howie Traynor. There was nothing of substance to report including his trip to the library earlier that day. Before he finished, Marcie Sterling returned from the women's restroom. Jefferson introduced them to each other and Marcie brought her chair from her desk around to sit next to Jefferson and join in.

"How's your investigation going?" Carvelli asked.

"I don't know," a clearly exasperated Jefferson began. "I probably shouldn't discuss it with you, but I know you can keep your mouth shut. So far, we got nothing. A list of possibles, and we're chasing our tails checking them out. We're not even sure he's on our list. The fact the judge up North handled several appeals from trials that Rhea Watson did is the only connection between them that we have.

"I was wondering," Jefferson continued. "How do you know for sure you're putting him to bed every night? How can you be sure he's not slipping out the back?"

"He could be," Tony shrugged. "I thought of that, so I put a guy in the alley to watch for it a few times. None of them ever saw him. Plus, his car is on the street. Pretty unlikely he slipped out, took a bus to Bemidji, did that judge and got back by morning."

"Yeah, okay," Jefferson agreed. "How much longer will you stay on him?"

"I need talk to Vivian Donahue tonight. This is getting to be a waste of everybody's time and her money. And, I have other business to attend to and so does Madeline. The other guys, the retired cops, they're starting to grumble a bit too about other things they want to do. Everybody's bored. What about you two? You got anything going?" Tony asked.

"Not much. I told you about our list, didn't I?" Jefferson said.

"Yeah, you did."

"We've managed to eliminate sixteen names. They're either dead or still in prison or out of state and alibied."

"That leaves....?"

"Fifty-eight," Marcie said.

"Too many," Carvelli said. "Hey, I'm taking off. If anything comes up…"

"You'll let me know," Jefferson finished for him.

Vivian Donahue was out on the front lawn of the mansion watching the groundskeepers work on the garden. It was late summer heading toward autumn and she wanted to be out enjoying the beautiful day.

Vivian saw a car pull into her driveway and watched with curiosity as it approached. As it got closer she realized it was the black Audi owned by Madeline Rivers. They made eye contact as Maddy drove by and waved at each other as Maddy continued to the house and parked her car.

"This is a pleasant surprise," Vivian said as she held out her arms to the younger woman. The women gave each other an affectionate hug. When they separated, Vivian continued by asking, "What brings you all the way out here on this lovely day?"

With a curious look on her face, Maddy asked, "Didn't Tony, I mean Anthony, call you?"

Vivian laughed at her use of the name Anthony, put her right arm through Maddy's left and started toward the main building. "You call him Tony, dear. I'll stick with Anthony. It sounds more natural that way. And no, he didn't call me. Why?"

They heard the quiet rumble of Tony's Camaro and both of them turned to watch him drive by.

"I'll let him tell you," Maddy said as they continued toward the house.

A few minutes later the three of them were seated at a table on the patio overlooking the lake and swimming pool.

"You've come here to tell me you want to call off the surveillance of this Traynor person," Vivian flatly stated before Carvelli could say it.

"Yes," Tony said sipping his iced tea, "We're getting nowhere. He's not doing anything and we both have other clients."

"You've spent enough money on this, Vivian," Maddy added. "He's not your problem and it's beginning to look like his religious, whatever it is, awakening or conversion is real."

Vivian took the news quietly. Tony and Maddy sipped their drinks waiting for her to respond. Vivian stared out across Lake Minnetonka seeing but not really watching a two-masted sailboat silently glide by.

"Chalk it up to being a foolish old woman..." Vivian started to say.

"Stop it. You're neither," Maddy mildly chastised her.

"Thank you dear," she patted Maddy's left had. "Very well. If you think you're wasting your time, I don't care about the money, then end it."

Howie Traynor arrived home from work at his normal time later that same day. He parked in a spot in front of his building and was surprised to see the car that had followed go past and drive away. Believing he was still being watched, he kept to his normal routine and went into his building and up to his apartment.

For the next hour, every few minutes, he would peek through the vertical blinds in the windows of the small living room. Howie believed there was someone on station in front of his building to relieve the man who followed him home. He checked every car in sight and saw no one. After an hour or so he was satisfied they were gone.

Howie went into the small bedroom and laid down to take a nap. He decided he would break his routine and go out later around eight o'clock to see if they were really gone.

TWENTY-TWO

Jeannie Peterson waited patiently on the curb at the passenger drop-off area. Her husband of almost forty years, Ross Peterson, was removing the two medium size pieces of luggage from the trunk of his car. He placed the bags on the street and slammed the trunk lid down. The trunk didn't close, and it took him two more attempts before the latch caught and locked. Jeannie stood on the sidewalk trying not to look amused while her husband fought with the old car. By the time he made the third attempt, he was cussing, and she was almost laughing.

"Maybe it's time to buy a new car," she said for at least the hundredth time. The twelve-year-old Taurus had seen better days.

"Its fine," he snapped at her. "I'm not wasting retirement money on a car." He continued by saying, "I'm not going to eat dog food when I retire." While he stated this last line, Jeannie was reciting exactly the same words in her head knowing he would say them.

"I'll do my best not to cook dog food for you," she said as he set her bags next to her. "I hate having to carry luggage onto the plane."

"They'll fit in the overhead. I'm not going to pay fifty bucks to check a bag. That's ridiculous," he grumbled as he turned to go back to the car and left his wife standing on the sidewalk. "Call me when you get there," he practically ordered, then got in the old car and drove off without even saying goodbye.

Jeannie Peterson could not have cared less that he didn't say goodbye to her. In fact, she barely noticed. She was flying out of the Minneapolis-St. Paul airport to Massachusetts to spend time with their daughter and new grandson. This was their third grandchild; one by their son and his wife and this second one by their daughter and her husband. Even though she didn't need the help, their daughter Ellen had asked Jeannie to visit. Both offspring had moved as soon as they were old enough in order to get away from their father. Their son Mike had moved to Texas and Ellen to Massachusetts.

Defying the old cheapskate, Jeannie checked both bags and charged it to a credit card Ross knew nothing about. She passed quickly through security and headed toward her gate. While walking down the concourse to catch the people mover she again thought to their future. Three more years until her husband reaches mandatory retirement. The old curmudgeon had no hobbies, no interests, nothing to keep him occupied. What was she going to do with him underfoot every day?

The man found a seat in the semi-crowded courtroom of Judge Ross Peterson and sat behind two large women. There was a trial taking place and the defendant was on the stand. He listened for fifteen minutes while the young man testified to the jury. Apparently it was a homicide trial involving drugs and the twenty-something defendant was obviously lying. It was almost painful to watch as he talked himself into a quick conviction. Or at least that's what the stranger thought.

He had been watching the judge for a couple of days. He followed him to the airport this morning and watched from a space in front of the terminal a couple of cars down as the old man dropped off his wife. Now he was in the courtroom checking on the judge to finalize his plan.

The defense lawyer finished his exam of his client and Peterson had the lawyers come forward. When the two prosecutors and defense lawyer reached the bench, Peterson asked, "You got any more witnesses after this?"

The defense lawyer, a well-known African-American said he did not.

Peterson then asked the prosecution about their cross-examination. The lead attorney told him she had at least an hour.

When the lawyers returned to their chairs, the judge informed the jury they would take a short break. It was almost 5:30 p.m. and Peterson was determined to finish taking testimony that evening.

While Peterson was leaving the bench, the out-of-place stranger in the back quickly fled to the hallway. He exited the courtroom and went right to the elevators.

Judge Peterson parked the old Taurus in the attached garage and looked at the dashboard clock. It was 8:18 and almost dark outside.

The trial would be given to the jury tomorrow, two days ahead of schedule. Peterson took pride in running a tight ship. He had been on the bench for twenty-one years and knew how to be in charge and keep a trial moving.

On the drive home he had indulged himself with a meal at a small restaurant by his home. He rationalized the expense by convincing himself it did not cost much more than if he ate at home.

He went into the house through the door to the kitchen and to the refrigerator. The judge allowed himself one or two lite beers each night, his one and only vice. He reached for the door handle as a shadowy figure dressed completely in black appeared in front of him. The man stood in front of the elderly judge, his right hand in the pocket of his black windbreaker.

The judge jerked backward at the sight and awkwardly said, "Who, what, ah, who are you?"

"I'm hurt," the sinister figure said, "I thought you would remember me."

At that moment, the light of comprehension came on in the judge's head. He immediately thought of two names: Robert Smith, an acquaintance and appeals court judge and Rhea Watson, a lawyer who had tried many cases before him.

"Wait, no please..." Peterson started to say as he held up his hands and extended his arms. What stopped him was the 50,000 volts the intruder sent through him. Unfortunately, the fun he expected to have torturing and killing his third victim was not to be.

Unknown to the judge's assailant, Peterson had been fitted with a pacemaker a little over a year ago. The voltage from the Taser produced a cardiac arrhythmia and in less than two minutes, Judge Ross Peterson was dead.

By 9:05 a.m. the next day, Marty Colstad had become quite concerned with the missing judge. Marty was Ross Peterson's clerk and in the year and a half he had clerked for the judge, Peterson had never been late to work.

Marty, a student in his final year of law school at William Mitchell in St. Paul, had taken it upon himself to find out what happened. The first thing he did was discuss it with the lawyers. Both sides were ready to give closing arguments and the jury was getting impatient.

Marty then called the police and asked them to check at Peterson's home. Within a half hour they called back with the grim news.

Officer Rhonda Dean parked her squad car on the street in front of the Peterson's home. The first thing she did was ring the front doorbell and look through the windows in the front of the house. Next she went around the side to the back door, knocked several times and looked into the kitchen. Seeing nothing noticeably amiss she walked around the garage to check the yard.

She came around the back corner of the garage and saw him. He was sitting up, his back to the garage, his hands nailed to the garage wall and what looked to be a crown of some type on his head.

Owen Jefferson parked his car at the mouth of the Peterson's driveway. He and Marcie Sterling followed the small crowd of police and first responders around to the back of the garage. The head of the crime scene unit was already there, and the two detectives walked over to her.

"Hey, Barb," Jefferson said as he shook hands with her. "Lieutenant Barbara Langer, Detective Marcie Sterling," he said introducing the two women.

"I have a team in the house and your guys are canvassing the neighborhood," Langer said. "So far, we haven't found anything inside. Whoever did this is really careful."

"Yeah, I know," Jefferson quietly agreed. "Wait here," he said to Marcie.

Jefferson walked carefully across the grass and knelt down in front of the body next to Clyde Marston, the man from the medical examiner's office.

"No blood this time," Marston said referring to the front of Peterson's shirt. "No crushed fingers either."

"What do you think?" Jefferson asked.

"Don't know. He could've had a weak heart and if he was hit with a Taser like Watson that could've killed him. We'll see."

Jefferson took a minute to look over the victim's fingers and the wound where the nails were driven through his hands. "He died before our guy got around to the fun part," he quietly said.

"Looks like it," Marston agreed.

"Put a rush on it, will you Clyde? And let me know right away."

"You got it Owen. I may even know yet today."

That afternoon Jefferson commandeered one of the private conference rooms in the detective's squad room. He and Sterling moved their case files into the room and set up on the table inside. There was a large whiteboard along one wall and the tech department set up two PC's for their use.

Marcie was finishing listing seven names on the whiteboard when Selena Kane entered the room.

"These are the ones from our list who are attached to all three victims. They were all tried by Rhea Watson with Ross Peterson on the bench. And all seven had their appeals rejected by the judge up North, Robert Smith."

"When these cases go up on appeal," Kane said, "they are not decided by just one judge. Have you thought of that?"

"Marcie did, yeah," Jefferson answered making sure he gave his new partner the credit. "And you're right, there are three judges on each case. We have figured out who and we're having them all notified. The state can provide them with protection until this is over. That's the best we can do."

"Okay," Kane said. "Good catch," she said to Marcie.

"I think it's one of these three," Marcie said pointing to three names on the board. "Eugene Parlow, Aaron Forsberg or Howard Traynor.

"Why them?" Kane asked.

"They're the ones who were recently released because they were convicted with falsified DNA test results," Jefferson answered.

"Oh, okay. I see what you mean," Kane said. "Did this start after they got out?"

"Yes, a few weeks later," Marcie answered her. "There was a fourth one two," she continued, "a rapist named Angelo Suarez. He was the guy shot and killed by that woman in St. Paul…"

"I remember that," Kane interrupted. "We should send her flowers, a congratulatory card and a shooting merit badge. Now what?"

"We'll get them in here for questioning," Jefferson said. "But, I'm not sure. My bet would be Traynor, but he's got a solid alibi for the first two."

"Try to catch this guy and soon. The media will be all over this before much longer."

TWENTY-THREE

"Mia slow down! Don't cross the street without me," Katie yelled at the little girl. Katie Gibbs was a twenty-three-year-old, part-time nanny for three-year-old Mia Harper. Mia stopped at the corner and Katie hurried to catch up with the child. Katie was a student at the University of Minnesota in their dental hygienist program. The Harper's were a post forty couple with successful careers who had Katie as their little showpiece accoutrement. Their total parental involvement with Katie was to make sure she had good nannies and to get her into the best schools and occasionally display the beautiful, brown-eyed brunette to their wine and cheese friends.

Mia waited impatiently for Katie at the corner of Twenty Fifth and Bryant in south Minneapolis. It was almost 10:00 a.m. and Katie was taking her to Mueller Park for some play time. The Harpers had spent a small fortune renovating a ten room house a block away. They had chosen this neighborhood to demonstrate their trendy side but were not thrilled about their little trophy fraternizing with the locals. The Harpers disapproved of both the small park and its inhabitants.

Katie held Mia's hand while they hurried across Twenty Fifth and entered the park by the wading pool. As soon as they reached the park's grass Mia jerked away from Katie and took off. Katie walked quickly behind her as Mia ran toward the large sandbox play area. Mia knew her two best friends, a three-year-old girl named Kyra and another three-year-old girl Sailee, would already be there.

Katie sat down on a bench next to the small park facilities building to watch the girls. The day care provider for Mia's friends and a couple of the other younger children was also there. The two women watched as the children ran in, out and off of the various swings, slides and playground equipment. A couple of other regulars with children joined them and for a half-hour or so they gabbed and watched the kids play.

Several times Katie turned her head toward the park's picnic area. Finally, after the fourth or fifth time, she asked her friend Darlene, the day care provider, about the man sitting at a table. He was about a hundred yards away from them, his arms spread out on the table top and his head tilted forward.

"I think he might be a passed out drunk," Darlene answered her.

Both women looked toward their left at the man and Katie said, "He hasn't moved since I got here. What's that all over the front of his shirt?"

"He probably got sick and threw up on himself," Darlene said.

By now, the other women in their little group were looking at him as Katie said, "Maybe someone should go over there and check on him."

"Go ahead," the others said in unison. Katie turned back to Darlene and said, "Come with me, please."

"Okay," Darlene answered reluctantly.

The two of them walked slowly toward the man. He was in the Southeast corner of the park sitting at a picnic table. His back was against the table, his head facing away from it west toward Colfax Avenue. His arms were stretched out to both sides and his head tilted downward, his chin touching his chest and they could see he was barefoot.

Katie and Darlene slowly came to within fifty feet of him when Darlene exclaimed, "Oh my God! That's not vomit, its blood!" Darlene grabbed Katie's arm as if to stop her and almost yelled, "What should we do?"

By this time Katie was already doing it. She removed her phone from her pocket and started to punch in 911 on it. As she did this she calmly said to the horrified Darlene, "Go back to the kids and make sure to keep them away from here."

Owen Jefferson and Marcie Sterling listened quietly while Katie told the story for the fourth or fifth time. They were standing on the south side of the little building. While they talked, the CSU people were combing over every inch of the park and an M.E. doctor was examining the body.

When Katie finished, Jefferson asked, "Do you think you could do something for us? We'd like you to take a look and see if you can identify him."

"Oh, God, I don't know," Katie said wrinkling her face in revulsion. "I guess I could try." She turned around to check on Mia. All of the children had been hustled into a corner of the play area directly opposite from the body. The park's building blocked their line of sight but none of them were playing. With the police all over the park even the little ones knew something was wrong and they all quietly sat watching. All of the adults had been asked to stay to give statements to the police.

The medical examiner had set up a three-sided portable screen around the picnic table and body. A crowd was gathering along the streets bordering the park. There were also houses along the little park's south side. The screen would shield the grisly sight from the gawkers and the media. The latter were starting to arrive. Channel 8 had a van and crew on site that was being held back by uniformed officers.

The two detectives, with Katie in between them, walked back toward the body. When they got within ten feet of him, Katie could see his hands were nailed to the tabletop and he was wearing a barbed wire crown.

"You okay?" Marcie asked her.

"Barely. What kind of sicko could do this?" Katie said.

The M.E. looked at them and when Jefferson nodded at the doctor he gently lifted the man's head, so Katie could see his face.

"You still okay?" Marcie asked again.

Katie stared at the gruesome white face, completely drained of blood and said, "Yeah, I'm alright and, I shouldn't be."

"Do you recognize him?" Jefferson quietly asked.

"No," she said. "I've never seen him around here."

They walked her back to the group of civilians and children. There were two other police officers there who told Jefferson they had taken statements from the adults. Jefferson then gave the okay for them to get the kids home.

Before leaving the scene themselves, Jefferson had the M.E. get the fingerprints from both of the victim's hands. While watching him do this, Jefferson again looked at the crushed and bloody fingers and toes of the man.

While they were walking to where their car was parked on Bryant for the ride back to headquarters, Marcie said, "That's two in two days. First the judge and now this guy, whoever he is."

Jefferson was looking at a Polaroid of the ghastly looking man. Just like the others, he thought. Throat cut from behind by a left-handed person from ear to ear, blood covering his abdomen, the crushed fingers and toes and the macabre crown of barbed wire thorns.

They reached the car and he slipped the photo into his inside coat pocket.

"You check missing persons and I'll run his prints. Let's see if we can find out who he is," Jefferson said.

Before they could get in the car a woman reporter with the Channel 8 van yelled at Jefferson and caught his attention. Gabriella Shriqui was politely but firmly being held back by an MPD cop.

Jefferson heard his name being called and looked toward the source. He saw Gabriella and decided he would take a minute to talk to her. He motioned to the uniformed officer to let her through. She started to come forward with a camera operator, but Jefferson quickly held up a hand to stop the cameraman.

When Gabriella reached him, the three of them, including Marcie, walked silently across the street. When they reached the edge of the park Jefferson turned to Gabriella and held up a hand before she could ask a question.

"Here's the deal," Jefferson began. "I'll talk to you only, no cameras and this is completely off the record."

Gabriella stood in front of them with her back to the park. She took a quick look at each of the detectives then said, "Owen, that's not fair…"

"What's fair got to do with it?" Jefferson said.

"Okay," Gabriella shrugged. "We're getting reports…"

"Leaks," Jefferson again interrupted.

"Okay leaks…" she started again.

"Rumors actually," Jefferson corrected her.

"Fine, goddamnit," an annoyed Gabriella said. "Rumors, leaks, whatever. We're hearing there's a serial killer out there and this guy is victim three or four. You guys need to start coming clean or we'll start reporting using the 'sources close to the investigation' bullshit attribution."

Jefferson thought it over a minute before saying, "Call me later this afternoon. I have to check with some people first, okay?"

"Fair enough but, if I don't get anything we'll run with what we know. I'll keep your name out of it, but we will report this. We have to."

On the drive downtown, the two detectives talked over the case. The first thing they needed was to identify this latest victim. From that they would see if there is a connection with the other victims.

"These cannot be random," Marcie said. "There has to be a connection."

"And when we find the connection we'll find our psycho," Jefferson agreed.

Jefferson electronically submitted the fingerprints taken from the body into IAFIS, the automated Fingerprint Identification System. IAFIS is used by law enforcement throughout the nation to identify people by their fingerprints. It is maintained by the FBI and contains over one hundred million sets of fingerprints obtained by a number of ways, especially from criminal subjects.

While he waited for a response, Jefferson leaned back in his chair, his arms folded across his chest and stared at the names on the whiteboard. Marcie was on the phone talking to someone in missing persons. Whoever she was speaking with placed her on hold to check on something.

"We may have a hit," Marcie said while holding the phone to her ear. Jefferson sat up and wheeled his chair around to look at her but before he could respond, Marcie held up an index finger to him and said into the phone, "Yes, I'm here. What do you have?"

She listened for a minute and took some notes while saying, "Uh huh, uh huh. Okay. Yeah, I got it. Thanks, we'll check it out."

Marcie hung up the phone and made a few more notes on the tablet she had written on.

"What?" Jefferson impatiently asked.

"They got a call from a woman a couple of hours ago. Her name is Marilyn Kuhn. She was supposed to meet her dad for breakfast this morning and when he didn't show she got worried and went to his house. When she got there his car was in the garage, but he wasn't there. She called, and we sent a squad car to get a statement. The description she gave sounds like our victim."

"Okay. You go check her out. Here," Jefferson said as he tossed the Polaroid of the victim across their desks to her. "Take this with you but only show it to her if you absolutely have to. She doesn't need to see her dad like that. See if she has a picture of him for you to look at. If it's him take her to the morgue to identify him. Can you do that?"

"Take her to the morgue?"

"Yeah."

Marcie hesitated for a moment, a sad look on her face, and then said, "Yeah, I can. It's part of the job and I better get used to it."

"You never get used to it," Jefferson said. "You just learn how to deal with it."

As she was packing up to leave she asked him, "What will you be doing?"

"I'm waiting for IAFIS to run its program and see if he's in the system. It takes a half hour or so. While I'm doing that I need to talk to Selena about the media."

Fifteen minutes later, Selena Kane and Jefferson were ushered into the office of the mayor. Waiting for them were the chief of police, the city attorney and the county attorney. Introductions were made then Jefferson was given the floor. Jefferson quickly brought them all up to date on the victims and the investigation.

"So, we have a serial killer on our hands," the mayor said. "Why wasn't I told sooner?"

"That was my call," the chief interjected. "Until yesterday we weren't sure."

"I'm still not sure we have a typical serial," Selena Kane interjected.

"How so?" Mayor Gillette asked.

"Serial killers usually act on some psychological need. Motives can vary but they are typically things like anger, thrill, attention seeking or even a financial gain," Kane answered. "We believe this is some type of vengeance or revenge thing. At least that's our best guess. He's going after specific people who we believe wronged him through the courts."

"What about the man who was found this morning?" the chief asked. "What's his connection?"

"We don't know yet, Chief," Jefferson answered. "We're still checking into him to find out who he is."

"Could this maniac be one of the people who were convicted with doctored DNA reports and recently released?" asked the mayor.

"They're on our list," Jefferson said.

"All four of them?" the county attorney asked.

"No," Selena Kane interjected. "One of the four, Angelo Suarez was shot and killed during an attempted assault by him on a woman in a St. Paul parking lot."

"I heard about that," the mayor said. "Good for her."

"What about the press?" the chief asked.

The mayor thought it over for a few seconds then said, "My office will prepare a statement. We'll have to admit we believe these killings are connected but we're still investigating blah, blah, blah. We'll run it by you," she said to the chief. "Then we'll release it in about an hour. We'll have it for all of you to look at in about a half hour. Thanks for the information and keep us all up to date."

"We will, your Honor," Kane said.

Jefferson sat down in the same chair of the conference room they were using. The IAFIS report was finished and it came up negative. If the man had ever been fingerprinted he was not listed in the data base. While he was looking over the printed report his cell phone went off.

"Yeah, did you find out anything?" Jefferson asked Marcie.

"We're on our way to the morgue. She's following me in her car. I think it's him, her dad. She showed me a picture and it looks like him," Marcie said. "His name is Elliot Sanders. I asked her about any connection he might have to the courts, judges or lawyers. I didn't give her any specifics."

"And?"

"The only thing she could come up with was he did jury duty about twelve or thirteen years ago. She couldn't remember for sure.

Hey! Watch out asshole," she yelled as a driver cut in front of her then stuck out his left hand and flipped her off. "I wish I still had my ticket book," she said.

"No, you don't," Jefferson reminded her.

"Yeah, you're right. Anyway, can you check with the courts? See if they have a record of him on jury duty back then?"

"Sure. I even know who to call. Call me back when you're done at the morgue."

Jefferson was on hold for over fifteen minutes waiting with growing impatience. A record's clerk with the clerk of courts office was checking their records for Elliot Sanders.

"Found him," the woman said when she got back on the phone.

"What did you come up with?"

The woman gave Jefferson all of the details of the trial on which Sanders had served. When she finished, Jefferson had her repeat it just to be sure. He thanked her profusely, made her swear to keep it to herself, then hung up the phone and softly whistled. He stood up and went to the whiteboard where the list of names was written, circled one and quietly said, "Gotcha, you sonofabitch."

His cell phone rang, and he checked the ID. He answered the call and asked, "What did you find out?"

"It's him, her dad. Boy that really sucks doing that," Marcie glumly added.

"She sure?"

"Yeah, she's sure. I'm on my way back. I'll be there in five minutes."

"I'll tell you what I found out when you get here."

Jefferson ended the call with Marcie and put down his cell phone. He picked up the department's phone and dialed a number to a cop in the surveillance unit. Jefferson requested a high priority surveillance team to be put on his suspect. The man he called, an MPD lieutenant and a good friend, had surveillance in place within an hour and the suspect would be closely and professionally watched.

TWENTY-FOUR

Marc Kadella was seated at one end of the dining room table and Margaret Tennant was at the other end. They made dinner together and cleaned up afterwards. Now each was engrossed in work brought home and enjoying a quiet evening at Margaret's house.

Marc was going over his case notes and witness statements for a trial starting scheduled for the next day. His client was charged with second degree burglary, a serious felony. He was accused of entering a home with intent to steal from its contents. Fortunately, no one was home at the time. It was the man's second offense and the prosecution had offered nothing in exchange for a plea.

The fool had entered the house through an unlocked window. When he tried to leave through the same window, there were two uniformed Minneapolis cops standing beneath it waiting for him. Having been unable to exclude any of the evidence, the trial was likely a waste of everyone's time. Especially damning was the client's statement to the cops. "Well, I guess you got me for robbing this house." Marc was no longer amazed or even amused at how stupid these people are. Once in a while it would be nice to get a client who knew how to keep his mouth shut.

His phone went off and he picked it up, looked at the ID and answered it by saying, "Hey goombah, what's up?"

"What's this goombah shit?" Tony Carvelli said. "I call with serious news and you try to imply I'm a gangster. I'm offended," he continued trying to sound serious.

"That's perfect," Marc laughed. "Except you don't know what the word offended means," Marc looked at Margaret who was listening with an inquisitive look and mouthed the word "Tony" to her.

"Say hello," she said.

"Margaret says hello."

"Tell her she's way too good for you and should dump you for a real man and not some wussified lawyer," Tony replied.

"Tony says hello too," Marc said to Margaret.

"So, what's this serious news you have?" Marc asked his P.I. friend.

"I got a call from Owen Jefferson a little while ago, you remember him?"

"Sure," Marc replied.

"You see the news about Judge Peterson and the guy they found in the park this morning?"

"Yeah, the six o'clock news claimed there's a serial killer loose."

"Yeah, well sort of but not exactly," Carvelli said. "All the victims have something in common. I'm not at liberty to go into detail about this but the thing they have in common is Howie Traynor's trial for the death of Vivian's aunt, Lucille Benson."

"What!?" Marc practically yelled which caused Margaret to raise her head up from the file she was working on. "Are they sure?"

"Pretty sure, yeah," Carvelli answered.

While Marc listened, a bead of sweat lightly broke out on his forehead. Carvelli went over each victim. He started with the first one, the appellate judge who had presided over Traynor's appeal. Then he revisited Rhea Watson who had prosecuted the case and Judge Ross Peterson who was the trial judge.

Before Carvelli got to the man found that morning in Mueller Park, Marc interrupted him. "What about the guy found this morning? He wasn't a judge or lawyer. I was his lawyer."

"Elliot Sanders. Does the name sound familiar?" Carvelli asked.

"No, should it?"

"No, probably not. It's been a while. Anyway, you ready for this? He was the jury foreman."

"Holy shit, sonofabitch," Marc quietly said. "Do you think I'm..."

"Yeah, Marc. They do think you're on the list. Probably me too."

"Why you?"

"I arrested his ass. Me and Jake Waschke and a few others."

"Jesus Christ. Now what?

"What?" a concerned Margaret almost yelled.

Marc held up an index finger to her and softly said to her, "I'll tell you in a minute. Relax."

"Jefferson has surveillance on him and…"

"Wait a minute," Marc interrupted. "I thought you and Maddy were doing that for Vivian. What happened?"

"We stopped a few days ago. He hadn't done anything so…"

"Were you watching him when any of these other victims were killed?"

"Yeah, we were," Carvelli said.

"Then how…"

"That's the question, isn't it?" Carvelli replied. "I don't know. We had him covered for the time frame of the first two but not Judge Peterson and this Sanders guy."

"That's a pretty solid alibi," Marc, the lawyer in him said. "What do you think?"

"I don't know what to think. He could've slipped past us, but his car never moved. How did he get out and get up to Bemidji, do that judge up there then get back by morning in time for Sunday church?"

"The cops could have it all wrong," Marc said. "They could be looking at the wrong thing entirely."

"Yeah, they could. The Minneapolis cops are contacting everyone involved with this case, so I told Jefferson I'd get a hold of you. You want some protection?"

Marc thought about that for a moment then said, "No. I have a carry permit and I'll start using it for now."

"Yeah, me too," Carvelli said. "Be careful."

"I will, you too," Marc replied.

Before Marc could set the phone on the table, Margaret started in. "What the hell was that?" she almost shouted. She was staring at him with an astonished look on her face because of what she had overheard. "You're going to start carrying a gun?"

It wasn't the fact that he was going to start carrying a gun. She knew he had a concealed carry permit as did she. A lot of judges do. In fact, Margaret knew of at least two Hennepin County judges, both very liberal, who kept a gun hidden on the bench. What concerned her was the reason why Marc told Tony he would. She wanted to know why.

Marc relayed the conversation to her and explained the police suspicions about Howie Traynor. "I can't see how it could be him. He was under surveillance for all but a couple of the killings," he said

"Don't you think you should demand police protection?"

Marc simply shrugged and said, "They can't protect everybody all the time. I don't believe it's Howie so I'm not too worried about it."

The next day George Lynch and his ten-year-old black lab were taking their usual mid-morning walk. It was cloudy and cool with a forecast of rain predicted for later that afternoon. George was a retired fireman and still married to his high school sweetheart. Because of the chill he had on a hat and coat. Zeus was loosely held by a long leash which allowed the dog a little freedom to roam.

The two of them were on the walkway surrounding Lake Harriet, one of the chain of lakes in Minneapolis. The weather being what it was there were far fewer people out than normal.

Up ahead, about a hundred yards, George could see and hear a flock of about twenty crows. The birds were on and around a small copse of birch trees standing between the asphalt trail and the lake. As George and his companion got closer, he could tell that something on the ground among the trees had the scavengers' attention.

When they reached that point on the walkway, George decided to find out what it was. He tightened Zeus' leash and the two of them walked toward the commotion. Being city birds and used to people, they didn't fly off until George got within ten feet and set Zeus loose.

At the bottom of the half dozen or so trees was some brush about three feet high. Because of this, George had to walk around the trees to see what had attracted the birds. When he got there he almost wished he had not.

The first police officer to arrive had been at Mueller Park the day before. He spoke to the retired fireman who was waiting on the walking path and called it in on his shoulder mic right away. George described to him the pose of the body and the cop knew immediately what to do.

When Jefferson and Marcie arrived, the M.E. was examining the body and a CSU team was combing over the area. They took a few minutes to hear the dog walker's story. They thanked him then walked over to the first cop on scene, Officer DeJohn Carver.

"When are you getting your sergeant stripes?" Jefferson asked him as they shook hands.

"Next month," Carver replied.

"Really? Good. About time." Jefferson introduced Marcie then waited for Carver to fill him in. The patrolman told the detectives what he found and did upon arriving.

"Write it up and get it to me by the end of today," Jefferson said when Carver finished.

"Owen," the patrolman continued. "I know this guy. Or, he looks really familiar, but I can't remember his name."

Jefferson and Marcie stood behind Clyde Marston, the on-site M.E. The victim was posed exactly as the others. His arms were spread apart, and his hands were nailed to two trees. His throat had been slit open, his shirt covered in blood and the crown of barbed wire thorns atop his head. Even from a few feet away the two detectives could see the damage done to the man's fingers and toes.

"Lift his chin and let me take a look please, Clyde," Jefferson said.

Marston complied and as soon as he did so Jefferson quietly said, "Sonofabitch. You've got to be kidding."

"You know him?" Marcie asked.

"Yeah, I know who he is," Jefferson answered. "He ripped me to shreds on the witness stand a few years ago, before he was appointed to the bench. It's Julian Segal, a Ramsey County judge. I think I better give St. Paul a call."

Jefferson found the number of a St. Paul detective he knew and called him. The man answered immediately and without a greeting said, "So, you've got yourself a shit storm over there. Glad I'm not you," John Lucas said.

"Yeah, well suck it up buddy 'cause I'm about to drag you into it."

Jefferson explained the most recent victim to Lucas. When he finished Lucas told him he would put together a search team to go through Segal's house. While on the phone Lucas had looked up the judge's Summit Avenue address and Jefferson agreed to meet him there.

Jefferson, Marcie and Lucas were the first to arrive at Segal's home. It was their responsibility to inform the new widow of what had happened to her husband. She told them she had called the St. Paul police to report him missing.

"We're Jewish," she said through her sobs. "He's supposed to be buried…"

"Within 24 hours," Jefferson said. "I know ma'am."

"Do they have to do an autopsy?" she asked.

"Yes, legally it must be done. I've already requested that it be done as quickly as possible to get him back to you," Jefferson answered. "Mrs. Segal, we need to search your home. We would like to have your permission to do so."

"Why?" she asked.

"It's a routine request," Marcie politely said. "To look for any clue as to who might have done this. We'll be as careful as we possibly can."

"Oh, yes, I see," the widow answered. "Yes, sure. Do what you have to do."

An hour later Jefferson told John Lucas they were leaving and to let him know if they found anything.

"You taking this?" Lucas asked referring to jurisdiction.

"The body was found in Minneapolis. Unless we find out he was killed somewhere else, it's ours."

"Let me know if you need anything else," Lucas said.

Marcie Sterling was on the phone with Jeff Miller, the MPD computer tech, while Owen Jefferson stared at the whiteboard. They were back at the office trying to find a connection between their theory and Julian Segal.

'Thanks, Jeff," Marcie said into the phone. "Get anything you find to us as soon as you can."

"He has a thing for you," Jefferson said after Marcie hung up the phone.

"Shut up!" she said which made Jefferson laugh. Their boss, Selena Kane entered the room at that moment and sat down at the head of the table.

"Tell me you have something," she said.

"We're looking," Jefferson dejectedly answered.

"Maybe we're looking at this all wrong. What if it's something and someone else?" Kane said looking at the names on the whiteboard.

"I'm open to suggestions," Jefferson answered.

"It's here," Marcie interjected referring to the names on the board. "That's the only thing that makes any sense. Otherwise, what, someone's randomly murdering judges, lawyers and this guy who was a jury foreman? That's too much of a stretch."

"What do I tell the chief and the mayor, three victims in three days?"

"Tell them it's time to be honest. Tell them we have a serial on the loose," Jefferson said. "We've contacted everyone we can think of who might be connected to Traynor's trial…"

Jefferson's cell phone went off, he looked at the ID and answered it.

"You wanted a run down on Howie Traynor?" he heard the head of the surveillance unit; Lieutenant Rod Schiller say.

"Yeah, what do you have? We got another one last night."

"I heard," Schiller replied. "We picked him up yesterday at the church at 4:10. My guy was there by 3:00. Traynor's car was in the lot and he came out of the church at 4:10.

"We took him straight home and he stayed there until 5:45. He went to a gym called *A Plus Workout*. He was there from 6:00 until 7:25. On the way home he stopped at a small grocery store. He was in the store for twelve minutes. From there he went straight home and didn't come out."

"Did you sit on him all night, Rod?"

"Yeah, including a guy in the alley. He didn't come out and his car didn't move."

"Shit. Well, thanks Rod."

"We'll stay on him."

When he finished the call Kane said, "I take it there was nothing there."

"No," Jefferson replied then told the two women what Schiller told him.

"So, it's not Traynor," Kane said.

"Unless he's working with someone else," Marcie said.

"I just thought of something," Jefferson said. He picked up his phone and dialed a number he had recently memorized. It was answered on the third ring.

"What's up? I heard you got another one, third one in three days," Jefferson heard Tony Carvelli say.

"Yeah and it'll be a shit storm around here and soon. Listen, you know Traynor's ex-lawyer," he continued. "Do me a favor. Call him and ask him if Julian Segal had anything to do with that trial; anything at all to do with Traynor."

"Is that who it was?" Carvelli asked. "I hadn't heard that."

"Yeah, we'll release that later today. Keep it to yourself for now, okay? Will you call him for me?"

"Sure, no problem. He'd talk to you. He's a good guy, not your normal defense lawyer but I'll call him and call you right back."

About the same time Owen Jefferson was identifying the third victim in three days, Marc Kadella was arriving at his office. His burglary trial had been resolved with a last-minute plea bargain. His client pleaded guilty to third degree burglary which is still a felony. The judge agreed to a sentence of eighteen months in prison and suspended twelve months of it. As part of his three years of supervised probation, he agreed to complete an accredited drug rehab program. He would also submit to random drug testing and remain law abiding. If he did this, the conviction would reduce to a misdemeanor. It was a good deal if he completed all of the terms. Marc believed there was maybe a ten percent chance that he would.

"He's with a client, Tony," Marc heard Sandy say into the telephone. Marc and Connie Mickelson were showing a client out and he heard Sandy say his name. The woman was a very well-off divorce client of Connie whose nineteen-year-old son had a criminal problem. Marc had agreed to take his case and the woman had written a nice check as the retainer. Knowing Carvelli was calling, Marc used it as an excuse to get away from the woman.

"What's up?" he said when he got back to his desk.

"Owen Jefferson asked me to call you again and ask you a question."

"Okay," Marc curiously answered.

"You know who Julian Segal is?"

"Sure. Everyone in the Cities knows him. Why?"

"Have you seen any news today?"

"No, I haven't. God, don't tell me…"

"Yeah, they found him this morning alongside Lake Harriet. Same deal. Keep that to yourself for now. They haven't released his name. Did he have anything to do with Howie Traynor's trial way back when?"

"Let me think," Marc said. After ten to fifteen seconds he said, "No. Not that I can think of, unless he was somehow involved in the appeal which I doubt. That was handled by the state P.D. office."

"You're sure?"

"Yeah, I'm sure."

"Okay, Marc. I'll tell him."

TWENTY-FIVE

"Thanks Tony," Jefferson said into his personal phone, "I owe you one." He ended the call and looked across the conference room table at his partner. They were still in their squad room looking for a connection of Segal to their case. Marcie was on the phone with her admirer, Jeff Miller, giving him more instructions for his computer search.

When she hung up the phone, Jefferson said, "That was Carvelli. He spoke to Traynor's lawyer. As far as the lawyer knew, Segal had no connection to Howie Traynor. I've been thinking," Jefferson continued, "maybe Kane is partially correct."

"I'm not following," Marcie said.

"Remember, she said maybe we're looking at this all wrong. Maybe it's none of these guys."

"Yeah, okay."

"But, we're pretty certain that's too much of a coincidence. Maybe it is one of the guys on our list, but he has an accomplice."

The phone on the table rang and Marcie answered it. She said hello then listened for a moment.

"Are you sure? You did. Okay and thanks, Jeff," she said. Marcie hung up the phone and without a word, stood up and went to the whiteboard. She picked up a marker, drew a red circle around a name and next to it wrote the name "Segal".

"What?" Jefferson asked.

"His lawyer," Marcie replied. "Jeff Miller caught it right away and double checked it to be sure."

Jefferson got up from the table, slipped into his sport coat, looked at his watch and said, "It's almost suppertime. Maybe he'll be home."

"Should we call first?" Marcie asked as she grabbed her things to join him.

"No, let's try to surprise him. I think it's time you and I had a chat with Mr. Aaron Forsberg."

Having parked the department issued sedan in front of the house, the two of them walked up the sidewalk to the front door. Jefferson rang the bell and a moment later they heard someone moving inside the house. An older man with a friendly face and smile opened the door. The two detectives showed the man their badges and ID's and Jefferson asked if Aaron was home.

"No, I'm sorry, he's out," the affable elderly man said speaking through the screen door.

"Are you his uncle, John Forsberg?" Jefferson asked.

"Yes, I am."

"Do you know when he might be back?" Marcie asked.

"No, I don't. He comes and goes. He doesn't keep regular hours."

"I noticed you didn't ask us what this is about or why we're here," Marcie said.

Uncle John hesitated for a moment, sighed then said, "Why don't you come in and we'll talk?"

The three of them took chairs in the living room and John Forsberg said, "You're here about these killings that are in the papers. I recognize you," he continued looking at Jefferson, "from TV."

"You seem like you have something you want to tell us," Marcie quietly said.

The older man said, "I believe Aaron was innocent of killing his wife. I'm about the only one that stuck with him. But, prison changed him. He was never a real touchy-feely kind of guy. Prison hardened him and made him real angry and bitter."

"Prison does that to a lot of people," Jefferson interjected.

"Yeah, I'm sure it does," Forsberg agreed. "On the nights of these killings, starting with that judge up North, I've been keeping track and he's been out every night. I don't know where he is or what he's doing. If I ask him he gets annoyed and acts like it's none of my business. I'm worried about him." Forsberg was seated in a chair that matched the sofa the detectives sat on. While he told them about his nephew being out on the nights of the killings, he was kneading his hands with his head down looking at the floor. He didn't notice the quick glance Marcie and Jefferson exchanged.

Forsberg looked up and quickly added, "But he's been out a lot of nights when nothing happened, either. So…"

"You're right," Jefferson said. "Just because he's out sometimes when there's been a killing, doesn't mean he did them." Jefferson pulled two cards from his cardholder and handed them to Forsberg. "Here are a couple of my cards. Give one to Aaron and tell him we need to talk to him. You keep one and if you think of anything else, give me a call."

Marcie handed him two of her cards as well and all three of them stood. As they were leaving, Jefferson said, "Nice neighborhood. I noticed there's a house for sale across the street. I'm thinking of moving. Are the owner's home?"

"No, they've already moved. His job took them to Texas. You could call the realtor. It might be nice to have a cop in the neighborhood."

"I'll do that," Jefferson replied.

They shook hands and Forsberg showed them out. On the walk back to their car Jefferson told Marcie to write down the name and phone number of the realtor on the sign.

"I thought the place was empty," Jefferson said. "No curtains in the windows. Good place for a surveillance team."

"I didn't notice that," Marcie said, a bit embarrassed, as they reached the car.

"Don't worry," Jefferson said. "You will. It comes with experience."

Jefferson arrived at the office the next day shortly after 7:00 a.m. He went straight to the coffee pot then headed toward the conference room they were using as an office. He was surprised to see the lights in the room were already on. When he opened the door, Marcie and Jeff Miller were there to greet him.

"Be careful," he growled at them. "I hate people who are already cheerful at this time of the day. It's not natural."

"Okay," Marcie said. "I'll be a sure to be a crab ass for the next hour. Anyway, Jeff has some news."

"Marcie called me before I left last night, and we talked about expanding our search. I stayed late and did a 'known associates' check on the guys on our list who have a connection to the last three victims. I came up with another seven names. Guys who might fit the burglary profile and are not dead. None have a connection with Aaron Forsberg..."

"That would figure," Jefferson said. "He did his time out of state and had no criminal past."

"Right," Miller agreed. "But, three of these guys have prison connections with both Eugene Parlow and Howie Traynor."

Miller handed several sheets of paper across the table to Jefferson. "Here's a list of the names with bios, criminal histories and their connection to our guys," Miller said.

"Have you been through this?" Jefferson asked Marcie.

"Yeah. I think we need some help. We can probably eliminate some of these guys, but we'll need more people to check them out."

"Agreed," Jefferson said while scanning through the pages. "Good work, Jeff. If you can think of anything else, go ahead and check it."

An hour later, Jefferson began a meeting with four more detectives plus Selena Kane. There were two teams of detectives, one with two men and one comprising a man and a woman.

Jefferson had divided the list of seven new names giving three to one team and four to the other. He explained the situation to them and what was expected of them.

"You've been pulled from your current cases to work exclusively on this," Selena Kane told them. "This is maximum priority."

"We want to know everything we can about them. Especially prison records, who they did time with and what they've been up to since they get out," Jefferson added.

"Shove a microscope up their asses and get anything and everything you can," Kane said.

"You think one of these guys is involved with the Crown of Thornes killer?" a male detective named Mark Cullen asked.

"Crown of what?" Jefferson asked. "Where did you get that?"

"It's in this morning's paper," Kane said. "Apparently they needed some cutesy name to sell papers."

There was a sharp knock on the door and a man walked in, nodded at Kane and Jefferson and took a seat.

"All of you know Lieutenant Schiller from surveillance," Jefferson said. Everyone silently nodded in assent.

"We've got one of these guys, Howie Traynor under surveillance now," Jefferson continued pointing at the whiteboard. "We'll put two more, Parlow and Forsberg, under as well. We think those are our most likely suspects."

"Why?" the female detective asked.

"They have direct ties to the victims, at least most of them and these killings started shortly after they got out of prison," Jefferson said.

"And they all have reason to be pissed at these people for their convictions," Kane added. "That's it for now. You have assignments. You know what to do. We'll meet again at nine o'clock tomorrow morning and I want some results."

After the four detectives left, the meeting continued with Lt. Schiller saying, "I'll need more people for this if we want them all covered twenty-four seven."

"The chief and mayor say we get whatever we want," Kane said. "If you need more guys, we can pull all you need from patrol into civilian clothes."

For the next hour the four of them went over the list of potential cops to use. They also set up a surveillance plan for Kane to take to the chief and mayor. Satisfied they were doing all they could for now, Kane ended the meeting to go upstairs to what she called a come to Jesus meeting.

TWENTY-SIX

Three murders in three consecutive days had ignited a firestorm in the media. The national media, through local affiliates and wire services, also picked it up. The cable news networks, with twenty-four hours per day of air time to fill were having a glorious time with it. Never shy about fanning the flames for ratings and to sell more papers the reporting was barely a notch below hysterical. To make things even worse, the connection that all of the victims except one were judges or lawyers was leaked from the MPD. Within hours of this fact being reported, almost every judge, prosecutor and criminal defense lawyer in the Cities were calling the police insisting on round the clock protection.

The recipient of the leak, Gabriella Shriqui, was on her way to a meeting with Channel 8 management. She received a call from the station's news director, Hunter Oswald, inviting her to the meeting. Hunter had not elaborated on what it was about, and Gabriella's curiosity was definitely piqued. A meeting with upper management was not a daily occurrence.

Gabriella knocked lightly on the office door of the station's general manager, Madison Eyler. She hesitated for one second then turned the door handle and went in at the same time she heard Eyler's response.

"Hi, Gabriella," Eyler greeted her. "Come in and have a seat."

"What's up?" Gabriella asked looking back and forth between Oswood and Eyler.

"We want you to take charge and coordinate the coverage of this Crown of Thornes killer story," Oswood said.

"Right now, we have people running around like chickens all trying to get in on it," Eyler added. "We need one person in charge and to be the main on-air personality."

"You seem to have a knack for getting information," Oswood said. "For getting men..."

"And women," Eyler interjected.

"...to talk to you," Oswood finished.

"I have a good teacher," Gabriella said referring to her new friend, Madeline Rivers. "She could get the Sphinx to speak. Okay, I'd be happy to do it. But you'll put the word out to all of the staff that everyone backs off and I decide who does what?"

"Absolutely. That's exactly what we have in mind," Eyler said.

"And you're likely looking at network air time also," added Oswood. "You will report only to me. You and I will have final say about what goes on the air. Okay?"

"Great," a delighted Gabriella said.

Her bosses gave each other an odd look and Gabriella sensed there was something more.

"What?" she asked.

"We want to tell you something that I know is a little sensitive," Eyler said. "We're bringing back Melinda Pace."

"I thought she was fired," Gabriella quickly said.

"She was," Oswood replied. "But…"

"Never say never," Eyler interjected. "We've heard she is negotiating with a couple of competitors…"

"So, let her turn them into a tabloid news sleaze factory," an obviously angry Gabriella said.

"Gabriella," Eyler firmly said, "we're not here to ask your permission. You're a terrific asset to this station and the job we're giving you to handle this serial killer was given to you because of merit, not to placate you. The truth is, with Melinda gone, ratings are down and so are revenues."

"She claims to have cleaned up her act," Oswood said. "She's quit drinking and is contrite about what happened. She's got a couple of job offers but is practically begging to come back to us."

"Gabriella," Eyler continued much more softly, "no decision has been made. We just wanted to have you hear this from us first. We know your history with her from the Riley case and respect your feelings. Frankly, I share them. But, Hunter and I also share some responsibility for her behavior. We should've done more to reign her in."

"No argument there," Gabriella said. "Whatever you decide, I'll live with it. Personally, I hope that sick bitch rots in hell."

When Gabriella arrived back at her cubicle she checked her phone and found five messages. She had no interest in four of them. They were from a guy she stopped seeing when she found out he was married, and he didn't want to let it go. As she deleted the calls she thought about using Maddy Rivers to get him off of her back and out of her life. Maddy could teach him a lesson, Gabriella thought which brought a smile to her face.

The fifth one was the police source from whom she had received the information about lawyers and judges as victims. Gabriella sat down and called him back.

"Hey, Gabriella," the plain clothes officer said. "Thanks for keeping my name out of the story."

"I told you I would," Gabriella replied to the man who was clearly smitten by her. "Anything new come up?"

"Well, yeah," Josh Feherty said. "I was wondering if we could get together later for a drink or dinner and I could tell you then."

There it is, Gabriella thought, the date question. "Geez, Josh. I can't, sorry. I'm working tonight. I work Friday evenings as a backup for the anchors and if we get any breaking news… sorry. I could really use what you have…."

"I'm not sure you should use this," a disappointed Josh said. "I got a line on one of the suspects but it's an ongoing investigation."

"You're right. I won't use it," Gabriella said while thinking, unless I can get confirmation of it from another source.

Josh hesitated then, wanting to stay in good with Gabriella said, "His name is Howard Traynor. He's one of the guys who got released from prison because his DNA test was doctored by a lab tech."

"I remember that," Gabriella said. "Interesting. Look Josh, someone just came in and I have to go. Stay in touch if you come up with anything else. I really appreciate your help."

Gabriella ended the call then took a minute to think about Josh Feherty. He was a fairly good looking and a nice, solid guy. The problem was he wasn't the brightest bulb, had risen about as far as he would as a cop and Gabriella just didn't feel it.

Putting him out of mind she pulled her chair up to her desk and plugged Howie Traynor's name into Google. For the next twenty minutes she read over everything listed about him. When she got halfway through the trial for the murder of Lucille Benson, she came across a name she wasn't expecting.

"Holy shit," she quietly said. "Marc Kadella was his lawyer."

Gabriella finished her research of Traynor and sat back in her chair. Then she looked at the clock and speed-dialed a number on her phone.

"Hey, Gabriella," she heard her new best friend, Maddy Rivers say. "What's up?"

"What are you doing for lunch? Can we meet?"

"Sure, what's wrong?"

"I'll tell you when I see you. I don't want to talk about it here. Same place?"

"See you in a half hour?" Maddy asked.

"That'll work," Gabriella replied.

Maddy strolled through the door of the faux French bistro in downtown Minneapolis and saw Gabriella wave to her from a booth by the windows. The two women greeted each other as Maddy sat down in the booth across from her friend.

"So, what's up?" Maddy asked.

Before Gabriella could answer, the server approached the table with the drinks Gabriella had ordered for them. The young man took a lot more time hanging around the two women than was called for looking back and forth at both of them.

"Cute kid," Maddy said as he wandered off.

With a sad look on her face Gabriella watched him walk away then turned to Maddy and said, "Are they getting younger or are we…"

"Getting older," Maddy finished for her.

"Thanks, I can hear my clock ticking which means I'll probably get a call from my Mother tonight. The reason I called," Gabriella continued, "is I got a tip from a cop about that Howie Traynor, remember him?"

"Sure," Maddy answered.

"He's a prime suspect in the Crown of Thornes case. Did you know Marc was his lawyer? Someone should warn him."

"Marc knows," Maddy said. "Tony Carvelli called him to tell him about Howie Traynor. When Tony told Vivian Donahue what was going on, she offered to pay for security for Marc. You can't use that as part of a story."

"I know. I'm keeping it to myself for now. If my boss finds out I'm sitting on a piece of information like that he'll have my ass. I'll tell him I couldn't independently verify it, so I can't ethically use it."

TWENTY-SEVEN

The office intercom buzzed on Marc's desk phone. His door was closed so he could work at his desk while eating a sandwich for lunch. He answered the phone and Carolyn told him Maddy was calling.

"Hello, gorgeous," Marc said when Carolyn put the call through.

"This is a professional call so, behave accordingly and knock off the flirting," Maddy good-naturedly chided him.

Madeline's phone was on speaker and Gabriella leaned toward it and said loud enough for the phone to pick-up, "You can flirt with me all you want."

"Is that Gabriella?" Marc asked.

"Hi, Marc," Gabriella said.

"She says her clock's ticking, her mother will call any day and she's getting desperate," Madeline said while Gabriella stared at her with a horrified look on her face.

"Wow, that's very flattering, especially the desperation part," Marc said with a touch of sarcasm. "But tell her I'm a little busy right now. Maybe some other time." Gabriella heard this and almost choked trying not to laugh. "What are you two up to?"

"We're having lunch. Gabriella got a tip about your old pal, you know, the one who just got out," Maddy said not wanting to use Traynor's name.

Gabriella took the phone from Maddy and quietly said, "I just wanted to make sure you knew about him. Maddy says Tony already told you. Be careful."

"That's kind of you Gabriella but Maddy's right and I am being careful. I don't believe it though. My understanding is he's been under surveillance for a while. And don't use that unless you want to get sued."

"I know, and I won't," Gabriella said.

"Was that you that got the leak about the victims being judges and lawyers?" Marc asked. "I heard it was your station that first reported it."

"I can neither confirm nor deny," Gabriella coyly answered.

"So that's a yes and I figured it was you. Listen you two, I need to get ready for a hearing this afternoon. Let's get together next week. I'll buy you lunch."

"Deal," Gabriella said.

"But Madeline, you only get a salad."

"What? Why?" Maddy said into the phone.

"Well, um, because the last time I saw you I noticed you were putting on a few pounds, especially on the hips."

Gabriella tried to stifle a laugh as Madeline snarled, "Give me that phone!"

Gabriella held it in the palm of her hand and pulled it away as Maddy reached for it. They could hear Marc laughing as Maddy tried vainly to reach across the table to retrieve the phone.

"I love saying things like that to her," Marc said. "Even though it's not the least bit true it keeps her ego in line. Plus, Gabriella," he continued, "you watch, she won't eat anything but carrots for the next month. I'll call you next week. Bye."

Before Marc entered the fourteenth-floor courtroom he took a few seconds to look through the small window in the door. It was ten minutes before 9:00 o'clock, the time his hearing was scheduled to begin. Marc could see eight or ten people inside including his uncle sitting in a chair behind the rail. Marc wasn't looking forward to this knowing the judge would want to see the lawyers right away.

He saw Earl Bicknell, the lawyer for the city, already at his table. The judge's clerk was next to the empty bench and several cops were seated in the gallery behind Bicknell.

Marc opened the door and all eyes turned to look at him. He greeted Uncle Larry and the two of them went through the gate to the defense table.

Before Marc sat down as the clerk said, "The judge wants to see both lawyers in chambers right away."

The two men shook hands as they both walked across the well toward the rear doorway.

"Are you really going through with this?" Bicknell whispered to him.

"I don't know," Marc said shaking his head as the two of them went through the door. "It's not up to me."

They greeted the judge, Lucinda Gilbert, who promptly asked the prosecutor, "What are you offering?"

"Two hundred dollar fine," your Honor.

"And?" she said looking at Marc.

"My guy won't plead," Marc said.

"Why not?"

"Because it's his right not to."

"You're right," the judge said. "I'm sorry, I shouldn't have asked."

Never having appeared in front of this judge before, a new appointment to the bench, Marc was a little surprised at the apology.

"How about an *Alford* plea? He admits there's sufficient evidence to convict while maintaining his innocence?" Bicknell asked.

"I've listened to the recording, counselor. I have a little trouble with him maintaining his innocence. But if he wants to go that route, that's his right but...," Gilbert started to say.

"So, your Honor," Marc said sitting up and leaning forward to stare directly at the judge, "you've already decided he's guilty?"

"I didn't mean that," a perplexed Gilbert said.

Marc continued to stare at her and she avoided eye contact with him. Bicknell sat quietly, mildly amused at the display he was witnessing.

Without blinking or taking his eyes off the judge, Marc said, "I'll put it to my client and let him decide."

When they reached the hallway behind the courtroom Bicknell asked, "You going to file on her?"

"I don't know," a still angry Marc answered. When the two men reached the door to the courtroom a calmer Marc added. "She's new. She needs to learn to be a little more careful about what she says."

Marc took the chair at the defense table next to his uncle and quietly explained to him what had been offered. An *Alfor*d plea is one in which the defendant maintains his innocence but admits there is sufficient evidence to support a conviction. It is usually offered as a way to obtain a reasonable plea bargain with a recalcitrant defendant. It is also normally coupled with a threat of more dire consequences if the defendant rejects it.

"No," was Larry's one-word reply. "Marc, my boy, this is the most interesting thing I've done since Ellen passed. What can they do, put me in prison?"

"She could give you some jail time."

"I'll worry about that when it happens. When does the trial start?"

"This isn't a trial, Larry," Marc said. "I told you, this is what's called a *Rasmussen* hearing or, a suppression hearing. We'll get a look at the evidence and witnesses. Then we'll argue about whether or not the evidence the cops have should be allowed in court. It's to let the judge see if the cops entrapped you into doing this."

"They did," Larry said.

Patiently Marc replied, "To legally entrap someone the cops have to get someone to commit a crime he otherwise would not have done. In other words, but for the cop's behavior this would not have happened."

"It wouldn't have," Larry replied.

"We'll see," Marc said.

The hearing itself lasted about an hour and a half. There were five witnesses called by the prosecution. They were the four MPD cops who had operated the sting including the woman who had posed as the prostitute. This would also give Marc an opportunity to see the witnesses on the stand and gauge the strength of the prosecution's case.

The first witness called was the female decoy. She had been sitting with the other three cops and the tech and Marc had not noticed her before this.

As she was being sworn in Marc whispered to his uncle, "You only offered her fifty bucks? I would have arrested you, too. She's gorgeous for God's sake."

Hers was the longest testimony and it was through her that the audio recording of the transaction was presented to the court. She was emphatic that Larry had approached her, and she did nothing to entice him. The audio was clear that Larry had offered fifty dollars for oral sex. It was then that she identified herself as Officer Jennifer Hall and arrested him.

One at a time the three male cops testified that the defendant was read his rights and taken to a local precinct for processing. Larry used a credit card to post bail and was released; every step done strictly by the book and in conformance with police procedure. Not wanting to tip his hand and show the prosecution his case, even though he didn't have one, Marc had not asked a single question.

At the conclusion of the testimony Marc went through the formality of requesting that the evidence and testimony be excluded. This was quickly denied.

"Your Honor," Marc said. "I want the prosecution to produce a picture, an exact duplication of how Officer Hall was dressed and what she looked like on the day this event occurred."

"That's reasonable. So ordered. You will provide the photo to Mr. Kadella. When can you get it?"

"A moment, your Honor," Bicknell replied. He turned to the officers who were still in the court and waved one forward. He was the detective who was in charge of the sting. Bicknell whispered to him then turned to the judge and said, "Tomorrow, your Honor. I'll messenger it to him tomorrow."

"Good enough," Gilbert said.

"Since it is obviously available now, I'm wondering why I haven't been given it before this?" Marc asked.

"He didn't ask, your Honor."

"I shouldn't have to…"

"All right. Enough you two. You'll get the photo. Anything else?" she asked Marc. He gave her a negative reply and she waved the lawyers up to the bench.

"What about a trial date? How's next week look?" she asked.

"I'm booked," Bicknell replied.

"The week after? Find a day Mr. Bicknell. Let's get this over with."

"My client wants a jury, your Honor."

"Okay, that's his right," Gilbert answered. She looked at the small calendar taped to the bench and said, "How about Wednesday, October 6? Even with a jury we won't need more than a day."

"I'm okay with that," Marc said.

"Me, too," Bicknell agreed.

"Okay, Wednesday, October sixth at 9:00 a.m. All discovery and witness lists to be done no later than Thursday, October one. I'll put out an order today."

On their way out of the courtroom after waiting for everyone else to leave, Marc spoke with the man seated in the back by himself. When he finished, Marc escorted his client out of the front of the building to the light rail platform. He waited for the train with his uncle then found his car and drove back to the office.

TWENTY-EIGHT

Cara Meyers hurried quickly down the back steps of the Church of Christ church on Forty Eighth and Dupont in South Minneapolis. She nodded and pleasantly said good night to several of the people in her group before heading to the parking lot. Her Addicts Anonymous meeting had lasted longer than normal, and she wanted to get home, shower and go to bed.

"Hell of a way to spend a Sunday night," she muttered.

Cara pushed the button on her key fob and unlocked her two-year-old Accord. She had parked under a light and took a moment to cautiously look around. There were several people from her group getting into their cars and she did not see anything unusual in the lot.

Cara was a thirty-eight-year-old senior associate in an insurance defense firm in downtown Minneapolis. The firm, Howard, Caine and Nugent, took up two floors of the U.S. Bank Plaza, a forty-story glass and chrome building in downtown Minneapolis. Cara had just completed her sixth year with the firm. She had been rejected for partnership three times. After the most recent rejection about a month ago, she had been flat-out told by the managing partner that a partnership would not happen. Cara was under no threat of being fired and could stay as long as she met her billable hours requirement, an average of fifty per week.

On her drive home, Cara again pondered her situation. The money was good, with bonuses and 401k benefits over two hundred per year. The simple truth was she hated the place. Hated the firm; hated what she did; with few exceptions she could barely tolerate most of the lawyers and she hated herself for selling her soul for money. Cara was also quite trapped.

At one time she had been a very good criminal defense lawyer. Cara had originally joined up with a local heavyweight criminal defense lawyer and was soon well on her way to becoming one herself. Even though she made less than half of what she made now she actually had a life and was happy.

Six years ago, Howard, Caine and Nugent had offered a lot more money and a phony promise of partnership. A good friend who knew the firm warned her, but she didn't listen. And now she was driving away from an Addicts Anonymous meeting because she had become addicted to speed and meth. The drugs were mostly to help her keep up and bill enough hours to keep her job.

Cara pulled the Accord into the underground lot of her condo building. She lived six blocks from work which allowed her to walk to work; the only exercise she had time for.

While walking toward the elevator she moved her head around in a circle as if taking the kinks out of her neck. Cara walked past a concrete support pole and the next thing she knew she was sitting on the floor of the garage, her back against that same pole, in a lot of pain and unable to move or speak.

Owen Jefferson was leaning against the trunk of a car casually watching the M.E. examine the body. The car's owner was steaming mad because it was parked inside the police tape surrounding the crime scene. He was late for work and needed his car. Ten minutes ago, he had given up and called a cab cursing at the cops for making him spend the money. On top of that it was raining, and his umbrella was in his car but because he had raised such a fuss none of the cops would get it for him.

Marcie Sterling was standing a few feet behind the M.E. looking over his shoulder. After a few minutes she walked across the parking ramp aisle to join Jefferson.

"What do you think?" she asked.

"He didn't have time to do the job completely. Looks like her throat was slit the same way and she has the barbed wire crown. Her fingers are still intact, and he had no way to finish posing her."

"Or a copy cat," Marcie said.

"Could be but I don't think so. Doesn't feel like it."

Marcie was holding the victim's purse. Both she and Jefferson wore gloves, and she held up the woman's driver's license. "Cara Meyers. Five foot seven, one thirty-five, brown and brown, thirty-eight years old. Address is here, in this building," Marcie cryptically read from the license.

Marcie set the purse on the back of the car Jefferson leaned on and started going through the bill fold. Jefferson turned back to watch the M.E.

A minute later Marcie held up a laminated card and said, "Check this out. Ms. Meyers is, was, a lawyer."

She handed it to Jefferson, who read it and said, "That probably takes care of the copycat theory."

The M.E., Clyde Marston, stood holding up a clear plastic bag for the two detectives to see.

"Tell me you have something!" Jefferson said as he straightened to greet Marston.

"Maybe," Marston said as he handed the little bag to the tall detective. "It's a hair and I don't think it's hers. Lighter in color and shorter."

"Can we get DNA off of it?" Marcie asked.

"Probably," Marston shrugged. "For sure if the follicle is still attached."

"I'm taking possession of this. Note that in your report for chain-of-custody. I'll run this over to St. Paul to the state crime lab myself. Anything else?" Jefferson said.

"Doesn't look like it," Marston replied. "I'll check more thoroughly when I get her downtown."

Despite the steady rain, with lights and sirens, Jefferson and Marcie made it to the East Side of St. Paul in under twenty minutes. While Jefferson drove, Marcie called Selena Kane and told her what they had. Kane called the deputy chief who called the chief and he called the mayor. By coincidence, Mayor Gillette was on the phone with Governor Dahlstrom when the chief called. One of the mayor's assistants interrupted the call with the news.

Jefferson pulled up to the BCA building on Maryland Avenue and, the wheels having been greased by a phone call from the governor, a crowd of lab people were already waiting for them. Leading the parade of BCA personnel through the rain was the BCA director herself, Anne Scanlon.

Jefferson illegally parked his car in a fire lane and the two detectives got out. Jefferson looked at Scanlon, a former MPD deputy chief and said, "Anne, what's going on?"

"I got a call from Governor Dahlstrom and he made it abundantly clear we're to give this a priority," she replied.

Marcie handed the precious piece of evidence to a man who introduced himself as the lead lab tech.

"We'll keep an accurate chain-of custody record," the director said.

"Call us when you know something," Jefferson said holding his trench coat at the collar against the rain.

Jeff Miller hurried to the homicide detectives' squad room. On their way back from St. Paul, Marcie had called him and told him to run a check on the latest victim. He had news for them and was taking this opportunity to deliver it personality. And, see Marcie.

"You could've called," Jefferson said when Jeff came through the conference room door.

"I, ah, yes, I suppose," Jeff stammered.

"Did you find something, Jeff?" Marcie politely asked while giving Jefferson a stern look.

Jeff looked at her, smiled and said, "Yeah, I did." He walked over to the whiteboard, picked up a marker and circled a name.

"Parlow! Are you sure she's connected to Eugene Parlow?" Jefferson asked with a bewildered look on his face.

"Cara Meyers was Parlow's lawyer when the faulty DNA was used to convict him," Jeff proudly told them.

"Are you sure she isn't connected to any other names on our list?" Marcie asked.

"I ran all of the suspects on the board and Parlow was the only one that came up," Miller answered. "And, Judge Peterson was his trial judge; Judge Smith, the victim up North, decided his appeal and Rhea Watson was the prosecutor."

"This is too much of a coincidence. What are the odds of this happening?" Marcie asked. "We need to get a hold of Lieutenant Schiller and double check their surveillance," Marcie continued. "According to the surveillance reports, Parlow is the one they're having the most trouble keeping track of."

Jeff took a chair next to Marcie and said, "The odds of this happening are probably better than you think. Rhea Watson, during that time, was the chief criminal prosecutor for the county. She had over a hundred cases."

"I remember it," Jefferson said. "Word was she was very ambitions and had her eye on the top job. Plus, the judge, Peterson, had a bit of a reputation for believing in DNA evidence. Most of the prosecutors with DNA cases tried to get him."

"Okay," Marcie said. "What about the appellate judge, Smith?" she continued pointing at his name on the whiteboard.

"That one could simply be a coincidence," Jefferson said. "Every homicide case gets appealed and he maybe just got unlucky. I need to go see someone, a civilian ex-cop. Marcie, I want you to go to the M.E.'s office and check on the autopsy. Then get a hold of the detectives who are running checks on the other suspects."

Jefferson wearily sat back in his chair and studied the whiteboard for a minute or so.

"I don't know where the hell we are," he said. "I still think its Traynor or, more likely Forsberg but…"

"We've had them under surveillance," Marcie said.

"Yeah," Jefferson said turning to look at Marcie. "And it's a helluva an alibi, isn't it?"

Marcie and Jeff Miller left, and Jefferson made a phone call. Tony Carvelli agreed to meet him, and the two men settled on a place to do so. Twenty minutes later, Jefferson entered a chain Italian restaurant, removed his trench coat to shake the rain off and took an empty booth in the bar.

A few minutes later Carvelli arrived and the two men shook hands. They both ordered coffee from the server then Jefferson said, "I need a fresh pair of eyes and an uncluttered mind."

The server brought two cups into which he poured their coffee. When the young woman left Jefferson went over everything they had about the killings while Carvelli quietly listened. When he finished, Jefferson said, "What do you think?"

"What about the hair that was found this morning?" Tony asked.

"You know something, the more I think about it, the more I wonder if it wasn't planted. Why, all of a sudden, does he get that careless and we find just one hair?"

"Maybe you're right. Or, maybe he had to hurry. He's in a parking garage with lights and people who could show up any time. Occam's razor," Tony said. "The simplest solution, the simplest answer is probably the correct one."

"Is that what Occam's razor is?"

"That's the simplified version," Tony said. Carvelli leaned forward almost halfway across the table. Jefferson did the same, so the two men's heads were inches apart. "In my gut, I think it's Traynor. I'm just not buying his 'I found Jesus' act."

"Yeah, but…"

"I know," Tony interrupted. "We've watched him like a hawk. I just remember what a goddamn psycho he was; is. I'm not buying that he could switch that off. Listen, let me think about it and if I come up with anything, I'll let you know."

"Thanks, Tony. I needed to talk to someone about this," Jefferson said. "It's making me a little crazy."

"Anytime."

TWENTY-NINE

When Jefferson got back downtown to the department, Marcie was back from the M.E.'s office. Jefferson hung up his coat and wearily sat down. He looked at Marcie and said, "I'm open to suggestions, Marcie, if you have any."

"I've been thinking," she said. "What if it's one guy and he did one or two victims just to confuse us."

"He's done a good job of that. How do you know it isn't two of them working together?"

"I guess I really don't," she agreed. "And we should keep an open mind to the possibility but, I just don't think so. One guy makes more sense. Do a couple of victims he has no connection with to create reasonable doubt. I also think it's one of the three DNA guys," she continued referring to Forsberg, Traynor and Parlow.

Jefferson remained silent for another minute then said, "Right now, it's as good a theory as any. In fact, I was thinking the same thing before I got back. I think you may be right."

The compliment from the veteran detective, a man Marcie greatly admired, gave her ego a nice boost. While she inwardly smiled, Jefferson's phone went off.

"Jefferson," he said answering it. "Okay, put him through," he told the MPD switchboard.

"Mr. Forsberg, this is Owen Jefferson, what can I do for you?"

Jefferson listened in silence to the man on the other end of the call. After a couple of minutes, while Marcie curiously looked at him Jefferson covered the phone and mouthed the word Forsberg to her. He listened some more then said, "Fine and thanks for calling." Jefferson ended the call and explained it to his younger partner.

"That was Forsberg's uncle, John. Seems Aaron slipped out last night and beat our surveillance. He left around nine o'clock and took his uncle's car. Didn't tell the uncle, just said he was going out for a while and grabbed the keys to his uncle's car. Our guys didn't realize it was him driving the uncle's car and let him go."

When Jefferson finished telling Marcie about the phone call there was a sharp rap on the door and Selena Kane walked in.

"We need to go upstairs to the mayor's office. There's a political clusterfuck taking place and the higher ups want some answers from you two," Kane said.

"Tell them we don't have any," Jefferson wearily said.

"That's not true," Marcie interjected seeing the pursed and narrowed lips on Kane's face. "We've narrowed the list down and we have a DNA test coming back probably by tomorrow."

"Okay," Kane said, the look on her face softening a bit, "that's something. Let's go Owen. We have people we have to answer to."

"Yeah, yeah, okay," Jefferson agreed.

The three of them were swiftly ushered into the mayor's office as soon as they arrived. Waiting for them were Mayor Susan Gillette and the Chief of Police, Arne Sorenstad. Also, in attendance were the County Attorney Craig Slocum and the chief prosecutor, Steven Gondeck. Three extra chairs had been brought in for the lieutenant and two detectives.

"I had an interesting call from the governor earlier today while you two were on your way to St. Paul," the mayor began. "The word is already out that another lawyer was murdered. Please tell us you have some answers."

Before Kane or Jefferson had a chance to speak, Marcie Sterling spoke up. "Of the six victims, the first three all have a connection to the same three men," she said. "Judge Smith handled the appeal of each of them. Judge Peterson was the trial judge and Rhea Watson was the prosecutor for Aaron Forsberg, Howard Traynor and Eugene Parlow. These are three of the four men recently released from prison because of doctored DNA test results."

"And they're all suing the city, county and state over it," Slocum reminded everyone.

"The next three," Marcie continued, "each have a connection to one of these three suspects but not the other two. We believe the hair found on this morning's victim will give us some DNA evidence."

With Marcie's clear and succinct update, Selena Kane relaxed a bit.

"Are you sure they are all the victims of the same man?" Chief Sorenstad asked looking directly at Marcie.

"We've kicked around the idea of more than one person being involved but it doesn't seem likely. Parlow and Traynor served time in Stillwater together and probably knew each other but, Forsberg was in Michigan City, Indiana. He has no link to the other two."

"Why do you think it's not Traynor and Parlow together?" Steven Gondeck asked.

"Because Howie Traynor has been under surveillance the entire time, even before the killings started. It's possible he has been directing Parlow but it doesn't seem likely. They travel in very different circles," Marcie replied.

Marcie looked at Jefferson who nodded and said, "Tell them."

"Aaron Forsberg slipped our surveillance last night. Plus, we know he was out and unaccounted for at the time of the first three," Marcie said.

"We'll lock him down for sure tonight and see what comes back from the BCA on the hair sample," Jefferson added.

"Pick him up," the chief angrily said.

"We have no grounds at all for that," Jefferson said. "No probable cause except he doesn't have an alibi. We'll know more when we get the DNA test back."

The room went silent for a moment then Mayor Gillette quietly said, "Owen, if he gets by you and there's another murder, it will be all three of your asses. I hope you know that."

"I understand," Jefferson answered her. He looked at the chief and said, "We will get him."

"Goddamnit, make it soon," the mayor said.

Vivian Donahue ended the call from Susan Gillette and leaned back in her father's old, leather chair. She was sitting at his walnut desk in the mansion's private study. Vivian loved this room above all others. The big chair, the desk, the solid, dark walnut paneling, the overstuffed couch that matched the desk chair, all reminded her of her father. Whenever she spoke of him she still referred to him as Daddy. She was and always would be Daddy's girl and she was quite comfortable with it. Best of all, he would be proud of her. Her strength, intelligence and commanding presence were all handed down from him with a large dose of her mother tossed in for good measure.

While she silently stared at the portrait of her father and mother hanging on the wall, she contemplated the phone call she received from Mayor Gillette. The mayor had given her a detailed report on the meeting that took place in her office. Gillette, having been made aware Vivian had a personal interest in the case, had called her even before she called Governor Dahlstrom to tell him about the meeting. Vivian listened politely and thanked her for the call. She thought it over then made a decision.

"Hello, Anthony," she said into her private iphone. "Could you find some time today to see me? I need to talk to you about something."

"Crown of Thornes?" Carvelli asked.

"I'm not sure I approve of that particular sobriquet. It sounds a little blasphemous," she said.

"I think it's meant to be," Tony answered. "But to answer your question, yes in about an hour or so."

"Good, you can come for dinner. And try to bring our beautiful friend as well. I think we may need her."

"I'll give her a call and see you around six."

At 5:45, Carvelli drove his Camaro up the long driveway toward the mansion. Trailing right behind him in her car was Maddy Rivers. They parked with Vivian's candy apple red Bentley sandwiched between them. As the two of them walked toward the door in the light rain, Maddy said, referring to the Bentley, "I want one of those."

"I'll mention it to Vivian. As much as she likes you, she'll probably have one delivered with a bow on it for your birthday," Tony said.

"Don't you dare!" Maddy said. Three seconds later as they reached the door, Maddy added, "You think she would?"

Tony looked at her, lightly shook his head and didn't answer. He rang the bell and stepped back from the door.

"I was just sorta, you know, wondering," Maddy sheepishly added.

"You were just sorta, you know, seeing yourself driving that car," Tony replied.

"You have to admit it's not a bad image," she added then turned back to look wistfully at the Bentley again.

The woman who answered the door and let them in led them to Vivian's private study. She opened the door for them and Vivian came around the desk to greet them.

"When would you like dinner to be ready, Mrs. Donahue?"

Vivian looked back and forth at her guests then courteously said, "A half an hour should be fine Gail, thank you."

The young woman left, and Tony asked, "You're not making dinner for us yourself? I was looking forward to it."

"Be thankful. I can do a lot of things, but cook is not one of them. The price of a spoiled upbringing," she said to Tony knowing he was poking fun at her. "And how are you my lovely girl? Give us a hug," she said to Maddy and the two of them embraced.

Vivian took a chair in front of the couch and Maddy and Tony sat down on it.

"Tony and I were admiring your Bentley and…" Maddy started to say.

"Worst car I've ever owned," Vivian stopped her. "They can't seem to get the timing right. The damn thing is in the shop every other week. I'll give them one more try then they get it back." This statement punched a huge hole in Maddy's fantasy and she dropped the subject.

"I received some information today I want to discuss with you," Vivian began. Ten minutes later, without telling them who her source was, she finished relaying what had taken place that afternoon in the mayor's office.

"They found a loose hair on this morning's victim?" Tony asked pretending he didn't know this.

"Yes, they believe they'll get a DNA match soon, maybe even today," Vivian replied.

"That should be enough to pick up whoever it matches," Tony said. "But, by itself, I'm not sure you've got a conviction."

"That's what I was wondering," Vivian added. "Is there anything we can do to help them along?"

Maddy and Tony talked it over for a minute then Tony said to Vivian, "Let's wait and see what comes back from the DNA test. There are some things we can do that I'm not going to tell you about if the cops need a hand."

"You mean things that might not be strictly legal?" Vivian asked.

"I didn't say that," Tony replied.

"Anthony, do you really think you need to protect me?"

"I just love the way she calls you Anthony," Maddy said. "Coming from her it fits you." Maddy looked at Vivian and added, "No, no we know you can take care of yourself. It's to protect us. The fewer people who know what we're up to, the better."

"Okay, dear," Vivian smiled. "Point taken." She looked at the clock on the wall then said, "I'm hungry let's eat."

THIRTY

The rain was back Tuesday morning coming down harder than it had the day before. The weather geeks were calling for one more day of it, off and on. The weather predicted for the upcoming weekend was supposed to be one of those glorious, early autumn Upper Midwest treasures.

Owen Jefferson pulled his department issued Crown Vic into a "Police Only" spot on Third Avenue alongside City Hall. He waited for a large delivery truck to go by which sprayed the car down with rainwater when it passed. Jefferson sat in the car's silent interior for a full minute staring through the window. The engine was still running, and the wipers swished back and forth. He could not remember another case like this, one so completely devoid of physical evidence with these many victims. So far only one misplaced strand of hair.

Jefferson turned off the wipers and the car's engine. He checked for traffic and as he exited the car, muttered to himself, "That goddamn strand of hair better tell us something." He hunched his shoulders, ducked his head against the rain and sprinted to the door.

Marcie Sterling was on the phone when Jefferson entered their conference room. "Hang on," she said into the phone, "he just walked in."

"Who?" Jefferson quietly asked as he shook the rain off his trench coat and hung it on the coat rack.

"Lieutenant Schiller," Marcie answered referring to the commander of the department's surveillance unit.

While taking his seat at the table opposite Marcie, Jefferson picked up his extension and said, "Don't give me any more bad news. I'm not in the mood."

"No, no," Schiller quickly answered. "No, I'm calling to let you know we got a bug on Forsberg's uncle's car. He cooperated with us."

"Yeah, he said he would," Jefferson said. "Anything going on last night?"

"No, all quiet and Owen, again, I couldn't be sorrier about Forsberg slipping past us."

"Forget it, Rod. Shit happens."

"Just between you and me, I got the feeling his uncle thinks he's doing it. Says the nephew is really angry. I'll email a complete report later this morning," Schiller told him.

"Thanks, Rod. I'll talk to you later."

"How much trouble is he in?" Marcie asked after Jefferson ended the call.

"Not as much as we are if we don't break this pretty soon," Jefferson glumly replied.

"Did we get a written report on those other seven guys who came up as possibles after Judge Segal was killed?" he asked her.

"Yeah," Marcie replied pulling a stapled document from a pile on the table. "Here," she said as she slid it across to him.

"Have you read it?" he asked while paging through it.

"Yes, and it's just what they told us. A couple of them are remotely possible because of past violent felonies. Pretty thin, I think. They've all been out for at least a couple of years and..."

"This started when our three assholes got out," Jefferson said completing the thought.

"You are in a rotten mood this morning," Marcie observed.

"Here's what we're going to do this morning," Jefferson said ignoring her remark. "We'll both read through everything we have again and try to find something."

Shortly after ten a.m., Jefferson's personal cell phone rang. He looked at the I.D. then quickly answered it. "Tell me something good," he said.

The woman calling was slightly taken aback by the abrupt greeting. She quickly recovered and said, "Detective Jefferson? This is Anne Scanlon at the BCA."

"I'm sorry, Anne," Jefferson apologized. "That was no way to answer your call. Did your guys come up with something?"

Scanlon quickly told him who's DNA the hair matched.

"Do you have a written result you can email me? We'll need it for the warrants," he said as he gave Marcie a thumbs up. He listened for a moment then said, "Great news, Anne. In fact, I think I want to have your baby."

Scanlon laughed then said, "I'll have it emailed in a couple minutes. You'll have it right away. And I have all the babies I need, thanks."

Jefferson ended the call, looked at Marcie and said, "Guess."

"Forsberg," she said.

"Howie Traynor," Jefferson answered. "Ninety-nine-point six percent match. It's his hair."

"How the hell did he get past us?"

"I don't know but we'll get a search warrant now and tear that apartment apart till we find it."

Using the department's phone, Jefferson placed a call to Steve Gondeck, the lawyer with the county attorney. He told the receptionist who he was, and the call was extremely urgent. Within ten seconds,

Gondeck was on the phone. Jefferson gave him the good news and Gondeck told him he would get both a search warrant and an arrest warrant.

When he finished talking to Gondeck, Jefferson looked at Marcie and said, "For the first time since this started, I actually feel the stress lifting."

"We'll get this fuckin' asshole and put him away for good," Marcie said.

Jefferson laughed then said, "Why Detective Sterling, your language."

"I've been around too many cops," she slyly replied.

Normally Steve Gondeck, because he was the lead felony litigator at the county attorney's office, would hand this off to an assistant to get the warrants. This time it was a little different and very personal. Rhea Watson was not only a colleague but a good friend. She had also been a mentor and her death felt like a kick in the chest. Plus, Gondeck had been a second chair for the prosecution of Aaron Forsberg. He had been more than a little worried he might be on the list. Gondeck also admitted feeling a wave of relief knowing Traynor was the guy and he had no connection to him.

Jefferson forwarded the email with the DNA results attached. This document would go with his affidavit in support of the warrants he would request. While typing up the affidavit and warrants for the judge to sign he called the court clerk. One of the court administrators told him which judge was assigned today for signing warrant requests. Gondeck heard the name and swallowed hard hoping she was not wearing her ACLU membership badge.

Fifteen minutes later Gondeck found himself waiting in the outer office of Judge Karen Fisher while the judge reviewed his warrant requests. The judge's clerk was at her desk working on her computer when the judge buzzed her.

"Yes, Judge," Gondeck heard the clerk say into her phone. "Certainly, I'll send him in."

When Gondeck heard this, he stood, and the clerk smiled while pointing to the door to Fisher's chambers. Gondeck lightly knocked on the closed door and went in with a feeling of dread.

"Mr. Gondeck, have a seat please." Gondeck sat down and the judge continued saying, "Howard Traynor. Isn't he one of the recently released inmates suing about a false DNA test used to send him to prison?"

"Um, yes, your Honor, I believe so," Gondeck replied.

"What else do you have tying him to this victim?"

"Well, um, nothing your Honor but the DNA result..."

"I'm not going to stick my neck out and the state, county and city's as well with one strand of hair. Sorry. Give me something more. His lawyer will take a large bite out of all of us if that's all you have," she said as she handed him the paperwork across her desk.

Gondeck stood up, took the documents from her and realizing it was futile to try to argue with her, said, "I'll see what I can do."

"Look Steve," the judge said. "I get it. This is a big deal and I want to get whoever is doing this too. But, one loose strand of hair for a suspect whose already been screwed by DNA testing isn't enough. And, if you try to shop this around to another judge, I'll remember it."

"Yes, your Honor," Gondeck said then turned and left before the steam started coming out of his ears.

THIRTY-ONE

Owen Jefferson hung up the department's phone and heavily sighed. Steve Gondeck had called with the news about the warrants. Jefferson looked across the table at Marcie who stared back with an inquisitive look on her face.

"Serenity now," Jefferson said.

"What?"

"No warrants," he answered her. "No search warrant, no arrest warrant. That was Steve Gondeck, with Slocum's office..."

"Yeah, I know who he is."

"The judge he had to take the applications to refused to sign them. Said she needed more than a single strand of hair. Steve thinks Traynor suing everybody over the last time DNA was used against him caused her to pause."

"Now what?" Marcie asked.

Jefferson didn't answer her right away. He swiveled his chair toward the whiteboard. He leaned back while staring at the names, reflecting on what they could do.

"I say we go pick him up anyway," Marcie said. "We have enough to haul his ass in here for questioning."

Jefferson turned his chair back to her, stared directly at her for several seconds before saying, "You're right. Go get him. Grab a couple of uniforms and get him downtown. He should be at the church, but you can check with Rod Schiller to make sure."

Marcie started dialing the phone to call Schiller and while doing so said, "What are you up to?"

"I have someone I need to talk to. Make sure everybody wears a vest and has a Taser. I don't trust this guy one bit. And keep quiet about this. I don't want the media hanging from the rafters when you get him back here."

Jefferson quietly waited for his partner to finish her calls then pack up and leave. As soon as she was out the door, he made the call he was waiting to make.

"Hey, you busy right this minute?" Jefferson said when Tony Carvelli answered this phone.

"No, I was about to call you anyway. I hear you got the DNA results back from the hair sample found on Cara Meyers and it's our boy Howie," Carvelli said.

"How did you find that out?"

"I'm not telling you and I'm not sure you want to know."

"Okay, I need to talk to you. You got some time now?" Jefferson asked.

"Why aren't you out arresting the sonofabitch?"

"That's one of the things I need to talk to you about."

"Okay," Carvelli replied. "I could use some lunch anyway."

Barely fifteen minutes after the phone call between the two men, Carvelli entered *Rosa's* on Lake Street and Graham Avenue. He looked along the wall on the right-hand side and checked the booths until he spotted Jefferson.

"Best Mexican in town," Carvelli said as he shook Jefferson's hand and sat opposite him.

Within fifteen seconds Rosa herself was at their booth.

"Bad enough I got cops coming in here now you're bringing him with you," she lightly chided Jefferson referring to Carvelli. "You know Tony, I think you have a tab around here that you still owe," she kidded Carvelli.

"You say that to me every time I come in here," he said.

"Cause you ain't paid it."

Tony gently took her right hand, gently kissed the back of it and said, "But I still love you. Let's run off together."

"You're too old for me. You couldn't keep up," the sixty something Rosa replied.

"Probably true," Jefferson said.

Rosa winked at Jefferson with a sly smile then took a pen from behind her right ear. She took their order and left the two men to talk.

Jefferson quickly explained where he was with the investigation and the problem with the arrest and search warrants. When he finished he said, "We need a boost. We need to figure out how he's doing this."

"If he's doing it," Carvelli corrected him. "The guy's been under surveillance except for a couple of days since he got out. He has the best alibi ever. What about the other two, what's their names...?"

"Forsberg and Parlow," Jefferson said.

"Yeah, what about them?"

"I don't see Parlow being smart enough to pull this off," Jefferson told him. "Forsberg, to be honest, looks as good for it as Traynor does. But, we got DNA on Traynor..."

"Okay, but don't kid yourself about Parlow. He's as big an asshole as Traynor..."

"...and we've been having more trouble keeping track of him than Forsberg or Howie," Jefferson added. "Look Tony, I don't know why but my gut tells me that it's Traynor. At this point we're chasing our tails and I want to either nail his ass or eliminate him."

Rosa brought their lunches and the three of them engaged in a little more good-natured banter. She left, and the two men went to work on their meals.

"Okay," Tony said a few minutes later. "I know what I can do but you are not going to be told. The less you know the better. You'll just have to trust me."

"You got it," Jefferson said while wiping his mouth with a paper napkin. He slyly smiled to himself knowing perfectly well what the former MPD detective had in mind.

While Owen Jefferson and Tony Carvelli were meeting for lunch, Marcie Sterling parked in the lot of St. Andrew's Catholic Church. She was followed and accompanied by two large MPD uniformed cops, Sergeant Paul Hemer and Officer Kyle Fulton. Hemer was driving the squad car and he parked it behind Howie's car effectively blocking it in. Having seen them arrive, Father John Brinkley opened the door for them before they reached it.

Marcie introduced themselves to the priest while showing him her credentials. She politely asked Father John to take them to Howie Traynor.

The priest led them downstairs into the basement where Howie was eating lunch. All the way down Father John kept asking questions about why they were there and what they wanted. Marcie courteously deflected each question with a standard inability to divulge this information response.

"Howard Traynor?" Marcie asked when they arrived at his table. Howie had seen them coming across the floor of the basement's common area. He quickly shoved the last bite of his sandwich in his mouth then turned back to look at them.

"Yes," Howie said to Marcie's question while still chewing.

"We need you to come with us," Marcie answered.

"Is he under arrest?" the priest asked.

"Am I?" Howie also inquired.

"No, we just want you to come downtown for a chat."

At that moment, the younger uniformed cop, Fulton, the larger of the two, step forward in a menacing manner. When he did this the old Howie Traynor returned for a brief moment, enough to make a point. The expression on his face changed enough to let the cop know Howie was not to be intimidated by a mere cop. Fulton got the message and so did Marcie and Sergeant Hemer.

"This building is a place of worship and a sanctuary," Father John reminded them trying to find cover for Howie.

"It's his place of employment," Marcie corrected the priest. She looked at Howie and asked, "Are you requesting sanctuary from the Church?"

Howie thought it over for a second then stood up and said, "No, I'll come with you. I have nothing to hide and I would like to get this over with."

The priest started to say something, but Howie interrupted him. "It's all right, Father. I know what they want. They think I have something to do with these murders, but I don't. So, I might as well go with them and see if I can convince them. Will you call a lawyer for me, please Father? His name is Marc Kadella," Howie asked him then spelled Marc's name. "Ask him to meet me there."

"I will, and I'll be downtown myself right behind you," Father John replied.

While he was being led out of the church, Howie said, "I'll tell you right now, I'm not answering any questions until my lawyer gets there."

"That's your right and we will respect that," a disappointed Marcie Sterling replied.

Marcie drove her car into the underground parking of the Old City Hall. The two uniforms, with Howie Traynor in the back of their squad car, followed her down the ramp. Within minutes they hustled him upstairs to the police department and into an interrogation room. Marcie left Officer Fulton in the conference room at the door to watch Howie while she went to find Owen Jefferson.

Marcie stuck her head into the conference room they were using as an office and found it to be empty. She turned to the detectives in the room and said, "Anybody seen Jefferson?"

Before anyone could answer he came into the room through the hallway doors.

"Never mind," Marcie said.

They greeted each other, and Marcie held the door for him as they went into their private office space. Selena Kane saw Jefferson arrive and she entered the room right behind him.

"He lawyered up," Marcie told them. "Says he won't talk to us without a lawyer."

"Let's get him one," Kane said.

"His priest is calling one for him," Marcie said. "A guy Howie told him to call."

"What do you want to do?" Kane asked Jefferson.

157

"Wait for his lawyer. In the meantime, I'll call Steve Gondeck at Slocum's office and have him come over," Jefferson answered his boss as he started dialing the department phone.

There was a sharp knock on the door, a detective stuck his head in and said, "There's a priest here. Says he is this Traynor guy's priest and insists on seeing him."

"I'll take care of it," Kane said.

A minute later Kane opened the door to the interrogation room and let Father John go in. She then motioned for Officer Fulton to step out and she told him to watch the door from outside the room.

THIRTY-TWO

An hour after Father John called him, Marc Kadella arrived at the police department. He was escorted into the detective's room where he was spotted by Steve Gondeck.

"What's going on?" Marc asked Gondeck as the two men shook hands.

"Are you the lawyer the priest called, and do you represent him?" Gondeck asked.

"Yes, and for today I represent him. We'll see about anything more than that," Marc replied. "I was in court across the street and got a text from my office. You guys picked up Howie Traynor?"

"Yeah, we did."

"For this Crown of Thornes business?"

"Well, um, yeah. For questioning about it," Gondeck said.

"Why?"

"Can't tell you that," Gondeck said.

Marc looked at his friend for a moment then said," What do you mean, you can't tell me that?"

"He's not under arrest yet."

"What does that mean, yet? In other words, you don't have enough for an arrest warrant or a search warrant so you're fishing. Where is he?" Marc asked without waiting for an answer.

The two lawyers had been standing by an empty desk. By this time Kane, Jefferson and Sterling joined them. It was Jefferson who answered Marc about Traynor's whereabouts.

"He's in an interrogation room with his priest. I'll take you there."

Jefferson led the way with Marc trailing behind, briefcase in hand. He was followed by Gondeck, Kane and Sterling. When they reached the room, Fulton opened the door to let Marc go in.

"If I find out you're listening in on this…" Marc started to say to the cops.

"Hey, you know me better than that," Gondeck indignantly replied.

"A friendly reminder," Marc smiled.

Marc entered the room and found Traynor and the priest seated at the table together. Both men's hands were folded as if they had been praying. Howie had a contrite and worried look on his face.

"Mr. Kadella, I swear I had nothing to do with any of this," Howie blurted out before the door was closed behind him.

"Relax, Howie. Nothing's happening yet," Marc said. He introduced himself to the priest then politely asked him to leave.

"He can stay," Howie said.

"The priest-penitent privilege might not apply to our discussion," Marc said.

"It's okay, Howard," Father John said, as he pushed back his chair and stood to leave. "I'll wait right outside."

"Did the cops say anything to you?" Marc asked when the priest left.

"No, nothing," Howie replied. "I been around the block a few times. I got a past, I know that. But I ain't done nothing and the cops know it. They're just hassling me 'cause they're desperate."

"Why do you think they know you haven't done anything?"

"Because they've been following me. Almost since the day we were in court and I got out."

"How do you know that?" Marc asked.

"Cause I've seen them. They sit outside my apartment all night and follow me everywhere. I'm not that stupid."

Marc thought about what his client had just told him then said, "Just a second."

He stood up, opened the door and said, "Come on in."

Gondeck, Kane, Jefferson and Sterling all filed into the interrogation room along with Father John who sat down next to Howie as the three cops and Steve Gondeck stood along one wall. Marc closed the door behind them, sat down and abruptly asked, "Have you been following my client? Have you been conducting twenty-four hour a day surveillance of him?"

It was Jefferson who answered. "We are not at liberty to discuss police procedures regarding an ongoing investigation."

"So, the answer is yes, you have," Marc said. "This means his alibi for these murders is about as good as it gets." This last statement was made by Marc while he looked directly at Steve Gondeck. "We're leaving," Marc said as he stood up.

"Wait, Mr. Kadella," Howie said. "I'll say one thing."

"I'm advising you not to," Marc told him as he sat down again.

"It's okay," Howie told Marc. "I know you think that somehow I have done these murders. I haven't. But I've been thinking about it and my money is on the Forsberg guy and probably Gene Parlow."

"Why do you say that?" Jefferson asked.

Howie looked at Marc who said, "Go ahead. Tell him why."

"Because every time we go to the lawyer, that woman who's suing the city for us, they're both there before me and pretty chummy. Then when I get there they clam up. And, I know Forsberg is really angry about the whole thing. He's pissed about getting screwed when he was convicted, and he's pissed about the settlement offer.

"I knew Gene Parlow when I was in prison. He used to bitch all the time about how his lawyer screwed him over and he'd like to get even. If I was you guys, I'd look at them."

"Is my client under arrest?" Marc asked when Howie finished.

"No," Gondeck replied.

"Is he willing to take a lie detector test?" Selena Kane abruptly jumped in.

"There's no such thing as a lie detector," Marc said. "It's a fantasy for TV. If he passes the test will you guys leave him alone? No. If he fails it, then what? So, to answer your question, no, he will not take a polygraph."

Marc looked at Gondeck and said, "I want the harassment of my client to stop. No more surveillance."

"No one's harassing Mr. Traynor," Gondeck replied.

Marc stared at Gondeck, realizing he had not admitted to the surveillance but had also not agreed to end it.

"They better not, Steve," Marc said.

"Is that a threat?" Kane asked.

"Don't even try that 'is that a threat' line with me, Lieutenant. I'm not impressed. Let's go," Marc said. Marc, Howie and Father John stood up and walked out.

Steve Gondeck, Jefferson and Marcie Sterling were seated at the table in the conference room. Selena Kane was on the phone giving the chief an update. Gondeck was looking at the names on the whiteboard, specifically the ones with a circle around them.

"Could he be right?" Gondeck asked. "Is it this Parlow guy or Forsberg or maybe both of them?"

"Maybe," Jefferson answered him.

"Maybe? You do realize that alone is enough to create reasonable doubt," the prosecuting attorney said.

"Something's been bothering me. How would Parlow or Forsberg know who Elliot Sanders was? How did they know he was the jury foreman at Traynor's trial?" Marcie asked. "We're assuming that at least two of the last three victims were killed to cast doubt and confuse us. The lawyers for Parlow and Forsberg, Segal and Meyers, would have been easy to find out. But Traynor's jury foreman…"

"I don't know. How did you find out?" Gondeck asked.

"We called the court clerk's office and they looked it up for us," Jefferson said.

"They should have a record of anyone else making that inquiry," Gondeck said. "But Forsberg could easily be computer savvy enough to find out on his own."

"Parlow, probably not," Marcie said.

"That doesn't eliminate him," Gondeck said. "So, we're back to these two guys could be involved."

"What about all three together?" Jefferson asked.

The small room went silent while the three of them thought this over. A minute later it was Marcie who broke the silence.

"Possible, but not likely."

"Why?" Gondeck asked.

"Because Traynor just handed us the other two," Marcie said. "Would he do that if he was involved with them?"

"Good point," Jefferson glumly agreed.

"Hey," Gondeck leaned across the table and looked at the cops. "We can't dismiss anything right now. Keep digging, we have to find something. But, one thing's for sure, Traynor's lawyer is right. He has an air tight alibi courtesy of the MPD."

THIRTY-THREE

It took the better part of two years after the trial of Howie Traynor for the murder of Lucille Corwin Benson for the dreams to stop. Jimmy Oliver spent fourteen months in the correctional facility at Lino Lakes expecting to be shivved in his cell at any moment. At night, more often than not, his sleep would be disturbed by the image of Howie Traynor's hands reaching for his throat. Jimmy would wake up in a sweat checking his cellmate, worried he had awakened him. Upon his release, it was another seven or eight months before the dreams began to subside.

Jimmy originally planned to remain in the Cities just long enough to build up a stash then hit the road. Over the years his fear and desire to leave waned. One thing led to another and he never quite got around to it, that and a taste for crystal meth he needed to feed.

Jimmy was never someone who paid attention to the news. He knew nothing about Howie's release until the man himself showed up at *Tooley's*. Jimmy was in the back fetching a case of beer and when he walked out of the storeroom, Howie was standing at the bar. At first Jimmy's mind couldn't grasp what he was seeing. Then the image changed to the Grim Reaper; scythe, hooded cloak and dead eyes.

His worst nightmare was standing a few feet from him when something almost miraculous happened. Howie Traynor broke into a broad grin and extended his right hand across the bar; a sight Jimmy Oliver would have not thought possible.

Without wetting himself or dropping the beer, Jimmy composed himself enough to shake Howie's hand. For the next ten minutes the two men conversed like old friends. Finally, Howie apologetically informed him that he was a changed man, and all was forgiven. Jimmy wasn't sure he believed him though he seemed sincere. That night and each night since, the dreams were back.

Tonight, the crowd in *Tooley's* was light even for a weeknight. Jimmy was starting to feel a little on edge and decided he could use a little toot of the meth burning a hole in his pocket. He served one of the regulars then asked the other bartender if he could take a smoke break.

"There's some trash by the back door, Jimmy," the man said. "Toss it in the dumpster will you?"

"Sure thing Dave. I'll be back in a bit," he told his co-worker who knew exactly where Jimmy was going and why.

Forty minutes after Jimmy went out back into the bar's parking lot he still had not returned. Knowing what Jimmy was up to and with the sparsely patronized bar, Dave wasn't too concerned. A few minutes later the bar's owner, Richie Mayfield, came in and asked Dave about Jimmy.

"Goddamnit, I should fire his ass."

"He's okay," Dave said sticking up for him.

Annoyed, Richie said, "I'll go get him and kick his little junkie ass back in here."

Richie went out the back door and walked through the almost empty parking lot. He had installed two bright pole lamps in the lot and Richie could easily see Jimmy was not there. To his right, the apartment building next door had put up a cedar board privacy fence. It ran along *Tooley's* property line and took a ninety degree turn at the back corner of the parking lot to run parallel to the alley. When Richie reached the alley, he turned to his right and, from the light from the pole lamps, he could see Jimmy sitting on the alley floor up against the fence.

Owen Jefferson's cell phone went off waking up both the detective and his wife. In his line of work, midnight calls were simply a part of the job. Because of his current case this one was particularly unwelcome.

"Yeah, Jefferson," he answered sounding completely awake.

"Owen, it's Dan Fielding. Sorry to bother you..." the MPD sergeant began.

"It's okay Dan. What do you have?"

Fielding had been the first cop to arrive at *Tooley's*. He took one look at the displayed body of Jimmy Oliver and immediately called in for Jefferson's personal phone number.

"I think it's one of yours. The guy's displayed like the others. Barbed wire crown and his hands nailed to a fence. Looks like his throat's been slit ear-to-ear."

"Where are you, Dan?" Jefferson asked.

"In the alley back of *Tooley's* bar. The owner says the victim is..."

"Jimmy Oliver," Jefferson quietly finished the uniformed cop's sentence.

"Yeah, how'd you know?"

"Take charge and seal off the area," a dejected Jefferson said. "You know what to do. I'll be there as soon as I can. Thanks, Dan."

By now Jefferson was sitting on the edge of the bed in his underwear. He quietly said to himself, "Goddamn sonofabitch. I should've seen this coming."

"They found another one?" his wife of thirteen years, Clarice asked.

"Yeah, babe," he answered her while making a phone call. "Rod, it's Owen Jefferson. Who you got sitting on Howie Traynor?"

"I'm not sure. What time is it?" Schiller replied.

"We found another one. Get up and whoever it is get somebody in that apartment and knock on his door right now. Kick it in if they have to. If Traynor isn't home, tell them to wait for him and arrest his ass the minute he shows up."

"You got it Owen. What if he is home? You want him brought in?"

Jefferson thought this over for a moment then said, "No, I guess not. Get them up there to check on him. Oh, and while you're at it, check on the other two guys, Parlow and Forsberg."

Natalie Musgrave had been in uniform with the MPD for seven years. A black woman in her late twenties she had earned outstanding performance evaluations and, more importantly, the respect of her peers. She felt like she was approaching a crossroad in her career. Does she stay in uniform or try to go into plainclothes and make detective? Her current assignment, helping surveillance of the Crown of Thornes suspects, was initially an opportunity. For the past ten days or so she had begun to find it routine and more than a little boring. Watching Howie Traynor was not exactly a suspenseful thriller. All he ever did was go to work, go home, go to the gym most evenings and three or four times a week stop at the grocery store.

Tonight, she was sitting by herself in a nondescript van one door down from Traynor's apartment. She was on the midnight to morning shift and just checked in with the cop in the alley, Troy Lenoir.

Natalie barely had time to get settled in for her shift when the van's phone went off. She checked the caller I.D., answered the call and in less than fifteen seconds was out of the van and speaking with Lenoir on the radio.

"Schiller just called, Troy. We need to go in and get up there and check on him. I want back up so hurry," she said as she trotted across the street toward the building.

Natalie used a master key the cops and fire department were issued to get in the building and started up the front steps. On her way to the third floor she was relieved to hear the back door open and footsteps on the back stairs.

Lenoir joined her at the door to Howie's apartment and she pounded on it loudly several times. In about a minute they heard footsteps in the apartment. The door opened, and a groggy Howie Traynor peered at them.

"What?" he angrily asked.

"Have a nice evening, Mr. Traynor," Natalie said. They made a hasty retreat and heard Howie slam the door shut. Lenoir followed her out the front and Natalie said to him, "I think someone's going to be disappointed he was home."

Owen Jefferson parked his car in the middle of the street alongside *Tooley's*. The street and the area all around the scene was crawling with cops. Two TV media vans and their crews were being held back about a block away. Using bright lights and directional sound detectors they were filming the scene and trying to pick up whatever could be heard.

Jefferson walked under the yellow crime scene tape and into *Tooley's* parking lot. When Sergeant Fielding saw him, the two men walked toward each other.

"What do you have, Dan?"

"Okay. The bartender says Oliver went out for a break at a couple minutes past eleven. He says he specifically checked the clock because Oliver sometimes takes a little too long. About eleven forty, eleven forty-five, the owner comes in just to check on the place. Oliver isn't back yet so the owner goes out back to look for him and finds him along the fence in the alley."

While Fielding was telling him this, the two of them were slowly walking toward the alley. The CSU team had set up several powerful flood lights to illuminate the scene.

When they reached the alley, Jefferson looked toward Jimmy's body just as his phone went off. He checked the I.D. and decided to take the call.

"What do you have, Rod?" he asked.

"Traynor was home and looked like he'd been sleeping," Schiller told him.

"Shit," Jefferson glumly replied.

"Aaron Forsberg was also home and mightily pissed at being bothered."

"Tough shit. I don't much care."

"But," Schiller continued, "our boy Eugene Parlow was nowhere to be found. He managed to slip away from us."

"Put a BOLO out on him and pick him up," Jefferson said.

"Already done," Schiller replied.

Jefferson spent a half hour at the crime scene. He took a close up look at the body, talked to the CSU people and the assistant M.E. on the scene. He checked Jimmy's fingers and noted they were all crushed but not his toes. Probably in a hurry, he thought.

Jefferson went inside and questioned both the bartender and owner to be sure of the time frame. Satisfied there was little more he could do, he decided to leave. While he was opening his car door, a thought occurred to him.

Jefferson looked at his watch then covered his mouth with the palm of his hand. He stood in the street staring at nothing but obviously in thought for a moment.

"Officer," he said to a uniform he didn't know who was watching the street.

"Yes, sir," the man responded.

"Keep an eye on my car. I'll be back in a while for it," Jefferson said as he started walking.

Exactly fifty-six minutes later he rapped on the door of the van with Natalie Musgrove sitting inside. Without waiting for a response, Jefferson slid the door open and found Musgrove with her handgun at her side.

"Jesus Christ, Sarge, I about jumped a foot."

"Sorry, Natalie," he said. "What time did you knock on his door?"

"12:17," she replied.

"Are you sure?"

"Yeah, I logged it."

"Okay, good. I need you to run me back to the crime scene and my car."

"You sure it's…"

"Yeah, he's not going anywhere else tonight."

THIRTY-FOUR

Owen Jefferson parked his department issued Chevy sedan in an open spot on Third Avenue alongside the Old City Hall building. It was barely past 6:00 a.m. and the downtown traffic was still very light.

Jefferson got back to bed shortly before 3:00 a.m. and had dozed off and on for a couple of hours. Every time he closed his eyes the black, dead eyes of Jimmy Oliver were staring at hm. This one bothered him more than all of the others. He knew why, too. He should have seen this coming. He should have done something, anything to at least warn Oliver if not give him more protection.

"Don't take it out on Marcie," he quietly said to himself as he opened the car door and got out.

Twenty minutes after he arrived at the conference room they were using Marcie Sterling came in.

"Why didn't you call me last night?" she said without speaking a greeting.

"Good morning, Marcie," Jefferson.

"I thought we were working together on this," she continued. Marcie was standing at the front of the table, an annoyed look on her face.

"I thought about it," Jefferson sighed, "but decided not to. It was after midnight and I saw no reason to drag you out of bed. There was nothing you could do."

"Oh, you mean you were being considerate," Marcie said almost apologetically.

"Yes, I was," Jefferson said realizing he had just talked himself out of trouble. "Sit down and we'll go over it," he continued while Marcie hung up her coat.

When he finished, Marcie said, "So, Parlow was missing again."

"Yeah, but…"

"I'm beginning to lean toward him. We got nothing on anybody else and he's the least alibied one of the three of them."

"You didn't let me finish. We found Parlow shacked up with a woman friend. She swears he was with her from ten o'clock until we found him. But could've been Traynor," Jefferson said referring to the walk he had taken from the crime scene to Howie's building.

"Yeah, possible," Marcie agreed. "But it just doesn't seem likely. How did he get out again without being seen? We've had his ass covered and…"

"I know," a dejected Jefferson said.

Marcie sat back, furrowed her brow and stared at her partner for a moment then said, "You want it to be Traynor. Why?"

Jefferson thought over her statement then said, "I guess I do. I'm not sure why. Probably because it makes the most sense. Who else would have a motive to go after Jimmy Oliver?" He paused for another ten seconds or so then continued. "I'm just not sure I buy his 'I found Jesus' act. You had to know him from the old days. I have a report to write."

At 7:30 Selena Kane came into the room carrying a cup of coffee. She took the seat at the head of the table, looked at Jefferson and said, "Tell me."

While verbally giving her the report of Jimmy Oliver's murder, Jefferson finished typing his official one. He hit the print button on his laptop and the printer began spewing out several copies.

Before he could finish giving Kane his report, the department phone rang, and Marcie answered it. She listened for several seconds then said, "I'll tell him, just a minute. It's the M.E., Marston. They found three more hairs and…"

Before she could finish Jefferson grabbed his extension and said, "What do we have?"

While Jefferson listened to the M.E., Marcie told Selena Kane what Marston had told her. They found three hairs on Jimmy Oliver that were not his and examined them. They appeared to be an exact match to the one found on victim number six, Cara Meyers.

"We'll be right there. Give us ten minutes. We'll run them over to St. Paul ourselves," Jefferson said then hung up the phone.

"Call St. Paul, the BCA. Give them a heads up what we have and we're on our way," Jefferson said to Selena Kane. "Let's go," he said to Marcie who was already up and holding the conference room door open.

While the two of them were hurrying down the hall leading to Jefferson's car, his cell phone went off. He checked the caller I.D. and answered it.

"I heard about last night," Tony Carvelli said. "Should we go?"

"Um yeah, that will be fine," Jefferson cryptically answered not wanting Marcie to know what the call was about.

"What was that?" Marcie asked.

"Personal. Nothing to do with the case," Jefferson said after ending the call.

The two of them walked a few more steps while Marcie continued to look at him and Jefferson obviously ignored her. "Bullshit," she said.

"Leave it alone," he answered her. "Trust me this one time."

Tony Carvelli and Maddy Rivers were parked in front of the apartment building next to Howie Traynor's. Maddy was dressed in a mild disguise. She wore dark blue slacks, a lighter blue blouse and a somewhat floppy blue wool hat. She was wearing stylish black-framed glasses and carried a leather satchel briefcase. Her long hair was tucked under the hat and anyone who saw her would think she was a businesswoman making a call.

"Six minutes, no more," Tony reminded her. "Even that's pushing it. We should keep it to three minutes."

"I'll be okay, Daddy," Maddy said mocking his concern. "You just keep an eye out and stay in touch," she continued referring to their comm. system.

Maddy was wearing a small ear piece that she would receive calls on from Tony and allow her to transmit to him. They had also taken the precaution to drive by St. Andrews to be sure Howie and his cop surveillance were both there.

Maddy held two small metal instruments in her right hand and the briefcase in her left, as she approached the door to the apartment building. With her experience and training she believed she could get the lock open in under thirty seconds. But, barely two steps from it the door opened, and an elderly tenant came out.

"Oh, hello," the woman said to Maddy, a little startled to find her at the door.

"I'm sorry," Maddy replied with a friendly smile, "I didn't mean to startle you."

"Oh, it's all right, dear. You go on in," the woman said as she held the door open for Maddy.

"Why, thank you and you have a nice day," Maddy said as she entered the building.

Barely ten seconds later she was on the building's third floor kneeling on one knee at Howie's door. Using her lock picks, she had the door open and was inside n under twenty seconds.

"I'm in," she quietly said to Tony.

"The clock's ticking, get moving," he answered her.

Before arriving at the apartment, the two of them had gone over how Maddy should conduct her search. They had come up with a list of where to begin and how much time to spend in each room.

"I'm in the kitchen," Maddy said for Tony's benefit.

She quickly but not carelessly began going through all of the drawers and cupboards. Wearing surgical gloves, she pulled the drawers out and went through each and even looked under them. Using a small penlight, she checked behind the stove and refrigerator looking for anything out of the ordinary.

"Time's up, move on," she heard Tony say.

"Heading for the living room."

Maddy smoothly repeated the same process in the living room and finished seconds before Tony told her to. She did the same thing in the bathroom and so far, found nothing. This wasn't a surprise since the two of them had not expected Traynor to be that careless.

Maddy worked her way through the bedroom with Tony giving her a running reminder on the time. She searched the dresser, the bed and opened the bedroom closet and began shining the light around thinking this might be how Traynor was getting out somehow.

"Oh, shit," she heard Tony say. "Traynor just pulled up in front of the building. Get your ass out of there!"

Not one to panic, Maddy closed the closet door, looked around the bedroom to make sure it appeared in order then started toward the door.

"Jesus Christ, he's running toward the front door. Are you out?"

"Almost," Maddy answered him. She took a quick look around the living room then, satisfied, grabbed the satchel she had placed by the door and stepped into the hall. As she did a short stab of fear hit her when she heard Traynor's footsteps pounding up the front stairs.

Maddy started walking quickly down the hall to the back stairway but realized she wouldn't make it. Halfway there she came to a door on her right without an apartment number on it. She tried the handle and it opened. Maddy looked into the dark room, realized it was a janitor's closet then stepped into it and quietly closed the door behind her seconds before Howie reached the top step.

She listened and could hear Howie unlocking his apartment door then closing it when he went in. All the while this was taking place, she had Tony Carvelli barking in her ear. Satisfied that Howie would not hear her, she finally answered Tony and told him where she was.

Less than a minute after entering his apartment, Maddy heard him come out and then heard his feet thumping down the stairs. While she listened, she felt along the wall by the door for a light switch. She found it and switched on the light.

"He's coming out, I think," Maddy told Tony. "Let me know."

A few seconds later she heard Carvelli confirm that Traynor was out and headed back to his car. He was carrying something with him that he did not have when he went in.

"Must've forgotten something when he went to work," Carvelli said. "Give it a couple minutes then…"

"Wait, I found something," Maddy responded.

She had noticed what looked like a trap door with a handle on it in the ceiling. Maddy reached up for the handle and was just tall enough to grab it. She pulled down on it and when it opened several steps of a stairway opened up and unfolded.

"What the hell are you doing?" an anxious Carvelli asked.

"I think I found a stairway to the roof. I'll go up and check it out," she said as she started up the stairs.

When she reached the top there was another small trap door. She pushed it open and sunlight came streaming in causing her to blink several times.

"It's the roof," she said. "I'm going to check it out."

Maddy went through the trap door and onto the roof. It was flat and covered with asphalt and gravel. While she walked around she gave Carvelli a running account of what she observed. She stood along the three-foot wall that surrounded it and looked out over the neighborhood. The apartment building next door was eleven or twelve feet away and she wondered if Howie could jump it.

"Time's up," Carvelli said while she stared at the gap between the buildings. "Get out of there."

"Yeah, okay," she replied. It was when she turned to go back to the stairs she noticed a small pile of loose lumber. "Hey, there's something here," she said to Tony while moving a few of the boards. "It looks like there is a plank of some kind nailed together. It's a pair of two by sixes put together and it looks long enough to reach the other building."

"Can you check it?"

Maddy tried to lift but could barely pick it up. "No," she said. "It's too heavy. I can lift it but not carry it over there. But, I'll bet Howie could."

"Okay. Let's check with Jefferson and tell him what we found. Get out, now."

An hour later, Owen Jefferson entered the *Lakeview Tavern* in south Minneapolis. It was still mid-afternoon, and it took a few moments for his eyes to adjust to the dimly lit bar. The booths were along the side to his left opposite the bar and he noticed Carvelli wave to him from one of them.

"Hey, Owen," Maddy said as Jefferson sat down next to her.

Jefferson greeted the two of them then said, "Okay, what did you find."

Carvelli let Madeline tell the detective what she did, admitting to at least one felony, and what she found. Before she could finish the bartender appeared and chatted with Tony and Jefferson. He brought the three of them soft drinks and when he left Madeline finished her story.

"What do you think?" Owen asked her. "Could he get up on the roof and get to the next building and get by our guys?"

"Yeah, it's possible," Maddy said. "Those two by six planks I found are probably strong enough to hold him. But, they're pretty heavy. I could lift them, but no way could I carry them to the edge of the building and lay them across."

"He could," Tony said. "He was a strong guy and in prison there's not much else to do but work out."

"And he still does, at least four or five times a week," Jefferson added.

"Then he has to walk across them three stories up to the next building," Maddy said. "Not too many people could do that."

"He could, "Tony said again. "He's a burglar and a damn good one. I never met one that didn't have nerves of steel and Howie was one of the best."

"What about Parlow? Did he have an alibi?" Tony asked Jefferson.

"Yes," Jefferson admitted. "At least one we can't crack for now. We're still looking at him and the other guy, Forsberg."

"Now what?" Maddy asked.

"I'm not sure," Jefferson said. "If the hair samples we took for testing come back as a match to Traynor, we should have enough for an arrest and a search warrant, especially with his history with Jimmy Oliver. We'll have the test results within a day or two, probably tomorrow. Then I'll go help with the search and find the ladder leading up to the roof."

THIRTY-FIVE

Marcie Sterling would never admit it, but she was feeling absolutely euphoric. Someone had leaked it to the media that an arrest was being made in the Crown of Thornes killer case. Marcie was in the lead followed by two male detectives and a male and female uniform cop with a handcuffed Howie Traynor in the middle. Marcie was wearing her best "I'm in charge" look as she marched down the crowded hallway toward the detective's room. A small mob of both print and broadcast journalists jammed the hallway and Marcie charged directly through them. All the while the bright lights lit up the scene, the cameras recorded her, and the reporters shouted the questions.

"I am innocent. I'm a patsy. I haven't done anything," was repeated over and over by Traynor.

Gabriella Shriqui squeezed through the crowd and fell into step beside Marcie. Gabriella asked several questions of her as they made their way down the hall, all of which were answered with a stern, "No comment".

The entire scene would have been laughably ridiculous except for how serious the underlying crimes were. The best part, the one that would be played on air over and over and go national occurred as Marcie opened the squad room door.

One of the male detectives, tired of Traynor proclaiming his innocence, grabbed Howie by the arm and snarled "Shut the fuck up you pond scum asshole."

A week-long suspension was in his immediate future. It would also teach him to control himself when the cameras were rolling.

The DNA results had come back from St. Paul as a positive match. They were exactly the same as the single hair found on Cara Meyers and a ninety-nine plus per cent match to Howie Traynor.

This time Steve Gondeck had better luck with the signing judge, a different one than the previous one. An arrest and search warrant had been quickly issued and the MPD needed no motivation to move quickly.

Traynor had been arrested outside of his apartment building when he arrived home from work. Jefferson had intentionally waited until then not wanting to go into a church again. He also didn't want a nosy priest interfering right away.

A very cooperative Howie Traynor was read his rights and acknowledged he understood them. He was shown and given a copy of both the arrest warrant and search warrant. The only comment he made was to politely say he wanted a lawyer. Marcie and her crew of cops then put him in a squad car and drove him downtown.

A half hour later, while watching the forensics team go through Howie's apartment, Jefferson decided he had waited long enough. It was time for him to "discover" the janitor's closet with the stairs to the roof.

He casually left Howie's apartment and strolled down the hallway to the janitor's closet. A minute later he was back getting one of the forensic team members to follow him up to the roof.

"What are we looking for?" the man asked.

"Not sure," Jefferson said. "Something that might explain how he managed to get out and slip past our surveillance."

In less than two minutes they found the twelve-foot planks that had been nailed together. Whoever had done so had nailed four two by four boards crosswise on the underside of the longer boards. These were obviously to hold the large boards together. The two of them carried the plank to the edge of the building. They laid it across the space to the next building and it made a perfect walkway between the buildings.

"That doesn't explain how he got out, Owen."

"Yeah, it does. If he got over to the building next door, he could go out the back door. See those lilac bushes in back along the alley?" Jefferson continued pointing at the thick, leafy bushes behind the next building. "Our guys wouldn't have seen him sneak out that way."

"Pretty circumstantial," the other cop said.

"It works though."

"Hey, Owen," the two of them heard a man yell.

They turned and saw another cop with his head sticking up through the open trap door.

"You better get down here and see what we found."

"Just a second, Paul," Jefferson yelled back.

He turned back to the other searcher and said, "Scott, see if you can lift this plank by yourself and put it back."

"Don't let me fall," Scott said as he grabbed the long boards with both hands. He struggled a bit and it wasn't easy, but he did manage to lift the plank up and bring it back. He put it back where they found it and said, "It's not easy. The thing probably weighs one fifty to one sixty, but it can be done."

"Wait here, I'll send someone up to take pictures," Jefferson told him.

Jefferson went back down the stairs and into Howie's apartment. He dispatched the photographer up to the roof then followed Paul Thornton into the bedroom.

"Sara found this," Thornton said pointing out the objects lying on the bed.

"Holy shit. Now we gotcha you sonofabitch," Jefferson quietly said as he leaned over to examine the items on the bed.

The three things lined up on Howie's bed were what looked to be ten to twelve feet of coiled barbed wire, a pair of heavy wire cutters and thick leather work gloves. Without touching them, Jefferson carefully examined each.

"Where were they?" Jefferson asked.

"In between the mattress and box spring," Sara said.

"Did you photograph them...?"

"Yes, as soon as I found them."

"Great work," Jefferson replied as he straightened up. "Bag'em, tag 'em and get them to the lab ASAP. And Paul, there's stuff on the roof to place into evidence. Scott will show you. I have to take off. Have Carly email me a photo of this stuff, right away," he continued referring to the items on the bed.

There was a soft knock on Marc Kadella's office door. Before he could respond, Carolyn opened it and seeing him on the phone, quietly told Marc that she needed to interrupt him.

"I have another call I have to take Uncle Larry," Marc said as an excuse to end the call. He listened for a moment then replied, "Yes, I'll deposit your check. Relax. I'm ready for your trial. I have to go."

Marc hung up the phone, shook his head then looked at Carolyn who was suppressing a laugh and said, "What?"

"You need to come out and see this. It's all over the news."

He followed her into the office common area where he found a crowd gathered in front of the television.

"Check it out," Barry Cline said to him, referring to the TV.

Marc peered between the shoulders of Barry and the office paralegal, Jeff Modell. On the screen was Gabriella Shiriqui in a hallway at the police headquarters reporting the arrest of Howie Traynor. The entire office watched in silence for several minutes while an anchorwoman asked Gabriella a few questions, most of which Gabriella could not answer.

The TV went to a commercial and Sandy, the other full-time legal secretary, hit the remote and shut it off.

The office landlord, Connie Mickleson, was leaning against Carolyn's desk. Marc looked at her and she asked, "You going downtown to see him?"

"I don't know, I suppose," Marc sighed. "I guess I'm his lawyer, at least for now."

The office phone rang, and Sandy answered it while the lawyers were discussing Marc's obligation. Sandy spoke into the phone by saying, "I'll see if he's available." She put the caller on hold, looked at Marc and said, "Guess who."

"Is it him?" Marc asked.

"Yep. What do you want me to tell him?"

"I'll take it," Marc answered as he walked toward his office.

He left his door open, so everyone could crowd in and listen. There wasn't much conversation and it only lasted a minute or so. Marc ended it by saying, "Okay, Howie, I'll be there in about fifteen minutes. Until then, don't talk to anyone."

He hung up the phone, looked at the faces crowding into his doorway and said, "Why do I get a bad feeling about this?"

Marc finished reading the copies of the search and arrest warrants that had been given to Howie. They both seemed to be in order and he placed them on the table. He was in a small attorney-client conference room at the jail alone with Howie. Marc reached in his inside suit coat pocket and removed a photo print Steve Gondeck had given him.

"What can you tell me about this?" Marc asked as he handed the photo to Howie.

Howie looked at it and with a puzzled expression said, "I don't know. It looks like some kind of wire, wire cutters and gloves."

"You've never seen them before?"

Howie looked at the photo again and said, "The gloves are mine, I think. They look like the ones I had at work. They've been missing for three or four days. Where were they?"

"The cops say they found them in your apartment between your bed's mattress and box spring."

"Then they put 'em there," Howie angrily replied. "Are they charging me with something?"

"Did you tell anyone your gloves were missing?" Marc asked ignoring his question.

"Sure, Father John. He gave me the money for a new pair. I bought them at the store I go to and they're at the church."

"Are you sure? Will he remember it?"

"Yeah, I'm sure. He should remember it," Howie answered him.

"Okay, good," Marc said. "I'll check with the priest. To answer your question, yes, they're charging you with second degree murder for the death of your old partner, Jimmy Oliver," Marc told him.

"I knew it. I knew as soon as it happened they'd try to lay it on me. Sonofabitch, sonofabitch, sonofabitch..." Howie quietly replied with despondence in his voice.

He lowered his head and looked down at the table top. Only silence passed between the two men for almost a minute. Finally, Howie looked at Marc and said almost pleadingly, "I didn't do this Mr. Kadella."

"Marc," Marc corrected him.

"I didn't do this, Marc," Howie repeated more emphatically.

"Okay," Marc replied. "What do you want from me?"

"Aren't you my lawyer?"

"Not on this I'm not. Is that what you want?"

'Well, yeah!"

"Relax," Marc said holding up a hand to calm him. "We need to talk about this and get it straight, okay?"

"Okay, sure."

"Do you have any money or any source of money?"

"Not really," Howie said. "Do we need to talk about this now?"

"Yes, we do," Marc said. "A case like this will consume me for months. I need to know I'll get paid. I'm not a rich lawyer. Very, very few are. There are other lawyers around, a few who would be willing to take your case…"

"I don't want one of them. I want you."

"Okay," Marc nodded. "I can take a lien against your lawsuit with the city. I'll talk to your lawyer about that, Albright."

"She already loaned me some money maybe she'll loan me some more," Howie said hopefully.

"We'll see. For now, here's the deal. I talked to the prosecutor who will try this case. He told me they're taking this to a grand jury. I think they might want to charge you with some of the other so-called Crown of Thornes killings. We'll see.

"Tomorrow or the next day they're going to bring you to court for arraignment on the second-degree charge. Once the judge hears this is the Crown of Thornes case, you can forget bail. Until then, keep your mouth shut. Call Albright and talk to her about money. She was on TV last night promoting herself, so I know she's back in town. Sign this," Marc said as he slid a two-page document and pen to him. "It's a retainer agreement."

Without bothering to look it over, Howie signed both pages and handed it and the pen back to Marc. Marc placed it in his briefcase, stood up and tapped his knuckles on the door.

"I have to take off. I have some things to get started on. I'll tell the cops no one is to talk to you without me being present. Remember what I told you. Talk to no one, especially other inmates and call Glenda Albright. Don't tell her anything either. Have her call me or I'll call her tomorrow. I'll be back to see you tomorrow."

Later that same evening, Maddy parked her Audi almost two blocks away from her destination. She had been to the *Lakeview Tavern* three or four times, always with Carvelli and always work related. Each time there had been parking available almost in front of the place. Tonight, the cars were lined up on both sides of the street for two blocks in each direction.

Maddy entered the usually quiet, neighborhood bar and was stopped in her tracks by the size of the crowd. One of the customers, mostly men with a smattering of a few women, turned to her when she came in. Maddy recognized the man as an MPD burglary detective she slightly knew.

"Hi, Maddy," the man said.

Like a light bulb coming on, just before she spoke to respond to him, his name popped into her head. "Hi, John. Have you seen Tony Carvelli?" She almost shouted to be heard above the din of the crowd.

"Yeah," the detective said leaning close to her ear. "He's up at the bar."

"Thanks," she said back. It took her a couple of minutes, but she managed to squeeze her way through the crowd. While she did this she saw the large banner on the wall to her left. "Welcome Home Jake" was what it read.

Carvelli saw her approaching and waved her forward. When she got to him he said, "Hey kid. Glad you made it." Tony turned to the guest of honor standing next to him. He pulled on the man's arm to turn him toward himself and Maddy.

"Jake," Tony said, "this is Maddy Rivers..."

"I remember you," Jake Waschke said as he extended his hand to her. "You were the P.I. that worked for that defense lawyer, Kadella. How are you?" he pleasantly said with a friendly smile.

"Oops," Maddy replied taking his hand. "I was hoping you'd forgotten."

Waschke laughed and said, "You're not easy to forget. How's the lawyer, is he coming?"

Maddy looked at Tony who said, "I don't think I invited him. I'm not sure how well a defense lawyer would do in a bar filled with cops."

You look good," Maddy said to the former MPD lieutenant.

"Prison agreed with me," Waschke laughed. "I quit smoking, lost weight and exercised a lot."

"Well, welcome home," Maddy said a bit uncomfortably. She leaned into Carvelli and whispered in his ear, "I need to talk to you, outside."

The two friends made their way back through the crowd and onto the sidewalk. Maddy lead Tony a half block away, stopped and said, "I heard the cops found barbed wire, gloves and a wire cutter in Traynor's apartment."

"Yeah," Tony said, "between his mattress and box spring."

"That's what I heard," Maddy said. "Tony, I checked between the mattress and box spring when I was in there yesterday. There was nothing there."

The two of them looked at each other for a few seconds then Carvelli said, "You're sure?"

Maddy said nothing but gave him a look with a raised eyebrow, "What do you think?"

"Sorry, dumb question." Tony answered her. "What the hell…"

THIRTY-SIX

Gabriella Shriqui knocked on the office door of her boss, Hunter Oswood, the News Director at Channel 8. Without waiting for a response Gabriella opened the door and entered. Waiting for her were the station's General Manager Madison Eyler, Oswood, Melinda Pace and Melinda's personal producer, Cordelia Davis. Gabriella greeted everyone and sat down on Cordelia's right in front of Oswood's desk.

"Thanks for coming, Gabriella," Madison Eyler said, starting the conversation.

Madison Eyler was leaning against the window sill to Gabriella's left. Oswood was seated behind his desk and Melinda, whom Gabriella despised and with good reason, was seated to Cordelia's left.

Gabriella knew what this meeting was about. Melinda Pace, after a suspension lasting several months, was going back on the air. Her show, *The Court Reporter* had been a huge success and money-maker for the station. It was also used as a half-hour lead in to the five o'clock news. As its name implied, the show was about court activity both locally and nationally. Especially interesting to the audience were notorious criminal cases. With the arrest of Howie Traynor, the day before, Gabriella knew Melinda was circling like a vulture to cover the Crown of Thornes case. Knowing what was coming Gabriella was determined to handle herself in a calm, objective, professional manner.

"How do you feel about working with Melinda on the Crown of Thornes case?" Oswood asked Gabriella.

"That depends on her," Gabriella calmly replied. "I won't be a party to another fiasco like the Riley case. So, ask her, can she conduct herself like a professional?"

"I resent...." Melinda started to sputter.

"What? You resent what, Melinda?" Gabriella interrupted her leaning forward and turning her head to look at Melinda.

"She has a good point, Melinda," Madison Eyler said. "Let's not rehash the past. Do you understand Gabriella's concerns?"

A thoroughly chastened Melinda meekly replied, "Yes, I understand."

"We need to get on top of this," Oswood said to both women. "This is a huge story. This station's credibility took an enormous hit..."

"We got our ass kicked," Eyler interjected.

"...and I want it restored." This last point was made while Oswood stared directly at Melinda Pace.

"I have a question," Gabriella said.

"Go ahead," Oswood told her.

"You put me in charge of the coverage of this case. I make all of the decisions subject only to your approval. Is that still the deal?" Gabriella asked.

"Yes," Eyler said. "That's still the deal."

"Then she works for me," Gabriella said referring to Melinda.

"Yes, that's correct," Oswood agreed.

Gabriella leaned forward again to look around Cordelia Davis who had remained uncomfortably silent. Gabriella looked at Melinda and said, "You work for me; I don't work for you. What I say goes. You don't put anything on the air that I disapprove of."

"Mine is an opinion show," Melinda tried to argue. "Sometimes the audience likes strong opinions."

"The main thing I want to get through your head," Gabriella started to say, her anger becoming apparent, "is the concept of innocent until proven guilty. Are you clear about that? For Christ sake, Melinda, you went to law school. Didn't anyone mention that to you in the three years you were there?"

"I got it," Melinda softly replied. "I know I went too far with Brittany Riley and I feel terrible about it. It won't happen again."

"Hand it to her," Eyler told Oswood.

"I've taken the liberty of writing an apology you will make at the start of your show today," Oswood told Melinda. He reached across his desk and handed a single sheet copy of a paper to Gabriella, Cordelia and Melinda.

Melinda took hers and without even glancing at it said, "I'll look it over and tell you what I think."

"You will read it verbatim or I will fire your ass here and now," Eyler sternly said. "It's already on the teleprompter. Make sure you get it right."

"Yes, ma'am," Melinda replied while Gabriella and Cordelia read over the apology.

When Gabriella finished reading the apology, Oswood asked, "Anything you want to add?"

"No," Gabriella said. "This should be fine."

"Okay," Oswood continued. "We're all on the same page?" he asked looking at Melinda.

"Can I say something?" Melinda politely asked.

"Sure."

"I know I can be a total pain in the ass prima donna, but I really did learn my lesson. I have to live with what happened to the Riley family and well, I just want to say I'll do my best. I am grateful for another chance and I won't let you down."

Gabriella stayed behind when Melinda and Cordelia left. "Is she really off the booze?"

Oswood shrugged and answered her by saying, "Cordelia says she is but, we'll see."

"I think she is," Eyler said. "She looks a lot better and seems better."

"Do you believe her?" Gabriella asked.

"I don't know," Oswood sighed. "I think so but, keep an eye on her."

"Traynor is being arraigned at one o'clock. I'll be there. No TV though," Gabriella said.

"We've joined in with the other TV stations to bring a motion to have the case televised," Eyler told her.

"The judge has discretion and Traynor's lawyer is the same guy who represented Brittany Riley. I doubt he'll want this on TV," Gabriella replied. "I'll see if I can get an interview with him today."

Marc waited with growing unease and impatience for the deputies to bring Howie Traynor to the courtroom. He was seated at one of the tables inside the bar anxious to get Howie's arraignment over with. At the other table was Steve Gondeck, the head felony litigator with the county attorney's office and a man Marc knew well.

The two of them had been in here since noon and had just come from the judge's chambers. While Judge Annette Koch ate lunch at her desk, she heard a motion concerning TV coverage of the arraignment. There were seven lawyers present all representing various local or national TV news outlets plus Marc and Gondeck.

The judge patiently heard each lawyer take his or her turn making the same basic argument. When they finished, Judge Koch looked at Marc and Gondeck sitting together on the judge's couch.

"What do you think, Mr. Gondeck?"

"We do not oppose the motion, your Honor," Gondeck replied while the court reporter continued to make a record of the hearing.

"Mr. Kadella," the judge said turning her attention to Marc.

"Absolutely not. The defense is totally opposed, Judge. This is going to be a media circus as it is, and I have enough experience to know that the courtroom cameras only make it worse."

"There are important first amendment issues..." one of the older TV lawyers started to say.

"Yeah, I heard you the first ten times," Judge Koch replied holding up a hand to stop him. "I remember reading something about the defendant's right to a fair trial, too. I'll go with that one. You are all free to file an appeal but until then, no cameras."

While Marc waited in the courtroom twirling a pen through his fingers, Gondeck rolled over to him while seated in his chair.

"Hey," he whispered when he got next to Marc not wanting the crowded gallery to overhear him.

"Yeah?"

"I just thought of something. Is Maddy Rivers going to be around for this trial?"

Marc stared at him for several seconds before saying, "Do I have to call your wife and tell her what's going on in that tiny little head of yours?"

"Hey," Gondeck said leaning back in the chair and held his hands up in mock protest. "I was just wondering."

"Uh huh," Marc replied. "Now, get back over on your side and behave yourself."

"Mr. Kadella," Marc heard a voice say. It was Judge Koch's clerk, Andy Combs. "Your client's here."

The gallery was almost full including a gaggle of media. Marc got up from his seat to go meet privately with Howie. When he did this, he glanced at the crowd and made eye contact with Gabriella Shriqui who wiggled her fingers at him. The two of them had become friends during a previous case and knew each other well. Gabriella was one of the few journalists Marc liked and respected. Of course, the fact that Gabriella was stop traffic gorgeous didn't hurt the relationship.

Marc found Howie already seated at a table in a small conference room adjoining the courtroom. Howie was dressed in clothes Marc had provided for him; tan khakis and a blue buttoned-down shirt. Judge Koch had already ordered that the shackles be removed from him and a deputy had done this.

"How you doing?" Marc asked while taking a seat.

"Okay, I guess," Howie shrugged. "It's not like I haven't done this before," he added with a weak smile.

"The place is full of spectators, including a lot of people from the press. When we go out there, I want you to show no expression at all. Don't laugh, don't smile, don't look sad, nothing. Act as if everything is going exactly the way we figured it would."

"Okay, yeah I get it," Howie said.

"They'll call your case, we'll go stand before the judge. She'll tell you you're charged with second degree murder and ask you to plea. Plead not guilty."

"I am not guilty," Howie said.

"Then there will be a discussion about bail. The judge will deny bail and that will be that. I'll tell her we won't waive your right to a speedy trial. I want to get that clock ticking today."

"Will there be more charges?"

"Yeah, I talked to the prosecutor and he admitted they're taking this to a grand jury. He wouldn't tell me any more than that except it will happen soon. Probably by the end of the week."

"You know him, the prosecutor?"

"Yeah, I've known him for a while. He's a decent guy but, don't let his looks or demeanor fool you. He's a damn good lawyer and he'll do whatever he has to do to put you away for life. He's tough as nails but honest.

"Now," Marc continued removing a two-page document from his briefcase. "I need you to sign this. It's a lien against your suit with the city and county. I talked to your lawyer and she thinks she'll settle it for a good piece of money up front and payments over time. She's agreed to front you twenty-five grand for me. I'll put it in a trust account and use it for fees and expenses and hopefully she'll get the case settled. One last time, you sure you want me? There are a lot of good lawyers who would love to have your case."

"No, no. I want you," Howie said as he signed the document. "I know you've had some big cases and can handle this. God won't let me go back to prison for something I didn't do. Is Father John here?"

"Yes, he is. He's in the front row right behind where we'll be sitting."

There was a soft knock on the door, it opened, and a courtroom deputy sheriff stuck her head in and told them the judge was coming out.

"Let's go," Marc said to Howie.

Marc entered his office through the hallway exit door and found everyone crowding around the TV set. He knew what they were watching. Melinda Pace was on the screen finishing her mandated apology and looking sincerely contrite and fully chastened.

"Did you know she was back?" Carolyn asked him.

It was a highly publicized trial that Marc had done that had led to the TV personality's suspension. Her behavior, fueled by a quest for ratings and her drinking problem, had driven Melinda Pace far over the line of ethical conduct. She was now back on the air just in time for the upcoming media circus about to swirl around Howie Traynor.

"Yeah, I heard," Marc answered Carolyn. "I saw Gabriella in court."

"How did it go?" Barry Cline asked him.

"About as expected," Marc answered.

"Oh, look at this!" Sandy said when Marc appeared on the screen. He had done a brief on-camera interview with Gabriella after the arraignment and it was being aired by Melinda.

"You just can't say no to her, can you?" Chris Grafton asked giving Marc a mild shot.

"Yeah, like you could," Marc replied.

The room went quiet until Marc and Gabriella were no longer on screen. When the camera went back to Melinda, Marc said, "You know, I get better looking every day."

The laughter died down and Marc followed Connie Mickelson, Chris and Barry into the conference room. The lawyers took chairs at the table and looked at Connie.

"What do you think?" she asked Marc.

"I don't know what to think," Marc replied. "He insists he's innocent. I haven't been given a lot of the discovery yet, so I don't know what's going on here yet."

Marc and Barry both handled criminal defense work. Connie did personal injury and family law. Chris was developing a nice list of small business corporate clients. Both Marc and Barry had handled notorious, highly publicized trials in the past. The publicity generated could be both a boon and a detriment to their business.

The four of them tossed it around for another fifteen minutes. At the end of it they all agreed, once again, to help Marc in any way they could. Marc admitted money could be a problem and Connie assured him he could count on her for help if and when he needed it.

THIRTY-SEVEN

Marc exited the semi-crowded elevator in the Hennepin County Government Center and found his Uncle Larry pacing in front of the elevator doors nervously waiting for him. They shook hands and walked together to the appropriate courtroom for Larry's trial. It was only a few minutes past 8:00 a.m. but the judge's clerk was in the courtroom waiting for him. Marc checked in with her then took a seat at the defense table next to his uncle. At 8:30 Earl Bicknell, the Minneapolis Assistant City Attorney arrived. The clerk immediately hustled the two lawyers back to see Judge Gilbert.

"Does your client really insist on going through with this?" Gilbert asked Marc even before the two lawyers could be seated.

"Yes, your Honor, he does," Marc respectfully answered. "He wants to exercise his constitutional right to have his day in court. Don't laugh Earl," Marc quickly added to a grinning Bicknell.

"He's right, counselor," the judge admonished the city attorney. "How about this," she continued turning back to Marc. "How about he pleads no contest, I put him on probation for six months and it goes off his record then. And he pays two hundred and we'll call it court costs?"

Marc sighed and said, "I'll ask him."

Marc left to check with his uncle. Two minutes later he was back in the judge's chambers.

"No deal," Marc told the judge and prosecutor.

"Okay. We'll take an hour for jury selection, no more than that. Then twenty minutes each for opening statements. You can put your first witness on and we'll get going. I want this done by one o'clock. No break for lunch. Any questions? Good. I'll be on the bench at nine. Be ready to go."

Marc walked past Larry who was still seated at the table in the courtroom, through the door and out into the hallway. He was relieved to see the two people he was hoping to find when he got there.

"Hey, thanks for coming," Marc said greeting Danh Vang, a reporter with the Minneapolis Star Tribune and Gabriella Shriqui.

"You owe me an interview on the Traynor case," Gabriella reminded.

"Me too," Vang chimed in.

"Yeah, yeah, I got it," Marc said. "We'll start at nine and pick a jury. It shouldn't take long to find six people. Probably no more than a couple hours for testimony," he explained to them. "Then closing arguments. The judge wants to be done by 1:00. I really appreciate this."

"This guy is your seventy-five-year-old uncle?" Vang asked him.

"Yeah but, don't use that," Marc said.

"We'll see," Gabriella said. "Depends on what we need to juice up the story."

"Come on, Gabriella. Give me a break. I don't need my mother, his sister to find out about this," Marc basically whined.

"We'll see," Gabriella winked at him.

True to her word, Judge Gilbert was on the bench precisely at nine. She immediately noticed seven or eight spectators which was not unusual. There are always people hanging around the courts watching trials for entertainment. In addition to those there was a woman from an anti-prostitution group sitting in. She was there to see to it that justice was done or at least the justice she believed should be done.

The presence of these people was not a surprise. Nor was the presence of the reporter from the Strib, Danh Vang. He worked the court beat and was around the courts every day. It was the attendance of Gabriella Shriqui that caught the judge's attention, as well as everyone else in the room. TV rarely bothered with routine misdemeanor cases but, of course, she had every right to be there. Uncle Larry was beaming with pride and joy at the sight of her.

To start the jury selection a panel of ten prospective jurors was brought in and seated in the jury box. The judge made a few preliminary remarks to them and asked a few general questions of the group as a whole.

Marc began the jury voir dire. He started with general questions to indoctrinate the jury about innocent until proven guilty; beyond a reasonable doubt; the burden of proof and to make sure each juror would keep an open mind. Forty-five minutes later the six lucky ones had been selected; three women and three men. None older than forty which was what Marc had hoped for.

Bicknell gave his opening statement and quickly walked the jury through the case. Marc had previously brought a motion to preclude the recording the cops had of Larry clearly soliciting the policewoman. His motion was denied, and Bicknell told them what they would hear and what the police witnesses would testify to.

Marc used his opening statement to again remind them of their promise and duty. While he spoke, he made eye contact with each of them and emphasized innocent until proven guilty and it was up to them to make that determination. Not the judge or the prosecutor. It was solely their decision.

Bicknell started calling witnesses and brought the detective who was in charge on first. Detective Paul Cannon was a solid veteran cop and had little trouble explaining to the jury what had happened. When he finished, Bicknell turned him over to Marc.

"Your testimony is that you, the sound technician and two uniformed police officers were parked a half a block away from your so-called decoy officer Jennifer Hall, is that correct?"

"Yes, that's right." Cannon replied.

"And none of you had a direct line of sight with Officer Hall did you?"

"No."

"You could not see what she was doing?"

"No, we could hear them clearly..."

"Is that a no to my question, Detective?"

"Um, yes, you're right we could not see her."

"She could have been doing a pole dance and..."

"Your Honor, objection," Bicknell interrupted him. "Assumes facts not in evidence."

"Sustained," the judge ruled.

"May we approach?" Bicknell asked. Judge Gilbert answered affirmatively, and the lawyers went to the bench. Gilbert pressed a button to emit a white noise in the courtroom so the three of them could converse without being overheard.

"Your Honor, he's trying to lay a claim for entrapment. If he wanted to plead that he should have done so before this," Bicknell said.

"Who said anything about entrapment?" Marc innocently asked.

"You are," Bicknell replied.

"He has a point, Mr. Kadella. You're getting awfully close to it. That's enough. Move along," Gilbert said.

"Yes, your Honor."

When the lawyers got back to their respective tables Marc let the detective go with no more questions.

The next two witnesses, male uniformed police officers, both testified to the same basic thing as Detective Cannon. With each of them, Marc made the same point that they could not see what actually occurred.

"Is this your primary function with the police department?" Marc asked both Sergeant Alan Schmidt and Officer Kenneth Lindborg.

Both men answered negatively to this specific inquiry.

"Isn't it true that you were taken off patrol duty, specifically for this prostitution sting?"

"Yes," both men answered.

"Normally you would be in a patrol car cruising for criminals and helping protect citizens, isn't that correct?"

"Yes," both men answered.

Next up was the sound technician who testified to the validity of the recording. His was mostly technical testimony and Marc had no questions for him.

The final witness was the policewoman decoy, Officer Jennifer Hall. Even in a cop's uniform with little makeup and her hair done up in a bun, she was still an attractive young woman. Five feet ten, slender dark blonde hair, the twenty-six-year-old made all of the male jurors sit up and pay attention.

It was during her testimony that the jurors heard the recording. There was no ambiguity about it all. The first voice was that of the policewoman and all she said to entice Larry was a soft hello. The two of them chatted for maybe fifteen seconds about the weather then Larry clearly blurted out the question.

"Is fifty bucks enough for a blow job?"

The officer asked to see the money and the recording was clear that both the decoy cop and Larry verbally acknowledged that he showed it to her as an offer. The remainder of the recording was mostly Larry being arrested and read his rights. Bicknell quickly finished Hall's direct exam after that and turned her over to Marc.

Before Marc asked his first question a deputy wheeled a large, flat screen TV into the courtroom. He placed it in front of the jury box, so the jurors would have a clear view of it.

"Officer Hall," Marc began, "I notice you're in your police uniform today and your hair is done up in a bun. Is that how you were dressed and how your hair was styled on the day of my client's arrest?"

"No," she answered. "I wouldn't make a very good decoy standing there in a police uniform."

This remark elicited a hearty laugh from the people in attendance and Marc smiled also.

"Probably not," he agreed. He picked up the TV remote the deputy had placed on his table and clicked the power button. On the screen was the picture of the way she looked on the day of the arrest.

"Is this how you looked that day?" The difference was stunning. She barely looked like the same person.

"Yes," she admitted.

"I must say, you look like a very attractive hooker, would you agree?"

"Objection to the use of the pejorative, hooker," Bicknell said trying to draw attention away from the TV.

"Overruled," Judge Gilbert said.

"That's the whole idea," Hall defiantly answered.

"I have nothing further, your Honor," Marc said leaving her picture up on the TV screen.

Bicknell thought for a moment about a redirect but decided the picture didn't hurt his case. He rested ending the prosecution's presentation.

Larry tugged on Marc's coat sleeve and whispered in his ear. "I want to testify."

Judge Gilbert ordered a short break before Marc could respond.

The jury was led out for a bathroom break and Marc took Larry into a small conference room.

"I want to testify," Larry repeated after the door closed.

"Why?" Marc said.

"I don't know," Larry said. "It well, looks like fun."

"Fun! This isn't a game. If the judge thinks you're playing games she'll nail your ass. Besides, what will you say? 'I saw this really hot chick hooker on the corner and I got really, really horny?' I don't think so!"

"It's my right to testify and…"

"No! This one time you are going to listen to me. You cannot do yourself any good on that witness stand."

"What will you say to them in your closing?" a chastened Larry asked.

"I have something I'll try. We'll see if it works but, you're not getting on that witness stand and that's final."

"Okay," Larry sullenly agreed.

Earl Bicknell, the prosecutor, was first up to give his closing argument. Believing he had a slam dunk conviction, Bicknell kept it short and simple. He led the jury through the pertinent testimony of each of his witnesses and a summary of the law regarding the solicitation of prostitutes.

"I realize that many people believe prostitution is a victimless crime. Believe me, ladies and gentlemen, it isn't. Those of us in law enforcement, (a subtle reminder whose side he was on) who have to deal with the dark side of it every day know how young women are abused and victimized for years. We fight it all the time and we need your help.

"Finally," he continued slowly strolling to the defense table to stand in front of Larry Jensen, "I can understand how you might be sympathetic to a lonely, widowed, elderly man," he said pointing at Larry. "But do not be swayed by your sympathy. The truth is he blatantly, deliberately broke the law and must be held accountable for it. We have proven beyond a reasonable doubt that the defendant is guilty of solicitation for the intent to commit prostitution. Thank you for your time and service."

Marc waited until Bicknell returned to his seat and for the judge to give him permission to begin. He walked over and stood barely three feet from the jury box. He held up his right hand with all five fingers extended and slowly moved that hand across the jurors in front of each one.

"Five, ladies and gentlemen," he started out saying as he continued to hold up the five fingers, "Five. Five members of the Minneapolis Police Department."

Marc changed to hold up just his index finger. "One detective with eighteen years of service. Another, a sergeant with thirteen years," he continued now showing two fingers. Two patrol officers," four fingers, "and a technician," he said back to showing them all five fingers.

"Five, including three patrol officers who are normally patrolling the streets to catch criminals and keep our city safe. Five," he said one last time for emphasis still showing them the five fingers.

He lowered his hand and gently held both hands in front of himself while he continued.

"Five members of the Minneapolis Police Department out fighting the scourge of prostitution and what did they get? A seventy-five-year-old, lonely widower. Quite a day in the annals of police work for the MPD."

"Objection," Bicknell said.

"Overruled but cool it on the sarcasm, Mr. Kadella."

"Thank you for your time and service. Ladies and gentlemen," Marc concluded without responding to the judge. He then walked back to the table and sat down.

Judge Gilbert gave the jury their instructions and they were led out to deliberate. The judge left the bench and Marc and Uncle Larry followed the small crowd into the hallway.

Marc spent the next twenty minutes being interviewed by the two reporters. Gabriella's cameraman had arrived, and he filmed for about ten minutes while Gabriella asked questions. Uncle Larry was also briefly filmed and answered a couple questions. When they finished, both reporters reminded Marc that he owed them an interview regarding Howie Traynor.

They began to pack up to leave when the judge's clerk came out and informed them the jury was back. Larry of course wanted to know if the short duration was good or bad. Marc had no idea either way.

Ten minutes later Bicknell came back in through the hallway doors just as the jury came back.

"Madam Foreman," Gilbert said when everyone appeared ready. "Have you reached a verdict?"

The woman who was the jury foreman stood up, answered affirmatively and read the verdict form.

"Not guilty," your Honor.

THIRTY-EIGHT

Marc was back at his desk. The unexpected not guilty verdict had displeased Judge Gilbert and angered Bicknell so much he stormed out of the courtroom. Marc had all he could do to contain his laughter. He had basically winked at the jury and encouraged them to stick it to the cops for wasting their resources and the jury's time. Best of all, it had worked.

Larry was a little ambivalent about it. On one hand he was quite pleased to avoid the conviction. But he wasn't sure how it would play with the women at his retirement complex.

Marc was still chuckling to himself about it while at his desk when there was a knock on his door. Connie stuck her head in and told him to check out the show on TV. Marc joined the small crowd in front of the office TV in time for the start of Melinda Pace's show.

"I usually like to end the show with a lighter side of the courts and law," she began. "I'm going to begin today's with it because it happened locally."

Melinda told the audience about Larry's trial and its outcome. She placed special emphasis on the tape recording of the defendant offering the undercover officer fifty dollars for oral sex. Melinda didn't have the recording itself but used the "several sources confirmed" line to assure the audience it happened. She then showed more than a minute of Marc and Larry being interviewed by Gabriella.

"I'm not sure whether to laugh or be upset," she said. "The whole thing is kind of amusing, but he was clearly guilty. I'll leave it to each of you to decide for yourselves."

At that exact moment the phone rang, and Carolyn quickly answered it. While the other office members laughed and congratulated Marc, Carolyn put the call on hold.

"Marc, it's your Mother."

"Oh, God no," he said hanging his head. "I forgot. She watches this show. I don't need this. This is the last thing I want, to deal with her about her brother."

By now everyone was barely containing their laughter over his dilemma. Connie pushed him toward his office while saying, "We'll take it in here."

"What do you mean, we?" he asked as Connie gently pushed him through the door. He sat down behind his desk while everyone crowded into his office.

"Hi, Mom," Marc lightly answered acting as if nothing was amiss. He held the phone to his ear, but Connie reached across the desk, punched the speaker button and held the base of the phone away from Marc.

"Give me that," he whispered almost panic stricken.

"What have you and that idiot brother of mine been up to and why wasn't I told?" the entire office heard Marc's mother say. "He offered a policewoman fifty dollars for a blow job!"

"Mom, stop!" Marc practically yelled, almost in a panic amidst the stifled laughter. "Stop, I don't need to hear my mother talking like this."

"Oh shut up. What, you don't think I know what a blow job is? Grow up. Now…"

"Mom, please, would you want to hear Grandma talk like this?"

"Where do you think I learned it? Now what have you two…?"

"Mom, call Larry! I'm not going to do this. Call your brother. I'm hanging up now," he said looking at Connie with pleading eyes as he punched his index finger up and down, gesturing for her to hang up.

Connie was watching with her lips pursed tightly together. Several of the others had left and were laughing in the common area.

Marc put his hands together as if praying and mouthed the word "please" several times to Connie.

"Fine, I'll call him but both of you are on my shit list!" Marc heard his mother say just before Connie ended the call.

By now the entire office was practically rolling on the floor at Marc's embarrassment. After a minute it died down. Connie wiped the tears from her eyes and took a deep breath.

"So, you found out your Mommy knows what a blow job is," she said.

Marc sat staring at the wall, too embarrassed to speak. A few seconds later he heard Carolyn yell at him.

"Hey, get out here. Melinda's talking about Howie Traynor."

Melinda was staring directly into the camera when Marc and Connie arrived in front of the TV. "Here it is folks," Melinda said holding a document in her right hand. "This is a copy of the indictment handed down by the grand jury. We received it earlier today and I read through it before today's show.

"The county attorney's office and the police are obviously positive that Howard Traynor is the Crown of Thornes killer. As I said, I read through it but, I haven't had a chance to study the facts and allegations contained in it."

She thumbed through the pages of the indictment, held it up again and continued.

"Forty-four pages, fifteen felony counts including ten counts of murder involving five victims."

By this point, Marc was practically seething with anger. "How the hell did she get a copy of it before me?" he growled.

The office phone rang, and Sandy stepped away from the TV to answer it.

"Marc, its Steve Gondeck from the…"

"Put him on hold!" Marc snapped. "Wait better still, tell him I'll call him back when I've had a chance to calm down. Tell him that exactly as I said it, so he'll know how pissed I am."

Marc turned back to the TV while Sandy passed the message along to Gondeck.

"I've also received information about the evidence they have against him. They searched Traynor's apartment and found barbed wire, wire cutters and leather work gloves hidden in his apartment. Forensic testing has matched the barbed wire to that found on the victims. The wire cutters are an exact match to the cuts used on the barbed wire crowns and they found Traynor's DNA inside the gloves."

By now, Marc had begun to calm down. He had been through this before, seeing news of evidence on TV that should have been sent to him first. There wasn't much point in getting angry about it; better to deal with it in court.

"Finally, ladies and gentlemen, let me remind you that Howard Traynor is innocent until proven guilty. That, at this point, these charges are only allegations and he must be given the benefit of the doubt. We'll be back after a short break."

Marc was seated on the front edge of Carolyn's desk staring at the screen. A commercial came on and he picked up the TV's remote and shut it off. Everyone in the room had gone silent waiting for Marc to speak. Marc sighed heavily then said, "First my mother and now this. Quite a day. Can someone remind me why I went to law school instead of getting a job at, oh, I don't know, maybe a grocery store or car wash?"

"Because you wouldn't have this much fun and meet such interesting people. Of course, you'd probably make more money," his friend and officemate, Barry Cline said.

"Oh yeah, that's right," Marc lightly replied. "I forgot how much fun this is. Thanks for reminding me."

He stood up and headed toward his office while saying, "At least I get to chew Gondeck's ass."

"Marc, I'm sorry. I don't know how she got it. There's a messenger on the way right now with a copy of the indictment and all of the discovery we have for you," Gondeck said even before he said hello. Knowing Marc was royally and rightfully fuming about

Melinda's show, Gondeck tried to preempt the blast he was about to get.

Instead, Marc calmly but passive aggressively said, "Okay. I'll look it over when I get it. Thanks," and hung up the phone without another word. Fifteen minutes later Gondeck's messenger arrived.

Marc was now in his car going north on Lyndale toward downtown. It was after five o'clock and the staff was packing to leave when he finished scanning the documents. Marc made a copy of the indictment and was in a hurry to meet with his client.

While Marc was seated on the edge of Carolyn's desk seething over Melinda Pace, Howie Traynor was in the jail's common area also watching her show. *The Court Reporter* was a favorite among the inmates in the various jails scattered throughout the Cities. Melinda was a particular favorite among the guests of Hennepin County. Occasionally one of them would be featured, usually in the "dumbest criminals" segment of the show. Being the level of intellectuals that most of them are, seeing themselves featured as the dumbest criminal was considered a badge of honor. Melinda's show was never missed and always attracted a large and attentive, if somewhat captivated, audience.

When Melinda finished reporting the information she had about Howie's case, several of the inmates turned to look at him. A couple of them even tried to give Howie a little good-natured ribbing about it. Instead, as they started to speak, Howie gave each a look that turned their blood cold. Not another word was spoken to Howie as they all stood and moved away from him to other seats.

Marc looked up when a knock on the door broke the silence of the room he was in. He was seated on a cheap, molded plastic chair at a small, metal table in a conference room at the jail. Marc had been there for almost twenty minutes waiting for a deputy to bring Howie down to him.

The door opened, and Howie shuffled in while the deputy held it open.

"Hey, Big Train," Marc said smiling at the large black man. "How you doing? Haven't seen you for a while."

"I'm good, Mr. Kadella," the deputy said flashing a large, toothy grin. Carl "Big Train" Johnson was a Viking offensive lineman until bad knees ended his career. Ever since he had been one of the most respected and liked guards in the jail.

"Knock when you're done," he told Marc.

Fifteen minutes later Howie finished scanning through the indictment then looked at his lawyer. "They're throwing everything they can think of at me," he calmly said.

"Hoping something sticks. They're hoping if the jury buys some of it maybe they'll buy all of it," Marc answered. "Or, if they cannot make the case on all of it the jury will believe you must be guilty of some of it."

"What do you think?" Howie asked Marc.

"Nothing at this point," Marc replied. "Here's the deal. They're going to arraign you again on the indictment. We'll waive reading of the charges, you plead not guilty and we'll argue about bail which will be denied again.

"We'll schedule an omnibus hearing to argue admissibility of the evidence. We'll see about that. I'm inclined to push for an early trial date. I don't want to give them more time to find more evidence. What do you think about that?"

"Sounds good. I'm innocent and I believe God will not let them convict me of something I didn't do."

"The downside of pushing for a speedy trial is that it gives us less time to prepare. But, they don't have witnesses except cops and technical people. We'll have their reports.

"For now," Marc continued, "you take that with you," he pointed to the indictment. "Read it over carefully. Memorize it. Go over every fact. Every claim they're making especially dates and places. Let me know where you were and what you were doing. Okay?"

"Yes, sir, Marc. I'll get right on it," Howie politely replied.

THIRTY-NINE

Marc was, as usual, early for Howie's second arraignment. Being a criminal defense lawyer, punctuality was mandatory. Because the news of the hearing was leaked to the media, by the time he arrived, there was a mob of people jamming the hallway of the fourteenth floor. Before Marc realized how bad it was, he had become stuck in the middle of it. He couldn't go forward, and he couldn't go back either.

Marc pressed forward, eliciting several dirty looks, snarls and barely concealed cursing. When he got within twenty feet of the courtroom doors, one of the four deputies guarding the doors recognized him. Two of the deputies brusquely shoved their way through to him and led him past the unruly crowd.

Once inside he looked over the gallery, shook his head a couple of times and smiled. It always amazed him how many people would stuff themselves into uncomfortable benches for a meaningless court appearance. Marc walked up the aisle dividing the gallery and just before he reached the gate, a woman stood up to block him.

"You still owe me an interview," Gabriella Shriqui said.

"Why are you people even here?" Marc said loud enough for the entire quiet crowd to overhear. "Nothing's going to happen today."

"When will I get my interview?" Gabriella asked a little too loudly.

Marc leaned down and whispered in her ear, "Thanks for putting that on Melinda's show so my mother could see it."

Gabriella looked up at him with a puzzled expression and said, "How was I supposed to know and why would I care? You were the one that asked me to do it, remember? I'll call you to schedule the interview."

"Yeah, yeah," Marc muttered then walked past her through the gate.

He dropped his briefcase on an empty table and an older, burly man seated in the first row leaned over the rail. Marc recognized him as a local news reporter for the Star Tribune.

"What's up, Gary?" Marc asked.

The man motioned Marc to come closer then whispered, "How does she merit an exclusive interview?"

Marc looked at Gabriella who was not paying any attention to them. He turned back to the man and answered loud enough for the media people in the front two rows to hear him.

"Are you blind or are you getting to the age where it doesn't matter anymore?"

When the laughter died down a deputy approached Marc and said, "Your client is in the jury room, counselor."

Marc followed the deputy across the courtroom to the jury room door. Just before he opened the door for Marc, the deputy quietly said, "The judge told me to tell you to take all the time you want. She has nothing else on the calendar for this afternoon so she's in no hurry."

"Okay and thanks," Marc replied. A moment later Marc took a seat across the jury room table from Howie. He was a little surprised to see the priest, Father John, seated next to his client.

"I realize you know the drill for what we're doing today," Marc said. "But, I just want to be sure, so I'll go over it again. Yours is the only case on the docket this afternoon. When the judge comes out she'll call your case. We'll get up and stand in front of her. She'll ask if you'll waive reading the charges and I'll say yes. She'll ask if you understand your rights; you say yes then she'll ask you to plead. Oh, I almost forgot, she'll ask if you have received a copy of the indictment.

"Again, I know we've been over this, but I want to make sure. The courtroom is overflowing with media and spectators. When we go out there, no matter what happens or is said, show no emotion. No matter what you do, the media will misinterpret it and blow it all out of proportion. So, don't give them anything that they can use to make it worse."

Marc looked at Father John and said, "You can sit at the table with us but, when his case gets called I want you to stay there when we go up. If the judge addresses you just answer her questions. I doubt she will. She may have you come forward to stand with us. If she does, come on up."

"Okay," the priest replied. "Will there be cameras in the courtroom?"

"No," Marc said. "The TV people are appealing the judge's order, but they'll lose. It's totally in her discretion and I am completely opposed to it. So, no TV."

"Good," Howie said.

The three of them went into the courtroom and Marc saw Steve Gondeck seated at a table. Marc quietly told Howie and Father John to sit at the table on which he had left his briefcase. He then motioned to Gondeck to come to him.

Anticipating Marc's question as soon as Marc closed the jury room door behind them, Gondeck said, "I know you're pissed, I get it, but it wasn't my fault. I can't prevent others from leaking stuff to the media."

Marc stared at him for several seconds showing no expression on his face at all. Finally, he said, "I know. I just wanted to see you squirm a little."

"I wasn't any happier about it than you," Gondeck said. "If I find out who's doing it I'll have their ass. You want a gag order, I won't oppose it."

"A gag order only stops me. Your cops will still ignore it. Actually, the reason I wanted to talk to you is I'm surprised to see you here. Isn't an arraignment a little beneath your totally lofty status?"

"Kiss my ass, Kadella," Gondeck replied smiling. "Tell you the truth; I got Slocum looking over my shoulder. He wants a conviction on this one desperately. He knows you're defending and..."

"So tell him to try it," Marc said.

"...he still hates your guts. But he's too busy with political crap, or so he says."

Marc smiled, turned the handle on the door and said, "Let's go get this over with. Oh, you will allow bail, right?"

"Take your best shot," Gondeck said as he went through an open doorway.

Marc shook hands with Howie who then turned to be led back to jail by two deputies. Without being consciously aware of it, Marc wiped the hand he used to shake with Howie on his pant leg.

The hearing had gone as predicted. Howie pleaded not guilty; Marc argued futilely for bail and the whole thing was over in less than fifteen minutes.

The sheriff's deputies had cleared the hallway mob beforehand, so the courtroom spectators were filing out unimpeded. Gondeck had made his exit through the back hallway and Marc took a seat at the table to wait for the crowd to leave. Gabriella came through the gate, took the chair Gondeck had used and rolled it next to Marc.

"You got a camera out there?" Marc asked referring to the hall.

"Yeah, can I get a quote from you? I see Gondeck snuck out the back."

"What's the deal with Melinda Pace? I thought she got canned," Marc asked.

"Money," Gabriella answered. "Ratings are down, and her show is cheap to produce, and the station makes buckets of money off it."

"I thought you were news," Marc said.

"We are but the lines get blurry sometimes. She's mostly entertainment dressed up as news. Stop looking at my legs."

"Don't wear dresses. Will I be on her show again?"

"That's not up to me," Gabriella said. "The station management assured me she's cleaned up her act and she's on a short leash."

Marc thought about what she just told him then said, "I'll believe it when I see it. I don't trust her but, I do trust you. I'll have to be careful what I say. Plus, she's not my problem to deal with."

That afternoon, Melinda's show, *The Court Reporter* went live. Normally she taped the show to allow for editing, but she had to wait for Gabriella's report.

Melinda spent the first half of the show indignantly reporting about judges sentencing decisions. She had two cases; one from California and one from Vermont. Both involved very lenient sentences for child molesters.

When Melinda returned from the commercial break she reported the arraignment of Howie Traynor. Melinda held a law degree from the University of Minnesota. She also spent several years as a reporter covering the various courts around the Twin Cities. In fact, this was how she came up with the idea for her show. Because of her legal background she was very well qualified to explain the legal process and court proceedings.

"Basically, folks," she said concluding her description of an arraignment, "it's pretty much a formality. The idea is to make sure the defendant understands the charges against him. It's also to make a formal plea and to be sure the defendant understands his rights.

"The lawyers can then argue for or against bail. In this case, given the severity of the many crimes Traynor allegedly," Melinda held up both hands and made air quotes around the word, allegedly, "committed, no judge would allow bail."

She then aired about a minute of the interview of Marc Kadella and Gabriella Shriqui. Melinda and Gabriella did a live two-minute Q & A about the case before the show went to another commercial.

"It's time for my favorite part of the show," she said when the show came back. "Our dumbest criminals segment.

"Today the award goes to Steven Walker of Tampa, Florida. After robbing a liquor store three blocks from his house, he went directly home and posted a notice on *Snapchat* that he was hiding there. The liquor store owner, having seen our genius many times and knowing his name because he had carded him many times, told the police who he was.

"A police monitor of social media found the Snapchat post. While searching his house the suspect mischievously posted another message proclaiming that the police were in his house at that moment searching for him. He then decided to let the internet world know he was hiding in a cabinet, certain the cops would never find him. Of course, this little tidbit was seen by the officer monitoring his Snapchat account.

"The resulting arrest completely shocked Mr. Walker. Have a great day folks."

During and after her on air Q & A with Melinda, Gabriella was watching the show on a small monitor she had on-site at the government center. The moment she finished it Gabriella was on the phone.

"I saw it," Hunter Oswood said without even saying hello when Gabriella called.

"What the hell is the matter with her?" Gabriella angrily asked. "Doesn't she get it that those little air quote gestures she makes are the equivalent of her winking at the audience?"

"I'll talk to her," an exasperated Oswood said. "I already put in a call to her producer to have her call me as soon as she gets off the air."

"Okay," a calmer Gabriella replied. "I'll see you when I get back."

FORTY

Something had been bothering Marc ever since the arraignment of Howie Traynor. It was a thought just below the surface at the back of his mind, a tickle or a minor itch that he couldn't scratch. It wasn't there all the time, but it wouldn't completely dissipate either.

Marc was seated at one end of Margaret Tennant's dining room table working on a tricky divorce case. Margaret was working on several files at the other end of the table.

His divorce case was between a couple in their mid-seventies and was quite acrimonious. Marc represented the husband and the reason for the difficulty was entirely on him. In fact, the wife had started the divorce because, as her lawyer told him, she was, "Tired of waiting for the mean old bastard to die."

While he worked on his pleadings for a discovery motion made necessary by the recalcitrance of his client, it suddenly occurred to him what was bothering him. Marc put down his pen, folded his hands, looked past Margaret and thought about what had just popped into his head. Marc stared straight ahead like this for over a minute until Margaret looked up and noticed him.

"What?" she asked.

"Hmm?" Marc murmured.

"You're thinking about something, what is it?"

"Oh, um, something about the Traynor case," he quietly said.

"You want to talk about it?"

"Put your judge hat on and let me ask you a question."

"Okay, go ahead."

"The cops get a search warrant...this is all hypothetical, of course, okay?"

"Sure."

"Anyway," he continued, "the cops get a valid search warrant for a specific apartment in a specific apartment building."

"Okay," Margaret nodded.

"During the course of the search, one of them wanders down the building's hallway, finds a janitor's closet and goes in. Inside he finds evidence, I won't tell you what yet, to use against the defendant. Is it admissible?"

Margaret thought about it for a moment then asked, "Was the closet door locked?"

"You know, I don't know, but I'd guess not. For now, let's assume it was."

"If it was locked then you could argue the cop had no right to go inside and it would be inadmissible."

"What if it wasn't locked?"

"Then, I'd want to see some case law on it, but my guess is the closet would be considered a common area for the tenants and anyone lawfully in the building. The person they were searching would have no expectation of privacy for anyone lawfully in the building. If that's true, then the evidence would be admissible."

"Which is probably the case since I know this cop and I don't see him picking a lock to get into a janitor's closet."

"Why did he go into it in the first place? What caused him to look in there at all?" Margaret asked.

Marc hesitated for a moment then said, "You know, that's an excellent question. Why would he bother? Why would he, during a search of the defendant's apartment, expect to find something in a janitor's closet, especially one that all of the tenants can access?"

"Worth checking," Margaret said.

"You're very smart," Marc said with an admiring look.

"I know," Margaret replied and patted herself on the back.

"That's why I keep you around."

"That's disappointing. I thought it was my smoking hot body and insatiable sex drive."

"That too."

"Speaking of which," she continued rolling her eyes toward the stairs leading to her bedroom. "Getting to be about that time, don't you think?'

The next day Marc skipped up the backstairs leading to his office taking them two at a time. When he reached the building's second floor he was light headed and out of breath. The life of a practicing lawyer did not always allow for regular exercise. He regained his composure and went into his office.

That morning on the drive from Margaret's to his apartment to change clothes, an idea came to him. Someone must have told Owen Jefferson to check out the janitor's closet and what to look for, especially on the roof. And Marc had a pretty good idea who that someone might be.

The day before, after the arraignment, Marc had left a message for Maddy Rivers. He was going to need an investigator and he believed she would jump at the chance. Normally she would have called him back within minutes. Oddly, so far, she had not returned his call.

His number one suspect for the heads up to Jefferson about the closet was Tony Carvelli. Providing a little clandestine information to them is something Marc could see Tony doing. Madeline's failure to return his call was starting to make him wonder if she was involved as well.

He settled into his office chair and placed calls and left messages for both Tony and Maddy. The rest of the morning was spent with other cases and billing his time. Shortly after eleven, Carolyn buzzed him for a call from Maddy.

"I was beginning to wonder if you got my message," he said.

"Yeah, I did. Listen, um, we need to talk. Can we meet for lunch in a half hour or so?"

"That 'we need to talk' line usually means your girlfriend is about to dump you. I know that's not the case so, what's up?"

"I don't want to talk over the phone. I'll buy you lunch for a change."

They agreed upon a place and time and Marc arrived at the restaurant to find her already waiting for him.

"Okay, so what's going on that you haven't returned my call?" Marc asked.

Maddy hesitated to answer and then the waitress appeared. The two of them ordered their lunch and she left.

"I can't work for you on the Traynor case, Marc. I have a conflict and I'm not sure how much I can tell you," she finally replied. "I'm really sorry. You know I love working with you, but I can't this time. Don't hate me," she added with a sorrowful, pleading look.

"Hate you?" Marc said completely taken aback by that comment. "Of course, I don't hate you. Why would you say such a thing?"

"Thanks," she said, obviously relieved. "I was worried you'd be mad."

Marc silently stared at her thinking about what she had told him and knowing why.

"What? Say something," she nervously said.

"Did the cops send you into Howie's building or did you and Tony come up with that on your own?"

At that moment, the waitress reappeared with their lunch salads. Maddy used the time she was serving the two of them to gather her thoughts before replying to Marc's surprising but accurate question.

"Why, ah, why would you think…"

"Madeline!" Marc sternly whispered. He was leaning across the table, the lawyer cross examining a hostile witness now. "Stop it. I know it was you and Tony. I know who your client is, and she shall remain nameless. But, I have every right to know what the hell is going on here. Don't try to play me, okay?"

"Yes, sir," she meekly replied.

"I'm going to rephrase the question. I want you to listen carefully and answer only this question. Okay?"

"Yes, I get it."

"Was it you that found the stairway to the apartment roof in the hallway janitor's closet?"

"Yes," she quietly answered.

"Did you break into the building at the behest of the police?"

"No," she defiantly answered. "The cops knew nothing about it. And I didn't break into the building at all. I went to the front door and a woman, I assume she was a tenant, came out and let me in."

For the next few minutes the two good friends picked at their salads in silence. Madeline had convinced herself that she could beg off working with Marc on the Traynor defense by simply claiming a conflict of interest. When he verbally slapped her by asking her about being in Traynor's apartment building, she was almost stunned. Now that fact was out in the open and she could not put it back.

At the same time, Marc was contemplating the dilemma he was in. His legal, moral, and ethical responsibility was to go after her on behalf of his client. If he did, she could lose her P.I. license and maybe go to jail. Marc knew she broke into Howie's apartment. He knew she was quite capable of it and that was the real reason she went into the building. He made up his mind he would not ask her about it unless he absolutely had to.

"Your opinion of me means a great deal to me," Maddy said. "I don't want to ruin that."

"My opinion of you hasn't changed a bit," Marc replied with a smile. "He reached across the table with both hands to hold both of hers. "I will do everything I can to protect you, but my first duty is to my client. Do you understand?"

"Of course," she said with a weak smile and a squeeze of his hands.

He released her hands then leaned back in the booth. After a moment he sighed and said, "I won't ask you what else, if anything, you did in that building unless I absolutely have to, which I may have to do. Okay?"

"I understand," she said. "Marc, there's something I want to tell you, but it has to be off the record. Will you promise me that?"

"Madeline, I can't do that," he said. He hesitated then added, "Or at least I shouldn't. Okay, you have my word, it will be just between you and me."

She leaned forward as did Marc and their noses were barely inches apart. "The evidence the cops found in his apartment, the barbed wire, wire cutters and gloves were not there the day before."

"Are you sure?" he asked then quickly added, "Never mind. Don't answer that."

Remaining in her position leaning across the table, she added, "I'll tell you something else, too. This you can use. Tony and me and a few retried cop friends of his did surveillance on your guy for about three weeks."

"When?"

"Tony will have a record. Lay a subpoena on him and he'll give it to you. I don't have all the details. But, I know it was during the time of the first three killings. That judge up North, that woman prosecutor, what's-her-name…"

"Rhea Watson," Marc said.

"Right and the judge, the second one…"

"Peterson?"

"Yeah, him. Then we dropped it because Traynor wasn't doing anything."

"Why did Vivian Donahue want him watched?" Marc asked. "Off the record, of course."

"Because he murdered her aunt and she wanted someone to check him out. Keep an eye on him. She didn't believe his 'I found Jesus' act and neither do I. Do you?"

"I don't know," Marc said. "It really doesn't matter what I believe."

FORTY-ONE

Gene Parlow and his younger brother Troy were heading south on I-35W. At Burnsville, the freeway coming out of Minneapolis, I-35W joined I-35E coming from St. Paul to re-form to become southbound I-35. About a mile past the junction of the two parts of I-35, the brothers opened up their Harleys. Traffic was still fairly heavy but concern about ending up on a slab in a morgue was never high on their list. Weaving in and out of traffic also made it impossible for the two MPD cops to keep up with them.

They covered the fifty miles to Faribault in less than forty minutes. Approximately half-way through the small city they exited the freeway. Heading southwest the brothers drove four miles and arrived at their destination; a public beach and picnic area on Cannon Lake. Because it was an October weekday the area was completely empty. As instructed they parked their bikes and found a picnic table to sit at and wait. Thirty minutes later a black Escalade parked next to the bikes and four men got out to join them.

One of the four men was nattily dressed in a charcoal gray three-piece suit. He sat on the picnic bench opposite the Parlows and, as Troy began to speak, held up a hand to stop him.

"Stand up, both of you," one of the bodyguards said.

The brothers were quickly searched for weapons then the same bodyguard pointed a finger at Gene Parlow and said, "You, shed those clothes including pants and underwear."

"What the hell is this..." Troy sputtered looking at the man in the suit.

He returned the look and again silenced Troy this time holding an index finger to his lips.

Gene Parlow quickly stripped and proved he was not wearing a wire. While this was taking place, the fourth man did a search of the two motorcycles looking for tracking devices.

"I'm a careful man, Mr. Parlow," the man in the suit said. Gene had put his clothes on and the two of them were again seated at the picnic table. "That's why I've never spent five minutes in a police station." The man's name was Sandy Baker and he was the head of the meth business Troy Parlow worked for.

"I understand, Mr. Baker..." Gene began to say.

"I don't think you do," Baker interrupted him. "Troy asked me to meet you about a job. I'm afraid I can't do that. You see, you're still very toxic."

"What do you mean?" Troy asked.

209

Baker turned to Troy and said, "The fact you don't know tells me everything. The cops are all over both of you. I'm surprised they don't have a tracking device on your motorcycles. They will after today. Did you know you were being followed today? You lost them south of Lakeville. I had a car on them following you. I have it on good authority they're still on you and this Aaron Forsberg guy because of this serial killer business in the Cities."

"They arrested someone for that!" Gene protested.

"Tell that to the police," Baker quietly replied. "Until the heats off, I can't use you."

"How do you know this?" Troy asked.

"That's irrelevant, Troy. I know it and that's all that matters. In fact, you're out too."

"You can't do that!" Troy yelled as he started to stand. "This is bull…"

One of the burly men standing behind Troy hit him with a quick, sharp shot to his right kidney. The pain spread up to his neck like a flame and Troy dropped quickly back down on the bench seat.

"Yes, I can, and I just did," Baker replied. "And you'd be well advised to keep your mouths shut."

As instructed, the brothers waited fifteen minutes after Baker and his thugs departed. While they waited, they discussed what could be done about it.

"Forget it, Gene. You'll never get close enough to him. You saw his guys. I'll piss blood for a week after the shot I took. My kidney still hurts like hell."

"We'll see," Gene said. "You know where he lives and where his businesses are?"

"Yeah but, I'm telling you, you'll never get close enough."

Gene looked at his younger brother and angrily said, "Who's this asshole? We could run the business. Let's go."

While the two men walked back to their bikes Troy said, "I might know a way. I know he makes trips to the Cities. Maybe then."

Aaron Forsberg was seated in the reception area oblivious to the very attractive female receptionist working on her computer. He was alone for this meeting with Glenda Albright. It was a meeting she requested.

When he first arrived, the receptionist informed him Albright was on a phone call. That was ten minutes ago, and Albright was apparently still on the call.

Forsberg stood and walked the few steps to the window overlooking Seventh Street. He looked across the street toward Second Avenue and saw the car he expected to find. It was a dark blue Chevy sedan with a man, and a woman sitting in it. What should have annoyed him, and did when the surveillance first started, now brought a smile to his otherwise dour countenance.

He heard the receptionist inform Albright that he was waiting. She ended the call and pleasantly said "Ms. Albright will be right out."

Forsberg perfunctorily thanked her and went back to his chair. Two minutes later Albright appeared.

"I was able to convince them that you deserved more money than the others," Albright told him when they were seated in her office. "They've upped their offer, just for you, to one point eight million. And," she continued by handing him a one-page document, "I've agreed to reduce my fee to twenty per cent. This is a new agreement spelling out the new fee arrangement," she said referring to the document in her hand.

"My net, after fees would be a little less than a million five, all of it paid up front?" Forsberg asked.

"Yes, all of it up front."

"When do you need to know?"

"There's no deadline yet, but soon."

Forsberg slid the unsigned retainer agreement across the desk to her and said, "Give me a couple of days to think about it. It should be ten times that much for what they did to me."

"It's up to you," Albright replied hiding her disappointment. "I don't think we'll do any better dragging this out any longer. You can look into getting the conviction expunged from your record and get your security licenses back."

"I've thought about that," Forsberg agreed. "We'll see."

As he was leaving her office Albright said, "Aaron, you need to get some counseling. This anger you're carrying around is only hurting you."

Forsberg paused at the door, looked at her and said, "I'll think about it. Right now, this anger is exactly what I need."

Forsberg drove the exact speed limit and went directly back to his uncle's. It was mildly amusing to watch the two cops maintain their distance while the traffic went past him. They were having a difficult time staying back and keeping one or two cars between them.

He parked the van in the driveway and walked the front sidewalk to the door. When he reached the door he turned, looked across the street at the empty house and waved at the surveillance team inside.

On the drive home he realized there might be a way to get the cops to back off. Once inside the house he went right to the phone and dialed information. He received the number he wanted then placed the call.

"Marc," Sandy said when Marc answered the intercom. "There's an Aaron Forsberg on the line and he says it's urgent."

"Put him through," Marc replied immediately recognizing the name.

"Mr. Kadella, my name is Aaron Forsberg, I'm one of the men who was wrongfully convicted with a doctored DNA report…"

"I know, Mr. Forsberg. I recognized the name. What can I do for you?"

"I thought you might be interested to know that the police are still following me. And I think they're following Gene Parlow as well."

"Really?" Marc asked.

"Yeah, and, since they arrested Howie Traynor I'm wondering why? Why continue to follow us if they think he did those killings?"

"Good question," Marc said. "Are you sure?"

"Do you have something to write with? I'll give you the license plate number of the car they were using today."

Forsberg told it to him while Marc made a note of the plate number, make and model of the car.

"And there's a team of cops still set up in an empty house across the street." Forsberg told Marc the house's address and Marc made a note of that as well.

When he finished, Marc thanked him for the call then thought about the best way to use the information.

FORTY-TWO

It was almost two weeks since Marc Kadella received the call from Aaron Forsberg. During that time, he had made up his mind about what to do with the information that Forsberg was still under surveillance. Clearly the police were still uncertain that his client was guilty. Instead of confronting the prosecution with this information and giving them an opportunity to correct it, Marc decided to keep it to himself for now.

Marc and at least twelve other people got off the overflowing elevator on the fourteenth floor. The mob headed toward the hallway and Judge Koch's courtroom. Marc went to the inner hall security doors and pressed the buzzer to notify a deputy. A few seconds later a deputy opened the door and let him in.

"Good afternoon, Mr. Kadella. Come in," the deputy said.

"Hello, Shirley. Big crowd today?"

"Full house," she replied.

Marc went into the courtroom through the judge's door then placed his briefcase on the table nearest the jury box. Knowing the trial would take place here, he wanted to stakeout his claim to that table. A few minutes later he sat down at the table in the juror's room across from Howie.

"Did you talk to Father John about the gloves?" Howie asked.

"Yeah, a couple of weeks ago, why? I thought I told you. He backs up your claim that you told him they'd been stolen, and he told the police."

"Sorry, I'm nervous. I couldn't remember if you told me that," Howie said.

"It's okay. Relax. This is not the trial. It's a hearing to look at probable cause, some evidentiary problems and a couple motions."

"What if the judge decides they didn't have probable cause?" Howie asked.

"Then you walk. Don't hold your breath. She won't second guess the grand jury," Marc answered. "But, it's also an opportunity to look at their evidence. They'll have to put a couple people on the stand to testify."

"Who?"

"I'm guessing the lead cop, Owen Jefferson; the medical examiner and someone from the BCA to testify about the hair."

There was a knock on the door, a deputy looked in and told them Steve Gondeck had arrived. Marc and Howie went into the courtroom and a slight buzz went through the crowd. Because Marc knew the media would be in full attendance he made sure Howie looked

213

presentable. Marc again provided him with tan khakis, a blue button-down dress shirt, clean socks and brown loafers.

Marc had filed pleadings to support the motions to be decided today. Gondeck had also filed his pleadings to counter Marc's requests and to argue for an aggravated sentence in the event of a guilty verdict. Gondeck wanted the judge to go way beyond the prison time the sentencing guidelines recommended in the event of a second-degree murder conviction. If there was a first-degree conviction, Traynor would receive an immediate sentence of life without parole.

Owen Jefferson was the first witness. He was called because Marc wanted the evidence obtained from the roof of Howie's apartment excluded. Jefferson testified about searching the janitor's closet and how he found the stairs to the roof.

When Jefferson finished, Marc argued the search of the entire building was illegal. First he argued the search warrant for Howie's apartment was not obtained by sufficient probable cause. This was quickly dismissed. He then tried to convince the judge that the search warrant did not cover the janitor's closet.

Attached to his pleadings was case law he found to support his argument. Gondeck had submitted more accurate case law to validate the search. It came down to the fact that the police were legally in the building. Given that fact, the unlocked closet was a common area in which Howie Traynor had no personal expectation of privacy and the search was valid. Judge Koch quickly dismissed Marc's argument.

The rest of the hearing was spent with testimony from the M.E., Clyde Marston and a tech from the BCA. Marston testified about the autopsy results of each victim and the cause of death. The BCA tech told the judge about the hair samples and the likelihood of a match to anyone other than Howie Traynor, roughly one in twelve million. Marc watched and quietly listened to the strength of the prosecution's witnesses and evidence. When his turn to cross examine them came, not wanting to show the prosecution anything, he passed on both.

After the testimony was finished and the judge found sufficient probable cause, the lawyers argued about Marc's change of venue motion. At times the exchange even became a bit heated. Due to the media coverage Marc had a strong argument to make. But, he also had the burden of proving to the judge that his client could not obtain a fair trial in Hennepin County. Gondeck argued successfully that finding twelve jurors and several alternates who had not followed the case would not be as difficult as it seemed. In the end, Koch ruled against the defense.

Finally, the hearing concluded after the argument about an aggravated sentence. Gondeck wanted an upward departure and consecutive sentencing on each charge. He argued the exceptional cruelty clearly backed him up.

Judge Koch told the lawyers she would take it under advisement and did not rule on it. Gondeck didn't seem to care. He got what he wanted. A little more publicity about the exceptionally vicious nature of the murders and the suffering the victims went through.

"Is your client willing to waive his right to a speedy trial?" Judge Koch asked Marc.

"No, your Honor, he is not," Marc replied.

"Very well. I'll see the lawyers next Thursday at 10:00 a.m. for a scheduling conference. Will that work for you?"

Both lawyers answered affirmatively, and the hearing concluded.

While the media hurried out to file their reports and the crowd dwindled, Marc met with Howie in the jury room again.

"We didn't do too good today," Howie glumly stated.

"About what I thought we'd get," Marc replied. "We did better than you think. I got some information today I didn't have before and some statements made under oath that we can use. This is just round one. We have a long way to go."

"Why didn't you want to waive a speedy trial?" Howie asked.

"You like sitting in jail?"

"No, you're right. I was just wondering."

"Mostly because I didn't want to give them more time to find more evidence. Some of these charges are weak. If we can convince the jury they overcharged hoping something would stick they might get pissed at the prosecution. Who knows? We'll see but we might as well get at it."

They rose to leave, shook hands and Howie ruefully said, "At least I'll get back in time to see that woman on TV, Melinda what's-her-name…"

"Pace," Marc said.

"Yeah, her. I'll get back in time to see her slander and convict me on TV some more."

While Owen Jefferson was on the witness stand the phone in his pocket vibrated. In fact, it went off four more times before he finished testifying and was dismissed.

When he reached the hallway, he checked it and saw the same number for all five calls. He put the phone to his ear, listened to the message and returned the call.

"What's up, Scott?" Jefferson asked the man who had made the calls, Detective Scott Brown.

"We got a homicide here you'll want to see." Brown gave him a quick description and the location. Jefferson assured him he would be there as quickly as possible.

Jefferson took a minute to call Marcie Sterling to tell her about what he had been told. She agreed to get their department issued car and pick him up. Less than twenty minutes after speaking with Detective Brown, Jefferson and Marcie were at the scene.

Marcie parked on the south Minneapolis street a half block from the crime scene. They passed through the yellow tape at the mouth of the alley and quickly walked to the small crowd of cops and forensic techs.

"Hey, Owen. Hi Marcie," Scott Brown greeted them.

"Scott, Aaron," Jefferson said in return to Brown and his partner, Detective Aaron Hernandez as he and Marcie snapped on protective gloves.

"Recognize this?" Hernandez asked while he held up a man's driver's license.

Jefferson and Marcie read the name and Jefferson said, "Eugene Parlow. Your vic is Eugene Parlow? The Eugene Parlow on our whiteboard?"

"Take a look, you tell me," Brown suggested.

Jefferson and Marcie went over to where a CSU tech was kneeling in between two dumpsters. The CSU saw them and stood to give the two detectives an unobstructed view of the body.

Lying on his back, his dead eyes still open staring blankly at the sky, was an obviously dead Eugene Parlow. There were two bloody spots on his gray T-shirt and a hole in his forehead with a trickle of blood leaking from it.

"That's him," Marcie said while Jefferson knelt to examine the body. "That's our Eugene Parlow."

"Three gunshot wounds," Maggie Dayton, the M.E. on scene said. "Two in the chest, one in the forehead. They appear to be nine-millimeter."

"Professional," Jefferson said as he stood. "This was no gangbanger."

"And he wasn't killed here," Dayton added referring to the lack of blood at the scene.

"No, he wasn't," Jefferson agreed.

"Owen," Scott Brown said, "I need to show you something."

Jefferson and Marcie followed Brown a few feet across the alley.

"This," Brown said pointing at a heavy canvass bag, the size of a gym bag, lying on the ground. "Look inside."

The two detectives knelt next to it, Jefferson unzipped and opened the bag. They looked inside at the objects it contained and Jefferson softly said, "Jesus Christ. What the hell..."

They continued to kneel while Jefferson moved a couple of the items in the bag to examine the others. A minute or so later he stood up.

"Scott, Aaron," he said to his fellow detectives. Jefferson took a deep breath while Marcie continued to check out the items in the bag he said, "Treat this like any other homicide. Bag and tag this," he continued pointing at the canvass bag and its contents. "But, keep quiet about it, for now."

"Owen, we have to put it in our report..." Hernandez started to protest.

"I know," Jefferson said holding up a hand. "Do what you have to do. Just don't advertise it. I need to talk to the county attorney and let him know what we found."

"Slocum?" Marcie asked.

"No," Jefferson shook his head. "Steve Gondeck."

FORTY-THREE

Jefferson waited with increasing impatience in the reception area to the county attorney offices. He looked up at the clock for at least the tenth time, annoyed with the realization he had been waiting almost an hour. Two minutes later, seconds before he was going to look at the clock again, Steve Gondeck appeared.

"I'm really sorry, Owen," he apologized as the two men shook hands. "Right after you called I got a call from a judge I had to go see. I didn't think it would take this long. Come on back," he explained as he held the door for the detective.

On their way back to the Gondeck's office he whispered to Jefferson, "Slocum wants to sit in."

"Is that good or bad?"

"It's never good," Gondeck answered.

Craig Slocum was the elected Hennepin County Attorney. At one time he was a successful civil litigator in private practice who decided to go into politics. A closet Republican, he had joined the Democrat party in order to win the election in Hennepin County. His ambition to obtain the Governor's mansion had suffered a severe blow a of couple years back. A high-profile case involving the murder of the current governor's daughter had landed on his desk. To further his political ambitions, Slocum tried the case himself only to have it blow up in his face. Ever since then the defense lawyer who had done this to him was, to Slocum, public enemy number one. The defense lawyer's name was Marc Kadella.

The murder of Eugene Parlow the day before had barely made the news. The Star Tribune ran a small story on page seven of the Metro section making it sound like a drug-deal, motorcycle gang killing. So far, no one in the media had made the connection between Parlow and Howie Traynor. Jefferson called Gondeck with the news and they decided to keep a lid on it as long as possible.

"We're in my office," Jefferson heard Gondeck say into his desk phone. "Okay, we'll wait."

Less than a minute later, Slocum joined the two men waiting for him in Gondeck's office.

"Should I have Jennifer join us?" Gondeck asked Slocum referring to another prosecutor, Jennifer Moore. "She's going to second chair this case."

"No," Slocum emphatically said. "We can fill her in later. Now, Detective, Steve tells me you say you have some important evidence to discuss with us."

"Yes, sir," Jefferson began. For the next twenty minutes, while the two lawyers asked questions, Jefferson filled them in on the murder of Eugene Parlow. He concluded with a description of what was found in the canvass bag in the alley near the body.

When Jefferson finished Gondeck turned his attention to Slocum and started to say, "We have to tell..."

Slocum held up a hand to cut him off and stop him.

"Do you have anything else, Detective?" Slocum politely asked.

"No, sir."

"Let me ask you," Slocum continued. "Do you have any evidence conclusively tying the bag and its contents to this Parlow person? Any fingerprints, DNA, hair samples? Anything at all?"

"Um, no. I don't think so. At least not yet," Jefferson answered a bit puzzled.

Slocum stood up and said, "Thank you, Detective. I need to discuss this with Steve alone. I'm sure you understand?"

"Sure, no problem," Jefferson replied.

Slocum opened the office door for him, shook his hand and said, "Keep this quiet for now. Thanks again and be sure to let us know if anything else comes up."

Slocum returned to the chair he was using, looked at Gondeck and said, "You were about to say?"

"We need to inform Traynor's lawyer about this," Gondeck said.

"No, we don't."

"Yes, Craig, we do," Gondeck said with unmistakable emphasis. "It's exculpatory evidence and we have an ethical obligation to tell him."

"I disagree. How do we know the bag belonged to this Parlow person? It was found on the other side of the ally. There is nothing to tie it or its contents to Parlow. No, it's my decision and we will not inform Kadella about it and that's final."

"Craig, you need to get past this hard-on you have for Marc Kadella and act like a professional."

"Stop! You don't need to lecture me about my professional obligation," Slocum interrupted him, the tension between them rising rapidly. More calmly Slocum said, "Look Steve, if the police come up with something more positive to tie the bag to Parlow, we'll revisit the subject. Until then, my decision stands."

Gondeck stared at his boss for several seconds then said, "Okay. It's your call but, you're about to get an email from me spelling out my objections to the decision. If anybody gets jammed up over this, it's not going to be me."

"That's not necessary," an obviously annoyed Slocum replied.

"Yes it is. I'm going to cover my ass on this one," Gondeck said.

"Very well, that's your prerogative," Slocum replied more calmly. "I believe I'm on solid legal ground. We do not have to disclose any of this to Kadella. Especially since the method of Parlow's murder is so different than the others."

"One other thing," Gondeck said. "I almost forgot. Kadella is requesting copies of the police surveillance records of Traynor, Aaron Forsberg and Parlow. He believes these may also be exculpatory."

"No, they are confidential police work product. Fight him in court over them. Make him prove they are or may be exculpatory."

"We're going to lose that, Craig," Gondeck patiently explained. "Those records are exculpatory."

"He can argue it in court on a motion or at trial. I will not help this guy any more than is absolutely necessary."

Early the next day, Marc Kadella was in his office on the phone with Tony Carvelli.

"What makes you think I did surveillance of Howie Traynor?" Tony coyly asked.

"Tony don't do this. Don't try to blow smoke up my ass like this. I'm having enough trouble with Slocum's office getting discovery. Ask Vivian if it's okay to give me the records. I know you, I know you're meticulous and you kept a running log of it. If Vivian objects it's okay. I'll get a subpoena or a court order if I have to."

Carvelli thought it over then said, "I'll get back to you."

"Today?" Marc asked.

"As soon as I can. Let me call her."

"Okay, thanks."

Marc went back to the motion pleadings he was working on. A scheduling conference was coming up next week. The prosecution was not providing any discovery of the evidence such as autopsy reports, DNA results, nothing. In the meantime, he was seeing these things reported on TV and in the newspapers. Knowing Steve Gondeck and having tried several cases with him, Marc believed it wasn't him. It was Slocum who was doing this.

Marc's office intercom buzzed and when he answered it, Carolyn said, "Gabriella Shriqui is on the phone. Do you want to talk to her?"

"What does she want?"

"Didn't say. Should I put her through?"

"Sure," Marc said setting aside the papers he was working on. "I'll give her a few minutes."

"Hello, Marc," Gabriella said.

"What's up and this phone call is off the record. I won't talk about Howard Traynor," Marc said.

"That's not why I'm calling…"

"I still don't have time to help you with your ticking biological clock problem either."

"What?" Gabriella asked, confused by Marc's statement. "Oh, I remember. I'm going to kill Maddy for telling you that."

While Marc laughed Gabriella continued by saying, "I called to find out if the Eugene Parlow in this morning's paper is the same guy as the one who was released from prison because of a doctored DNA test. Do you know anything about it?"

"What are you talking out?"

"In this morning's Strib, in the Metro section on page six. A Eugene Parlow was found murdered in an alley in south Minneapolis yesterday."

A stunned Marc Kadella didn't respond with the news. Finally, Gabriella said, "Marc are you there?"

"Um, yeah. Ah, I was just thinking," he said.

"So, I take it you don't know anything either. I can't get anything out of the cops or Slocum's office. No one seems to know anything about it."

"Bullshit," Marc said. "It's him. How many Eugene Parlow's are there in this town? For some reason they're keeping a lid on it. I have to go, Gabriella. I need to make a phone call."

"Can I call you back?"

Marc paused then said, "I tell you what, you know Steve Gondeck?"

"Yes, I know him."

"Call him in half an hour. If he won't talk to you, call me after lunch."

Two minutes later, Gondeck answered Marc's call.

"Why haven't I been told about the murder of Eugene Parlow?" Marc asked without even saying hello.

"Because we don't believe it had anything to do with Traynor or your case," Gondeck replied.

"At this point, Steve, that's not for you to decide," Marc said barely concealing his anger.

"Wait, Marc. Back it up. Yes, you have a right to know and I was going to call you today," Gondeck lied. "Parlow was found in an alley between two dumpsters. He was shot three times; twice in the chest, once in the forehead. It's a drug-deal, gang killing, Marc."

221

"I'll want all police reports, autopsies, everything. Speaking of which, when am I going to get the rest of my discovery? I've seen news reports on TV about hair samples and DNA but…"

"I don't know where that's coming from," Gondeck protested. "We're working on getting these things to you. I have people I answer to, you know."

This last statement was a clear message to Marc that Slocum was personally monitoring this case. Marc had suspected this all along and Gondeck just confirmed it. They were dragging their feet on Slocum's orders to make Marc's job difficult and to try to get him to waive a speedy trial to give the cops more time to find more evidence.

"Gabriella Shriqui, the reporter from Channel 8 is going to call you in a while. She wants to talk to you about Parlow. Either you talk to her or I will. I'll see you in court next week." With that, Marc ended the call.

Before Marc had a chance to go back to his motion paperwork, his personal cell phone went off. He looked at the ID then answered it.

"What did Vivian tell you?" he asked Tony Carvelli.

"She told me to make you buy me lunch and give you what you want. The lady likes you for some reason I can't explain."

"I'll see you at noon," Marc said.

FORTY-FOUR

The intercom on Steve Gondeck's desk phone buzzed. He looked at the ID and thought about ignoring it. He was busy and not in the mood to play "placate the idiot" as he liked to call it. Giving in against his better judgment he picked up the phone.

"Yes, Craig, what do you need?" Gondeck said as pleasantly as possible.

The county attorney abruptly said, "Come into my office. I have something I want to talk to you about."

"I'm a little busy. I have a scheduling conference for the Traynor case this morning."

"That's what I want to talk to you about. Bring your entire file," Slocum said.

An alarm bell sounded in Gondeck's head, but he acquiesced to his boss' demand anyway. He gathered up the Traynor file and headed out the door.

Ever since their meeting with Owen Jefferson concerning the murder of Eugene Parlow, Gondeck and Slocum had been at odds. In Gondeck's opinion, the Parlow murder and the evidence found at the scene were obviously pertinent to the Traynor case. He strongly believed the prosecution had an ethical responsibility to inform Traynor's lawyer and turn over the information about that crime to him.

Slocum had taken the opposite view. The canvas bag found near Parlow's body could not be positively linked to Parlow and therefore, so he argued, it was not relevant to Traynor's case.

The two men had gone around about this, three or four times, once or twice the argument became a little heated. While walking the short distance to Slocum's large, corner office a feeling of foreboding hung over Gondeck. He had an uneasy feeling he knew what was coming. In his opinion, a huge mistake was about to be made.

Gondeck rapped firmly on the office door, opened it, and went in. Seated in a chair was the mistake he believed Slocum was going to make.

"Come in, Steve," Slocum said. "Have a seat."

Instead of sitting down he stepped over to the man sitting in Slocum's office chair. He handed the man the Traynor file and said, "Here you are Tommy, good luck. You have a scheduling conference with Judge Koch in twenty minutes."

Tommy Harris was Slocum's number one ass-kisser. Slocum brought him into the county attorney's office from the firm they were with when both were in private practice. Harris was passed over for partner by that firm for the third time and jumped at the chance when

Slocum became county attorney. He was a fair trial lawyer but not in Gondeck's class. As far as Slocum was concerned he had a far more significant virtue. Harris could be counted on to strictly adhere to Slocum's bidding without question.

A slightly shocked Slocum said, "You're not going to argue with me about it?"

Gondeck look at Slocum shrugged and said, "You're the boss. It's entirely your decision."

"I appreciate that, Steve. I just think you're a little too close to Traynor's lawyer, Kadella. No hard feelings?"

"No, Craig, not at all," Gondeck lied while thinking Slocum was letting his personal, petty feelings toward Marc Kadella cloud his judgment.

When Gondeck got back to his office, he stood behind his desk staring out the large window overlooking south Minneapolis. Barely two minutes later, he heard a knock on his door and an angry Jennifer Moore stormed in slamming the door behind her.

"It wasn't my call," Gondeck said holding his hands up as if to ward her off. "He took the case away from me."

"Slocum?" she quietly asked somewhat mollified.

"Who else?"

"Who has it?"

"Guess," Gondeck smiled.

"Not Tommy Harris. Tell me that didn't happen," she replied.

"Yes indeed."

Jennifer paused then said, "Now I'm glad they took me off. Who's second chair?"

"Not sure. Probably one of the new guys. They'll want a gofer who will do anything he's told."

Jennifer shrugged her shoulders then said, "Okay, I guess. Sorry to barge in on you. I thought you did it."

"I wouldn't and don't worry about it."

Marc turned the corner away from the elevators to get to Judge Koch's courtroom. Once again he ran into a small herd of media members and court junkies in front of courtroom 1424. One of the media people spotted him and before he could react he was surrounded by them.

"I have no comment about anything," Marc quickly said as he retreated back from where he came. He reached the court chamber's area security doors and pushed the buzzer on the intercom. A moment later a deputy opened the door and while the reporters continued to harangue Marc with questions, the deputy let him in.

Marc found two men standing in the back hallway at the door to Koch's chambers. One of them he recognized, the other younger one, he did not know at all.

"Are you guys here for the Traynor conference?" he asked.

The lawyer he vaguely knew introduced himself as Tommy Harris. The younger man told Marc he was Paul Ramsey. The three of them shook hands.

"What happened to Steve Gondeck?" Marc asked.

"I've been assigned to handle this case," Harris said avoiding Marc's question.

Marc remembered what he had heard about Tommy Harris. Word was Harris was Slocum's toady and office snitch. Remembering this made Marc realize that Slocum, whom Marc knew despised him, had taken the case away from Gondeck for personal reasons. The realization could not have made Marc happier. Steve Gondeck was a far better and more experienced lawyer.

"I was wondering if we could talk about a continuance of today's hearing and your client waiving his right to a speedy trial," Harris asked.

"Sorry, no to both," Marc replied.

"It's just that we were assigned this case this morning and..."

"Craig Slocum should have thought of that before he threw his little temper tantrum and removed Gondeck," Marc replied.

"So, you won't..."

"No, I won't," Marc said smiling.

"Come in and have a seat, gentlemen," Koch said as the three lawyers filed into her chambers. "I want to do this in here to avoid the press. Where are Steve Gondeck and Jennifer Moore? I thought they were trying this case."

Tommy Harris explained to her that the case had been reassigned as the lawyers took their seats.

"I can't tell Craig Slocum who to assign to work his cases but, you tell him this had better be it. You two are the attorneys of record unless one of you dies. Is that clear?"

"Yes, your Honor," both men answered her.

When the court reporter indicated she was ready, Judge Koch took a moment to read the case information into the record. She then had each lawyer in turn state their names and representation for the woman to take down.

"Before we begin, your Honor," Harris said. "I'd like to request a continuance."

"This is exactly why I don't approve of Craig Slocum switching lawyers," Koch sternly admonished him. "My schedule is not subject to his whim. But, I'll let Mr. Kadella decide," she continued believing he had already turned down the request.

"No, your Honor. My client should not be burdened with the expense or delay," Marc said.

"No, it is," Koch said. Looking at Marc she asked, "Mr. Kadella, I assume they asked about waiving a speedy trial."

"Yes, your Honor. No again," Marc answered.

Koch looked at the two prosecutors and said, "There you are. You may have to put in some late nights. Again, something Craig Slocum should've considered. What's next?"

"My motions for discovery, your Honor," Marc said.

"I've read through your pleadings," Koch answered him. She looked at Harris and said, "What's the problem? Why isn't he getting what he needs?"

"I haven't had a chance to adequately review the pleadings," Harris protested.

"Too bad," Koch replied. She turned to Marc and said, "Why do you want the police surveillance records?"

"The police had my client under round the clock surveillance during the time of at least some of these murders," Marc answered her. "They create an alibi and are clearly exculpatory."

"Is that true?" Koch asked Harris.

"I'm not sure, your Honor, I..."

"He gets the records," Koch ruled. "What else?"

"Change of venue," Marc said.

"Do you have any evidence to submit other than what's in your pleadings?" Koch asked.

"No, your Honor. It just seems self evident that given the publicity, he can't get a fair trial in Hennepin County."

Koch thought for a moment then said, "I'm going to deny your request. I think we can impanel an unbiased jury. But, if we can't after a reasonable attempt, we'll revisit the issue."

"Sequester the jury," Marc said.

"We'll cross that bridge when we come to it," Koch said. "I'll take it under advisement."

"We would like a gag order issued your Honor," Harris said. "Mr. Kadella is very cozy with several members of the media. He even acted as a lawyer for one at one time, a Ms. Gabriella Shriqui at the Channel 8 facility."

"I remember that," Koch said looking at Marc. "Tell you what, I hate gag orders. They never work anyway. But I'll keep an open mind about it. If things get out of hand, I may impose it later.

"Okay," the judge continued. "Mr. Harris, I'm going to issue an order for you to turn over his discovery requests within ten days. I don't like prosecutors who try to keep things from defense lawyers. Am I clear?"

"Yes, your Honor," Harris replied.

"Now, what about scheduling. I am open in early December. How long to try it?"

"That's entirely too soon," Harris protested.

"It's not up to you," Koch said. "The clock is ticking. Unless the defendant changes his mind," she continued looking at Marc, "we'll start on Monday, November Thirtieth. That will give us almost four weeks to try to finish before Christmas. Clear your calendars.

"I want complete witness lists exchanged and all discovery completed by Friday, November twentieth. That will give us time to hear any last-minute motions the week of Thanksgiving. You wanted a speedy trial, Mr. Kadella, you're about to get one."

By the time the local noon TV news reports aired, the word about the trial scheduling had already been leaked. Marc knew it did not come from him. He was also certain it had not been leaked by the judge. Slocum's office, as usual, was a sieve.

FORTY-FIVE

"Hey," Carolyn said as Marc came through the office door when he returned after the conference in Judge Koch's chambers. "Take this, you'll want to see it right away," she continued holding a message slip for him.

Marc shifted his briefcase to his left hand and took the pink piece of paper from her. He read the brief note and asked, "He called about an hour ago? This is a relief. I've been trying to get a hold of him for two weeks," he continued without waiting for Carolyn to confirm the time of the call.

"He said he was in Europe on vacation and got back last night," Carolyn told him.

Marc looked at the wall clock behind Carolyn's desk. Noting the time and driving distance, he made a quick mental calculation. "He should be here around three this afternoon," he said out loud to himself.

"He said you could call him on his cell. That's the number," Carolyn said referring to a phone number on the message.

"I will. Thanks, Carolyn," Marc added hurrying to his office.

"Hello Jason and thanks for calling," Marc said when the man answered his call.

"Sorry I missed you, Marc. I was in Europe. But I'm on my way. Give me a quick update."

The man's name was Jason Biggs and he was a criminalist Marc had used before with very good results. A criminalist is basically an independent CSI type investigator. Briggs was in his early fifties, though he looked older because of his bald head and diminutive frame. He earned a bachelor's degree in forensic science from Northwestern and his masters from Boston University. Briggs then spent ten years with the Chicago police department and six more in the Chicago office of the FBI. He watched many people of lesser ability make a lot more money as independent agents and over ten years ago decided to go that route himself. Because of his reputation from the CPD and FBI, he immediately tripled his income and worked less doing it.

"Have you heard about my case?"

"I went online and looked it up this morning before I called. You've got yourself a nasty one."

"Yeah. Here's the deal. There's a lot of physical evidence connected to the bodies. You'll need to go over those. Plus, autopsy reports although the ones I've seen make the cause of death seem pretty obvious with the exception of one who appears to have died from a heart attack probably brought on when he was hit with a Taser. I haven't received any toxicology test results yet on any of them."

"What about crime scenes?"

"I've been through all of them. The Minneapolis cops are pretty good and thorough. You'll want to take a look but I'm not sure what you'll find."

"Witnesses?" Briggs asked.

"A few civilians but not many. No eyewitnesses to the crimes. Mostly people who found the bodies. I'll talk to them myself. A lot of cops, M.E. personnel and DNA techs."

"What was tested for DNA?"

"A few hair samples and the inside of a pair of gloves. We'll need to get our own test done."

"How many hairs?"

"Four total."

"Anything else we'll need to test for DNA?"

"Not so far. They haven't found my guy's DNA on anything else so…"

"We don't want to test anything else and find it for them," Briggs said completing Marc's thought.

"Exactly. There's a lot of metal to test. Barbed wire."

"No problem. I can do that myself. I have the equipment and know how to do that. I can't do DNA myself, but I know several excellent labs to do it for us," Briggs replied.

"If I decide to," Marc said.

"Why wouldn't you?" Briggs asked.

"My guy was convicted once before on flawed DNA testing. I'm not sure I want to verify the test results this time for them. I might be able to use the last faked results against them this time. I just have to figure out how to get it into testimony."

"I see," Briggs said, "interesting. Well, I'll be there between two and three. I'm an hour or so west of Madison now."

"Great Jason and thanks again. It's a relief to know you're coming. Do you want me to get a room for you?"

"Oh, yes, please. I didn't think about that," Briggs replied.

"I'll take care of it. Same place as last time. Do you remember how to get to my office?"

"Yes, I'll come right there when I get to Minneapolis."

"See you soon," Marc said ending the call.

Steve Gondeck was in a surly mood. For the first time in his career he was removed from a case and his ego had taken a hit. Intellectually he knew it was simply Slocum being a petulant ass, but it still annoyed him. Gondeck had even typed up an email to Slocum resigning from his job. He let it sit in his outgoing mail and went for a walk to think it over.

The walk calmed him down and made him realize he had not been removed from the Traynor case because of incompetence. In fact, it was just the opposite. Slocum knew that with Gondeck in charge of the prosecution, Slocum would be frozen out of any meaningful involvement. Slocum knew that giving the case to his personal office pet would put Slocum in total control.

By the time he got back to the government center building, Gondeck had made a couple of decisions. He took the street-level escalator up to the building's main floor and found a bank of pay phones. He looked up the number he wanted on his personal phone and, not wanting the call to be traced to his phone, called from the pay phone.

The woman answered, and he identified himself. They agreed to meet for lunch away from downtown right away. Gondeck then took an elevator back to his office. He deleted his resignation email and quickly typed and printed a note, found a blank envelope and left to meet his lunch date.

Gondeck entered the Applebee's in a suburb on the western fringe of the Metro area. Gabriella Shiriqui was sitting near the hostess stand waiting for him. She rose to greet him, and the hostess showed them to a table.

"I'm really nervous about this Gabriella. In all my years with the county attorney's office, I have never done this; meet with a reporter clandestinely like this," Gondeck said.

"And you're worried about your job," Gabriella stated.

"Yeah, I'd get fired in a heartbeat," Gondeck agreed.

"Tell you what," Gabriella smiled, reached across the table to pat his hand reassuringly and said, "if I use what you have, I'll refer to where I got it as 'sources close to the investigation' and I'll be sure to use the plural sources. I'll go to jail to protect you, okay?"

"Fair enough," Gondeck said more relaxed with Gabriella's assurance.

They ordered lunch and while they did, Gondeck gave her a quick rundown on the case against Howie Traynor. Almost everything he told her, at first, was already known to her. After their dishes were cleared he got to the good part. He gave her the inside scoop about what happened that morning when he was removed and why Slocum did it.

"So, Slocum's got a personal grudge against Marc Kadella," she said when Gondeck paused. "Interesting and unprofessional but hardly the stuff of headlines. I mean, I'll use it but…"

"That's not the worst of it," Gondeck interrupted her. "There's more. Slocum is deliberately withholding evidence, exculpatory evidence from the defense."

"Isn't that unethical? I thought he had a legal duty to…"

"Yes, he does," Gondeck agreed.

"What evidence is he withholding?"

"That, I can't tell you. He'll know where it came from. But," he continued as he removed the envelope with the note in it from his inside coat pocket, "I want you to do me a favor, please." He handed the envelope to her and said, "Call Marc Kadella and give him this. Then wait for him to read it. I have spelled it out for him and wrote in it that he can tell you as long as you protect me. He needs to get this."

She took the sealed envelope from him and said, "What if I decide to open this and read it myself?"

Gondeck shrugged and said, "Once we leave here I can't stop you, but I've heard you're honest and ethical. Besides you'll get an exclusive on it anyway."

"I'll call Marc and see him as quickly as possible."

Marc's phone buzzed and when he answered it Carolyn let him know Gabriella had arrived. When she left the restaurant, she called Marc to let him know she had something for him and wanted to see him right away. The reporter in her resented being used as a go-between like this but also realized Gondeck and Kadella would both owe her a favor. Besides, something told her she was about to get a juicy piece of information about Slocum.

"Hi, Gabriella. Come in," Marc said when he went into the common area.

Once they were both seated in his office, Gabriella handed Marc the envelope and said, "The letter inside will tell you why I'm here. At least that's what I was told."

Marc slit open the envelope with a letter opener he had in his desk. He leaned back in his chair and read the note from Gondeck.

"Sonofabitch," he softly said when he finished. He shook his head and continued by saying. "That goddamn Slocum. What a petty, petulant ass he is."

"What? Tell me," Gabriella eagerly said.

Marc leaned forward, pulled his chair up against the desk and handed the note to Gabriella. She took a minute to read it over and when she finished softly said, "Sonofabitch." She looked at Marc and added, "Does this mean what I think it means? That Traynor may be innocent and Craig Slocum is suppressing evidence that you could use to prove it?"

"We'll find out," Marc said. "How are you going to report it?"

"I'll ah, just say 'sources close to the investigation' as my source. I have to run," she added as she stood up still holding the note.

"Uh, uh," Marc said. "Give me the note. That's going in the shredder."

"Oh, sure," she said slyly smiling as she handed it back to him.

"Don't use the part about Slocum not disclosing this evidence because of personal antipathy toward me. He would know where that came from. And, keep my name out of it, too," Marc said.

"Good afternoon," Melinda began. "I'm Melinda Pace and this is the *Court Reporter*.

"I have a bombshell to bring you today and we are live because it just came in. With me in the studio is Channel 8 reporter Gabriella Shriqui with our exclusive news."

The camera moved away to show both women seated at Melinda's anchor desk. Melinda turned to Gabriella and said, "What do you have for us?"

Gabriella turned to face the camera and said, "Sources close to the investigation of the Crown of Thornes case have revealed information to me about the prosecution's office that could be both unethical and illegal.

"Last week the murdered body of Eugene Parlow was found in an alley in South Minneapolis. He had been shot three times. Parlow is one of the men, along with Howard Traynor, who was investigated for the Crown of Thornes killings. The police were closely watching him because he was one of the men released from prison after it was revealed the DNA test used to convict him was doctored by a lab technician. In fact, my sources tell me that Parlow and Traynor knew each other.

"At the scene where Eugene Parlow's body was found, the police discovered a bag nearby containing a coiled length of barbed wire, wire cutters, a Taser stun gun device and a hammer and nails. These are the exact same items that were used in all of the Crown of Thornes murders.

"It was also revealed that Craig Slocum, the Hennepin County Attorney personally made the decision that because these items were believed to be unconnected to Parlow's murder, there would be no lab testing done on any of the items found in the bag. Mr. Slocum also decided that because this was not to be used in the prosecution of Howard Traynor, the county attorney's office had no obligation to reveal any of this to Traynor's lawyer.

"In addition, the judge who presided over Parlow's trial in which the faulty DNA test was used against Parlow was Judge Ross Peterson. The prosecutor was Rhea Watson, the judge who handled his appeal was the man murdered outside Bemidji, Robert Smith and Cara Meyers was his lawyer. All of these people are victims and tied to the Crown of Thornes."

"That doesn't necessarily mean Howard Traynor is innocent," Melinda pointed out. "As you said, Traynor and Parlow knew each other."

"Vaguely," Gabriella said. "There's no evidence to believe they worked together."

"There's no evidence to believe they didn't either," Melinda said.

"I suppose that's technically true," Gabriella agreed smiling yet silently seething at Melinda playing Devil's Advocate for Craig Slocum. "But, at the very least, the prosecution has to legally tell the defense about this. And, I can't help wonder if this had something to do with Slocum's decision to change lawyers for the prosecution."

Within minutes of Gabriella's report the switchboard at the county attorney's office lit up like a Christmas tree. The receptionists taking the calls spent the next hour issuing no comment statements to the reporters, locally, statewide and nationally, who wanted answers from Slocum.

The next day Slocum put out a press release denying any intent to withhold evidence. He claimed the bag was not found with Parlow's body and there was no evidence to directly tie the bag to Parlow. It also stated he would release the information to Traynor's lawyer as soon as possible.

FORTY-SIX

The Twin Cities Metro area received four inches of snow during the night. This was the first measurable snow storm of the season and the heavy, wet, sloppy stuff made a mess of the streets. Despite the fact that snow was hardly a rarity in Minnesota, many of the natives drove as if they had never seen it before. Traffic was barely moving at a crawl, especially in Minneapolis where plowing was not always deemed a necessity.

Marc spent the Thanksgiving weekend at Margaret Tennant's relaxing and acting like a normal person. Fortunately, he was in a relationship with a woman who understood the stress he was under and realized trial work is not a nine to five job.

Marc pulled into the early morning line entering the underground parking at the government center. Waiting in line as traffic moved by on Third Avenue spraying his SUV with sloppy, dirty snow did nothing to calm his nerves. No matter how many trials he did, on the morning of the first day his nerves were always as tight as a bowstring. He drummed his fingers on the steering wheel and silently urged the line to move faster.

Marc found an empty parking space in the underground garage. The weather geeks were calling for two to three more inches during the day which would make the drive home a pain.

While still in his car before heading up to the courtroom, Marc took a few minutes to think over his case. He had crammed six months of trial preparation into as many weeks. The realization that the prosecution had the same amount of time was somewhat comforting. What brought him more relief was the fact that the cops had not discovered any additional evidence; at least none that he knew about.

Lost in his thoughts while gathering up his briefcase, he did not notice the man coming up the side of his car. Suddenly there were two sharp raps on his window which made him jump six inches and grab his chest. Staring down at him was the friendly, familiar face of his officemate, Barry Cline.

Marc opened the car door and as he was getting out said, "You just took five years off my life."

"Sorry," Barry insincerely said with a big grin. "What do you say we go upstairs and pick a jury?"

"Yeah, let's. The sooner I get at it the better I'll feel," Marc said.

"Marc, everybody goes through those first day jitters. You'll be fine."

"I know, let's go."

They checked in with Judge Koch's clerk who took both of them back to the judge's chambers. On their way back, Marc asked the clerk if the prosecution had arrived. He received a negative response then asked why they were seeing the judge ex parte.

"The TV lawyers are taking another shot at getting the camera's turned on. Judge Koch told me to bring you back as soon as you got here."

"Good morning, gentlemen," the judge said when they entered her chambers. As they sat down on her couch, she continued by asking, "Mr. Cline, to what do we owe the pleasure of your appearance?"

"I'm co-counsel for the defense, your Honor. I filed my appearance with your clerk," Barry said.

For the next fifteen minutes during which Tommy Harris and Paul Ramsey arrived, the lawyers for the broadcast media made one final pitch to the judge.

"The court of appeals said no, and I've said no. I gave you this opportunity as a courtesy but, I haven't heard anything new," Koch said when the last of the lawyers finished. "What do you think, Mr. Kadella?"

"I think they've billed enough time to this…"

"I resent that!" the lead attorney said glaring at Marc.

"… the answer is still no and it's time we started our trial."

"I agree," Koch replied. "Motion denied. Anything else?" she asked. The judge looked around the room and received no reply. "Good. I'll be out in a few minutes."

With that the small herd of highly priced corporate lawyers filed out followed by Marc, Barry and the prosecutors.

Howie and Father John were waiting for them, seated at the defense table. Marc introduced Barry to both men and reminded Howie that Barry would be helping him with the jury selection. The four of them discussed their seating arrangement and decided to have the priest at the table.

When Tommy Harris saw this, he came to the defense table and said, "I'm going to object to the priest sitting at defense table."

"Take your best shot, Tommy," Marc said.

During the past six weeks, Marc had come to know Tommy Harris and his assistant, Paul Ramsey. Harris was a steady, competent lawyer who wasn't going to excite a jury but likely wouldn't make a big mistake, either. Ramsey was a sharp if inexperienced kid who came from a well-known Minnesota family. In fact, he was a direct descendant of Alexander Ramsey, the state's second governor for whom Ramsey County was named. Despite that, the young prosecutor was a pleasant man and Marc liked him.

Tommy Harris, on the other hand, was obviously Slocum's boy. He never missed an opportunity to let you know of his close, personal friendship with the county attorney. As a joke, Marc had considered buying Harris a pair of knee pads and lip balm. Concern for his client prevailed and he let the thought pass, for now.

Judge Koch came out on the bench a few minutes after nine. She looked over the jam-packed gallery and spent ten minutes politely but firmly explaining court decorum to everyone. When she finished, Harris requested a bench conference.

The four lawyers went up to the bench and Harris argued that the priest's appearance at the defense table was prejudicial. Marc argued his client was allowed spiritual comforting and Koch split the difference. She ruled Father John could not sit at the table but could use one of the chairs in front of the rail directly behind the table but only during jury selection. During the trial she would have the deputies reserve a front row seat for him behind the bar.

While the lawyer's retreated to their seats, Marc looked at the empty chairs behind their table. Something about them bothered him and it finally occurred to him what it was. He missed having Maddy sitting there. In big cases like this, having her there was somehow a comfort and it didn't hurt to have a beautiful woman distracting the jurors.

The prosecutors and the defense had been given a list of one hundred prospective jurors. Each name contained some basic information about that person; things such as age, marital status, employment and a few minor details.

Marc and Barry, with Connie Mickelson and Chris Grafton providing occasional help, had gone over every name on the list. In addition, Sandy and the office paralegal, Jeff Modell, had conducted a thorough internet search of each of them. The two lawyers had put each name into one of three categories; yes, no and maybes. The maybes had then been further classified on a one to ten scale. One being almost a no and ten being almost a yes.

The prosecution was working with a professional team of people to provide jury selection guidance. The firm they hired consisted of sociologists, psychologists, a retired trial judge and lawyers. They believed theirs was a much more scientific method of selecting jurors. Some lawyers swore by them and some swore at them. The simple truth is every lawyer has an opinion about how to select a jury and they are all about as accurate or inaccurate as any. Virtually all of them agree you could probably take the first twelve people you meet on the street and do about as well. No one has the balls to do it.

Because this was a homicide trial, the jurors or, more accurately, the veniremen, by Minnesota court rules must be questioned and selected one at a time. Obviously this would slow the process down significantly.

The prosecution had requested that the identities of the jurors be kept secret. This was the subject of a very heated argument between Marc and Harris. The prosecution argued that since one of the victims was the foreman of Traynor's previous trials, the jurors were not safe from retribution. Marc countered by pointing out that to do so would have the practical effect of sending a clear signal to the jury. The jury could easily infer that the defendant was presumed guilty and must prove his innocence. Keeping their identities secret would tell the jurors they were not safe from the defendant. Fortunately, the judge agreed with Marc.

The first venireman to be brought in was a man named George Zimmer. He was a sixty-seven-year-old, retired firefighter with the Minneapolis Fire Department. Marc had him listed as a "no" for his selections. Likely a little too law and order conservative.

Judge Koch began the questioning of him to probe a bit for any obvious biases. Each prospective juror had received a questionnaire and their answers to these had been provided to both the prosecution and defense. Most of the questions the judge asked were covered in the questionnaire. She asked them anyway because reading a sterile, written document is not the same as having the live person in front of you.

Judge Koch completed the questioning then turned Zimmer over to Marc. By the rules of criminal procedure, the defense would question each juror first.

Marc wanted to use this opportunity to accomplish a couple of things. Since it was extremely unlikely anyone would admit to a blatant bias, although occasionally it did happen, Marc wanted to indoctrinate each juror in certain legal concepts.

Anyone in America with a TV set had heard the terms "beyond a reasonable doubt" and "innocent until proven guilty." Judge Koch had gone over these concepts with Mr. Zimmer, but Marc took the time to make sure he understood them specifically with a slant favorable to the defendant.

More importantly, this was each lawyer's opportunity to make a good first impression on the juror. After all, if this pleasant, well dressed, soft spoken man believed in his client, maybe the defendant is innocent. It didn't hurt to have a priest sitting directly behind the defendant, either. Marc did this by engaging Zimmer in a conversation getting Zimmer to talk about himself. Most people like to tell others about their lives, their families, their careers and Marc was becoming quite adept at conveying to a jury that he genuinely cared about what they have to say. Marc's original mentor, Mickey O'Herlihy, liked to say, "If you can fake sincerity, you're half way to an acquittal."

When Marc finished, Tommy Harris took his turn. He did his best to make Zimmer realize that "beyond a reasonable" is not beyond all doubt. It was here that Zimmer's change in attitude sounded an alarm in Marc's head.

While conversing with Marc, Zimmer had been polite, responsive and even friendly. But, while Harris asked him if he understood that beyond a reasonable doubt did not mean beyond any and all doubt, Zimmer almost lit up. He straightened and produced a broad grin while nodding his head in agreement. Barry Cline noticed it too and gently poked Marc in the ribs.

Harris turned to Judge Koch and announced that he had no objection to this juror. Marc quickly requested a conference at the bench which was granted.

"I want him rejected for cause," Marc said when all four lawyers arrived in front of the judge.

"What cause?" Harris quickly asked. "He didn't say anything to…"

"He lit up like a Christmas tree," Barry said. "He's covering a bias, your Honor."

"One at a time, gentlemen," Koch admonished them.

"He can use one of his peremptory challenges," Harris said.

Each side was given a specified number of peremptory challenges. Peremptory challenges are allotted to each side to allow them to dismiss a veniremen without the necessity of an explanation. The defense had fifteen and the prosecution nine. Because these were a limited number and jury selection was just beginning, Marc did not want to use his unless absolutely necessary.

"I'm inclined to agree with the defense on this one, Mr. Harris. I saw it too. Because of the extreme seriousness of this trial, I'm going to err on the side of caution and dismiss him. Please return to your seats," Judge Koch told them.

"Mr. Zimmer," she continued when the lawyers had been seated, "you are excused. Thank you for your time."

Zimmer, with a surprised look on his face, stood and stepped down from the jury box. When he did he asked the judge, "Does this mean I can go home?"

"Actually, no it doesn't. You'll have to go back to the jury pool," Koch replied.

While he walked past Marc, the excused Mr. Zimmer gave Marc a look that was obviously not friendly.

With a couple of short breaks and an hour for lunch, the process went on all day. Shortly before six, Judge Koch called a halt for the day. So far they had managed to select one juror, a twenty-eight-year-old Air Force veteran who was recently discharged and currently unemployed.

Normally, a vet would be considered maybe a little too law and order conservative. But, both Marc and Barry agreed they saw something in the young man that told each of them he would be fair and open-minded.

Before the judge let them go for the day, she called the lawyers up to the bench.

"I want this trial done by Christmas. You guys need to cut out the repetitive questioning. If a question has already been asked, move it along. Do I make myself clear?"

"Yes, your Honor," they all muttered in unison.

"Good," she said. "Tomorrow morning, nine o'clock; be on time and be ready to move it along."

FORTY-SEVEN

Craig Slocum rapped once on the conference room door then walked in. Seated at the table were his two assistants, Tommy Harris and Paul Ramsey and their jury selection team. These were from an outside business that specialized in jury selection; two women and four men. They traveled around the country profiling prospective jurors for both high profile criminal and civil cases. Of course, they did not come cheap and it was the rare criminal defendant who could afford their services. The Hennepin County taxpayers, of course, had no voice in hiring or paying them. They just got the bill.

"Excuse me," Slocum politely said to the group. "Tommy, I need to see you for a minute."

It was early evening of the first day of jury selection. The prosecution was working on the jury list trying to fine tune their selections. Everyone in the room agreed that Kadella screwed up allowing the USAF vet to be selected. Veterans were almost certainly pro-prosecution.

"Sure, Boss," Harris replied.

"Just Tommy, Paul," Slocum said to Ramsey when he started to stand up.

Harris walked with Slocum back to Slocum's corner office. When the two men were seated Slocum said, "I've been thinking. We should make a plea offer to Kadella."

Harris stared back at his boss for a few seconds then said, "I thought you were dead set against any type of offer."

"I am. I know this Kadella. He's an arrogant ass and I know he'll turn it down. Then we leak it to the media that he made the offer and we turned it down."

"His client will look guilty and you will look strong and resolute. You'll look like the people's lawyer out to seek justice for the victims," Harris said, never one to miss an opportunity to suck up to Slocum.

"Exactly," Slocum beamed. "I was thinking, we offer a plea to two counts of second-degree murder."

"To run concurrently or consecutively?" Harris asked.

"I checked Traynor's criminal history score. I would look both harsh and magnanimous recommending thirty-five years. But, I know Kadella will turn it down. The ego on him loves the spotlight. He wants to try this case. He eats the publicity."

Harris thought about this last statement for a moment before saying, "If that's true, why did he oppose cameras in the courtroom?"

"Trust me," Slocum said with a dismissive wave of his hand. "You'll see. He'll turn it down."

Marc and Barry Cline were back at their office that same evening doing the same thing. Trying to decide which jurors might lean their way was actually more art than science regardless of what the prosecution's "professionals" believed. More guess work than hard, factual evidence.

"We did okay today," Barry said. "We only had to use one preemptory and..."

Suddenly Marc looked up from the table full of printouts and interrupted Barry. "I'm going to get a plea offer," he said, slightly nodding his head up and down.

"No way," Barry firmly disagreed. "Slocum wants your guy's hide and the pleasure of beating you too. And, I'll tell you something else. There's no love lost between me and Tommy Harris, Slocum's little boot licker. I've gone around with him myself a few times. He's a smug little asshole that most of the defense bar despises."

"I know about you and Harris and what other lawyers think of him," Marc said. "I'd rather have him than Gondeck. Steve knows what he's doing. I'm telling you, Slocum is going to make an offer. Something he knows Howie won't take. Then he'll leak it to the media that I made the offer. In fact, he'll claim I practically begged for it."

"I'll believe it when it happens. I don't think Slocum's that clever," Barry said.

"I'll bet you ten bucks; a friendly wager that we get an offer by Friday. What do you say?"

"Done," Barry said.

Marc picked up his phone, found the number he wanted and auto dialed it.

"Hi, Marc," Gabriella Shriqui said when she answered his call. "What's up? Got something juicy for me?"

"Maybe but you have to promise to sit on it for a few days because it might not happen," Marc.

"I'm not sure I like this," Gabriella replied. "What are you up to?"

Marc told her about his suspicions regarding a plea offer. When he finished he said, "I just wanted to get on record with someone ahead of time. I am not, repeat not, authorized by my client to make any type of plea offer or agree to one. Howie Traynor maintains his innocence. I have not and will not make an offer to the prosecution for any plea agreement. I suspect they are going to make an offer to me that they know my client will not accept. They will then leak it to the press that I approached them."

"You're using me to make Slocum and Tommy Harris look like assholes."

"Yes," Marc agreed.

Gabriella thought it over then said, "I guess I'm okay with it but, you owe me one."

"Why do I always owe you one?"

"Because I let you gawk at my legs," she said with a hearty laugh.

"You let me? That's an interesting way of putting it. Good night, Gabriella. I'll see you in court tomorrow."

Margaret Tennant called around 8:00 o'clock to find out how the first day went. Marc tried again to get her to help him with jury selection. As a judge with many years on the bench her insights would be invaluable.

"You know ethically, I can't do that," she admonished him again.

"I won't tell."

"Oh, shut up," she laughed. "Besides I doubt I know anymore about it than you or anyone else. Pick 'em and hope for the best. Get home and get some rest and eat a decent meal."

"Yes, Mom. I'll do my best," Marc said while guiltily looking over the empty burger bags from McDonald's scattered around the table.

"Love you," she said.

"Love you, too."

By the Thursday lunch break there were only four jurors selected, two men and two women, a male African American and three whites. When they broke for lunch Judge Koch ordered the lawyers to see her in chambers.

"Here it is gentlemen," Koch began while she hung up her robe. "Mr. Kadella, by my count, you're down to six challenges, is that correct?"

"Yes, your Honor," Marc agreed.

"And, Mr. Harris, you have two left," she said.

"Yes, your Honor," Harris replied. "In fact, I was going to request an additional…"

"Not a chance," Koch said. She was standing behind her desk chair leaning on the back of it. The look she gave Tommy Harris was clear that she would not consider allowing either of them any additional peremptory challenges.

"We have selected a grand total of four jurors. We need twelve more including four alternates. I'm telling you right now, once your challenges are used up, and I can make you use them, then it will be pretty much up to me to select this jury by denying your bias claims.

"Don't make plans for Saturday. If we aren't done by Friday evening, we'll be here first thing Saturday morning and maybe Sunday if the mood strikes me. Understood?"

"Yes, your Honor," all four lawyers said.

"Have a nice lunch," she said in dismissal.

A little before 4:00 p.m. on Friday all of the jurors had been selected. Twelve total plus four alternates. The twelve were a decent cross section of the community and would likely be fair and impartial.

Of the total sixteen, nine of them had claimed they had heard about the case but had not really followed it very closely. Given the overwhelming media coverage this was hard to believe. Even so, it was also likely true. A significant percentage of Americans paid scant attention to the world outside their own self-made bubble.

Before leaving for the weekend, Judge Koch swore them in and gave them a stern warning to avoid the news concerning this case. They were not allowed to talk to each other and certainly no one else about it at all.

When she finished Marc repeated his request to have them sequestered for the duration. Koch denied it again but assured him she would keep an open mind about it.

"Your Honor, I have another request to make," Marc said while the jury was still seated. "The defense moves to have all charges dismissed. This jury is constitutionally invalid, your Honor. The sixth amendment requires that the defendant be tried by an impartial jury, a jury of his peers. None of these good people are his peers. Not a single one has ever been wrongfully convicted of a crime by the use of doctored evidence and then spent twelve years in prison…"

"Your Honor!" Harris practically exploded.

"Not another word!" Koch practically yelled at Marc. "Say another word and you'll spend the weekend in jail."

Marc stood with an impassive look on his face. He knew saying these things in front of the jury was going to get him in trouble. The mischievous little boy in him simply couldn't resist. Plus, there was a possibility, minuscule at best that Koch would agree. If she did, because the jury had been sworn in, jeopardy had attached, and the case would be over. Double jeopardy would prevent the state from trying Howie again.

"The jury is dismissed until Monday morning," Koch said still seething.

Harris and Marc sat down while the jurors were being led out. When they were gone, Koch turned back to the lawyers.

"Move for a mistrial your Honor," an obviously angry Tommy Harris said while still seated.

"Denied. I'm not going to begin over to pick a new jury," she calmly said to Harris. "But," she continued glaring down at Marc, "You will write a check for a thousand dollars to the court and you'd better not try to say something that inflammatory in front of this jury again. Do I make myself clear?"

"Yes, your Honor. I was merely zealously representing..."

"Give me a break," Koch interrupted him.

"I'll appeal the fine," Marc said.

Koch thought about it, and then said, "I'll tell you what. I'll suspend the fine, for now. But if you do it again, I'll make it five thousand and you can appeal all you want. That goes for you too, Mr. Harris."

"What did I do?" Harris whined.

"You've both been warned. I'm running this show and you will behave."

With that statement, she adjourned for the weekend.

The dozen or so media members who had stayed until the end, hit the door in a mad scramble to get this story out. This could be the beginning of an entertaining trial.

"Give us a minute," Tommy Harris said to the two deputies who were about to take Howie back to jail. "I've been authorized to make an offer," he continued looking at Marc while Barry Cline and Howie looked on. "He pleads to two counts of second degree and..."

"No," Howie said emphatically. "I ain't pleading to anything."

"You haven't even heard it all," Harris said.

"I don't care. The answer is still no. I'm ready to go," Howie said turning to the guards.

Marc held out his left hand to Barry, palm up. Without either of them saying a word to Harris and while Harris and Paul Ramsey watched, Barry laid a ten-dollar bill across Marc's palm.

"Told you so," Marc said still looking at Tommy Harris.

FORTY-EIGHT

Gabriella Shriqui hurried from the government center to the outside of the building onto the front courtyard. The most recent snowstorm had moved into western Wisconsin and, except for the mess it left behind, the weather was fairly nice.

Her cameraman, Kyle Bronson, was already set up and waiting for her when she arrived. Gabriella had called the station to let them know what she had, and the decision was made to put her on live with Melinda Pace.

The entire second half of Melinda's show was taken up by Gabriella's report. Melinda was at her condescending best, or worst depending on your point of view, when Gabriella explained Marc's attempt to have the case dismissed.

"So, Traynor's lawyer tried to pull a fast one on the judge and she didn't go for it," was the way Melinda put it to her audience. "Good for her. It's nice to know there are some sensible judges who won't put up with the sneaky tricks criminal lawyers try to use to get their clients off."

Gabriella bristled a bit at this last comment and found herself wondering why it bothered her. It was a sneaky lawyer's trick and he did not get away with it.

"He's just trying to defend his client," Gabriella calmly said. "That's his job, Melinda."

"Thank you for a wonderful report, Gabriella. I just wish there was a camera in the courtroom."

"The trial starts Monday, Melinda," Gabriella said finishing her reporting.

On the walk to the parking ramp where she had left her car, Gabriella made a phone call.

"Hey," Maddy Rivers said when she answered Gabriella's call. "What's up?"

"I need a drink," Gabriella said, "and a bite to eat. Can you meet me?"

"Seven o'clock?"

"Perfect. I'll see you then," Gabriella said.

Gabriella started her car and just as she was about to back it out of the parking spot, her phone rang. She dug it out of her bag, looked at the I.D. and decided to take the call.

"Hello, Gabriella," she heard the caller say. "It's Derrick Boone, from the…"

"I know Derrick," Gabriella agreeably said. Derrick Boone was a lawyer in the county attorney's office. Gabriella had wooed him as a source during a trial she had covered, and his information was usually quite good. Plus, despite the ring on his finger, he was hot to have her. "What's up?"

"Can we meet for a drink? I have something juicy about the Traynor trial," he said.

"Gee, Derrick, I'm sorry but I already have plans to meet a friend."

"Bring her along, we'll make it a threesome."

"And you can bring your wife," Gabriella tossed back in his face, immediately regretting it. She did not want to lose him as a source.

"Nice shot," he laughed. "Okay, here it is…"

When Derrick Boone finished lying to her about the plea offer he claimed Marc made to Tommy Harris, Gabriella called her boss, Hunter Oswood. Twenty minutes later she was in his office. Also, in attendance was Madison Eyler.

"This is bullshit," Gabriella said. "Marc Kadella called me Monday evening and told me this was going to happen. They're lying."

"How do you know Kadella wasn't lying?" Hunter asked.

"Positively? I don't except he swore to me this would happen and he wanted it on record that his client adamantly refused to even consider a plea. He knew Slocum's office would make an offer and his client would turn it down. And he predicted Slocum would leak it to the media that Kadella made the offer and the prosecution turned him down. Less than an hour after court adjourned today that's exactly what happened."

"Late Friday afternoon would be the perfect time to do it too," Eyler chimed in. "It'll be all over TV and the papers all weekend. The jurors are bound to hear about it."

"So, what do we do?" Oswood asked somewhat rhetorically as he leaned back, locked his fingers behind his head and looked at the two women.

"I say we scoop everybody and report the lie. I'll go on the air and report what I told you. Kadella called me and warned me this would happen," Gabriella said.

"And Slocum's office will deny it," Eyler said.

The two of them, Eyler and Gabriella politely argued about it for almost two minutes with Eyler mostly playing the part of devil's advocate.

"Okay, here's what we will do," Oswood announced. Madison Eyler was the station G.M. and Oswood's boss. Oswood, being the news director, normally had the final word on what went on the air. "I think we can have it both ways. We'll go with the story tonight that Kadella made the offer. 'Sources have informed us that...' blah, blah, blah. Then," he continued looking at Gabriella, "you try to get Kadella on camera tomorrow for a rebuttal."

"What if he refuses?" Gabriella said in a bit of a sulk.

"Then he does," Oswood said. "If that happens then he doesn't get to go on and confirm that he called you ahead of time and told you this would happen."

"I did not want to say this, Gabriella," said Eyler, "but, if we do it your way we'll have problems getting information out of Slocum's office in the future. We can't afford to damage that relationship."

"That's a crock!" Gabriella steamed.

"No, it isn't, and you know it," Oswood interjected.

Gabriella looked at both of them, took a deep breath, sighed and said, "Putting Marc on the air on Saturday won't correct the damage to his client. Slocum's office is using us and...."

"It really sucks," Oswood admitted. "But this is the way we're going to handle it. Life is a two-way street and after this trial we'll still have to deal with the county attorney on other matters."

Marc was seated in a client chair in front of Connie Mickelson's desk. It was almost 5:00 o'clock and the two of them were the only ones still there. Connie liked to kick the staff out a little early on Friday afternoons, at least as often as she could.

The two of them were going over the jury selection and Marc was bouncing a couple of ideas off his good friend. The office phone rang, and Connie answered it.

"Yes, he's right here," Marc heard Connie say.

She covered the mouthpiece on the phone and whispered, "It's Aaron Forsberg. You want to take it in your office?"

"No," Marc answered as he reached for the phone. "I'll talk to him here. Marc Kadella," he said into the phone, "what can I do for you, Aaron."

"I thought you'd like to know; the cops are still watching me. Even though they arrested Traynor and Parlow is dead, apparently they're not completely convinced I'm not involved."

Marc was listening as he jotted down the date, time and a note about the substance of the call.

"Thanks for the update. Anything else?"

"No, that's it. If anything else happens, I'll let you know," Forsberg said.

"This is very interesting. I appreciate the call and keep me informed."

Craig Slocum knocked once as a courtesy then went into the conference room that Harris and Ramsey were using. Paul Ramsey was gone for the evening leaving Tommy Harris to wait for Slocum.

"Did we get the information out to all of the media that we wanted to?" Slocum asked as he sat down.

"We did," Harris answered him. "It should be all over the news for the next couple of days. The jurors are bound to hear about it."

"Good. What about the flawed DNA test? The one that got this Traynor released from prison. What did you decide about it?" Slocum asked.

Harris paused for a moment then said, "I think I should bring it out right away in my opening statement."

"I agree. If you don't, Kadella will find a way to bring it up. He's a sneaky little bastard. Better to bring it out into the open, use it as a motive so you can control it. What about the surveillance by the police?"

"We have to tell the jury ourselves, Boss," Harris said.

Inwardly Slocum loved being called Boss. To him it was a clear, succinct statement of who was in charge. Harris made sure everyone in the office knew Slocum preferred the title. Because of this, very few of the staff or lawyers referred to Slocum this way.

"I agree. Since you can clearly show how he managed to slip away, don't leave it for Kadella. I'm off to a fundraiser," Slocum said. He rose to leave then added, "Win this Tommy and you'll soon be working for Governor Slocum."

FORTY-NINE

Marc found Howie and Father John already in the courtroom and waiting for him. He shook hands with both men then directed the priest to the empty chair with the "Reserved" sign on it. Marc made sure that the court deputies would reserve the aisle seat for Father John in the front row directly behind the defense table. Judge Koch would not allow him to sit at the table with Howie, but she did agree to set this seat aside for him.

While Howie took his seat at the defense table, Marc walked up to the clerk's desk and told Andy Combs, Koch's clerk he needed to see her. Marc motioned for Howie and the two prosecutors and Combs led them back to chambers.

"Your Honor," Marc said to her, "I want the jury polled before we get started."

"About what?" she asked although she suspected what it was.

"Friday afternoon, Mr. Harris made a plea offer to my client which was promptly turned down. Within an hour, every news outlet in the Cities and many national ones as well, were reporting that I made the offer to them and they turned it down. Obviously this was promptly leaked to make my client look guilty."

"I resent that!" Harris blurted out.

"Give me a break," Judge Koch said. "Did you or did you not make the offer as Mr. Kadella said?"

"Well, yes but..."

"Then why was it reported so quickly the other way? I saw the news myself and he's right, it does make his client look guilty," Koch said.

Paul Ramsey, who had nothing to do with this, looked calm and relaxed. Tommy Harris on the other hand, looked like a little kid who just got caught with his hand in the cookie jar up to his elbow.

"Before you open your mouth and lie to me," Koch continued looking directly at Harris, "there better not be any more of these little games Craig Slocum likes to play. Do I make myself clear?"

Harris sat silently not sure what to say.

"I'll be out in a few minutes. We'll start opening statements then," she finished looking up at the lawyers. "I don't think we need to poll the jury. That would only serve to make sure they know about this."

Marc had the same thought. In fact, the reason he brought the subject up was to let Koch know the prosecution pulled this little stunt. Prosecutors love to claim they won't try the case in the media but almost never miss an opportunity to leak damaging news to them.

Tommy Harris went first and for the next hour and a half did a very credible job with his opening statement. The opening statement is the first opportunity for each side to address the jury as a whole. It is also another opportunity to make a good impression on them of yourself and your case. Not wanting to bore them, Harris walked them through the case competently explaining what the witnesses would tell them and the evidence they would see.

"Ladies and gentlemen, you're going to be told that the defendant was under surveillance during the time of these murders. Originally, he was watched by private investigators and retired police officers. There was then a gap of a few days after which the police themselves put him under surveillance.

"Now, this may sound like an airtight alibi but, it's not. We will show you and present you with the physical evidence how the defendant evaded the police to commit these brutal, vicious murders.

"And when we are done, you will have the evidence to prove beyond a reasonable doubt that Howard Traynor is guilty. Thank you, ladies and gentlemen."

While Harris led the jury through the prosecution's case, Marc listened very attentively. It was the prosecution's burden to prove beyond a reasonable doubt every element of every crime charged in the indictment. If Harris told the jury they would see or hear evidence or testimony about something and then failed to present it, Marc would use that in his closing argument. A significant part of a defense lawyer's job is to make sure the prosecution delivered and made their case. If they failed to do so, if they were unable to provide sufficient evidence of a single part of a crime charged, then that allegation, the verdict for that particular crime, must be a not guilty,

Before Marc began, Koch called him and the prosecutors up to the bench.

"How long?" she asked.

"Not very," Marc replied. "I'll be done by lunchtime," he assured her.

"Okay, we'll take a short break then you can begin."

It was after 11:30 by the time Marc started. His job, which of course he did not tell the jury, was to poke holes in the prosecution's case and create reasonable doubt. Because of this, he used his opening statement to make a couple of significant points.

The first was to get the jury to like him and to make them start thinking that "if this amiable, well-dressed, nice looking man was on the defendant's side then perhaps Howie Traynor isn't the blood-thirsty monster the prosecution claimed."

Marc spoke slowly, clearly and even casually to them, walking up and down the jury box, making eye contact with each and smiling when appropriate.

The second part of his opening statement was to remind them of the law and the legal responsibility of the prosecution. Even though everyone with a TV in America has heard of the burden of proof, presumption of innocence and the legal term beyond a reasonable doubt, Marc made sure each juror heard and understood them again and promised to abide by their oath.

Before he began, he made the decision not to try to refute what Harris had told them. He would do that as the trial went along. Plus, there was no reason to reveal his strategy yet. He would keep that to himself and not warn Harris what he was up to.

In reality, Marc didn't have much of a case to present. The only real defense Howie had was an alibi and the small amount of physical evidence. The cops and Tony Carvelli had him under surveillance at the time of most of the murders. Harris' claim that they knew how Howie evaded this surveillance was mostly speculation backed up by virtually no physical evidence.

The first witness for the prosecution would be the lead investigator, Detective Owen Jefferson. He was called forward, sworn in and took the witness stand. Jefferson would spend the remainder of that day and most of the next two giving testimony.

Harris began by slowly tossing easy, open-ended questions to him. They spent the first fifteen to twenty minutes giving the jury a detailed account of Jefferson's record as a police officer. By the time Harris finished with this, even Marc was impressed. It was about this time that Marc noticed something that made him smile. Jefferson had removed the tiny gold stud he normally wore in his left ear. Marc made the decision not to bring this up on cross exam. It would be objectionable and could easily look petty, almost childish.

For a first-degree murder conviction there are several particular elements that must be proven for each charge. The first, of course, the death of the victim must be proven. Jefferson was not a qualified medical examiner but, as an experienced homicide detective he could testify that each victim was, in fact, dead. He could also tell the jury that he had read the autopsy and what it contained as to the cause of death. The M.E. would come later, to expertly verify that fact and testify as to what the cause of death was.

The prosecution must also prove that whoever killed each victim did so with the express intent to kill him or her. Jefferson would testify about what he personally saw when he looked over each body. He would testify about the type of wound he observed, the blood covered abdomen and, in most cases, the hands nailed down. The M.E. would later testify that the wounds and the slit throats could only be done with intent to kill. It is an opinion and not a fact but as an experienced M.E. he can give his opinion and the jury can take it or leave it. First degree murder requires that the act was committed with malice aforethought. Essentially this means that whoever did it planned it ahead of time. This does not require significant planning over any specific period of time. It does not require a confession. The jury can infer from the physical evidence of the wounds and how the bodies were posed that murder was what the perpetrator had in mind and planned it ahead of time.

The death must have occurred in Hennepin County. Since the victims were all found there and there was no evidence to believe the act took place elsewhere, the jury is free to believe this was where each happened.

Fourth, the defendant did not commit the homicide in the heat of passion. He must not have done it because he was provoked by the victim to such an extent that an ordinary person would have acted the same way. If this happened, if the defendant was provoked by the victim, then the defendant is guilty of first-degree manslaughter and not murder.

This is a claim to be made by the defense, the act was done in the heat of passion, is what is legally known as an affirmative defense. What this means is that it is up to the defense to prove that the defendant was provoked by the victim. Obviously this did not happen to any of the Crown of Thornes victims.

Finally, and this is the most crucial element and at the heart of this case, it must be proven that the defendant did it. Marc's job was to poke enough holes in the prosecution's case to create reasonable doubt about Howie Traynor's guilt, the SODDI, "some other dude did it" defense. The defense is under no obligation to prove who that is. They need only provide the jury with reasonable doubt that the defendant did it.

There were also several other charges included in the indictment. Howie was also charged with second degree murder for each victim as well. Second degree requires all of the elements of first degree except premeditation. If the jury believes the defendant did not plan to kill, they can fall back on second degree.

There were also several burglary charges involving the deaths of Rhea Watson and Judge Ross Peterson. Whoever murdered them broke into their homes with intent to commit a crime. And there was a single kidnapping charge in the death of Elliot Sanders, the foreman from Howie's original trial.

Most of these charges were added just to illustrate what a bad person Howie Traynor truly was, to inflame the jury to conclude he was, if not an animal, at least a bit subhuman, and someone of whom society needed to rid itself. This can also blow back on the prosecution. If they can't prove the lesser charges, did they really prove the big ones?

FIFTY

Through Jefferson's testimony, Harris explained each of the murders included in the indictment. They proceeded in chronological order and began with Rhea Watson first.

Jefferson began by testifying about a report from Beltrami County of an appeals court judge having been murdered. Marc objected to this testimony as irrelevant since Howie was not charged with this crime and highly prejudicial. This issue had been argued prior to the trial and Koch had ruled it admissible as to similarity of crime. Marc believed the judge was wrong and objected on the trial record in front of the jury to preserve the issue for appeal. Koch quickly overruled Marc's objection and Jefferson continued.

"After you arrived at the home of Rhea Watson, what did you do next?" Harris asked.

On direct examination this is the type of question that is supposed to be used. An open-ended question that does not suggest what the answer is. This kind of question allows the witness to tell the jury what he or she saw or did. Preparing a witness by literally practicing his testimony is not only allowed but any reasonably competent lawyer had better do this. Putting words in his mouth and telling him what to say is grossly unethical and not allowed. But practicing a witness' testimony to get it down smoothly is absolutely necessary.

"I spoke with the officer who was the first responder, Sergeant Norman Anderson. He told me what he found in the house and who the victim was."

"How did he know who the victim was?"

"We both knew her. She was a former prosecutor in the county attorney's office," Jefferson said.

"What did you do next?"

"I spoke to the two women from Watson's law firm, her new employer, who had called the police."

Jefferson went on to tell the jury what they had to say. This was technically hearsay but, since it was basically harmless and had nothing to do with who might have done it, Marc did not object. Objecting too much can give the jury the impression you are trying to hide something from them. Besides, Marc knew the women would be called to testify themselves.

The next part of Jefferson's testimony would bring gruesome shock to the jury. Jefferson told them how he went into the house and downstairs to the basement to examine the body. When Harris reached this point, he obtained permission to approach his witness. It was granted, and Harris handed Jefferson an 8 x 10 full color print of a photo.

"Detective Harris, I have handed you a photo marked State's Exhibit A, is this an accurate photo of what you found in the basement?"

"Yes," he answered holding the print, "that's her."

A wide screen, high definition TV had been set up in front of the jury. When Jefferson verified the photo of Rhea Watson, Paul Ramsey hit a key on his laptop and the same picture appeared on the screen. It was a shot of the posed, naked, blood covered body of Rhea Watson. She was wearing the barbed wire crown and her hands were nailed into the cinder block wall she was up against.

For the five victims Howie was charged with murdering, the police, crime scene techs and medical examiners had taken hundreds of pictures. Harris had presented at least a dozen of each victim that he wanted to present to the jury. Marc, Harris and Paul Ramsey spent the better part of an entire day arguing in Judge Koch's chambers about the photos. Most of them were quite inflammatory and Harris obviously wanted them all admitted to shock the jury. The angrier they became with the horror of what the victims went through, the more likely the jury would want someone to pay for it.

Judge Koch decided to limit the number of photos to be admitted to between two and four each. She would allow one shot of how the body was found, an autopsy photo and one showing the crushed fingers and toes of those who had been tortured.

With the grizzly photo of Watson's tortured, bloody corpse on the TV screen Jefferson continued his testimony. He described for the jury the action the police took and that he went back to his desk to review the report from Beltrami County.

The judge allowed Jefferson to testify that the case up north was very similar to Rhea Watson's. Koch allowed details to be given to the jury that were the exact match, the crushed fingers and toes, the wound across the throat, the barbed-wire crown and crucifixion type pose of both bodies.

"What else, if anything was found that was the same on both victims?"

"There appeared to be two burn marks on each that were caused by a Taser."

"The same Taser?"

"Objection," Marc said as he stood up.

"Did you personally conduct any tests to identify the burns on the bodies?" Judge Koch asked Jefferson.

"No, your Honor, I did not."

"Sustained. Move along Mr. Harris."

It took Harris and Jefferson almost two hours to complete his testimony about Rhea Watson. Before Harris started on the next victim, Ross Peterson, Judge Koch ordered a break.

When court resumed, Harris followed the same basic script to guide Jefferson through the discovery of Judge Peterson. The most noticeable difference between the photos of Watson and Peterson was the lack of blood on Peterson. Harris had Jefferson explain this from the autopsy report that gave Peterson's cause of death as a heart attack.

"Do you know what caused Judge Peterson to have the heart attack that killed him?" Harris asked.

"Objection," Marc said. "Lack of foundation for this witness to make such a claim." Jefferson was not qualified to testify that the Taser shock caused Peterson's pacemaker to malfunction and cause the heart attack. The M.E. would have to do that, and Marc could challenge him on it.

"Sustained," Koch ruled. "Move along, Mr. Harris."

Jefferson also explained to the jury that the police were beginning to find links between Peterson, Rhea Watson and Howard Traynor. Harris was a bit of a plodder, but he was also quite thorough. It was almost 5:30 by the time they finished. The first day of testimony ended when Jefferson and Harris completed their discussion of Ross Peterson.

The next morning, Judge Koch was on the bench at precisely nine o'clock. Within two minutes the jury was seated, and Jefferson was called back to the stand.

"We left off yesterday afternoon when you finished your testimony about Judge Peterson," Harris began the second day of testimony.

Jefferson and Harris repeated their process of leading the jury through each victim. This morning they started with Elliot Sanders, the man found in Mueller Park in South Minneapolis.

"After the murder of Judge Peterson," Jefferson said, "we concentrated our investigation on finding common links between the victims. We were looking for people who were tried by Rhea Watson in front of Judge Peterson. We found quite a few of them in our system. When we included those who also had Judge Smith, the murder victim in Bemidji, as a judge handling their appeal, the list narrowed down to eight names."

"Was the defendant one of them?"

"Yes, he was. There were two others that were noticeable as well," Jefferson continued.

"Who were they?"

Jefferson looked at the notebook he held on his lap and read their names. "Eugene Parlow and Aaron Forsberg."

"Why did those two catch your attention?"

"Those two men, along with the defendant and a fourth man, Angelo Suarez, had recently been released from prison. Their convictions were overturned, and they were released early. Each of them were convicted with the use of flawed DNA testing. Except for Suarez, we put these men under surveillance as well as the defendant."

"Why not Suarez?"

"Angelo Suarez was shot and killed when he attempted to attack a woman in St. Paul."

This caused a noticeable buzz to go through the courtroom. Judge Koch rapped her gavel three times and with an icy glare silenced the crowd.

"Was Angelo Suarez connected to the victims?"

"No, he was tried in Ramsey County. We could find no connection between Suarez and the victims."

"You said there were eight names, what about the other five?"

"We were able to eliminate each one," Jefferson answered and then went on to explain how they were checked out and why none of them were considered suspects.

For the next half hour Jefferson, with a few easy questions to keep him on track, explained the scene where Elliot Sanders was found. He told the jury how he was found, the condition of the body and what Jefferson himself did.

Some of this was objectionable. Jefferson did not personally find the body, but it was pointless for Marc to object to it. The two women who found him were going to testify anyway and Jefferson's testimony would be corroborated by them. Plus, it did not really matter how the body was found and who found it.

The detective went into detail telling the jury about how he and his partner, Marcie Sterling, identified the victim through missing person reports and his daughter. He then went on to explain how he found the connection between Sanders and Howard Traynor.

"And Detective, what was that connection?"

"Elliot Sanders was the foreman of the jury that convicted Howard Traynor of the murder of Lucille Benson," Jefferson solemnly said. "This was the crime he was convicted of with a flawed DNA test result. The one he was recently released from prison for."

Again, there was a buzz in the gallery and Marc saw a noticeable stir from the jurors.

"Was there anything else you noticed?" Harris asked.

"Yes, it was obvious he had not been killed in Mueller Park. A subsequent search of his home found no evidence he had been killed there either."

"Why is this important?"

"He must have been taken against his will somewhere…"

"Objection," Marc stood up. "This is completely speculative your Honor. They have no evidence he was taken against his will anywhere."

"Do you have any such evidence that you will be presenting?"

"No," Harris quietly, reluctantly admitted.

"Then the objection is sustained. Move along, Mr. Harris."

Marc sat down and quietly rejoiced at his small victory. Howie was charged with kidnapping Elliot Sanders. That charge was just eliminated.

Throughout all of this, Howie Traynor had done a very good job of maintaining his demeanor. Marc had prepared him for this, as all defense lawyers do, but it isn't always easy. Of course, the media would report that Howie looked as if he was bored and totally uninterested in the proceedings. They had to report something and, typically, they were wrong.

Following the morning break, Jefferson testified about Cara Meyers. This was a bit tricky since Meyers had no prior connection to Howie. Harris made sure his witness admitted this and told the jury that Meyers was Eugene Parlow's former lawyer.

When he reached the part where the single strand of hair was found, just as he started to testify about it, Marc requested a bench conference.

"Your Honor," Marc quietly began when the lawyers assembled. "They are about to get into DNA testing. Detective Jefferson did not…"

Koch held up a hand to stop him, looked at Harris and said, "Not a word about any test results. Am I clear?"

"Yes, your Honor," Harris said trying to look wounded. "We had no intention of it."

"Good, then we won't have a problem."

When Jefferson resumed he testified that he, along with his partner, personally delivered the single strand of hair found on Cara Meyers to the BCA in St. Paul.

"In your opinion, as a veteran investigator, why do you believe Cara Meyers was murdered?" Harris asked.

Marc was on his feet in an instant. "Objection! Speculation, your Honor. There is no basis in fact for any answer to this question."

Judge Koch thought it over for a moment then said, "Overruled. He is a professional, experienced police homicide investigator. I'll allow a bit of it."

"To throw us off the investigation," Jefferson quickly said.

Not wanting to press his luck Harris decided to move on.

By now it was close enough to lunch time to take a break before the prosecution moved on to the last victim charged in the indictment, Jimmy Oliver. Knowing the testimony would be a little long, Harris suggested to Judge Koch that now would be a good time to break.

The afternoon was taken up with Jefferson's testimony of the murder of Jimmy Oliver. As they had done with all of the victims, one of the first things Harris did was to get the photo of Oliver's body as it was found on the TV screen. And, as they had done with the previous victims, the photo stayed up on the screen throughout Jefferson's testimony.

When the picture of Jimmy's bloody corpse nailed to the fence in the alley went on the screen, Marc was closely watching the jury. He saw a subtle but noticeable change in their demeanor.

They had clearly demonstrated shock and obvious revulsion when the first photo, the one of Rhea Watson was displayed. With each subsequent one, the jurors became less and less disturbed by the image. Jimmy Oliver's bloody body barely created a stir. Most of the jurors looked at it with an almost indifferent, impassive expression. Very likely each of them had seen much worse images on TV and in the movies many times.

Jefferson's testimony of the Jimmy Oliver murder was the longest and most detailed of all. He very thoroughly described all of it including timing his walk from *Tooley's* to Howie Traynor's apartment. He admitted the surveillance team at Howie's apartment had checked and found Howie home. But, he emphasized how easily he made it from *Tooley's* to Howie's implying Howie could have done it himself no problem.

Jefferson also spent quite a bit of time detailing the relationship between the two men. He made a special effort to tell the jury that it was the confession of Jimmy Oliver that led to the arrest of Howie Traynor for the murder of Lucille Benson and how frightened of Howie Jimmy Oliver had been because of it. Harris had decided not to have Jefferson testify about the meeting the two former burglary partners had during which Howie assured Jimmy he forgave him for giving him up to the police for the Benson murder. Even though this conversation between Jimmy and Howie was clearly exculpatory and should have been given to Marc, Slocum had ordered Harris to withhold it. Harris did not believe that Marc could know this and did not want to give it to him to use.

Jefferson finished his testimony regarding Jimmy Oliver with the discovery of the three hairs on Oliver's body. Once again the lawyers were called to the bench and Koch again warned Harris not to bring up any test results.

Harris finished his direct exam of the detective shortly before 5:00 o'clock. Koch called the lawyers to the bench and asked Marc if he wanted to start his cross examination. Marc would have liked to do so. It would have been a good idea to leave the jury with some points from the defense to consider that evening. The judge made it clear she wanted to adjourn and start in the morning and Marc reluctantly agreed.

FIFTY-ONE

Madeline Rivers parked her Audi in the restaurant lot. Marc had sent her a text asking her to meet him and suggested this faux French Bistro in Edina. While driving into the parking area she had seen Marc's SUV. Now she sat staring through the window thinking about their relationship.

Maddy had known Marc since shortly after arriving in Minneapolis from Chicago. Their mutual friend, Tony Carvelli, had introduced them and Maddy worked for Marc on several cases since then and developed a deep, almost loving friendship. In fact, Maddy did love Marc in the same way she would a close, older brother. And she knew he felt the same way toward her.

Something in the back of her mind was telling her this meeting was a problem. Maddy knew what was bothering her and she felt rotten about it. For the first time the two of them were on opposite sides of a case. Because of her involvement with the surveillance of Howie Traynor, Maddy had a conflict of interest and could not work for Marc. If she had known helping Carvelli was going to cause this, she certainly would have declined, she believed. On the other hand, turning Tony and Vivian Donahue down would have been difficult, to say the least.

Maddy entered through the front door and before the hostess got to her, she saw Marc. He was seated in a booth at the far end of the crowded bar waiting for her. He waved at her and a few seconds later she sat down opposite him.

"Hi," he smiled, "how are you?"

"I'm good," she answered a bit cautiously. "How's the trial?"

"Just starting," he answered.

"Marc, I'm so sorry I can't..."

"Stop. We've been through this. It's okay."

The waiter arrived and Maddy ordered a glass of house wine. Marc declined, still sipping a small glass of beer.

"It's getting late," Marc said after looking at his watch. "After nine and I need to get home and get a good night's sleep."

The waiter reappeared with Maddy's drink. Despite the obvious age difference, the young man hovered around her a lot longer than was necessary.

"That's why I wanted to see you," Marc said when the young man left. "I have to cross examine Owen Jefferson tomorrow and your name is going to come up. It can't be avoided."

When he said this, Maddy's shoulders visibly slumped, her heart sank a bit and she swallowed a large gulp of wine.

"I figured something like that," she said.

"Madeline, I'll do everything I can to protect you, but I have to defend my client."

"Marc," she leaned forward and whispered, "I told you what I did in confidence. Now you're going to use it?"

"Maddy, I wasn't your lawyer," Marc defensively answered her. "I'm Howie's lawyer and yes, I have to use it."

"It sucks," she said as she sulkily sat back.

The unspoken between them was the fact that Maddy had committed a felony going into Howie's apartment. If it came to light, she could go to jail for it and would certainly lose her P.I. license.

An awkward minute of silence passed between them. Maddy glared at Marc while he fidgeted with his almost empty glass.

"You know you're on both witness lists, don't you?"

"I am?" she asked genuinely surprised.

"Have you been served a subpoena by the prosecution?"

"No."

"Well, you'll love this," Marc said as he reached inside his suit coat and removed a single page of paper. It was folded in thirds and he placed it on the table. With a single finger he slid it across the table to her.

"Madeline Rivers, you've just been served by the defendant. Keep yourself available."

Maddy stared at it without speaking or touching it for almost thirty seconds. Finally, she picked it up, unfolded it and read it over.

"Is this really necessary?" she asked as she refolded it and placed it in her shoulder bag.

"I hope not..., yes," Marc quietly said.

"I have to go, I have to go," she said as she swallowed what was left of her wine, grabbed her bag and stood up.

While he watched her hurry through the crowd, ignoring the gawking men, Marc quietly said to himself, "Sometimes I really hate this goddamn job."

The waiter reappeared, and Marc told him he did not want anything else. Just as the young man was leaving, Marc stopped him and ordered a shot of Jack Daniels and a beer chaser.

On his way out of the office for the evening, Craig Slocum stopped at Tommy Harris' door and went in without knocking. Harris was at his desk working but set aside what he was doing when Slocum sat down.

"How did things go today?" Slocum asked.

"Good," Harris replied. "I finished my direct of Jefferson. We got in everything we could from him. The judge wouldn't let him testify about the hair samples, but I expected that."

"She wouldn't let him talk about them at all?" Slocum asked.

"No, no. He testified about them being found on Meyers and Oliver and that he took them to the BCA. She wouldn't let him tell the jury what the test results were."

"Oh, okay, sure," Slocum said.

"The jury got it though. They know what the DNA results were. Plus, I told them about it in my opening statement. They know. We'll get a couple of the techs to testify."

"Did Jefferson testify about the doctored DNA test that was used to help convict Traynor thirteen years ago?"

"Sure, we need it for motive, remember?" Harris said.

"What about the evidence found in Traynor's apartment?" Slocum asked.

"Jefferson identified all of it. He even told the jury that he was there and saw the cop use that board walkway to cross from Traynor's building to the next one. The jury now knows Traynor could have easily evaded the surveillance."

Slocum sat quietly for a moment staring at Harris' vanity wall behind his desk. The wall had his diplomas and admission to the bar proudly displayed.

"What about the ex-cop, Carvelli and the female P.I. Madeline Rivers?" he asked. "Are you planning on calling them?"

"No, I agree with you. We can't call them. It will look like we sent them into Traynor's building to find evidence for us. Let Kadella bring it up. Jefferson will deny it. He's a highly decorated police officer and he did a great job. He makes an excellent witness."

"And if Kadella puts them on the stand?"

"Then they go to jail for breaking and entering. But, we can legitimately claim they did it on their own, that the cops didn't put them up to it and it doesn't hurt our case."

After dinner, such as it is in jail, Howie Traynor settled into a chair to watch a rerun of Melinda Pace's show. It was being repeated following the 6:00 o'clock news. When it came on one of the other guests of Hennepin County stood up to change the channel.

"We already watched this bitch this afternoon," the bald man said as he reached a tattoo covered arm toward the TV.

"Leave it," Howie quietly, firmly commanded. Howie was seated in the middle of the third row of chairs. None of the other inmates were sitting within four chairs of him. He was watching Melinda do her intro and ignored the beefy, bald man.

"Who the fuck are you?" The man said to Howie as he turned toward him. Before Howie could answer, another inmate, a friend of the tattoo covered troublemaker, stood and whispered something in the man's ear. When he finished, the man grunted, sneered at Howie and said, "Whatever." Then he sat down in the front row.

The entire twenty-two minutes of airtime of Melinda's show was devoted to Jefferson's testimony. Locally the media had labeled this the most recent *Trial of the Century* and it garnered significant national attention as well.

Seated next to Melinda for the first half of the show was Gabriella Shriqui. Being the professional that she was, Gabriella completely suppressed her total contempt for the show's host. To watch the two of them interact would lead you to believe they were good friends.

When Gabriella's presence was initially televised, the crowd in the county jail, being the PC sensitive types, they were, let forth with a number of lewd comments. The one with the biggest, most foul-mouth was the one who had tried to change the channel.

Because Gabriella had been in the courtroom for Jefferson's testimony, she would serve as a substitute camera to explain in detail the day's events. During their discussion, an artist's rendition of the scene was put up on the screen for three different parts of the testimony.

During the second half of the show, Melinda had a former prosecuting attorney on the air. Her name was Denise Flagler. Melinda did everything she could to get Flagler to say Howie was guilty, but she refused to go there. Instead she reminded Melinda and her audience that the trial had a long way to go.

Later that night, a few minutes before lights out, Howie went into the bathroom to prepare for bed. The gorilla who had wanted to change the channel on the television saw him and followed him. There were three other men in there who scurried out as quickly as they could. Less than two minutes later, Howie laid down on his cot and within minutes he was sound asleep. The tattoo covered moron was found by a deputy and spent the next three days handcuffed to a bed at the Hennepin County Medical center. None of the inmates would testify to anything.

FIFTY-TWO

Marc knocked softly on the conference room door, quietly opened it and looked inside. A deputy told him Howie and the priest were inside waiting for him. Realizing they might be privately conferring, Marc did not want to unnecessarily disrupt or startle them. He found the two men seated at the small round table.

"Thank you, Father, for hearing my confession," Marc heard Howie say. "I feel better already."

Father John placed his right hand gently on Howie's shoulder and said, "Confession is always good for the soul," the priest replied.

Hearing the word "confession" being used, the lawyer in Marc quickly went on alert. Even though the priest could not be forced to testify about anything a penitent confessed to him, confession was not a word a defense lawyer ever wanted to hear.

"Good morning, Marc," Father John amiably said. He stood up, shook hands with Marc and continued, "I'll leave you two alone to converse."

The priest left, and Marc closed the door behind him. He pulled out the chair opposite Howie and said, "Should I ask what it was you confessed to?"

Howie hesitated for a moment then sheepishly turned his head away from his lawyer and said, "I ah, got in a fight, um, last night. One of the other inmates came after me in the bathroom."

Relieved, Marc said, "So you defended yourself..."

"Yes, I couldn't escape," Howie quickly agreed. "The old me took over and I hurt the man. He's in the hospital. I didn't mean to, I just..."

"Did the guards talk to you?"

"No, this man is a troublemaker and I don't think anyone really cares what happened."

"Okay," Marc said. "Keep quiet about it and let's move on."

The morning session would be starting shortly. Marc went over what was coming up and reminded Howie to remain calm and maintain an impassive look and demeanor.

Owen Jefferson sat down on the witness stand and Judge Koch politely reminded him he was still under oath. Tommy Harris had completed his questioning of the detective yesterday afternoon. It was now Marc's turn.

Before he asked his first question, Marc requested and was granted, permission to approach the witness. On his way to the witness stand, Marc dropped a document in front of Harris. He then handed a copy to Jefferson and one to Judge Koch. By the time Marc returned to his chair, Harris was on his feet.

"Your Honor, we object to this document being admitted into evidence as irrelevant and immaterial."

"May we approach, your Honor?" Marc asked.

"Yes," Koch said waving them to come forward while she reviewed the document. When the three lawyers assembled in front of her she hit the white noise privacy button and asked Marc, "What is this?"

"It's the autopsy report of Judge Robert Smith, murdered up by Bemidji," Marc replied.

"He's not charged with this crime," Harris interjected.

"Judge, their case hinges on the defendant evading their surveillance by somehow escaping from his building across the roof. I have the right to try to poke some holes in that theory. The murder of Judge Smith is relevant for that purpose. Plus, they opened the door when the witness testified about the method and cause of death being the same."

Koch considered it for a moment then said, "All right, I'll let you question the witness abut Judge Smith for that purpose only."

The lawyers retreated to their respective tables and Koch overruled the prosecution's objection.

"Detective Jefferson," Marc began, "I have given you an autopsy report from Beltrami County. Do you recognize this document?"

"Yes, I have seen it before," Jefferson answered.

"It is the autopsy report of the murder of Judge Robert Smith at his lake home outside Bemidji, isn't it?" Marc asked.

"Yes, it appears to be," Jefferson agreed.

"On the front page, I have highlighted the date of his death. Please read that to the jury."

Jefferson told the jury what it was.

"That was before Rhea Watson, the first murder my client is charged with, is it not?"

"Yes," Jefferson agreed.

"You personally received a copy of this report along with a copy of the police report of Judge Smith's murder the day after it happened did you not?"

"Yes."

"And you read through it that day?" Marc knew this because Tony Carvelli had told him this.

"Yes."

"Judge Smith, according to these reports, was found seated between two trees, his arms extended, his hands nailed to those trees and his fingers and toes were crushed, correct?"

"Yes, that's correct."

"And, his killer had planted a crown of barbed wire thorns on his head?"

"Objection," Harris said. "This witness has no personal knowledge of who placed the barbed wire on this victim's head." It was a foolish objection and Marc had to suppress a smile.

"Sustained," Koch ruled.

"I'll rephrase your Honor," Marc said. "Isn't it true that according to the report you read, Judge Smith had a barbed wire crown of thorns on his head when his body was found?"

"Yes, that's true."

"Without getting into the technical medical terms, isn't it true that the cause of death was loss of blood due to his throat being slit from ear-to-ear?"

"Yes, that's also true."

"When you arrived at the scene of Rhea Watson's death, isn't it true you saw her body in her basement, sitting with her back to the wall?"

"Yes."

"Her arms were spread, her hands nailed to the wall, her body covered in blood, her fingers and toes crushed and a barbed wire crown of thorns on her head exactly like Judge Smith?"

"Yes, she was," Jefferson agreed.

"And, Detective Jefferson," Marc began more softly, "isn't it also true that the moment you saw her you thought of the report you had read about Judge Smith?"

"Well maybe not the instant I saw her, but it did occur to me."

"Her cause of death is also loss of blood due to having her throat slit from ear-to-ear, exactly like Judge Smith, isn't it?"

"Objection," Harris said. "The witness is not a medical professional."

Judge Koch looked at Jefferson and asked, "Do you know her cause of death?"

"Yes, your honor."

"Overruled. The witness may answer."

"Yes," Jefferson said looking at Marc.

"To your knowledge, has the defendant been charged with Judge Smith's murder?"

"No, he has not," Jefferson said.

"Detective Jefferson, do you know a private investigator by the name of Anthony Carvelli?"

"Yes, I know him."

"In fact, Anthony Carvelli, a retired detective of the Minneapolis police is a friend of yours, is he not?"

"As he is of you, I understand," Jefferson managed to slip into the discussion.

"You're right," Marc admitted looking at the jury. "I've known Mr. Carvelli for several years. Do you know another private investigator by the name of Madeline Rivers?"

"Yes, I know her," Jefferson calmly said.

"And retired Minneapolis police officers Daniel Sorenson, Thomas Evans and Franklin Washington, do you know them?"

"Yes."

"Isn't it also true that Ms. Rivers, Sorenson, Evans and Franklin were all working under the direction of Carvelli doing surveillance of Howard Traynor on behalf of a private citizen at the time when Judge Robert Smith and Rhea Watson were murdered?"

"Yes, they were," Jefferson admitted.

"Isn't it also true that Carvelli was keeping you informed, sort of informally and off the record, of that surveillance?"

"Yes, he was."

"Isn't it true that Mr. Traynor is not charged with the murder of Robert Smith at his lake home thirty miles outside Bemidji, a distance of over two hundred miles from Minneapolis, because on the night it happened, Mr. Traynor was being watched and his car never moved?"

"I don't know why he has not been charged with that murder. It's not my case."

"Did Carvelli tell you they watched him all night that night?"

"Yes."

"Did he also tell you Mr. Traynor's car never moved from in front of his apartment building?"

"Yes," Jefferson agreed.

"So, isn't it true that he could not have sneaked out, somehow traveled to Bemidji without his car, murder Judge Smith and somehow get back to the Cities by morning undetected?"

"Yes, that's probably true," Jefferson admitted with obvious reluctance.

"And whoever murdered Judge Smith did it exactly the same way as the victims Howard Traynor is charged with murdering, is that correct?"

Jefferson opened his mouth as if to say something contradictory. He looked at Harris hoping for an objection. When none was forthcoming, he reluctantly said, "Yes, that's true."

"Is it reasonable to assume that the same person who murdered the victims charged in the indictment for this trial also killed Judge Smith and that person could not possibly be Howard Traynor?"

"Objection," Harris said jumping to his feet, "speculation."

"Sustained," the judge ruled. "The jury will disregard the question in its entirety."

Marc expected Harris to object and Koch to sustain it. He didn't care. He had made his point and even though Koch had ordered the jury to disregard it, the judge's order to the jury would not unring that bell.

Judge Koch looked over the jury and the gallery. Everyone in attendance was absolutely still and quiet. And, they were all staring directly at Marc and Owen Jefferson. However, needing a break herself, the judge ordered a short recess.

"Detective Jefferson, after the death of Rhea Watson, Anthony Carvelli told you he was going to discontinue the surveillance of Howie Traynor, didn't he?"

"Yes, he did."

"Because they had been watching him for almost three weeks and did not believe Traynor was doing anything criminal, did he not?"

"You'd have to ask Tony Carvelli that," Jefferson said.

"No, Detective, I'm asking you if he told you that."

"Objection, hearsay," Harris said.

"Overruled," Koch quickly said.

"Yes, he did tell me that."

"You made no attempt to persuade him to stay on the surveillance of Howie Traynor, did you?"

"No, I didn't."

"But, you had encouraged him to watch Mr. Traynor a couple of times before that didn't you?"

"Um, I guess so, yes."

"Because you believed Howie Traynor should be watched but the police could not do it, isn't that right?"

"Yes."

"And it was after the murder of Rhea Watson that Tony Carvelli told you he was calling it off and you did not object, did you?"

"No, because I didn't believe..."

"Non-responsive, your Honor," Marc quickly said to cut him off.

"You will answer only the question asked, Detective," Koch politely admonished him.

"When Judge Ross Peterson was killed, Mr. Traynor was not under surveillance by anyone, is that correct?"

"Yes, that's true."

"It was also at that time, that you compiled a list of people who were prosecuted by Rhea Watson, tried in front of Ross Peterson and whose cases were handled on appeal by Judge Robert Smith, isn't that true?"

"Yes," Jefferson acknowledged.

"Isn't it true you came up with a total of eight names?"

"Yes."

"None of these eight people were under surveillance by anyone at the time of the murders of Rhea Watson and Ross Peterson or Robert Smith, were they?"

"Not to my knowledge, no," Jefferson admitted.

"Was Mr. Traynor one of these eight people?"

"Yes, he was."

"And seven others including a Eugene Parlow and Aaron Forsberg?"

"Yes, that's correct."

"In fact, isn't it true, Detective Jefferson, you believed it was one of those three men, Howard Traynor, Eugene Parlow and Aaron Forsberg?"

"Well, not completely, no."

"But they were at the top of your suspect list, weren't they?"

"I suppose so, yes."

"Because all three of them had recently been released from prison and because their convictions were overturned due to the prosecution using DNA tests that were doctored by a lab technician, isn't that true?"

"Yes, and we found out the other five all had solid alibis."

"Really? They had solid alibis, but you didn't believe Mr. Traynor had a solid alibi by being under round the clock surveillance?"

"We believed he had a strong motive."

"Because of the way he was convicted by use of a tainted DNA test?"

Jefferson squirmed in his seat, looked at Harris, then the jury and back to Marc when he said, "Yes and he had ties to Smith, Watson and Peterson."

"As did both Eugene Parlow and Aaron Forsberg, didn't they?"

"Yes," Jefferson agreed.

"Isn't it true that neither Eugene Parlow nor Aaron Forsberg were under surveillance at the time Judge Smith, Judge Peterson and Rhea Watson were killed?"

"Objection," Harris said standing and interrupting. "He continues to bring up Judge Smith in an irrelevant manner."

"Overruled," Koch quickly said, "because of the similarities, his death is clearly connected to the others."

"Were they under surveillance?" Marc asked.

"No," Jefferson admitted.

"After Judge Peterson's murder, you decided to put all three of those suspects under surveillance by the police, isn't that true?"

"Yes."

"The very next day, Judge Julian Segal, a Ramsey County judge was found near Lake Harriet wasn't he?"

"Objection," Harris said. "The defendant is not..."

"Overruled," Koch said with a noticeable touch of annoyance. "The witness will answer the question."

"Yes, he was."

"He was found in between two trees, his arms spread, his hands nailed to the trees, his throat slit, fingers and toes crushed and a barbed wire crown on his head, isn't that true?"

"Yes."

"And exactly like the others, he had been jolted by a Taser?"

"Objection," Harris said.

"Sustained. Rephrase, Mr. Kadella."

It was a foolish objection. One way or another, the jury would hear about the Taser burns.

"If you know, did there appear to be Taser burns on Judge Segal's body similar to those on Robert Smith, Rhea Watson and Ross Peterson?" Marc asked rephrasing the question.

"Yes," Jefferson admitted.

"Isn't it also true that when you arrived at the scene where Judge Segal's body was found and saw him posed exactly the same way as the others, you immediately thought that the same man must have murdered Judge Segal, didn't you?"

This question was a little risky. Jefferson could easily deny it, but Marc believed the jury would doubt Jefferson's denial.

"Yes," Jefferson admitted.

"Isn't it also true that you had Howard Traynor under surveillance again, the night Julian Segal was murdered but not Aaron Forsberg?"

"Yes, that's correct."

"Mr. Traynor is not charged with the murder of Judge Segal because there is no physical evidence to connect him to Julian Segal's death, he was under police surveillance and you could not find any tie between Howie Traynor and Julian Segal, isn't that true?"

"Yes," Jefferson admitted reluctantly.

"Julian Segal, before being appointed to the bench, was a well-known criminal defense attorney, wasn't he?"

"I believe so, yes."

"In fact," Marc continued, "he was Aaron Forsberg's lawyer when Forsberg was sent to prison with the use of a flawed DNA test wasn't he?"

"Yes," Jefferson answered.

There was a noticeable stirring throughout the courtroom including the jury with this news. Harris was desperately trying to find something to object to but at this point it would not have mattered.

Judge Koch lightly rapped her gavel twice, looked over the crowd and sternly said, "Settle down. I won't have any disturbances during this trial. Will the lawyers please come forward?" she added when the quiet resumed.

"Mr. Kadella, is this a good time for the lunch break? I have a couple calls to make on other cases," she whispered when the three lawyers reached the bench.

"Certainly, your honor," Marc replied. He was inwardly delighted with the request. Let the jury go to lunch with the news about Segal and Forsberg. Let them think about it for over an hour and really sink in.

As the three men walked back to their tables, Koch gaveled and announced the lunch break.

While the courtroom was emptying for the lunch break, Marc, Howie and Father John went into the small conference room. The priest and Howie took seats at the table. Marc was a little stiff from sitting all morning. Add to that the stress of focusing on his exam of Jefferson and his lower back was a little sore. Instead of taking a seat he preferred to stand and stretch.

"I thought you did really well with that detective," Howie said.

"I agree," Father John chimed in.

"We scored some points. We're lucky the prosecution changed lawyers. Steve Gondeck would have known to go over all that in his direct examination of Jefferson. He would have brought it all out himself and taken most of its effectiveness away from me. Fortunately, Harris isn't that good."

"Now what?" Howie asked.

"You go back and get some lunch," Marc said. Not wanting to spend the lunch break with the priest. Marc said, "I'll go find a place to work on this afternoon's testimony and see you back here at one."

"I have to go back to the church for a while, Howard," Father John said. "But I'll be back later."

"Your seat is reserved," Marc reminded him. "You can come and go as you please. It will be there for you."

FIFTY-THREE

"Detective Jefferson, we left off before the lunch break with the death of Julian Segal, do you remember that?"

Jefferson answered the question affirmatively then Marc started in on the next victim, Elliot Sanders. Tommy Harris and Jefferson had thoroughly testified about Sanders and his ties to Howie Traynor.

Marc went slowly asking very short, specific questions the answer to each being obvious and self-evident. He asked individual yes and no questions concerning the lack of any physical evidence or witnesses that could tie the murder of Elliot Sanders to Howie Traynor. Marc also made Jefferson admit Howie Traynor was under round-the-clock surveillance by the MPD at the time of the Sanders murder.

In the end, Jefferson was forced to admit the only thing they had was motive. Elliot Sanders had been the foreman of the jury that convicted Howie Traynor for the death of Lucille Benson.

Marc finished this line of questioning and paused. He stared at Jefferson for almost a half a minute, absolute silence in the courtroom. Having obtained the admission about a lack of evidence of Sander's death, he probably should have moved on. Instead he silently weighed the consequences of breaking the cardinal rule of courtroom examination of a witness: never ask a question you don't know the answer to.

"Mr. Kadella, do you have any further questions of this witness?" Judge Koch finally asked him.

"Yes, your Honor. Detective Jefferson isn't it true when you discovered the connection between Elliot Sanders and Howard Traynor, that was the precise moment you made up your mind that Howard Traynor was the so-called Crown of Thornes Killer?"

Owen Jefferson almost imperceptibly flinched at the question. What was flashing through his mind at that moment was the question of how Marc could possibly know that. Jefferson hesitated wondering how he should answer.

Sensing Jefferson's dilemma, Marc quickly said, "You're under oath detective. Please answer."

"Yes, it was," Jefferson admitted.

A slight rustling sound went through the gallery while the crowd slightly stirred wondering why this might be significant. Many of them turned their heads from side-to-side looking at each other for an answer.

"Isn't it true that you discussed this conclusion you reached, your belief that Howard Traynor was the Crown of Thornes Killer, with other members of the police department?"

"Yes, a few," Jefferson admitted.

"The next victim, a lawyer by the name of Cara Meyers was found murdered and posed in her condo building's parking lot, was she not?"

"Yes."

"And on her body the M.E. found a single strand of hair that was not one of Cara Meyer's hairs, correct?"

"Yes."

"Subsequent DNA testing matched that single hair to Howard Traynor, isn't that true?"

"Objection," Harris said. "The witness was not allowed to testify about the DNA on direct exam, your Honor."

Koch thought it over for a moment then looked at Jefferson and said, "If you know."

"Yes, that was the result that was reported," Jefferson agreed.

"To your knowledge, was Howard Traynor ever represented by Cara Meyers?"

"Not that we were able to find."

"To your knowledge, did Howard Traynor and Cara Meyers ever even meet?"

"Not that I am aware of."

"Detective Jefferson, is it possible that the single strand of hair found on the body of Cara Meyers was planted to provide evidence against Howard Traynor?"

"Yes," Jefferson shrugged then looked at the jury and said, "anything is possible."

"When you received the DNA report from the crime lab, you were now convinced Howie Traynor was the Crown of Thornes Killer, were you not?"

"I suppose so, yes."

"And you discussed this with other members of the police, didn't you?"

"Yes," he admitted again.

"Did you tell your boss Selena Kane?"

"Yes, I'm sure I did."

"Did Lieutenant Kane have semi-regular meetings with the police chief and mayor about the case and the progress of your investigation?"

"Yes, she did."

"Who did the mayor and chief talk to about these things?"

"I do not know if they talked to anyone," Jefferson answered.

"Who else did your immediate superior, Selena Kane talk to?"

"I wouldn't know," Jefferson said.

"And who else did any of the people that the mayor, the chief and Lieutenant Kane talk to tell about the things they were told..."

"Objection," Harris said.

"For all you know, dozens if not hundreds of people may have known about these things," Marc continued ignoring Harris' objection.

"Sustained, Mr. Kadella," Koch ruled clearly annoyed. "Move along."

Marc turned his attention to the final victim, Jimmy Oliver. The relationship between Oliver and Traynor had been thoroughly disclosed to the jury during Jefferson's direct examination. Rather than rehash all of that in its entirety, Marc restated a few points to reestablish it in the minds of the jurors and then moved on.

"A short while after his release from prison, Howard Traynor stopped in at the bar where Mr. Oliver worked, did he not?"

"Yes," Jefferson admitted. Jefferson had warned Harris that Marc probably knew this, but Harris did not believe the detective and chose to ignore the possibility. He foolishly failed to realize that Howie Traynor himself could tell Marc all about this meeting. Now Marc could bring it out the way he wanted to.

"In fact, Mr. Traynor was under surveillance, by Anthony Carvelli at that time?"

"Yes, that's true."

"Isn't it true Mr. Carvelli told you that this happened and urged you to talk to Jimmy Oliver and find out what they talked about?"

"Yes, he did."

"Did you question Jimmy Oliver about this meeting?"

"Yes, I did."

"And what did he tell you?" This was an open-ended question in that it allowed Jefferson to narrate. Howie had told Marc exactly what happened so Marc knew what was coming.

"Objection, hearsay," Harris said rising from his chair.

"Overruled," Koch said before Marc could respond.

"Jimmy Oliver told me they had a nice talk, that Howie Traynor had converted to Catholicism and he forgave Jimmy for testifying against him for the murder of Lucille Benson."

"Did Jimmy Oliver appear to believe him?"

"Yes, he did."

Marc was a little tempted to go into greater detail about Jimmy Oliver being convinced Howie meant him no harm. It can be a trap lawyers sometimes cannot resist. Marc had obtained the admission he wanted that Jimmy believed Howie was sincere. He could now use that in his closing argument. To try to dig further could blow up in his face. Get what you need, shut up and move on.

"You testified earlier that three more single strands of hair were found on the body of Jimmy Oliver, is that correct?"

"Yes."

"Did you receive the DNA report on those hairs and did they match Howie Traynor's DNA?"

"Yes."

"Detective, is it possible that those three hairs were planted on Jimmy Oliver's body?"

Jefferson visibly squirmed a bit in the chair before admitting again, that it was possible.

Marc asked for and received permission to approach the witness. He stood, walked up to the detective and handed him a single sheet of paper.

Without returning to his seat Marc moved a respectful distance away from Jefferson and stood in front of the jury box.

"Detective Jefferson, I have given you a single sheet of paper marked Defense Exhibit Ten." This was said to be clear for the court reporter's record that Marc handed the witness something and exactly what it was. "Do you recognize it?"

"Yes."

"Tell the jury what it is please?"

"It's a page from a surveillance team log. It's the one from the night of Jimmy Oliver's murder."

"Jimmy Oliver was murdered sometime between 11:00 pm when he went outside for a smoke break and 11:45 when his boss found his body in the alley, is that correct?"

"Yes," Jefferson agreed.

"Read to the jury the highlighted entry made in the surveillance record you are holding, please."

Jefferson looked at the paper then toward Harris hoping for a reprieve. When he did not receive one he read out loud the entry Marc referred to.

"12:22 a.m. per orders from Lieutenant Schiller, Lenoir and I knocked on subject's door. Subject answered and appeared to have been asleep. Initialed by Natalie Musgrove," Jefferson said.

"Isn't it true that this is the surveillance team at Howie Traynor's apartment on the night of Oliver's murder and they went up to his apartment, knocked on his door and found him home and appeared to have awakened him?"

"Yes," Jefferson admitted.

This testimony caused enough of a stir to elicit a banging of her gavel and another warning from Judge Koch.

"Later you walked from the crime scene to Howard Traynor's apartment and determined it was possible he could have committed the murder then made it home in time to be there when Officers Musgrove and Lenoir knocked on his door and find him asleep. It was possible for him to have done that, is that correct?"

"Yes, that's correct."

He then moved on to question Jefferson about the search of Traynor's apartment.

"While the CSU team was searching the apartment, you were basically observing, is that correct?"

"Yes, that's true."

"After a few minutes you walked down the hallway and found the door to the unlocked janitor's closet?"

"Yes, I did."

"You then went inside and discovered the stairs leading up to the roof?"

"Yes."

"You went up on the roof, wandered around for a few minutes then found state's Exhibit A, the wooden boards nailed together," Marc said as he walked to the exhibit table and placed a hand on the boards. "Is that correct?"

"Yes," Jefferson said.

"Mr. Kadella return to your seat please," Koch politely told him.

Marc sat back down before asking the next question.

"You then brought a CSU team member up on the roof with you and between the two of you, you determined that it was possible for someone to use State's Exhibit A to cross over to the next building, isn't that true?"

"Yes, we did," Jefferson said.

"It's possible," Marc repeated.

"Yes."

"Madeline Rivers told you to look in that janitor's closet and up on the roof, didn't she?"

The abruptness of this question caught Jefferson completely off guard. He hesitated long enough for everyone in the courtroom to believe the answer was yes.

"Yes, she did," Jefferson admitted.

"Did she go into that building at your request?"

"No, she did not," Jefferson almost defiantly answered.

The audience and jury noticeably stirred again only this time Judge Koch ignored them. A moment later the room returned to absolute silence while Marc considered his next move.

"While you were on the roof discovering State's Exhibit A, Howard Traynor's possible means of escape so you claim, a discovery was made in Mr. Traynor's bedroom, is that true? State's Exhibits B, C and D were found between the mattress and box spring of the bed, correct?"

"Yes," Jefferson admitted.

"The coil of barbed wire, the wire cutters and leather gloves. There was DNA from Howard Traynor found inside the gloves, is that true?"

"Yes, there was."

"Was there anything found on the other objects? Any DNA or fingerprints or fibers or any physical evidence of any kind tying them to Howard Traynor?"

"You mean other than the fact that they were found in his bed?"

"Yes, Detective," Marc said while the audience chuckled at his mistake.

"No, there was not."

"Did Father John Brinkley tell you anything about the gloves?" By this time the priest was again in attendance and seated in the front row directly behind Marc.

"Objection, hearsay," Harris said.

"Your Honor, I can put him on the stand if need be," Marc said pointing a finger at the priest.

"Overruled," Koch said.

"Yes, he did."

"He told you Howie Traynor had reported the gloves missing from the church where both Father Brinkley and Howard Traynor worked. He also told you he gave Howard Traynor money to buy a new pair, didn't he?"

"Yes, he did."

"Detective Jefferson, based on your experience as a homicide investigator, would you say that a person being killed by having their throat slit open from ear-to-ear would cause considerable blood loss and spraying from the wound?"

"Yes, and all of these victims did."

Jefferson's embellished answer was technically nonresponsive. Marc let it go because it actually helped make the point he was after.

"During the search of Mr. Traynor's apartment, were there any items of clothing found with blood spatter on them?"

"Um, no, there were not," Jefferson admitted.

"Any items of any kind?"

"No."

"How about a knife? Was a knife ever found that matched the wounds of the victims?"

"No, it was not found."

"How about the knife found on the body of Eugene Parlow, another one of your suspects when he was found murdered in an alley? Was that knife tested to see if it matched any of the victims' wounds"

This was the first time Parlow's death had been mentioned. Most of the people in attendance, including all of the jurors, did not know about this except for a few of the media people. Marc's statement created a significant stir in the courtroom. Judge Koch hammered her gavel several times and it still took almost two minutes to get everyone settled down.

"Um, I'm, ah, not sure if that knife would match the victim's wounds."

"How about..." Marc began then caught himself. "Withdrawn. We'll come back to Mr. Parlow later. Was any physical evidence, hair, fibers, blood, DNA from any source other than Mr. Traynor found in Howie Traynor's apartment?"

"He must have been very careful," Jefferson blurted out.

"Your honor, nonresponsive," Marc almost yelled.

"Answer the question only, Detective. Don't pull a stunt like that again," she sternly admonished him. Koch turned to the jury and seriously said, "The jury will disregard that statement."

Realizing the jury could not possibly disregard what they had heard. Marc decided to use it.

"You believe he was so careful that you didn't find any hair, fibers, blood or any DNA but at the same time he was so careless that he left the barbed wire, wire cutters and gloves in between the mattress and box spring of his bed?"

Jefferson knew he had stumbled. He looked at Harris then Judge Koch for help.

"Answer the question," Koch said. "You opened this door."

"Yes," Jefferson meekly answered.

"Was a Taser device found in the apartment?"

"No," Jefferson admitted.

"Was any evidence found anywhere that could link the defendant to any of these crimes other than State's Exhibits B, C and D?"

"No," Jefferson had to admit.

Having scored a helpful point from Jefferson's faux pas, Marc moved on to Howie's car. During the course of his arrest the car had been impounded and thoroughly searched. Included was a complete vacuuming of every inch of the trunk and the car's interior. The detritus scooped up was analyzed under a microscope. Marc went over every part of this process and made Jefferson admit absolutely nothing was found.

Marc made sure Jefferson admitted nothing was found in the car connecting Howie to Elliot Sanders. Even though, according to the police, Sanders had been kidnapped and moved, there was no evidence Howie Traynor had anything to do with it.

"Isn't it true, Detective Jefferson, that a canvas bag was found near the body of Eugene Parlow?"

"Yes," Jefferson admitted.

Marc hit a button on his laptop and a photo of the bag appeared on the courtroom's TV set.

"On the television screen," Marc said for the benefit of the court reporter, "is a picture of a canvas bag. Is this the bag found near the body of Eugene Parlow?"

"Objection," Harris said. "Lack of foundation. This may be a similar...bag. We have no way of knowing."

"I am prepared to bring in the photographer and the CSU tech who witnessed the bag and the items being photographed if necessary, your Honor," Marc said when Koch looked at him.

"Overruled," Koch said. "You may answer if you know."

"Yes, it appears to be the same bag," Jefferson admitted.

Marc pressed the laptop button again and a coil of barbed wire took the place of the bag on the TV. This slide caused a noticeable gasp from the crowded courtroom.

"On the screen is a photo of a coil of barbed wire. It has a police identification tag on it. Was this barbed wire found in the bag?"

"Yes, it was."

The next picture was of the gloves found in the bag, followed in order by the wire cutter then the hammer and nails. Marc went through the same questions to have Jefferson identify them as being in the bag. The final photo he displayed was of the handheld Taser. Marc identified it by its product name and number. Jefferson acknowledged that this item was in the bag with the others.

"Isn't it true, that every one of the victims of the so-called Crown of Thornes Killer was shocked by a Taser such as this?"

"I believe so, yes."

"Was such a device ever found that could be linked to Howie Traynor?"

"No," Jefferson again admitted.

"Detective Jefferson let's go back to the janitor's closet and the roof at the apartment. Did the CSU team go over the closet looking for evidence?"

"Yes, of course," Jefferson admitted.

"Isn't it true they found absolutely nothing in the closet to indicate Howie Traynor had ever been there?"

"Yes, that's true," Jefferson answered somewhat wearily.

"Isn't it true they found evidence, including DNA that other people had been in the closet?"

"Yes."

"But nothing of Mr. Traynor correct?"

"Yes."

"How about the roof? Was it searched by the CSU team?"

"Yes."

"Was any physical evidence found on the roof to confirm Howard Traynor had ever been up there?"

"Not on the roof of his building but we did find three cigarette butts on the roof next door of the same brand he smokes and with his DNA on them," Jefferson blurted out catching Marc completely off guard.

The courtroom exploded.

FIFTY-FOUR

Marc sat slumped down in one of the cheap plastic chairs in the jail's conference room. He silently stared at the top of the table between himself and Howie Traynor. Howie was seated opposite his lawyer looking like a school boy waiting for the principal to bite his head off.

It had taken Judge Koch a few minutes and a serious threat to have the courtroom emptied before order was restored. The first thing she did was to order Jefferson's statement to be stricken from the record. She then spent several minutes instructing the jury to disregard Jefferson's answer about the cigarette butts and DNA results. All the while Marc sat staring straight ahead seething at what had just happened and trying to act as if it was not a big deal. He was also trying to decide who he was madder at; Howie for not telling him this or Tommy Harris for keeping it from him.

The judge finished instructing the jury then turned to glare at Harris. If looks could kill, Harris would have been impaled on a stake.

"Your Honor," Marc calmly said as he rose to address her. "The defense requests a conference in chambers."

"Granted," Koch said. "Deputy, please take the jury out." She looked at the wall clock then continued. "In fact, we're going to adjourn for the day."

"Your Honor..." Marc started to protest. Koch just verbally kicked him in the groin by making sure the jury would contemplate the last thing they heard from Jefferson, the news about the cigarette butts on the roof next door. Even though Koch had ordered the jury to ignore it, to do so was highly unlikely.

"No, Mr. Kadella, that's enough for today. I'll see the lawyers in chambers."

The three lawyers stood to follow her out while the media mob flooded through the exit. Howie was led away by the deputies without a word between himself and his lawyer.

"I want a mistrial," Marc said while the judge hung up her robe and before the lawyers had taken their seats.

"What do you have to say for yourself, Mr. Harris?" Koch asked. "Why wasn't this information given to the defense?"

"We just found out ourselves, your Honor," Harris whined in protest. "During the break I took a call in the hallway from the BCA. I haven't even seen the report yet."

"How did Jefferson find out?" Marc snarled.

"I guess, I ah, told him," Harris sheepishly admitted. "How could I know that would come up?"

"You only hoped it would," Marc said.

"Mr. Ramsey, did you know about this?" Koch asked.

Harris' assistant said, "No, your Honor. Like Mr. Kadella, I'm being treated like a mushroom."

Koch turned her head back to Harris and said, "If I find out you're lying, I will make it my life's business to have you disbarred. And Craig Slocum, if I find out he's involved.

"Now, as to a mistrial," she continued. "I'm not inclined to grant one but," she continued turning to Harris again, "you will not mention this again and the DNA results or any testimony about this again. Do I make myself clear?"

"Yes, your Honor," Harris said.

"Judge," Marc said, "that's not good enough. My defense was based on the belief they had no evidence putting my client on that roof. Now I find out that's not true and they kept it from me."

"It's my call and that's it. Appeal away. We'll pick up tomorrow morning."

Marc looked up at his client and said, "I just spent an entire day scoring points for us and creating reasonable doubt. Then it all blew up in my face because the jury now knows you were up on that roof and used the plank bridge to go over to the building next door. Or, at least that is what it looks like and what they believe. Just like the cops say you did. Our whole case hinged on the cops being your alibi and now…"

He heavily exhaled while staring at a silent, impassive Howie Traynor. "I needed to say that to vent a bit. Let's move on."

Marc looked at Howie, spread his hands apart and asked, "Is there anything else? Anything you need to tell me? Why were you up on that roof?"

"I knew I was being watched and I went up there to check on them. I had to go to the building next door to see the cops in the alley," Howie answered. "There's nothing else, I swear."

Marc pushed back his chair making a loud scraping noise on the floor. He stood and said, "Okay, I'll see you in the morning."

Howie took his usual seat in front of the television. Ever since his problem with the idiot in the bathroom, no one tried changing the channel when Melinda's show was on the air.

The Court Reporter was shown live in its normal time slot of 4:00 p.m. Because of the extraordinary interest in Howie's trial and the ratings the crass, opinionated Ms. Pace generated, it was repeated at

6:30. Fortunately Howie was usually back from court each day by then to catch the rerun.

Melinda was finished with the report by Gabriella Shriqui from in front of the Government Center. Gabriella had related the day's events including Owen Jefferson's outburst about the cigarette butts.

When the show came back from a commercial break Melinda turned to her guest. Denise Flagler, the former prosecutor was back to give her expert opinion of a trial she was not watching.

"I must admit," Melinda began, "I wasn't sure if the jury would believe Traynor sneaked out to kill these people the way the police said he did. Using a wooden plank to go to the next building seemed like a bit of a stretch."

"Juries aren't stupid, Melinda," Flagler said. "With the DNA of Howie Traynor found on the victims and the revelation that the police found proof he was on the roof of the building next to his apartment, I think his goose is cooked."

"What about the judge telling the jury to ignore the testimony about the cigarettes found on the roof?" Melinda asked.

"They're human," Flagler said looking directly at the camera. At that precise moment, Flagler was delighted she had spent two hours having her hair done and face painted. She looked great and knew it. "The jurors are not going to be able to ignore it. They'll say they did but it was a very powerful moment."

While this was being shown on the jail TV, several of Howie's neighbors stole quick glances at him. Howie ignored them and continued to watch the show with an impassive expression. When it was over he left the room without saying a word about it.

The next morning Judge Koch was late coming to the bench. She was delayed because she had to deal with an "emergency" motion on a civil case she was handling. It was a dispute between an insurance company and a corporate customer of the insurance company. To make sure that the lawyers billed enough time for this hearing which was no emergency and could have waited a month or two to be heard, there were a total of seven lawyers in Koch's chambers. Afterwards she took fifteen minutes to allow her exasperation to go away and it was past 10:00 a.m. when she entered the courtroom. She did not want her annoyance with the "emergency" hearing to affect the trial.

"Good morning, Detective Jefferson. I have just a few more questions," Marc began. "I'd like to be clear about something. Isn't it true that you believe Howie Traynor committed these murders because of some need for revenge?"

"I suppose you could put it that way, yes," Jefferson replied.

"Do you have a different motive?"

"No, I don't," Jefferson admitted.

"And, he is charged with the murder of Cara Meyers, a woman he had never met because it is possible he wanted to confuse the investigation, to throw you off the track, so to speak?"

"Essentially, yes."

"And, the single hair that was found on her body, you admitted it was possible it could have been planted is that correct?"

"Yes,"

"You believe it was possible he committed the other murders because they were involved in his original trial twelve years ago?"

"Yes."

"Detective Jefferson, are you aware I was his lawyer for that trial?"

"Objection," Harris interjected, "irrelevant."

"Sustained," Koch ruled.

Even though the objection was sustained as Marc expected the question still hung in the air. The message was loud and clear. Marc is alive and well and willing to represent him again.

"Isn't it true that Rhea Watson prosecuted both Eugene Parlow and Aaron Forsberg?"

"Yes, she did."

"And you knew this didn't you?"

"Yes,"

"Isn't it true that Judge Ross Peterson presided over the trials of both Eugene Parlow and Aaron Forsberg?"

"Yes, it is."

"Isn't it also true that Cara Meyers was Eugene Parlow's lawyer?"

"Yes."

"And Julian Segal was Aaron Forsberg's lawyer?"

"Yes."

"And they were both murdered by the Crown of Thornes killer and I'm still alive?"

"Objection!" Harris jumped up and yelled.

"Withdrawn," Marc said. "Are you aware that Judge Robert Smith the likely first victim in Beltrami County, was one of the appellate judges for Eugene Parlow, Aaron Forsberg and Howie Traynor?"

"Objection," Harris said again.

"Your Honor, I'm merely asking if the witness is aware of this," Marc said.

"Overruled. The witness will answer."

"Yes, we knew that."

"Do you believe beyond a reasonable doubt that Howard Traynor is guilty as charged?"

"Objection," Harris jumped to his feet again. "That is strictly for the jury to determine."

"Your Honor," Marc countered by saying, "the witness is a decorated, veteran, homicide detective. He can give his opinion."

Judge Koch thought it was an odd question for the defense to ask. She would never allow the prosecution to ask it but if the defense wanted Jefferson to give his opinion, it was their risk.

"Overruled. The witness can answer."

"Yes, of course I do," Jefferson said looking directly at the jury.

"Because even though he was under round-the-clock surveillance by private detectives and the Minneapolis Police Department, it's possible he could have slipped away, several times, evaded the surveillance, committed horrible, bloody crimes then slipped back past the surveillance again without ever being seen. It's possible he did that, isn't it?" Marc asked managing to keep any trace of sarcasm out of his voice.

Jefferson's reaction to the question was exactly what Marc hoped for. He paused at least ten seconds before answering. While he sat silently on the witness stand, the courtroom was absolutely still, and the question hung in the air.

"Yes," Jefferson finally agreed.

"A lot of things going on in this case that hang on the word *possible*, isn't there Detective Jefferson?"

"Your Honor, objection," Harris said again jumping out of his chair. "Argumentative."

"Sustained," Koch said. "The jury will disregard that last question." All the while Marc sat quietly staring at Owen Jefferson.

"One last question your Honor," Marc said without moving his eyes from the witness.

"Detective Jefferson, you are certain that Howard Traynor is guilty beyond a reasonable doubt yet, isn't it true that Eugene Parlow was under surveillance until his death and Aaron Forsberg is still under surveillance by the police?"

A slight murmur went through the crowd while Jefferson, Harris and Ramsey all wondered how Marc knew this.

"Yes," Jefferson quietly admitted "Because…"

"Nonresponsive," Marc said.

"Answer just the question as asked," Judge Koch reminded him which caused Jefferson to admit it again.

"I have no further questions at this time, your Honor. I request the right to recall."

"Granted," Koch ruled. "Mr. Harris, do you wish to redirect?"
"Yes, your Honor," Harris answered.
"Let's break for lunch first," she ordered.

The afternoon session also started a little late. It was almost 1:30 by the time Tommy Harris began his redirect examination of Owen Jefferson. The basic purpose of a redirect examination is to try to correct or rehabilitate statements made by the witness during the cross examination. It is not supposed to be an opportunity to bring out any new facts. These should have been handled during the original direct examination.

During Marc's cross exam of Jefferson, both Tommy Harris and Paul Ramsey made notes of statements to try to correct. Harris spent all afternoon basically going over the most important points Marc elicited from Jefferson that were favorable to the defense.

While Harris was doing this, Marc amused himself by listening carefully and objecting whenever he could. Almost all of the objections, at least a dozen, fell into one of two categories. Either "beyond the scope of the cross examination" or "already covered during the direct examination". Every one of them was sustained and with each one Harris became a little more flustered.

By the end of the day Harris did manage to get it out of Jefferson that the police believed Howie had an accomplice. They also believed it was either Eugene Parlow or Aaron Forsberg. When Harris finally finished, Marc was given an opportunity to re-cross exam Jefferson.

"Let me be sure I understand you, Detective Jefferson. Parlow and Forsberg were under surveillance because you believe it was possible that Howard Traynor had an accomplice?"

"Yes, that's correct," Jefferson sighed.

"There's that word *possible* again, isn't it Detective?"

"Objection," Harris said but didn't have the energy to stand.

"Sustained," Koch said hiding a smile.

"I have nothing further but, again, I do reserve the right to recall," Marc concluded.

FIFTY-FIVE

Marc was at his desk reviewing his trial book for approximately the twentieth time. He was going through it page-by-page trying to be careful and not miss anything.

When the testimony of Owen Jefferson finally concluded, the trial entered its middle part.

A real trial isn't like those depicted on TV or in the movies. They normally move at a snail's pace because the prosecution must build its case piece-by-piece, brick-by-brick. They must be sure that each and every element of every charge is proven beyond a reasonable doubt. And, they must do it for every crime charged. This requires a number of witnesses who add minor details that are important to the final product. The next witness to be called by Harris was Marcie Sterling, Jefferson's partner. She had taken the stand first thing this morning and was done by noon. Sterling had little more to offer than a confirmation of what Jefferson already told the jury.

The afternoon was spent with several witnesses who were only ancillary to the prosecution's case. There was a list of a dozen people who either discovered the victims or were first responder police officers. The only one who offered any real evidence was the tech who had performed the analysis of the items found in Howie's apartment. She testified that the barbed wire was the same as that found on the victims' heads and the wire cutters mostly matched the cuts made on those crowns. Marc had his own expert, his criminalist Jason Briggs to testify and dispute those findings. Hopefully Briggs could create some reasonable doubt about this evidence.

First up were the two women who called the police and went to the home of Rhea Watson. They were her assistant, Tricia Dunlop and Rhea's immediate supervisor and friend, Jacqueline Neeley. Paul Ramsey did the direct examination of both, his very first time questioning a real witness in a real case. He confidently guided each woman through her testimony then turned them over to Marc. Marc's cross exam amounted to little more than a few questions to elicit a confirmation that neither of them had anything to offer regarding who might have committed this crime.

The next witness was police sergeant Norman Anderson. His testimony was much more riveting. During his walk through of Rhea Watson house, he had used a small camera to take pictures. Prior to trial there had been an argument before Judge Koch about this. Marc tried to convince the judge that these photos were unnecessary and added nothing to the question of guilt. Koch had ruled that ten pictures could be shown and Koch herself selected those. When Anderson's picture of Watson's body went up on the TV it created virtually no reaction. By this time these gruesome photos had been seen too many times and their shock value had worn off.

The afternoon dragged along and by 4:30 the jurors were having a difficult time paying attention. Marc had noticed a couple of them even nod off. When Ramsey finished with the two women who found the posed body of Elliot Sanders at the picnic table in Mueller Park, Koch called a halt for the day.

Before she dismissed the jury she called the lawyers to the bench.

"Are you on schedule?" she asked Tommy Harris.

Assuring her that they were the judge dismissed the jury for the weekend. She also politely yet firmly admonished them they were not to discuss the case with anyone and were to avoid news reports concerning it.

Marc looked at the clock on his office wall, noticed it was already past 7:00 p.m. when his cell phone rang. He checked the I.D. and saw it was Margaret Tennant. Marc answered the call and for the next ten minutes found a little solace in her comforting voice.

Margaret not only knew Marc well, she also knew trial work. Before calling she expected Marc would beg off spending the weekend with her. The stress and significance of the case was all consuming and he would need some time to himself, to be alone and decompress a little. Plus, during a trial like this, the weekend, even if the trial was in recess, would not be time off for the lawyers.

Moments after ending the call with Margaret, Marc heard the front door being unlocked and opened. Knowing who it was Marc watched through his open door waiting for her to appear.

"Hey," Marc said when Connie Mickelson appeared in his doorway.

"I figured you'd still be here," she answered him.

Connie placed her large, leather purse on Marc's desk. She reached into it with both hands and when they emerged, she had two small glasses in her right hand and a bottle of bourbon in the other. She set the glasses on the desk blotter and poured three fingers in each one. She handed one to Marc, held hers toward him and he lightly touched it with his in a toast.

They each took a sip then Connie sat down and said, "Figured you could use a little pick-me-up."

Marc took another small sip while Connie tossed all of her drink down. She refilled her glass, held up the bottle to Marc who smiled and declined.

"So, how you doing?" she asked after setting the bottle back on his desk and leaning back in her chair.

Marc also leaned back, opened a desk drawer and put his feet up on it. "Okay," he answered.

"How's the trial going?"

Marc thought about his answer, sipped the bourbon again then said, "Okay but I've got a couple problems."

"The cigarette butts found on the roof?"

"Yeah," Marc agreed. "That's one."

"What are you going to do about it?"

"I'm not sure. How do you know…"

"It was on the news, of course. The Princess," Connie added sarcastically, "Melinda Pace, was practically giddy about it."

"It was excluded by Judge Koch," Marc said shaking his head. "They shouldn't report it at all."

"The jury heard it. They can't ignore it," Connie said.

"I know," Marc agreed. "I'll think of something. I hope."

"What's the other problem?"

Marc drained his glass, cringed a little as the liquid burned down his throat, then held the glass out to Connie. Connie had finished her second drink and splashed more into both glasses.

"Madeline Rivers," Marc said in answer to Connie's inquiry.

"I figured," Connie said. "You have to go after her."

"I know," Marc sighed. He looked away from Connie and stared vacantly at the drink in his hand. Up to this very moment he had been putting off dealing with this particular dilemma. He still did not want to but talking about it with Connie might help.

Marc was still leaning back in his brown leather desk chair, his feet on the opened drawer. He turned his head to Connie, drank half the bourbon in his glass and said, "I can either force her to commit perjury or admit to a felony."

"You didn't send her into Traynor's apartment. That was a choice she and Carvelli made," Connie reminded him.

"Connie, she's just like you. She's my pal; my girl. This sickens me." Marc looked at the wall clock, tossed down what remained in his glass and said, "I have to get out of here. If I don't, I'll stay until that bottle's empty."

"It might be just what you need," Connie smiled.

Marc dropped his feet onto the floor, swiveled his chair to face forward, handed the empty glass to Connie and said, "Probably but I don't think that would be a good idea."

Marc's personal phone rang at that moment and he checked the I.D. It was not a number he recognized, and he almost did not answer it. Marc's curiosity got the better of him and he picked up the phone and put it to his ear.

"Hey, Marc," he heard a man's voice say, a voice he recognized but couldn't place. "It's Steve Gondeck."

"Steve," Marc said. "What's up?" Marc continued as he looked at Connie with a puzzled expression.

"Look, Marc," Gondeck continued speaking almost in a whisper. "I have some information for you, but I can't tell you over the phone. Can we meet tonight?"

"What, you think the NSA is listening in? Trust me, Steve. I've been dealing with the IRS and the Feds for twenty years. They're not that competent."

"Marc, I'm serious," Gondeck said.

"Okay. Where and when?"

Gondeck gave him the name of a restaurant on the 494 strip in Bloomington and Marc agreed to meet him in twenty minutes.

Marc walked into the restaurant, stood in the dining room entryway and looked for Gondeck. At first he did not see him then finally noticed him waving from a table in the back. Approaching the table, Marc realized why he didn't recognize him. Marc had never seen Steve Gondeck wearing anything but a business suit, white shirt and tie. This man had on a cotton pullover and jeans.

The two lawyers shook hands and took their seats. Gondeck was sipping a short glass of beer and Marc ordered the same. While the waiter went to get it, the two of them made small talk about the Vikings, the weather and the upcoming Holidays.

"Okay," Marc said after a swallow of his beer while patting his mouth with a napkin. "What's up?"

Gondeck hesitated for a long moment once again thinking about the information he had. His professional responsibility divided between his ethical obligation to his job and clients, the people of Hennepin County and the State of Minnesota, and his ethical obligation as an officer of the court. He had been weighing these commitments most of the day. Normally they did not contrast as they did now. Gondeck had finally decided that his duty as an officer of the court and his responsibility to seek justice outweighed his loyalty to the county attorney's office.

"It's about Craig Slocum and your trial," he began.

"Okay, what?" Marc asked not the least bit surprised that Slocum might be trying to pull something.

Gondeck removed a folded single sheet of paper from his back pocket. On it was a handwritten list of names and job titles. He gave it to Marc who looked it over. There were a dozen names listed.

"So, what are these?" Marc asked.

"They're the names of people in the county attorney's office who know how much Slocum hates you personally. How much he blames you for damaging his political career."

"So what?" Marc asked.

"They also know the stunt he pulled to surprise you at trial," Gondeck said.

For the next ten minutes he explained to Marc what he was talking about. What Craig Slocum had done to abuse his power in an attempt to convict Howie Traynor and get even with Marc.

"You don't seem surprised," Gondeck said when he finished.

"I'm not," Marc calmly replied. "I'm not the only defense lawyer who has had problems with your boss."

"True," Gondeck admitted.

"How did you find out?"

"His secretary. She's on the list," Gondeck said pointing a finger at her name.

"This is all real nice," Marc said with a shrug. "But it's also confidential and privileged. None of these people can be forced to testify."

"Maybe," Gondeck agreed, "maybe not. This is at least unethical and probably illegal. You're a smart guy. You'll figure out a way to use this."

Marc silently looked at his friendly adversary for a while before saying, "Why are you doing this? You could get disbarred for this."

Gondeck drained what was left in his glass. "Because it is flat out wrong. Aside from whether or not it is legal, illegal, ethical or unethical, it is simply wrong.

"You know me, Marc. I like to win as much as the next guy and I still believe your client is guilty. But this is bullshit. And," he quietly continued, "this isn't the first time. Slocum has the attitude that rules are for others and don't really apply to him. He has that 'ends justifies the means' Christian hypocrite problem. Besides, like I said, you're a smart guy, you'll think of something and protect me."

"Okay and thanks for putting me on the spot," Marc replied with a touch of lawyer sarcasm.

He thought about the information he had been given then said, "Well, I'm not sure what I can do with it yet, but I'll give it some thought and figure out something, I hope."

FIFTY-SIX

Over the weekend temperatures climbed into the upper 40's. The snow was gone, the streets clean and clear and car washes were doing a booming business.

Monday morning Marc arrived at the government center shortly after 7:00. Both Friday and Saturday nights, having been relieved of the stress of trial for two days, Marc had slept the sleep of the dead. Last night, Sunday, he tossed and turned most of the night before giving up shortly after 5:00 a.m.

Judge Koch's courtroom door was unlocked when he arrived, and the media herd was not there yet. While he was arranging his table with the items he would need, the judge's clerk, Andy Combs, came into the courtroom. They greeted each other then Combs set up his desk next to the judge's bench.

"You're early," Combs said to Marc.

"Couldn't sleep," Marc replied. "Is the judge in yet?"

"Oh yeah," Combs replied. "She's here every day by 6:30. Do you need to see her?"

"No," Marc replied, "just curious."

"The state calls Martin Colstad," Harris declared after Koch gave him the go ahead.

Colstad was the clerk for Judge Ross Peterson. It was Colstad who alerted the police that Peterson was missing, and it was Colstad, along with Officer Rhonda Dean, who found the judge's body.

Martin Colstad and Officer Dean combined were on the stand for about an hour and a half. The trial was still in its slow boring phase. The witnesses to be heard for the next few days would offer little to the question of guilty or not guilty. They were essential to paint a complete verbal picture for the jury of the death of each victim.

Between the two of them, Colstad and Dean explained what they did and why, how they came to search for the missing judge and what they found at his house. When he finished first with Colstad and then Dean, Ramsey passed each of the witnesses over to Marc.

Colstad was a career government employee. He had a degree as a Para-legal and worked in the Hennepin County courts for over sixteen years, the last ten as Judge Peterson's personal clerk. Because of his position with the judge, Colstad would have firsthand knowledge of Peterson as a judge.

Marc amiably asked a few questions to establish that fact then quickly changed to a more serious manner.

"Isn't it true that Judge Peterson would not be described as a pleasant man?"

Colstad, despite watching hundreds of others testify in trials over the years was a little nervous. This question caught him off guard and he visibly shifted in his seat.

"Objection," Ramsey said rising to address the court. "Judge Peterson's personality is not on trial and is irrelevant."

"If you will indulge me a bit, your Honor, I'll be able to demonstrate the relevance," Marc said.

"I'll overrule the objection, for now, but I expect you to get there," Koch ruled. "The witness will answer."

"Well, um, yes, you could say that."

"Isn't it also true that Judge Peterson was known to be more favorable to the prosecution in criminal matters?"

"Well, I don't think..."

"You're under oath, Mr. Colstad," Marc sharply reminded him.

"Yes, he was," Colstad quietly agreed.

"Objection, relevance," Ramsey tried again.

"I'm getting there your Honor," Marc said in rebuttal.

"Overruled," Koch said again as Ramsey sat down.

"Isn't it also true that he was known as a law and order judge who gave out harsh, stiff sentences to guilty defendants?"

Ramsey started to rise but Koch held out a hand and said, "Keep your seat Mr. Ramsey. I see where he's going."

"Yes, that's true," Colstad reluctantly admitted.

"During the ten years you clerked for him, did the judge receive death threats from people he had sent to prison?"

"All judges do," Colstad said.

"Nonresponsive, your Honor," Marc said while continuing to stare at Colstad.

"Answer the question, Mr. Colstad," Koch firmly admonished him.

"Yes, he did," Colstad agreed.

"How many?"

"Oh, I don't know the exact number," Colstad answered.

"When the judge did receive a threatening letter, you notified the police didn't you?"

"Yes, I did."

Marc reached in his briefcase and removed a stack of paper that looked like copies of letters. He placed the two-inch-thick stack on the table and asked again, "How many did he receive?"

Colstad looked around the room hoping for a reprieve from answering. When one was obviously not forthcoming he said, "Over four hundred."

This answer caused a minor stirring in the courtroom which brought one sharp, loud bang from Judge Koch's gavel.

"Isn't it also true that not a single one of the more than four hundred threatening letters Judge Peterson received was written by my client, Howie Traynor?"

"I, ah, don't believe so," Colstad answered.

"Is that a yes, Mr. Colstad? None of those letters was written by Howie Traynor?"

"Yes, that's true," Colstad agreed.

"Judge Peterson had a lot of people wanting to do him harm, didn't he Mr. Colstad?"

"Argumentative," Ramsey objected.

"Sustained. You made your point, Mr. Kadella. Move it along."

Having obtained what he wanted from Peterson's clerk, the obvious admission that others wanted him dead also, Marc ended his questioning.

Marc had only a few questions for Rhonda Dean. These were designed to fortify the fact that there were differences in the way Peterson's body looked than the others. Since the M.E. and CSU people would have to testify, Dean's corroboration would verify that the body was found with no blood on it or mangled fingers and toes. The greater details of how he died would come later.

When Dean finished, Koch called for a short break. The judge and jury left the courtroom and the spectators filed out into the hall.

"How did you get copies of those letters?" Howie asked Marc referring to the papers Marc was putting back in his briefcase.

"I didn't. I was bluffing," Marc said and winked at Howie.

The rest of the day was used up by minor witnesses for each victim. After Judge Peterson, the prosecution continued with the victims in order. The next witnesses were the man who discovered the body of Eugene Parlow's lawyer, Cara Meyers. He was followed by the police officer who was first on the scene. While the photo of Cara Meyers was displayed on the TV screen, each described what they did. The idea was again for the prosecution to build their case brick-by-brick. The Cara Meyers witnesses finished after lunch and before the afternoon break.

"Your honor, we're running a little ahead of schedule and our next witnesses are not here," Harris quietly admitted. The lawyers were arrayed at the judge's bench.

"Do you have anyone else lined up to go this afternoon?" Koch asked.

"No, your Honor. We didn't expect to finish with these until later today. We anticipated a longer cross examination by Mr. Kadella," Harris said in a weak attempt to lay the blame on Marc.

"Nice try," Marc said.

"Very well," Koch said. "We'll adjourn for the day. But, you'd better be ready to go first thing in the morning."

"More gruesome details from the Crown of Thornes case," Melinda Pace began the show by saying.

The first half of her show was taken up with a live Q & A between Melinda and Gabriella Shriqui. The value of the news was somewhat minimal, but it did give Melinda an opportunity to display a picture of each of the victims. Of course, Melinda gave the audience the usual warning to get the kids away from the TV because of the graphic nature of the photos. This is, of course, designed to be sure to get everyone's attention by letting the audience know something really juicy was coming.

The use of the photos caught Gabriella completely off guard. She had no idea that Melinda was going to do this. Plus, Gabriella was extremely curious about how Melinda got her hands on these pictures. Melinda would never admit she paid a thousand dollars in cash out of her own pocket to a source in Slocum's office. It was a source who sold them with the full knowledge of Craig Slocum himself.

Later that evening, during the 6:30 rerun of Melinda's show, Howie Traynor showed no emotion when the pictures filled the jail's TV screen. Several of the other guests in the room made admiring comments while stealing short, quick glances at the celebrity inmate.

The finale of Melinda's show as usual, was a quick story of her selection for "Today's Dumbest Criminal." The county inmates sat enraptured by what they considered the best part of the show.

"From Tulsa, Oklahoma," Melinda began, "We have today's featured story.

"Jacob Canfield attempted to rob the Tulsa County Bank. He held a gun on the teller, a twenty-one-year-old woman by the name of Anna Sanchez, while she stacked the money on the counter. Instead of making Ms. Sanchez put the money in a bag for him, our would-be bank robber placed the gun on the counter, so he could use both hands to stuff the money in his pockets. Anna, brave girl that she is, picked up the gun and pointed it at today's idiot.

"Rather than surrender, Jacob turned and sprinted toward the door. Anna fired a couple of shots and one of them hit him in, well folks, I'll be blunt, his butt. As he was going down from being shot, Jacob did a header into the unbreakable glass of the front door. He knocked himself out, gave himself a concussion and compressed neck. The Tulsa police found him unconscious on the floor while Anna stood over him still holding the gun.

"The report is he'll be out of the hospital in a few days. He'll probably hire a lawyer to sue the bank and contact the ACLU to file a lawsuit against the bank for violating his civil rights for excessive use of force. Would anyone be surprised? As for me, I am just sorry that this guy will someday father children and pass his genes along."

FIFTY-SEVEN

Friday morning and Marc was again going through his ritual after parking his car. He opened the briefcase on the passenger seat and removed a yellow legal pad. While he remained seated in his car, he read through the notes he had made in anticipation of today's testimony.

True to his reputation, Tommy Harris did a competent, if not spectacular job of putting enough testimony into evidence to satisfy each element of each charge. The one exception being the kidnapping of Elliot Sanders.

For the past three days, Harris and Ramsey put on a parade of witnesses. Included were the people who found each body, the first responder, police officers and a CSU tech to testify about their procedures.

Harris saved the best for last. The medical examiner who performed the autopsies had to testify about the cause of death for each victim. The prosecution was also allowed to put more grisly photos in front of the jury. The ME explained the wounds from their throats being slit to the crushed fingers and toes when they were tortured. The real purpose of this gruesome display was to insight the jury with enough revulsion to get them to make somebody pay for this.

The medical examiner who conducted the autopsies, Clyde Marston, had to admit Peterson died from a heart attack. Marston insisted it was caused by the pacemaker being overcharged by the Taser and it was not natural causes. Marc also got him to admit that whoever did it, did not intend to induce a heart attack. This admission likely removed first-degree premeditation for the death of Peterson and probably second-degree murder as well. Given the list of murder charges Howie Traynor faced, this was a minor victory at best.

The number one issue facing the jury was still: who did this? All of the other issues, including the other first-degree premeditated murder charges were still there. There were no eyewitnesses and no confession, but the jury could easily infer premeditation from how the crimes were committed. The case would come down to whether or not the jury unanimously believed Howard Traynor did them. One conviction for first degree murder and Howie dies in prison.

Marc completed his last-minute review of what he believed was coming today. The prosecution had timed their case perfectly. It was Friday and Marc saw them finishing their case this afternoon with their psychiatrist.

Marc was previously provided with a copy of the doctor's report. His name was George Christie and of course he came with impeccable credentials. Dr, Christie was head of the Department of Psychiatry at Vanderbilt University. He was also an acknowledged leading expert in the field of sociopathic mental illness.

Christie had been given all of Howie's medical records back to his birth. According to his report, the doctor would testify that Howie Traynor was a sociopath from birth and as such his particular psychosis was untreatable. Therefore, his conversion to Catholicism and alleged transformation to a model citizen was a total scam.

Marc was too late to enter the courtroom through the front door. The hallway was already too crowded with the media and curiosity seekers. Instead, Marc used the security intercom and a deputy allowed him to enter through the back hallway.

When he did he was surprised to find Harris and Ramsey already seated at their table.

"We need to see the judge," Harris said while Marc hung up his coat. Without waiting for a reply Harris started toward the door leading to the chamber's hallway.

Marc watched Harris with Ramsey trying to catch up then said, "Is it okay if I come with?"

Paul Ramsey turned his head to Marc, smiled and lightly laughed. Tommy Harris completely ignored the sarcastic question and marched through the door.

Marc caught up with the two prosecutors as they were taking their usual seats in the judge's chambers. Before he could sit down Harris started in on the reason for this meeting.

"Judge, we want to reopen the issue of the cigarettes found on the roof of the building next door to Traynor's apartment."

An alarm went off in Marc's head and he said, "I want this on the record, your Honor."

Koch, seated behind her semi-cluttered desk looked at Marc and said, "I agree."

Koch called her clerk in and they all waited for almost ten minutes while the trial's court reporter came in and set up his equipment. When he was ready he let Koch know it. The judge then made a statement about the time and place of this in camera hearing.

"You may proceed, Mr. Harris," Koch told Tommy.

"Thank you, your Honor," Harris began hiding his disappointment that a complete record was being made. "We believe we should be allowed to submit testimony about the three cigarette butts with the defendant's DNA. The test was delayed through no fault of the prosecution.

"I have two affidavits to submit from the head of the BCA lab and the technician who conducted the test," Harris continued as he handed copies of both documents to Marc and Judge Koch. "Apparently there was some problem we were not aware of. We want to put the technician Burt Orland, on the stand. He is on our witness list. I also have copies of case law your Honor, to back up our position," Harris said handing copies of the cases to Koch and Marc.

"Mr. Kadella," Koch said to Marc.

"Absolutely not, your Honor. I received a copy of the test results the day Owen Jefferson blurted this information out in court and you ruled it was to be ignored," Marc began.

"Clearly he's had time to contest the report's findings," Harris interrupted.

Koch held up a hand to indicate Harris should wait his turn while Marc continued.

"A significant part of my defense was based on the fact that the police found no evidence that my client was ever in the janitor's closet or on the roof. Now I'm being told that was not true and I believe it was deliberately withheld from me."

Before Harris could protest Marc's accusation Koch again held up her hand to stop.

"That's a pretty serious claim, Mr. Kadella. If you can prove it, let's hear it. Otherwise, be thankful we're not in front of the jury or you'd be writing that check."

Koch then turned to Harris and said, "I'm not pleased about this, but I believe you're right. This evidence was inevitable, and the jury should hear it."

"Your Honor, this could easily be reversible error," Marc protested.

"Then your client will get me reversed on appeal," Koch told him.

Koch looked at the clock on the wall and continued, "I'll read this over," she said referring to the documents submitted by Harris. "We'll start at 10:00. Thank you."

The morning session was taken up with the testimony of three men. They were all Hennepin County Sheriff's deputies who knew Howie from his original trial; the one that got him sent to prison for the murder of Lucille Benson. Two were retired and one was still a deputy sheriff.

The three of them all had the same basic story to tell. They worked in the jail after Howie was convicted and heard his threats.

"Who were the people that Mr. Traynor threatened if you can recall?" was a question Harris put to each of them.

All three men answered almost exactly the same, having previously rehearsed their testimony. They all listed ten to twelve names including most of those he was charged with murdering. They also testified to remembering this because everyone in the jail, including the other inmates, were terrified of Howie Traynor.

Marc objected to them claiming what the inmates believed and was sustained. It was essentially a futile gesture. The witnesses could testify about what they felt about Howie. Each said the same thing. Howie Traynor was just about the scariest inmate they ever dealt with.

"What did you personally think of those threats? Did you believe him?"

"Absolutely," or a variation of this was given by each of the men n turn.

Harris also elicited an admission that convicted inmates often made threats toward the people who they believe are responsible for their incarceration.

"Sure," each agreed. Most of these threats are made in anger and after a while, the inmate cools down and nothing ever comes of it. Howie Traynor's threats were different. His were not made in anger. In fact, he was icy cool at the time and by the look in his eyes, he meant it.

Marc objected to their mind reading ability and was again futilely sustained. His cross examination was basically obtaining admissions that Howie's metamorphosis in prison could have changed him. Knowing what was coming from the prosecution's psychiatrist expert left Marc feeling his cross exam was a little weak.

"Previously, you heard testimony that the defendant's DNA was found on the roof of the building next door to his apartment," Koch said addressing the jury after lunch. "At that time, I ordered you to disregard it. You are about to hear from witnesses who will give testimony contrary to that order." The judge then turned to the prosecutor's table and said, "You may call your next witness, Mr. Harris."

The first witness was an officer of the MPD, Carrie Sinclair. She testified that she was the one who found the cigarette butts on the roof. She admitted that she found them three days after Howie Traynor's arrest. In order to maintain the chain of custody, she identified the evidence bag they were in and her initials on the bag.

Following Officer Sinclair was the CSU tech who checked them out of evidence and delivered them to the lab at the Bureau of Criminal Apprehension in St. Paul. It was there that they were to be tested for

DNA. They were delivered to the BCA the day after they were found on the roof of the building next to Howie's apartment.

Finally, the lab technician with the BCA took the stand. His name was Burt Orland. Orland was on the stand for over an hour and by the time he finished almost everyone in the courtroom was totally confused. His explanation about why the testimony took so long was barely plausible and his testimony about how DNA was tested almost incomprehensible. At the end, the only thing the jury or anyone else could grasp was his claim that the DNA was a 99.6% match to Howie Traynor.

Mark limited his cross exam to making Orland admit there was no way of knowing how or when the cigarettes came to be on the roof. Marc also obtained an admission that they could easily have been planted by someone else. It was possible that, because Howie's car was impounded, someone could have removed the three butts from the car's ash tray and placed them on the roof. The obvious inference being it was the police who did it since they had custody of the car. It was enough to at least argue reasonable doubt.

The final witness for the prosecution was the psychiatrist, Dr. George Christie. It was not a coincidence that he took the stand as the last witness for their case and the last witness on a Friday afternoon.

During the trial, Father John was in attendance seated directly behind the defense as much as possible. Both Marc and Howie made an effort to speak with him as often as they could to let the jury know the priest was there on behalf of the defendant. Of course, this was done deliberately to make a good impression on the jurors. Christie would try to convince the jury that Howie's conversion to Jesus and model citizen was a ruse.

Harris started off with a long dissertation of the doctor's credentials. By the time this was done, even Marc was impressed, especially by the number of books the doctor had published on the subject of sociopathology. Slocum had brought in the best hired gun to be found.

Marc and the lawyers and staff in his office went through every book, treatise and article Christie had published on the subject. In addition, Jeff Modell the office Para-legal and resident computer geek searched online for anything they might have missed.

What they hoped to find was some written statement from the doctor admitting sociopaths could change. The best they could find was a couple of references to serious drug therapy used to control this behavior. Even those references were qualified and of little use.

Essentially, what the doctor told the jury was that Howie was pulling a scam and that his sociopathic personality was not a learned behavior but was part of his DNA, as much as his height or eye color.

Marc's cross examination was about as good as one could be to show the doctor's bias. He tried to paint him, with some success, as a hired gun who testified exactly the way the prosecution wanted. He also admitted he only testified for the prosecution.

"Isn't it true, Doctor, you only testify for the state because your one hundred-thousand-dollar fee is too steep for all but the wealthiest defendants?"

At the sound of the amount Christie was paid, every juror sat up straight and looked wide-eyed at Harris. A hundred thousand dollars is still a lot of money to most people.

"I wouldn't know," Christie answered.

"Isn't it true you did not spend one minute with the defendant?"

"It wasn't necessary..."

"Nonresponsive, your Honor," Marc said.

"Answer the question," Koch ordered.

"Yes, that's true."

"You got all of your information and formed your one hundred-thousand-dollar opinion..."

"Objection," Harris jumped up. "Mischaracterization and argumentative."

"I'll sustain the objection on the grounds of it being argumentative," Koch said. "I'm not quite sure what mischaracterization means. Rephrase, Mr. Kadella."

"You obtained all of your information and formed your opinion about Howie Traynor from reading things that other people wrote, isn't that true?"

"Yes," Christie admitted.

Marc silently thought about if he should continue. He obtained about all he could from the shrink. Marc also knew he had his own expert to call who would refute what Christie said and she had spent several hours actually meeting with Howie.

"I have nothing further, your Honor," Marc finally said.

"Re-direct, Mr. Harris?" Koch asked.

Harris stood up to address the court. He decided Christie had handled Marc very well and wasn't going to push it.

"No, your Honor."

"Do you have any more witnesses?" she asked knowing they did not.

"No, your Honor. The state rests." Then Harris sat down.

"Mr. Kadella?"

"The defense moves the court to dismiss all charges for failure to bring a case against the defendant."

This request is normally a mere formality. The defense must request dismissal to reserve the issue for appeal. If the defense fails to do so, it cannot be argued on appeal. It is rarely granted, and Marc knew it would not be in this case.

"Denied," Koch replied. "We're adjourned until Monday."

Koch again admonished the jury not to discuss the case with anyone and avoid all news reports. This was probably a futile gesture.

Connie Mickelson poured a shot of her bourbon into three glasses and passed them across her desk. Marc and his friend and officemate, Barry Cline took them, clinked their glasses together and downed the fiery liquid in one gulp.

"Harris played it pretty well," Barry said. "He ended his case on the last day with three guards telling the jury Howie threatened these victims and scared everyone he met shitless, then was able to remind the jury Howie was on the roof next door and must have used the plank bridge to get there. Finally, he wraps it up with an expert who has credentials as long as my leg who tells them Howie's conversion is bullshit."

"That's about it," Marc admitted as he handed his empty glass to Connie.

"And all of this on a Friday afternoon so the jury has all weekend to let it sink in," Barry added.

"I have something in mind," Marc said. "This thing isn't over."

FIFTY-EIGHT

"Good morning, Mr. Kadella," the deputy said while opening the security door for Marc. "Your client and the priest are already in the conference room waiting for you," he added while the two men walked down the back hallway toward Koch's courtroom.

"Thanks, Clarence," Marc replied.

"Good luck today," Clarence said. In a whisper he added, "Just so you know, I got fifty bucks on you winning the case."

"Really?" Marc said and stopped at the courtroom door. "You think we're doing that good?"

"Well, um, no actually," the deputy said. "But I got five to one odds so what the hell…"

"Oh, great," Marc said feigning disappointment. "That makes me feel better."

Marc lightly knocked on the conference room door at the side of the courtroom. Without waiting for a reply, he turned the doorknob and entered.

He found his client and the priest kneeling on the floor, their hands folded on the small tabletop while Father John quietly prayed. Marc respectfully waited in a corner while they finished. When they did, the priest offered to leave but Marc stopped him and told him to stay. The three of them took chairs at the table.

"We'll start our case with our psychiatrist," Marc reminded them. He told this to Howie on Saturday but decided to go over it again for Father John. "I want to put her on first to refute what their guy said Friday afternoon."

"Will it work?" Father John asked.

"Who knows?" Mark shrugged. "The jury will believe what it wants to. We just need to create enough reasonable doubt for an acquittal or convince one of them to get a hung jury. Their shrink was a paid, hired gun spewing mostly bullsh…, um,"

"Bullshit," Father John said for him.

"Yeah," Marc smiled. "After she's done, I'll call you to the stand," Marc continued looking at the priest. "Until then, I don't want you in the courtroom. We've been over your testimony enough times that you'll do fine. Any questions?"

Father John and Howie both shook their heads in response.

"Okay, let's go."

"Is the defense ready?" Judge Koch asked Marc.

A criminal defendant is under no obligation to put on a case at all. If the defense lawyer believes the prosecution has not made its case or met its burden of proof, the defense may rest without calling a single witness. There are also other times when the defense simply has no case to present to a jury.

"Yes, your Honor," Marc said after standing, respectfully, to address the court.

"You may call your first witness."

"The defense calls Dr. Lorraine Butler," Marc solemnly intoned.

The deputy guarding the exit doors opened one and a petite woman with stylishly cut, light brown hair, entered. Marc slightly smiled at the sight of her. Normally she dressed for work much more casually, though still professionally, than she was today. This was only the third time in her career she would testify at a trial and the psychiatrist was determined to make a good impression.

Dr. Butler was sworn in, took the stand and looked to Marc to begin his questioning. The two of them spent four hours the day before preparing her testimony.

She appeared a little nervous which Marc had actually convinced her to do. It would send a clear message to the jury that, unlike the prosecution's expert, she was not a professional witness. Marc tossed her some easy questions and she admitted to being a little anxious. The doctor looked directly at the jury and with a sheepish grin confessed this was only her third time as a witness. Of course, all of this was carefully rehearsed, designed to win over the jury. Gauging by the friendly looks she was getting from the jurors, it appeared to be working.

Marc took her through a detailed listing of her credentials which were nowhere near as impressive as Dr. Christie's. Marc believed this could be an advantage. Hopefully the jury would simply like her better than the prosecution's hired gun and give her more credibility.

Marc led her through her testimony about her practice to be sure the jury understood this was not an academic. Relaxing after a short while, she comfortably explained to the jury what type of psychiatrist she was. Essentially she was one that dealt with real people with real problems every day. Unlike Christie who appeared somewhat imperious and a bit condescending, Dr. Butler came across as a real, down-to-earth, Midwestern person. Someone you would go to if you needed counseling and treatment.

"Were you able to read the report prepared by Dr. George Christie, the state's expert, regarding Howard Traynor?"

"Yes, I did," she answered.

"What, if any, opinion do you have about his report and diagnosis?"

"Dr. Christie is an intelligent, highly educated, respected academic. However," Butler said pleasantly looking toward the jury, "he hasn't seen a patient for thirty years. For him to make a blanket statement and claim anyone showing congenital sociopathic symptoms cannot be treated and cured is simply not factual."

"Have you formed an opinion about Howie Traynor and his condition today?"

"Yes, I have," she replied.

"Please tell the jury what that opinion is," Marc said.

"Based upon my time spent with Mr. Traynor and my years of dealing with all types of neuroses, I believe Mr. Traynor has overcome his sociopathic personality traits. His conduct and apparent conversion to Catholicism are genuine."

Marc thanked her and passed her to Tommy Harris for cross examination. During their preparation, Barry Cline conducted a mock cross exam of Butler. Based on what Marc had seen of Harris and what Barry also knew of him, they both believed Barry's preparation was more than adequate. Harris did not disappoint them.

Tommy Harris jumped right in asking her a series of yes and no questions designed to compare her credentials with those of Dr. Christie. He restated every one of the items on the curriculum vitae of Christie and Butler played along. She admitted Christie's academic and publishing credentials were impressive. Marc prepared her for this and she pleasantly made no effort to argue with Harris or inflate her own achievements. By the time he was done, Harris was coming across almost as condescending as his expert.

At the end, feeling pretty good about himself, Harris opened his mouth and put both feet in. He was simply unwilling to leave well enough alone.

"What makes you think you can sit there and tell this jury why they should disbelieve someone with as accomplished as Dr, Christie and believe you?"

It was a question any third-year law school student would know better than to ask, the open-ended question that you don't know how the witness will answer. Marc stifled a laugh when he saw the look on Paul Ramsey's face.

"Because I've been dealing with real people in the real world for over twenty years. Dr. Christie has been sitting in an Ivory Tower in academia dealing with theory all that time. It's the old saying, 'Those that can, do; those that can't, teach," Butler said hitting Harris right between the eyes.

To his credit, Tommy Harris knew he was in a hole and it was time to stop digging. He ended his questioning and Koch ordered a short recess.

Father John Brinkley was called to the stand. The salt and pepper haired, mid-fifties, handsome priest made the exact impression Marc expected. Even atheists and non-Catholics would give the man high marks for appearance.

The good Father was on the stand for the remainder of the morning. Marc took him through his personal history with Howie, having met him while Father John was providing religious guidance to inmates and then mentoring Howie through the conversion process. For the defense, his main contribution was to reinforce Dr. Butler's assertion that Howie's conversion was legitimate. Marc also scored points with the testimony about Howie's work at the church.

Of course, none of this had any bearing on the real question before the jury. Did Howie Traynor, commit these murders? This was a point Harris, having learned his lesson with his exam of Dr. Butler, quickly made then passed on the witness.

While the crowd was filing out of the courtroom and Howie was being led back to jail, Marc turned around and saw a sight that made him smile. Sitting in the seat normally reserved for Father John was Maddy Rivers. The serious look on her face made his smile vanish.

Marc stepped up to the rail and she asked, "What time do you want me?"

"Right after lunch," he replied.

"Okay," she said then turned to leave.

"Madeline, wait!"

She turned back to him and she said, "Marc, I'm scared. I'm..."

"Listen," he whispered. He looked around the courtroom and noticed Gabriella Shriqui watching them. Marc shook his head at Gabriella then held open the gate and gestured for Maddy to come through and sit down with him.

They sat down at the defense table and Maddy inhaled deeply and weakly smiled.

"What I did was stupid, and I could get in a lot of trouble for it," she softly said.

"Listen to me," Marc said. "I only have a few questions for you. I want you to be very careful. Don't anticipate what I'm going to ask. Listen carefully to the question, let me ask it completely and then think about your answer and answer only the question I ask, okay?"

"Okay," she nodded.

"We don't have time to prepare. I'll ask you about the surveillance and you going into the building. Be careful what you say. You were in the building itself legally. Tell them why you went into the janitor's closet and on the roof. But, go slow and don't get carried away. Don't volunteer that you were in Howie's apartment. Understand?"

"Yes," she said. "I get it."

"And to be honest, I don't think Harris will have much for you. He'll likely want you off of that stand as fast as possible. I'll see you after lunch."

"Ms. Rivers," Marc began after Maddy was sworn in and took the stand, "in the interest of full disclosure you and I are well acquainted are we not? You have worked for me as a private investigation on several cases I have handled, correct?"

"That's right," Maddy replied with a weak smile.

Since Madeline Rivers was a witness called by the defense she was technically a defense witness. Normally these questions could be objected to as leading. Asking leading questions of your own witness is normally not allowed. Because these were merely to inform the jury of their relationship and not to provide substance, they would be allowed.

"In fact, we're good friends, aren't we?"

Maddy pulled the microphone a little closer and said, "I hope so, yes."

Marc moved on and had Maddy tell the jury a bit about her background and what she did for a living. While she did this, Marc kept one eye on the jurors to gauge their reaction to her. Every one of them was totally captivated by her and could not look away, even the women. Marc could not help wondering if the men were hearing anything she said.

Because the two of them had been estranged during the trial, Marc did not have an opportunity to prepare her testimony. He hoped the little chat they had before lunch had repaired their friendship enough to allow him to get out of her what he needed.

Knowing he had Tony Carvelli on his list to testify, Marc would get a detailed report about Howie's surveillance from him. All he wanted from Maddy was the part that she played in it.

Maddy told the jury what she did when she was part of the surveillance of Howie Traynor. Being as intelligent as she is, Maddy caught on immediately to where Marc was taking her. Using her own record of the surveillance she went over every date and time she was watching Howie. For each day of this, Maddy was sure to emphasize that Howie Traynor did nothing to arouse her suspicions at all.

"In fact, we were, all getting bored with watching him. He wasn't doing anything."

Marc changed course and moved to her entry into Howie's apartment building.

Maddy explained that an elderly woman opened the security door for her and allowed her to go inside.

"Did the Minneapolis police direct you to go into the building for any reason whatsoever?"

"No, they did not."

"No one in the police department..."

"Objection," Harris said. "Asked and answered."

"Sustained," Judge Koch quickly ruled.

"Once inside it was you who discovered the janitor's closet and the stairs leading to the roof, wasn't it?"

"Yes."

"Was the closet locked?"

"No, it was not."

"Ms. Rivers, why did you go into the closet?"

Maddy turned her head to the jury and told them about the warnings she received from Tony Carvelli that Howie returned. She admitted she ducked into the janitor's closet to avoid being seen by him.

With a little prodding from Marc, Maddy carefully, slowly described finding the stairs to the roof. She also told them that she went up on the roof and did a walk about on it.

"Did you give this information to Detective Owen Jefferson?"

"Yes, I did," Maddy admitted.

"Ms. Rivers, did you go inside Howie Traynor's apartment and plant the barbed wire, wire cutters and leather gloves the police found in his bedroom?"

At first Maddy felt like Marc had just betrayed her. Here it was. She could admit to a felony or commit perjury. Maddy stared blankly at Marc for several seconds before realizing what exactly he had just asked her.

"No, I did not," she honestly said.

"Are you sure..."

"Objection," Harris stood again. "Asked and answered."

"Sustained. Move along Mr. Kadella," Koch said.

Trying to look dejected Marc paused for several seconds before saying, "I have nothing further, your Honor."

Tommy Harris, because Maddy admitted she did nothing at the behest of the police decided to pass and asked no questions.

A greatly relieved Madeline Rivers, with every head in the room following her, made a calm yet hasty, exit. As she passed by Gabriella, unnoticed by everyone else, Maddy gave her a quick wink and Gabriella smiled.

FIFTY-NINE

While Maddy Rivers walked toward the exit, Judge Koch called the lawyers to the bench.

"Do you have another witness lined up for today?" she asked Marc.

"Well, your Honor, um no, I don't. I thought..." he replied.

"Let's adjourn for today, then," she said. "I have some personal business to attend to."

"Your Honor," Harris started to object.

"Forget it, Mr. Harris. I don't need your permission." Koch said cutting him off.

Howie leaned over and whispered in Marc's ear, "Can I see you for a minute?"

Marc looked at him noticing a slight trace of annoyance in his client's voice. "Sure," he replied. He pointed to the door for the conference room and said to the deputies, "Give us a few minutes, guys. We need to talk."

Before Marc had a chance to sit down, an obviously agitated Howie, pacing around in the small room, snarled, "Why the hell didn't you go after her?" referring to Maddy.

"I got what I could out of her," Marc said a bit defensively. "She wasn't going to admit she planted those things in your apartment."

Howie stopped his pacing and a little too quickly said, "I know she didn't plant them..."

Startled, Marc cut him off by saying, "How? How do you know she didn't?"

Howie's back straightened, his eyes opened wide and he said, "Well, ah, you, ah, you must've told me..."

"No, I didn't," Marc said staring intently at Howie. "How would I know?"

The punch hit Marc dead center of his solar plexus. It happened so quickly it wasn't even a blur before it landed. In an instant all of his wind rushed out and Howie's left hand clamped over his mouth. Marc would have collapsed if Howie had not grabbed his right arm and held him. As gently as he could, Marc's eyes bulging, his mind uncomprehending what happened, Howie lowered his lawyer into a chair.

"Ssssh, ssssh, ssssh," Howie whispered in his ear. "Just breathe, you'll be okay. Just breathe. I'm gonna take my hand off your mouth. Breathe easy. Nod your head."

Howie removed his hand and Marc tried to gulp down several inhalations of air. He now fully understood what Howie had done. Marc stared wide-eyed and unblinking at Howie while he fought to normalize his breathing.

Howie pulled another of the chairs in front of Marc and sat down on it facing him, their knees almost touching. He leaned forward, his face inches from his frightened lawyer's nose and quietly said, "Well, I guess that lets the cat out of the bag. You got it figured out now?"

Marc, his breathing having normalized, almost silently croaked, "Yes."

"That's right counselor, I'm guilty. In fact, I'm guilty of all of it, including the old broad thirteen years ago," Howie confessed looking at Marc with a sinister smile.

"This whole thing, this has been a huge act," Marc muttered.

"Every bit of it," Howie acknowledged. "Pretty goddamn good huh? Had you and that faggot priest fooled. God! Laying on that prison bed night after night, dreaming of getting out and going after those people," he said still smiling his sinister smile. "And I knew sooner or later some hanky-wringing, bleeding heart liberal would kick me loose. This is Minnesota…"

Regaining some of his composure, Marc asked, "What about Judge Segal and Cara Meyers? They didn't do anything to you?"

"I threw them in just to give the cops something to think about," Howie said with a mild chuckle.

"Why not me?" Marc asked, "I was your lawyer back then."

"Here's your deal, lawyer. You win this trial, and all is forgiven. You lose it and well," Howie shrugged, "even in prison I can get at you. People owe me, and they'll pay a little visit to your kids, Eric and Jessica…"

"You sonofabitch," Marc almost yelled and started to come out of his chair. Howie stiff armed him back just as a voice came through the door. "Everything okay in there?" They heard one of the deputies ask.

Howie nodded his head at Marc indicating that Marc was to respond. "Yeah," Marc said, "we're good."

"I've been following your career," Howie said removing his hand from Marc's chest. "I have faith in you. But you should've gone after that P.I. bitch friend of yours. Although I must admit, she's a tasty little piece. Maybe I'll pay her a visit some day," he smiled.

Howie stood up, looked down at a still terrified Marc, smiled his cold, scary smile and said, "You'd better figure something out. If I go back to prison because of you, you'll watch your kids die before you do and maybe that little judge you've been banging, too."

Howie reached for the door knob to leave and Marc worked up the courage to say, "Do you know how bat shit crazy you are?"

Howie turned his head back to look at him and said, "Yeah, I do."

Over an hour passed since Marc's meeting with Howie Traynor and he still sat in his car. Marc was practically numb from Howie's revelation. The only thing he was capable of was reviewing the trial in his head. And the conclusion he came to was that he was likely losing. Or at least there was a very good chance of it.

With all of the blood, gore and gruesome details that had been presented to the jury, they could easily want to nail someone for this. The remainder of Marc's case was weak, to say the least. He obviously had to come up with something and pull a rabbit out of a hat,

Tony Carvelli was lined up to testify about his surveillance; Marc had counted on Carvelli and the police following Howie as a foolproof, absolute alibi. Not only had the prosecution found a way to negate this but, they were right. Howie did sneak past everyone exactly the way the cops and prosecution said he did. What they didn't have was a means of transportation. They had no evidence to show how he got around getting to his victims. Was this enough for reasonable doubt? Maybe.

Marc also had his criminalist, Jason Biggs prepared to testify. He would link the evidence found on each victim to the death of Judge Smith in northern Minnesota. This could help with reasonable doubt since the cops admitted there was no way Howie could have done that. Enough for reasonable doubt? Again, maybe at best.

He would wrap up his case with more character witnesses. Two priests, two nuns and a co-worker from the church. All of this might be enough but without the alibi of the police surveillance he could not count on it. Those three cigarette butts found on the roof of the building next to Howie's might be the final nail in his coffin. Why did this sick bastard leave them up there?

Driving back to the office he thought about his son and daughter. Obviously he had to get them out of town for a while. His ex-wife and Marc got along now probably better than when they were married. Karen and her new husband, Tom, would cooperate. They could all go to Karen's parents who had moved to Texas. They would be all right there at least through the Holidays.

He weighed the consequences of the outcome of this trial. If he lost, Howie Traynor would be back where he belonged; doing life without parole in prison. Were his threats legitimate? Could he really get others to do his bidding? Maybe but probably unlikely.

If he won, Howie Traynor would be back loose on the streets. How could that be good? Maybe he would really go after Maddy and she would put a bullet between his eyes. Too risky he realized.

An idea had been germinating in his head. As he drove, Marc came to the conclusion he had to try it. He had to pull out all of the stops and take a flyer to win the case. Protecting his son and daughter were the absolute priority. Losing this trial was no longer an option. He would worry about what to do about Howie Traynor on the loose later.

Marc hurried through the outer office, went straight into his private office and quickly closed the door. Unable to use Maddy during the investigation, preparation and trial, Marc worked with someone else he knew, a middle-aged man who did mostly divorce work. Marc used him primarily as a process server to serve subpoenas and line up witnesses.

Without bothering to remove his overcoat, Marc dialed the man's phone number.

"Al, its Marc Kadella," Marc said when the man answered.

"I know, Marc. What's up?"

"You know those subpoenas you have that you've been holding for me?"

"Sure," Al replied.

"Okay, for the first one, fill in the date and time for tomorrow at 9:00 a.m. For the tech guy, same date and make his for 9:30 and can you make sure he gets there?"

"No problem," Al said. "When do you want them served?"

"Tomorrow morning, early. Then call or text me when it's done."

"Will do."

SIXTY

Having barely slept the night before, a stressed-out Marc Kadella was on Third Avenue driving toward the government center. Around midnight his ex-wife called and told him they were on the road heading south to Texas. Persuading her had been a difficult conversation but she finally agreed for the sake of their son and daughter to spend the Holidays at her mother's. It was one less thing for Marc to worry about.

Around 4:00 a.m. Marc gave up trying to sleep. Instead he spent three hours preparing for today's testimony, especially for his surprise witness. Shortly after 7:00 his process server called with the news that he had served one of the subpoenas. Marc was walking through the second-floor courtyard when he received the text that the second one, the more important one, had also been served.

Marc went into the courtroom through the back door. Seated at the table doing his best altar boy impersonation, was his client. Marc took one look at him and his knees went weak, his palms started to sweat, and his stomach became queasy.

"Good morning, Marc," Howie greeted him as he took his seat. "Hope you slept well."

For the benefit of the audience Marc weakly smiled and nodded at Howie but did not say a word. Instead he opened his briefcase and set up the table for today's testimony. When Marc finished, a question he was curious about got the better of him and he quietly asked Howie.

"Why did you leave those cigarette butts on the roof next door to you?"

"I wondered if you were going to ask," he smiled. "For the same reason I put the barbed wire, gloves and wire cutters under my mattress. I wanted to get arrested and fuck with the cops."

"You may proceed, Mr. Kadella," Judge Koch informed him.

Marc looked up at the wall clock in the courtroom which read 9:15. The witness he wanted, the one subpoenaed to be there at 9:00 had not yet arrived. Marc was prepared to go forward. Tony Carvelli was out in the hall, but he wanted the shock value and was disappointed he would not get it.

"Your Honor," Marc said as he arose, "the defense calls..."

At that precise moment the exterior doors blew open and an obviously angry Craig Slocum burst in. He quickly stomped toward the gate in the bar.

"...Craig Slocum," Marc finished.

"Objection!" Harris yelled jumping to his feet as a loud buzz went through the courtroom.

"He's on our witness list, your Honor," Marc said.

"I thought that was a joke," Harris stammered.

As a sort of pain-in-the-ass type of move, witness lists are often loaded with names whose connection to the case is, at most, peripheral. This is done primarily to make your opponent interview witnesses you have no intention of calling. You are supposed to have a good faith basis for including someone on your list, but this is usually very flexible.

"How is that my problem?" Marc asked.

"This is preposterous," Slocum loudly proclaimed, trying to assert his authority.

"This is my courtroom, Mr. Slocum. You will speak only when I want you to. Mr. Harris represents the state here, not you," Koch admonished him.

Slocum owed her an apology, but his ego would not allow it. Instead he stood silently at the gate glaring back at the impertinent judge.

Ignoring him, Judge Koch rapped her gavel and said, "Recess. I'll see counsel in chambers." As she stood she indicated to the court reporter that he was to attend also. Slocum began to come through the gate to follow the lawyers into chambers. Koch was on her feet and saw him. "Have a seat, Mr. Slocum," she said indicating a chair behind the prosecution table. Slocum grumbled under his breath as he sat down.

Once the reporter was set up and ready, Koch began by asking Marc, "Okay, Mr. Kadella, what are you up to?" Koch was seated at her desk still in her robes, the lawyers arrayed in the chairs before her. Harris was obviously still steaming and Marc inwardly smiling.

"Your Honor," Marc began, "my client is fighting for his life. I have reason to believe that the county attorney has abused his authority in an effort to circumvent justice and…"

"That's a lie!" Harris burst out.

"That's an accusation you had better be prepared to back up with evidence, Mr. Harris," an angry Judge Koch said staring harshly at him. "Do you have such evidence?"

"I'm sorry, your Honor," Harris meekly said. "I apologize to both the

Court and Mr. Kadella."

For the next several minutes Koch heard the lawyers, in turn, make their arguments for and against allowing the county attorney to testify. When they were done Koch sat silently for a full minute. Her hands were together as if in prayer on which she lightly rested her chin. She looked past the silent lawyers apparently thinking over her decision.

The judge put her hands down. Looked at Marc and said, "I'll allow this but, you'd better have something. Do I make myself clear?"

"Your Honor!" Harris tried to protest but was cutoff when Koch held up a hand to stop him.

"Yes, your Honor," Marc replied.

"I'll be out in a minute," she said.

As the lawyers were filing out of the judge's changers, Marc whispered to Harris, "What's the matter, Tommy, got something to hide?"

Slocum was sworn in and took the witness stand. No longer angry, his arrogance took over. Dressed in a two thousand-dollar three-piece suit, he fiddled with the knot on his hand painted silk tie while smugly waiting for Marc to begin, all the while allowing himself to believe that he would make a fool out of Kadella.

"Please state your name and occupation," Koch told him.

"Craig T. Slocum. I am the duly elected county attorney for Hennepin County, Minnesota," he said.

"You may begin," Koch told Marc.

"Mr. Slocum," Marc politely began, "As the county attorney you are the chief law enforcement officer for Hennepin County are you not?"

"Yes, I am."

"You must have at least a hundred lawyers working for you in the various departments, don't you?"

"Objection, relevance your honor," Harris said.

"Overruled."

"More than that, actually," Slocum replied.

"How many cases do you personally try each year?"

"Well my duties are such that..."

"Nonresponsive," Marc said to Judge Koch.

"Answer the question," Koch said. "How many cases do you try yourself each year?"

"None lately," he admitted.

"Isn't it true, Mr. Slocum, you have not tried a single case since you personally tried the case of The State of Minnesota vs. Carl Fornich, several years ago?"

"Objection, relevance," Harris said again.

"I'm getting there your Honor," Marc told her.

"Very well, overruled for now."

"Mr. Slocum?" Marc said.

"Yes, that's true," Slocum admitted.

"That was a highly publicized murder case concerning a serial killer similar to this case wasn't it?"

Slocum hesitated for a moment then admitted it was.

"And you tried that case yourself because you believed it would be a slam dunk easy win and the publicity would do wonders for your political career, isn't that true?"

"That's absurd," Slocum said as he shifted in his seat.

"Mr. Slocum," Marc said staring straight at him. "I am prepared to subpoena at least twenty people in your office who know that to be true. I'll put them on that witness stand and force them to testify. You're under oath. Would you like to change your answer now?"

This was almost certainly a bluff. It was highly unlikely that, because of attorney-client privilege, any of them would be allowed to testify. But no one, not Tommy Harris, Craig Slocum or even Judge Koch thought of it or knew it for sure.

Slocum's eyes narrowed, he drew a deep breath then said, "All right. Yes, I suppose that's correct. I have political ambitions. There's nothing wrong with that."

"In fact, you were going to run for governor, isn't that true?"

"Oh, I'm not sure, maybe I had thought about it," Slocum tried to hedge.

"Mr. Slocum, you're still under oath in front of a jury. Should I ask it again?"

"All right, yes. I was going to run for governor after that case. So what?"

"Your dream of becoming governor went up in smoke after you lost the case, didn't it?"

Once again, Slocum's eyes narrowed, he uncrossed and re-crossed his legs and his face became visibly red.

"It was a setback," Slocum said.

"It was more than a setback," Marc said. "The Democratic Party told you to forget it, did they not? You're still under oath and I can find witnesses," Marc continued.

"Your Honor! This is absurd. Where is the relevance?" Harris said.

"I'm almost there, your Honor," Marc replied without taking his eyes off Slocum.

"I'll give you a little more Mr. Kadella but you'd better get there soon."

"Isn't it true Mr. Slocum, your dream of becoming governor crashed after losing that case?" Marc repeated insistently.

Slocum hesitated, clearly aggravated then said, "All right, yes, it did."

"And who was the lawyer for the defense in that trial?"

Again, Slocum hesitated then finally admitted, "You were."

Most of the media in attendance knew this but none of the jurors did. When they all heard this there was a slight shifting in their seats as they looked back and forth at the two antagonists.

"Isn't it true, Mr. Slocum, you have harbored a deep, personal animus toward me ever since?"

"I wouldn't say that," Slocum said although his expression noticeably belied his words.

"You're still under oath," Marc quietly reminded him. "You want to try again?"

"Argumentative, your Honor," Harris said.

"Sustained," Koch ruled.

"I can still get those subpoenas served," Marc said virtually ignoring Koch's ruling.

"All right, yes. I admit I find you to be a loathsome defense lawyer like..."

"Isn't it true," Marc jumped in cutting him off from embellishing his answer. "You originally assigned this case to your head felony litigator, Steven Gondeck?"

Annoyed at being cutoff Slocum reluctantly said, "Yes."

"Isn't it also true you replaced Mr. Gondeck with Mr. Harris because you believed Mr. Gondeck and I got along too well? That we were too friendly with one another?"

"That's none of your business. I..."

"Why are you trying so desperately to keep information from this jury?" Marc asked.

"The answer to your question is no that is not why I replaced Steve Gondeck with Tommy Harris," Slocum haughtily said to a skeptical courtroom.

"Mr. Slocum, does the name Eugene Parlow sound familiar?" Marc asked abruptly changing the subject.

Slocum shifted slightly again in his seat and his tongue flicked briefly across his lips. "Yes, I think so."

"Isn't it true he was one of the men the police suspected of committing these murders?"

"Yes, I believe so."

"He was found murdered in an alley in south Minneapolis?"

"Yes."

Marc hit a couple of keys on his laptop and an image appeared on the TV screen. It was the picture of the bag found near Parlow's body.

"The canvass bag being shown on the television now was found near his body, was it not?"

"I don't think it was near the body..." Slocum began.

"It was less than twenty feet away," Marc said.

"Okay, yes I suppose that was near the body."

For each of the next few questions Marc displayed a photo of each of the items found in the bag. He elicited a positive response that these items were, in fact, found in the bag.

"Isn't it true that it was solely your decision to withhold the discovery of these items from the defense?"

"Objection," Harris said as he started to stand.

"Overruled," Koch abruptly told him. "The witness will answer."

"Um, yes. I didn't..."

"Nonresponsive, your Honor," Marc said cutting off Slocum's explanation.

"Answer only the question," Koch reminded him.

Marc asked for and was granted permission to approach the witness. He stopped at the exhibit table and picked up several items. Marc placed them on the rail in front of Slocum then walked over to the back of the jury box and stood there while Slocum looked at the exhibits.

"Mr. Slocum, I have given you the items found in Howie Traynor's apartment; the barbed wire, wire cutter and gloves. When the police found them, you were told about it, were you not?"

"Yes," Slocum admitted.

"Yet, when these exact same items were found by the body of Eugene Parlow, you decided that was not relevant, isn't that true?"

Slocum paused for a moment and started to say something. Instead his shoulders slumped, and he quietly said, "Yes."

"Mr. Slocum, was it you that had someone plant these items in Howie Traynor's apartment?"

"Objection!" Harris exploded jumping to his feet.

"Overruled," Koch quickly said, "The witness will answer."

Marc was stunned that the judge did not chastise him for asking such an inflammatory question. Overruling Harris' objection sent a clear message to the jury that it might be true.

"Absolutely not," Slocum indignantly replied.

Marc walked back to the exhibit table and picked up a clear plastic evidence bag. In it were the three cigarette butts found with Howie's DNA. He handed the bag to Slocum and resumed his position standing by the jury box.

"Mr. Slocum, you are holding the three cigarette butts found on the roof of the building next to Howie Traynor's apartment. These items were found a few days after he was arrested, is that correct?"

"Yes, I believe so," Slocum answered.

"And they were sent to the BCA lab in St. Paul for analysis the next day, isn't that true?"

"Yes."

The entire courtroom was as quiet as a funeral. The only sound being the exchange taking place between these two antagonists. The two men themselves seemed totally oblivious of it but the tension in the air was rising with each moment, each question, each answer. Everyone seemed to instinctively realize the trial had reached its make or break moment for both sides.

"And the result of that analysis was not received until last week, more than two months after these items were sent to the BCA?"

"Yes, that's correct," Slocum shrugged. "I don't run the BCA lab," Slocum continued with a haughty smile.

"Really? Mr. Slocum, did you use your influence on the BCA lab to slow down and delay the report on the cigarette butts, so they could be used as a dramatic surprise during the trial?"

"No, of course not," Slocum answered but with noticeably less arrogance.

"Mr. Slocum let me remind you that you are under oath and I have subpoenaed a man by the name of Richard Fletcher, who is currently in the hall waiting to testify. Isn't it true he is the head of the BCA lab whose son is currently awaiting trial in Hennepin County on drug charges and did you use this to influence him to delay the analysis of the cigarette butts?"

"Objection," Harris tried to say.

"Overruled and sit down," Koch ordered him.

Time froze in the courtroom. Slocum sat in the chair, leaning forward, his eyes shifting about the room. A bead of sweat broke out on his upper lip and he noticeably licked it.

What seemed like an hour but was barely a half a minute went by in total silence. Everyone in the courtroom, especially the jury, knew what the answer was but waited for it anyway.

"I'll wait all day," Marc quietly said.

"All right, yes, I did," Slocum finally admitted, the arrogance having returned.

"Did you order someone to take those cigarette butts from the ashtray in Howie Traynor's car and plant them on the roof?"

Harris started to stand but Koch stopped him with a stern look.

"No, I did not," Slocum denied but it sounded weak and uncertain.

Immediately Marc slapped his left hand down hard on the rail in front of the jury box. The sharp, loud crack startled the jurors and caused both Judge Koch and Slocum to sit up.

"Isn't it true," Marc practically yelled, "all of this was done because you wanted to get even with me, personally? Don't look at him," Marc yelled at Slocum when Slocum shifted his eyes to Tommy Harris. "Answer me and tell this jury the truth!" Marc angrily almost screamed and slapped his hand on the railing again.

"All right, yes goddamnit. I'll get you, you sonofabitch!" Slocum snarled back at Marc.

The entire courtroom inhaled and froze, especially Marc Kadella. No one breathed, no one moved, no one even blinked. After a stunned moment, Marc thought, *Holy shit! He admitted it!* Another second passed as the image of Tom Cruise and Jack Nicholson the movie *A Few Good Men* flashed through his mind.

"I have no further questions, your Honor," Marc quickly said as he retreated to the defense table. When he got there, he remained standing and continued, "Your Honor, the defense moves for immediate dismissal of all charges due to obvious prosecutorial misconduct."

Before Marc finished saying this Tommy Harris was on his feet. "Objection your Honor. The defense badgered the witness into making an obviously false statement in an excited response."

"Overruled," Koch said to Harris. "Recess," she said then continued by saying, "I'll see counsel in chambers now. Mr. Slocum, you stay right where you are."

While the three lawyers followed the judge out of the courtroom, the gallery broke out in a stunned discussion. Howie Traynor leaned back in his chair, smiled and inwardly laughed at the spectacle.

"Your Honor, we demand a mistrial," Harris said before anyone even had a chance to sit down.

"Absolutely not," Marc countered. "They want a chance to clean their mess up and make another run at my client. That's reversible error."

"He's right, Mr. Harris. There will be no mistrial," Koch said.

For the next ten minutes Koch sat back and listened to the lawyers make their respective arguments. When they finished, she said, "Thank you, gentlemen. Let me think about it. I'll be out in a few minutes to make my ruling."

Less than ten minutes later, Judge Koch came back out to the bench. No one had left even for a quick trip to the restroom. Apparently everyone lucky enough to be there did not want to chance missing a single word.

The first thing Judge Koch said was, "I want absolute silence in this courtroom while I make my decision. If anyone interrupts me, they will go to jail."

She took a moment to gather her thoughts then started by saying, "I have three choices. One, I can declare a mistrial. That I will not do. Two, I can let the case continue and go to the jury or, three, dismiss the charges in the interest of justice.

"After careful consideration, I cannot in good conscience, allow this travesty to continue. Therefore, I am dismissing all charges contained in the indictment due to the misconduct and abuse of power by the county attorney."

She turned to the jury and said, "I want to sincerely thank you, the members of the jury. My decision is in no way a reflection of you. It is part of my responsibility and I bear it alone.

"Mr. Slocum," she continued staring down at the shriveled sight of the man in the witness stand, "I will be sending a full and complete report of your conduct and the transcript of your testimony to the Office of Professional Responsibility. You, sir, have some serious explaining to do.

"Mr. Traynor," she said looking at the defense table, "you are free to go. Case dismissed, with prejudice." Judge Koch hammered her gavel once, rose and quickly fled.

Bedlam erupted as she went through the door.

SIXTY-ONE

Marc heard his neighbor across the hall from his apartment close his door to leave for work. He was sitting in the dark on his couch, his feet on the coffee table, the television off. The front door was locked, and a chair jammed under the doorknob. The digital read from the small clock by the TV glowed with the numbers 6:47. This early in the morning in December, it was still quite dark outside as the new day began.

Marc had been sitting like this the entire night with a couple of bathroom breaks his only disturbance. He was still dressed in the same clothes he wore to court the day before except for the coat and tie. They were removed and carelessly tossed on his bed.

Up until midnight his phone had rung with at least twenty calls from various people including Margaret Tennant. Not in the mood to speak to anyone and knowing Margaret was safe, Marc ignored the calls and let them go to voice mail.

Marc remained on the couch all night barely sleeping. He would doze off occasionally for short stretches, fifteen minutes here, thirty minutes there. Each time the leering, sinister, sadistic image of Howie Traynor smiling at him would enter his mind and snap him awake. By morning he was starting to feel like a teenage victim in a slasher movie. Howie Traynor was out of jail and on the loose and Marc wondered if he would ever sleep soundly again.

He did have one significant, comforting advantage. On the couch next to him was his 1911 Model Colt .45 fully loaded, one in the chamber and two extra magazines lying next to it. In fact, he had held the handgun in his right hand for most of the night half expecting Howie to somehow magically appear. Marc noticed the read on the clock change to 6:48 as he again replayed in his mind the scene from the court the previous afternoon.

While Judge Koch explained herself to the jury, the parties and the spectators, Marc sat stoically, almost numb at what she was saying. When Koch dismissed the charges and freed Howie Traynor, it took all of Marc's self-control to prevent him from jumping up to object. His mind was having an argument with itself over freeing this monster, protecting his children and maintaining his ethical responsibility.

The judge quickly left the bench and Marc remembered looking at Craig Slocum. He was still sitting on the witness stand, ashen faced and shrunken while the gallery exploded.

Howie slapped him on the back as Marc quietly said, "My God, she actually did it." At least he believed he said something along those lines.

Marc stood up and turned to Howie who grinned and offered his hand to shake with his lawyer. Marc ignored the hand and softly told Howie the deputies would take him to the jail to process him out. Father John was at the table by this point, grinning like an idiot. Marc ignored him also as he gathered his things to leave.

Waiting for him at the gate in the bar with a puzzled look on her face was Gabriella Shriqui. She witnessed the attempted handshake by the newly freed defendant and Marc ignoring him. This should have been a moment of triumph for Marc. Instead the look on his face, a man Gabriella knew fairly well, was the face of a lawyer who had lost the case, not won.

"Marc," she said to him as he approached her, "can I get an interview?"

He abruptly stopped, looked over at the other reporters waiting for him and curtly said, "No comment."

Marc turned his back to them, walked through the courtroom and out the back. To avoid the media, he even went down the hall to the stairs and walked down the fourteen flights to get out of the building.

The clock changed to 7:02 and his phone rang. He picked it up from the coffee table, looked at the I.D. and answered it. Margaret was spending the Holidays with her parents in Florida. This was the third time she tried calling and Marc decided it was time to rejoin the world.

"Hi," he said when he answered her.

"Are you all right? You have everyone who knows you worried sick, especially me," she said a little anger mixed in with her concern. "Why didn't you answer your damn phone?"

Fighting the urge to hang up on her, he said "I didn't want to talk to anyone. I needed to be alone for a while."

"Why?" she asked concern back in her voice. "Marc, what's going on? I heard what happened. It was all over the news down here."

Marc took a moment to think about his response. He finally said, "I can't talk about it. Look, I'm okay. I need to work some things out. If you need to call me, I'll answer the phone. Stay in Florida. Have a nice time. Say hello to Mom and Dad for me, okay? I love you. Just give me some time."

"I don't understand..." she began.

"I know, and I can't talk about it," Marc said.

At that moment the light in Margaret's brain went on and she blurted, "Oh my God! He's guilty. You found out he's..."

"I have to go," Marc said to cut her off. "I'll talk to you later," and he ended the call. "Smart lady," he quietly said to himself.

Marc looked across the unfrozen surface of Lake of the Isles at an attractive young woman jogging on the path on the other side of the lake. He was sitting on a park bench, by himself, waiting for someone.

For December, the weather was quite mild. The snow was long gone, the ground was dry, and temperatures would go into the forties again. The weather geeks were predicting a brown Christmas in a few days. Not normal but not necessarily unusual either. Northern Minnesota had two feet of snow and temps in the teens. Because of the size of the state this was not atypical either.

After talking to Margaret, he decided it was time to get moving. He shaved and showered, made a phone call and set up this meeting. It was now almost 9:00 and he felt much better than he did after the trial ended.

"Hey, how you doing?" Marc heard Tony Carvelli say as his P.I. friend sat down on the bench next to him.

"Been better," Marc replied shaking hands with his friend.

"So, counselor what's up?"

"I hadn't thought of this when I asked you to meet me here," Marc said ignoring the question. "Look familiar?" he added holding his arms out to indicate the area.

"Yeah, it's Lake of the Isles," Tony said. "So?"

"Turn around," Marc told him. Tony swiveled to look behind them as Marc again asked, "Look familiar?"

"Yeah, it does. That's the house where your psycho client murdered Lucille Benson," Tony said referring to the big house on the corner with the wrought iron fence. Tony turned back to Marc and said, "Is there something Freudian going on here? What do you need to tell me?" he added.

Marc took a deep breath and started by saying, "I'll tell you because I know you'll know what to do and keep your mouth shut to protect me. I could get disbarred for this."

"No problem, Marc," Tony quietly, seriously said.

"The cops need to keep an eye on Howie Traynor. He's on the loose and..." Marc paused.

"He's not done," Tony said completing the thought.

"I didn't say that," Marc said. "But, I won't dispute it either. I have to be very careful what I say."

"I get it," Tony said patting Marc on the shoulder. "Open your coat," Tony said.

Marc was wearing jeans, sneakers, a light sweater and a coat more suited for autumn than December weather. Tony, being the cop and investigator that he was, noticed a slight bulge under Marc's jacket. Marc unzipped it and showed Tony the .45 in its shoulder holster.

"I have a permit," Marc said as he zipped the jacket closed.

"I just wanted to know. Is it that serious?" Tony asked.

"Absolutely," Marc answered.

Marc's phone rang, and he removed it from his coat pocket. He looked at the I.D. answered it and said, "Hi, sweetheart. I'm glad you called."

"Are you okay?" Maddy Rivers asked him. "Gabriella called me after court yesterday and told me what happened and how you were acting. I tried calling you last night. Is everything all right?"

"I'm here with Tony," Marc said. "Are you at home?"

"Yes," she said.

"Good, stay there and keep the door locked and a gun handy. Tony will call you in a little while and tell you what's going on, okay?"

"All right," a puzzled Maddy answered.

"Talk to you later and I'm really, really happy you and I are okay," Marc said.

"Me too," Maddy agreed.

The two men discussed Marc's dilemma with his ethical obligation and client confidentiality. While not once overtly admitting to anything, Marc let the savvy P.I. know that Howie was guilty as sin. Tony assured Marc he would quietly inform the appropriate people, especially those who might be on Howie's list. This included himself as one of the original arresting officers for the Benson murder.

They parted company and on his way back to his SUV, Marc took a call from his office. It was from Carolyn who had news and questions.

"Are you okay? Are you coming in? Everyone is wondering," she asked.

"I'm fine and no, I won't be in probably for a few days. I don't know, maybe I'll stop by. Maybe Monday, which is what, the 21st?" he said. "I don't know for sure."

"Okay, I just heard from Glenda Albright, Howie's personal injury lawyer. She has his settlement money. She wants a final bill from you. Says she'll pay you first, before him."

Marc stopped walking, held the phone to his ear and said, "I don't want any money from him. I have trial expenses to pay and I'll pay those out of my own pocket. Tell her I got enough."

"Marc, I have a couple more time sheets I printed off for you on this case. He owes you…"

"I don't care, Carolyn. I want nothing else from him," he sharply said.

"All right, sorry. I'll call her back and tell her," Carolyn replied, slightly taken aback by Marc's tone and attitude.

"I'll call or maybe come by later, we'll see," Marc said as he continued toward his car. "Hey, wait," he said and stopped again. "Did Albright say what time he was going to be there?"

"Ten this morning," Carolyn replied.

"Thanks," Marc said and abruptly ended the call.

He took a moment to call Carvelli to tell him where Howie could be found at 10:00 a.m. If the cops could set up surveillance, they might find him there.

SIXTY-TWO

"How did you find this out?" Tony asked Marc.

Carvelli was in his black, sleek Camaro already on his way downtown to the Old City Hall Building and police headquarters. He was on Lake Street heading east to Hennepin Avenue when Marc called with the news that Howie would be at Albright's office at 10:00. In answer to Tony's question, Marc told him about the call from Carolyn.

"I don't know if the cops can get a surveillance team set up by then. I may have to do it myself. I'll get back to you," Tony said.

Carvelli ended the call tossed his phone on the passenger seat and punched the gas. The big eight-cylinder engine kicked in and the car jumped forward. He blew through a light as it turned red on Hennepin and took a left to go downtown. Halfway there he retrieved his phone, found the number he wanted and hit the auto dial.

"Jefferson," he heard Owen Jefferson say when he answered.

"Hey, it's Carvelli, you busy?"

"Licking my wounds. Why?"

"Meet me out on Fourth Street in about five minutes. I'll pick you up."

"Why? What's up?"

"I'm driving too fast to talk right now. Just meet me and I'll explain when I get there."

At 9:52 Carvelli found a parking spot on Seventh Street with a clear view of the Raines Building. Owen Jefferson was in the seat next to him.

"He may be in there already," Jefferson said.

"Yeah, he could be," Carvelli agreed.

"So, I don't get to know the name of the source of your information. I just have to take your word for it, even though I could probably guess who it is," Jefferson said.

"Yes," Tony answered.

"If I need to get a warrant for something, this could be a problem."

"We'll think of something. And there he is," Tony said pointing a finger across the street as Howie Traynor reached the building's front door. "No car."

"It's probably still in impound. Hasn't had time to get it out," Jefferson commented as the two men watched Howie go into the office building.

While they waited Jefferson made a call to Rod Schiller, the head of the MPD surveillance unit. Jefferson explained what they were up to and asked the lieutenant about setting up a surveillance team.

"I'm not sure I can justify that, Owen," Schiller replied. "Is this a new case? What's going on?"

Jefferson covered the phone with his hand and said to Carvelli, "He needs to know why. How much can I tell him?"

Tony thought about it for a moment before saying, "Don't tell him about Kadella, that's between you and me. Yeah, yeah, you knew where it came from," Carvelli said when Jefferson raised his eyebrows at the mention of Marc's name. "Give him the usual 'reliable source' bullshit for now."

Jefferson went back on the phone and said, "Rod, we have a very solid reason to believe Traynor is guilty and not done. I believe it and…"

"That's good enough for me," Schiller said. "I'll get right on it and get back to you."

"Thanks," Jefferson said and ended the call.

"You have to keep that to yourself about Kadella. He's got his neck sticking out and is doing the stand-up thing on this," Tony said.

"A lawyer doing the right thing. I should mark my calendar," Jefferson answered him.

"That's bullshit, and you know it," Carvelli growled. "Most lawyers are good guys. They have a job to do just like we do."

"True enough," Jefferson agreed. "There he is," he continued when Traynor came through the door and onto the sidewalk.

Howie turned to the right to walk away from where they were parked. When he did this, Jefferson opened his door to get out.

"I'll follow him on this side of the street," Jefferson said referring to the opposite side of where Howie was walking. "Wait for me to call."

Carvelli impatiently waited while Jefferson casually tailed Howie west on Seventh Avenue. Fifteen minutes after Jefferson left the car, Carvelli's phone rang.

"Pick me up. I'm still on the south side of Seventh about a hundred yards from Hennepin. I can see Traynor. He's at a bus stop on Hennepin probably waiting for a bus to go home."

"I'll be right there," Carvelli said.

Two minutes after the call, Jefferson was getting back into the Camaro when a bus pulled up in front of Howie.

For the next half hour, the two men followed the city bus through traffic across the river into Northeast Minneapolis. At Central Avenue

Howie disembarked and ran to catch a bus headed up Central toward his home.

"Where's he going," Tony rhetorically asked when the bus went past Howie's street corner. They continued to follow him then at Eighteenth Street, Howie got off and Carvelli pulled to the curb.

"Why are you parking?" Jefferson asked.

"I know where he's going," Carvelli said. "That's his bank," he continued referring to the bank on Eighteenth and Central. "We followed him there a couple of times."

"And he just got a check from his lawyer and he's going to deposit it," Jefferson said. "I wonder how much he got."

"From the hanky-wringers that run Minneapolis? A lot, I'm sure," Carvelli answered.

Less than ten minutes after he went in, Howie exited the bank. He turned down Eighteenth and began walking east.

"He's heading home," Carvelli said. "It's only a few blocks," he continued as he pulled away from the curb. Barely a minute later they were strategically parked close enough to Howie's building to watch him go in when he arrived.

When he got inside his apartment Howie went to the front windows in the small living room, the windows overlooking the street in front. Howie used two fingers to carefully, slowly separate the vertical blinds just enough to peak out. He saw the black Camaro and the corners of his mouth turned up in a tight smile.

"Forget it, assholes," he quietly said out loud. "I won't make it that easy for you."

For the next twenty-four hours the MPD surveillance team stood watch at Howie's apartment. Not once did any of the watchers see him at all. Not even a movement by a window. The church was also being watched with the same result.

"Owen, we haven't seen anything of him since we started. Nothing. He hasn't moved and last night no lights, no TV, nothing. I don't think he's in there," Schiller said when he called Jefferson to let him know.

"What do you think Rod? Do we send somebody up there?" Jefferson asked.

"Yeah, I think we should. Let me call our on-site team. I'll send them up. They can ask him if he's going to pick up his car. That will give them an excuse to go in," Schiller said.

"He hasn't picked up his car yet?" Jefferson asked. "Oh shit," he quickly added. "I just realized, he must have another car stashed somewhere. That's how he got around when he slipped the surveillance before. Get your people up there. Call me back, I'm on my way."

Jefferson stood up, grabbed his overcoat and told Marcie Sterling to come with him. Marcie knew Howie was being watched again and why. While they hurried down the hall toward their car, Jefferson told her about the call he had received from Schiller.

Halfway to Howie's apartment, Schiller called him back.

"He's gone," Schiller told him.

"Kick the goddamn door in," Jefferson yelled.

"We did. The refrigerator is empty, his clothes are mostly there but it looks like he packed up some and left. He's gone, Owen," Schiller repeated. "Now what?"

"Sonofabitch," Jefferson muttered. "I don't know. I'll be there in a few minutes."

For the next few days there was a quiet manhunt taking place throughout the Twin Cities metro area. It was kept quiet because no one wanted it leaked to the press that a psycho was on the loose because the cops and county attorney made a total mess of their case. The search for Howie rapidly spread to the entire state, the Upper Midwest and eventually went national. By that point the media knew what was up and were making uncomfortable inquiries. Howie Traynor had vanished like a puff of smoke.

Owen Jefferson tried to trace the money Howie deposited from his lawsuit. Without a warrant the bank, although wanting to cooperate, was prevented from doing so. Without a case or at least some probable cause, no judge would issue a warrant. The bank manager, off the record, did inform Jefferson that the money was gone but did not know and could not say where it ultimately ended up.

The Christmas Holidays passed; December turned into January and gradually life went back to normal. There was only so much the police could do, and the feds were not very cooperative. No charges were pending against Howie Traynor and after a while the search for him took on a low priority for everyone.

A week after New Year's Craig Slocum resigned. He had deluded himself into believing he could ride out the storm and keep his job. A visit to the Governor's Mansion in St. Paul and a stern warning from Governor Dahlstrom dispelled that idea. Even though Dahlstrom was a Republican, he let Slocum, a nominal Democrat, know the Democrats wanted him gone ASAP. The next day, Slocum emptied his office. Besides, he was looking at spending the next year trying to keep his attorney license. A fight he would eventually lose.

The governor appointed an interim county attorney, a woman from the state attorney general's office. An election was scheduled for early May to fill the office for the remainder of Slocum's term. Steve Gondeck considered running then decided he wasn't a politician and declined. The woman appointed as interim county attorney would win the job which almost caused a mutiny among the staff and lawyers. She was turning out to be at least as bad as Craig Slocum.

By mid-January Marc Kadella stopped carrying a gun, at least not every day. His, son, daughter and ex-wife were home and back to normal. Margaret Tennant was no longer being guarded by sheriff's deputies and the world was still turning. Gradually, even in Minnesota, winter turned to spring and Howie Traynor would fade from memory and was no longer a source of significant concern.

SIXTY-THREE

June

Madeline Rivers and her date were finishing their meal. Gabriella Shriqui had convinced Maddy to try her luck on a couple of dating sites. Gabriella had met someone whom she claimed was a really good guy and between them, things were going quite well. Maddy had no way of knowing that Gabriella, at this very moment, was entertaining second thoughts about online dating and the "really good guy" was now history because he had been seeing at least three other women.

This was Maddy's fourth first date with men she had met online. So far the results were not encouraging. Gary something, she couldn't remember his last name, was this evening's first and last date. It seemed to be going well until a moment ago when he slipped up and mentioned a wife.

"You're married? Your profile said you were single," Maddy said leaning forward and staring straight at him.

"Well, ah, yeah. Sort of technically married," he stammered. "We're ah, separated. Probably getting divorced."

His use of the word "probably" caused an alarm to go off in her head. A thought occurred to Maddy and she asked, "Where are you living?"

"Um, ah, just temporarily, with my parents," he admitted.

"Why are you separated?" her curiosity getting the better of her, Maddy had to ask.

"Because my wife's an unreasonable bitch!"

"In other words, she caught you cheating and threw you out."

"I ah, wouldn't put it that way," he said avoiding Maddy's piercing eyes.

"No, but I'll bet she would. So, you cheated on your wife and now you're living with your Mom," Maddy said still glaring at the man. "You do realize you a have a giant 'L' for loser stamped on your forehead, don't you?"

"Hey, you don't talk to me like that way bitch," he snarled as he reached across the table with his right hand. It was a big mistake.

Maddy calmly grabbed his hand with her left, bent it back and twisted his arm in a direction it was not meant to go. She then applied just enough downward pressure to cause his elbow to almost snap eliciting a sharp yelp from him.

"Don't try to touch me again," she said with a soft voice and nasty look. "Oh, and you get the check."

"Hey, goddamnit," Gary whined. "That hurt. And, ah, look um, I was hoping you would, you know, help out with the bill, first date and all."

Maddy was on her feet preparing to leave when he said this. She bent over the table and said, "Wash dishes, asshole. Be thankful I don't find a good lawyer for your wife. I know a great one."

By this time the customers of several tables in the area were watching this little drama. Maddy turned to leave and saw them looking at her. "Just a little disagreement about the bill, folks. It's all settled now," she said smiling and walked away.

Maddy was at a restaurant called Trapper Jack's on the 494 strip in Bloomington, a decent place for a first date. Not too expensive and the food was good. It also had a patio area and on a pleasant early summer Saturday night like this one, every table on it was full.

Maddy walked through the dining area, virtually everyone there watching her. When she was twenty feet from the front door, she turned toward the bar area. Every man there was looking at the tall, slender beauty that she is including a man with whom she made brief eye contact. Angry and in a hurry to leave, the man's face did not register right away. Maddy took two or three more steps and then realized who it was she believed she had just seen.

She stopped dead in her tracks, turned back toward the bar in time to see the man reach the patio door. He hesitated before going out, looked back at her for an instant then casually went outside.

Maddy immediately hurried after him and as she did, she reached in the purse she had draped over her shoulder. She wrapped her hand around the reassuring butt of the Ladysmith 9 mm handgun in her purse as she went through the same door to the patio searching for the man.

She stood in the doorway and looked over the crowd. Not finding him, she asked a table filled with people next to the door if they had seen him. None of them had noticed anyone and after a couple more minutes, she gave up looking over the crowd. Maddy went back inside and, despite the noise, took out her phone and made a call.

"What's up kid? Saturday night shouldn't you be on a date somewhere?" she heard Tony Carvelli say.

"I was. Listen, I'm not sure but I think I just saw Howie Traynor." Maddy went on to tell him what she had seen and done and where she was.

"Stay inside. Do not, repeat, do not go out there after him. You know what he's like. He could be waiting for you. Wait right there. I'll have the Bloomington cops there in five minutes and I'll be there in ten myself."

"Okay," Maddy said.

"Do not go after him, Madeline," he repeated. "I know what you're like. Don't do it."

"I won't, I promise," an obviously annoyed Maddy said. "I'll be at the bar with one hand on my gun."

"Good," Tony replied. "Wait right there."

Carvelli was a little optimistic about the timing. It took ten minutes for the Bloomington cops to get there. When they did, six squad cars came roaring into the restaurant's parking lot, all with lights flashing. The restaurant patrons all believed they were caught up in some type of raid.

Maddy went out to greet them and before she could, Carvelli pulled into the parking lot and drove up to the front door where she was standing. While the patrol officers spread out through the parking lot, a BPD lieutenant joined Carvelli and Maddy at Tony's car.

"Hey, Mike," Carvelli said to the lieutenant. "This is Madeline Rivers. She's a P.I. friend of mine. She's the one who called."

"So, you think you might've seen this Traynor guy?" the lieutenant asked. Every cop in the Metro area still remembered who Howie Traynor was.

"Maybe," Maddy said. "It was just a glimpse of him then he was gone. Sorry, but I can't be more positive than that."

"It's okay," Tony said. "Better safe than sorry."

Another car with emergency lights flashing pulled into the parking lot. It was an unmarked sedan with Owen Jefferson at the wheel. He spotted the trio waiting by Carvelli's Camaro and drove over to them.

Madeline repeated her story for Jefferson including her most recent date from Hell. The Bloomington cops spent a half hour searching the parking lot, using flashlights to look into and even under every car. All the while the restaurant patrons watched wondering what was going on.

Satisfied, the cops gradually began to go back to their normal patrol duties. Finally, Maddy, Tony and Owen Jefferson were the only ones left.

"I wish I could've seen him better. It might not have even been him," Maddy said.

"It's okay," Jefferson said.

"Now that I think about it," Maddy continued. "I've had this weird feeling I was being followed for the past couple days. Did you call Marc?" she asked Tony.

"Yeah, I did. I told him about your call. He asked me to call him back with any news. He's at Margaret's house. They're fine."

"I don't know what else we can do tonight," Jefferson said. "You be careful," he told Maddy.

"And sleep with a gun tonight," Tony added.

Pavel Gorecki shuffled along the street in Northeast Minneapolis toward his destination, St. Andrew's Catholic Church. Pavel was 78, a retired railroad worker and a volunteer custodian at St. Andrews. A devout Catholic, he lived for his duties at the Church. His wife of almost fifty years passed six years ago and there was little else left in his life.

This Sunday morning for Pavel was the same as all Sundays. He hurried along as best as his weary, old legs could carry him. Pavel liked arriving early at the church to spend some quiet time communing with the Lord without the intervention of a priest. He would then go up and down the aisles and pews to make sure they were neat, tidy and ready for the 7:00 a.m. Mass.

Pavel took his normal seat in the pew farthest from the altar. The church was dimly lit and at first, he noticed nothing usual. Then as he knelt to pray, he looked up at the altar and noticed something out of the ordinary. Because of the weak lighting and his fading old eyes, he could not make out what it was. Something up there was amiss, and his curiosity got the better of him.

Pavel stood and made his way up the center aisle. He got within thirty feet of the object that had caught his attention before realizing what it was. The old man gasped, slapped his hands to his face, turned and hurried back down the center aisle, horrified, stumbling and gasping to get to a phone.

SIXTY-FOUR

Owen Jefferson's cell phone rang awakening both him and his wife. Because of his status in homicide, these calls were not unusual, especially on a Sunday morning which naturally followed Saturday nights with its usual assortment of violent stupidity.

"Yeah, Jefferson," he croaked then cleared his throat.

"Owen, it's Dan Fielding. I'm at St. Andrews in Northeast. You'll want to get down here. I think your boy is back. It's the priest..."

"Father Brinkley," Jefferson said. "Shit. Is he posed?"

"Yeah, just like Jimmy Oliver and the others," Fielding said. It was Sgt. Dan Fielding who was first on the scene when Jimmy Oliver was found in the alley behind *Tooley's*. "You know where St. Andrews is?"

"Yeah, I'll be there," Jefferson said.

"I got CSU and the M.E. on the way."

"Okay, Dan. I'll be along."

After Jefferson ended the call his wife, Clarice asked, "What?"

"Howie Traynor's back. Maddy Rivers, a P.I. friend of Tony Carvelli, saw him last night or, at least thinks she did. Now we got another victim, Traynor's priest over at St. Andrews."

Jefferson took his time getting to the crime scene. The first thing he did was call Marcie Sterling and Tony Carvelli. He awakened both of them but figured if he could get an early call, why not share the misery?

By the time Jefferson arrived at the church, Marcie was already inside. Jefferson went in and found Marcie, an assistant M.E. and the CSU team at the front of the church.

Marcie was bent down in front of the body watching while the M.E. examined it. Jefferson stood back, hands in his pants' pockets as he surveyed the scene.

Father John was sitting on the floor, his head slumped forward, his cassock covered in blood. His back was against the oak altar, his arms spread, and hands nailed into the wood. He had a barbed wire crown and even from this distance, Jefferson could tell his fingers were crushed, his feet were bare, and his toes had been similarly mangled.

Marcie noticed her partner watching. She stood up, stepped back to him and said, "Traynor's back or we've got a copycat."

"It's him," Jefferson said. He then explained what had happened the night before.

"Why didn't you call me last night?" Marcie asked.

"Because I figured you were with Jeff Miller and I didn't want to bother you," he said.

"What makes you think I was with Jeff Miller?" she asked a little too defensively.

"You didn't think I knew?"

"No, maybe, I don't know. Oh shit, who else knows?"

"Well let's see," Jefferson began. "There's me and pretty much the entire police department."

A uniformed officer tapped Jefferson on the shoulder and told him Tony Carvelli was outside.

Jefferson and Marcie hurried down the aisle toward the front door. While they walked, Marcie whispered, "How long have you known?"

"Since day one. I'm a cop, remember? Relax, you're an adult, he's more or less an adult, you're entitled. It's okay. Besides, word is he's really hung," he said with a smile.

"Oh shut up!" she said as she slapped him on the shoulder. They walked a few more steps and just before they reached the door she said, "Besides, it's not true but, he'll do."

Carvelli was standing on the concrete steps leading up to the front door of the church. Jefferson looked around and saw at least two hundred people watching from across the street. It was a little after 7:00 and most of the crowd were parishioners who were there for the 7:00 a.m. Mass. Word of Father John's murder had leaked and quickly spread. Jefferson stopped on the top step and saw a couple of media vans pull up a block away.

"So much for keeping a lid on this," he muttered.

The two MPD detectives joined Carvelli who was sipping a large Caribou coffee, looking as dapper as ever.

"Is it our boy?" Carvelli asked.

"Looks like it," Jefferson answered. "Did you call Maddy Rivers and Marc Kadella?"

"Yeah, I did, had the pleasure of waking them both up. They're fine. I'll call them back when we're done here. Can I get in to take a look?"

"Sure, come on," Jefferson said.

Jefferson and Marcie spent the morning notifying every police department in the Metro area. The local media was all over the story and all over the MPD looking for information. The public relations office issued denials and warnings that it was too early to tell if the Crown of Thornes Killer was back. Ignoring the denials, the media ran with the story that it was the Crown of Thornes Killer. By the end of the day, every judge and a number of prosecutors were clamoring for police protection.

Because the police had done a good job of keeping Howie Traynor's name out of it, he was not named as a suspect. A couple of media people specifically asked the MPD about him but received firm denials.

By the end of the day, an exhausted Owen Jefferson was happy to be home.

While all of this was taking place, Howie Traynor was smugly watching the TV news from his motel room in Hudson, Wisconsin. Hudson is a small city on the St. Croix River. The river serves as a border between the two states and is barely twenty miles east of St. Paul. Howie could be back in Minneapolis in less than an hour.

Melinda Pace hurried down the front steps of the Lutheran church. She was in a hurry to get away from the AA meeting and a small crowd of people in the evening's group gathering in front along the sidewalk. Melinda went along with this farce to satisfy the station's higher-ups, but she really did not buy into it. The other people who attended she considered to be nothing but whining, simpering, pathetic losers and drunks with whom she had nothing in common. For their part, Melinda was a huge celebrity who was one of them and was so much nicer than her reputation portrayed.

Playing her role Melinda smiled and politely nodded at several of them as she walked toward the street. Most of them were smoking and Melinda also lit up while she walked.

Following her normal routine, she was parked on the street of the next block away from the church where the meetings were held. She was in a spot where none of the others would be, so they would not want to walk along with her. Plus, she could make a quick getaway.

Listening to the heels of her shoes clicking on the concrete sidewalk, all Melinda could think about was the silver flask filled with vodka in the car. She had arrived for the meeting before dark and the street lights were not turned on. Because she was thinking about her flask of vodka she failed to notice the streetlight next to her car was out.

Three feet from the driver's door Melinda hit the unlock button on her key fob. She reached for the door and Howie hit her in the ribs with his Taser. Melinda hit the asphalt face first and hard, immobilized and bewildered but still conscious. Before she even began to comprehend what was happening her mouth was taped shut, her hands tied together, and she was in the trunk of a car.

Howie Traynor, one hand on the trunk lid, tossed her purse in with her. A terrified Melinda Pace stared up at him, conscious, immobilized and finally comprehending the fate that awaited her.

"Hello, Melinda," Howie said grinning down at her. "I've been looking forward to meeting you."

Howie quietly closed the trunk lid and took a quick look around to see if anyone was watching. Satisfied he drove off down the dark, tree-lined street.

"Who found her?" Jefferson asked a uniformed MPD cop.

"A groundskeeper. He was out checking the course just before 6:00," the man answered.

Jefferson, the officer and Marcie Sterling were standing in the rough along the eleventh hole of the Columbia Golf Course. Melinda Pace was nailed to two small trees in an all too familiar pose. A CSU tech and an M.E., Clyde Marston, were examining the body. The entire area surrounding the scene had been roped off with yellow crime scene tape. A half dozen CSU people were searching for evidence while another dozen cops were milling about. A vehicle from the medical examiner's office was parked on the fairway nearby waiting to transport the body. Two CSU vehicles were there but everyone else had ridden in on golf carts. Jefferson turned at the sound of one approaching and saw the chief of police himself being driven toward them.

"Good morning, Chief," Jefferson and Marcie both said when Chief Sorenstad reached them.

The chief stood silently for a minute staring at the body. His driver came up behind him and Sorenstad said, to no one in particular, "This will create one helluva shitstorm. When something like this happens to one of their own, the media goes nuts about it. Same guy?" he asked Jefferson.

"We think so," Jefferson said.

"This Traynor nut job?"

"Probably."

"Jesus Christ," Sorenstad quietly said. "We had the sonofabitch and messed up the case against him. We'll all get crucified, pardon the pun," he added nodding toward the displayed corpse of Melinda Pace. "Find this sick bastard, Jefferson."

Before Jefferson could respond his phone rang. He looked at the I.D. and answered it. Jefferson listened to the caller, his face showing more and more concern as he did so.

"What?" Marcie asked.

Jefferson held up a finger to stop her and said, "I'll be there as quick as I can. The Chief's standing right here. I'll tell him."

Sorenstad and Marcie looked curiously at Jefferson. He ended the call, replaced the phone in his coat pocket and heavily sighed.

"We got another one, Chief. It's Bobby Conlin. Detective Bobby Conlin."

SIXTY-FIVE

Tony Carvelli parked the Camaro on the street one building down from his destination. He got out and walked the two hundred or so feet on the sidewalk and strolled across the asphalt entrance to the building. Tony saw the man he was there to meet, cleaning the limousine he drove for a living.

"Hey Jake," Tony said as he extended his hand to his friend, former MPD lieutenant, Jake Waschke.

The two men shook hands and Waschke said, "I was about to call you."

"You heard about Bobby?" Tony asked.

"Yeah," Waschke said as he tossed the towel he was holding into a laundry hamper. When he was released from prison, Jake's many friends around the Cities had a number of jobs lined up for him. Limo driving seemed like a sensible, easy way to merge back into society.

"How's this gig going?" Tony asked.

"You wouldn't believe it," Waschke smiled. "I'm making more money, working fewer hours and with less stress than I did as a cop. What about Bobby? What's going on there?" Waschke asked.

"It's Howie Traynor. He's back," Carvelli answered him.

"You're sure?"

"Yeah, Maddy Rivers saw him a couple nights ago. You remember Maddy, don't you?"

Waschke smiled and said, "Pretty hard to forget. Why Bobby?"

"I think because he was with us when we busted Traynor for the Lucille Benson murder. Remember? At the *East End,* Bobby was the one who hit him with the Taser..."

"And that psycho Traynor pulled the leads out of his chest, threw them back at him then busted his jaw," Waschke interrupted finishing the story. "What do you think, is he after us too?"

"Probably," Tony shrugged as if to say, let him try.

"I just remembered, the woman who was with us when we busted him, Helen Barkey..."

"She got married a few years back," Tony said. "She moved somewhere out west. She should be okay."

"Good. What are we going to do about this psycho?"

Tony nodded his head toward the building's exit and said, "I got an idea."

The two men walked out through the garage door toward the street. While they did, Maddy Rivers pulled up in her black Audi parked and joined them.

The three of them quietly conversed and after a few minutes, Waschke asked Maddy, "You sure about this? You could be working without a net," he told her.

"Yeah, I'm sure," she answered him. "I'll be okay."

"Is Conrad Hilton still around town," Jake asked Tony, referring to a man who was an expert at wiretapping and electronic surveillance systems.

"Yeah, in fact I talked to him this morning. I told him what we needed," Tony said.

"Does he know why?" Maddy asked.

"No," Tony answered her.

"Have you talked to the other guys yet?" Jake asked him.

"No, I wanted to talk to you first. You know these guys. If I'm in and you're in, they're in."

Waschke thrust his hands in the pockets of his pants. He stared up at the sky for a few seconds then began to stroll about deep in thought. While he did this, both Tony and Maddy leaned against the front of her car waiting.

A minute later he came back to them and said, "Is there any other way? Have we thought of everything?"

"I'm open to suggestions about what else to do and hell no we haven't thought of everything," Tony replied.

Waschke smiled a wry, nervous smile and said, "I can't think of anything better either."

Jake looked at Madeline again and asked, "You're sure about this?"

"I'll be fine, Jake. Yes, I'm sure," she replied.

Madeline was sitting at a table in the patio area of a hookup bar on West Lake Street in the Uptown area of Minneapolis. With her was Officer Karen Anderson. Between them they had received quite a few looks from the single guys in the semi-crowded establishment. The two women were unacquainted, so they made small talk about the difficulties of being female police officers.

Roughly forty-five minutes after being seated, a man from the bar approached them. Without invitation he grabbed an unoccupied chair from another table and sat down with them. By all appearances, the two women appeared quite annoyed by the unwanted intrusion. The man's name was Mitchell Cavanaugh, and like Maddy's companion, he was an MPD police officer.

He leaned forward and above the din of the bar, said, "I haven't noticed anyone out of the ordinary paying too much attention to you.

The problem is, you're getting a little too much and it's hard to spot anyone unusual."

Maddy said, "I'm going to slap you then get up and leave. Karen, you stay with Mitch and watch for anyone following me out."

True to her word, Maddy suddenly slapped Mitch across the face. Both he and Karen looked shocked while Maddy looked angry. As she stood up, grabbed her purse and fled quickly out the front door, several of the men at the bar, all too young for Maddy anyway, heartily laughed and made lewd comments.

A bearded man with dark glasses and hair over his ears briefly smiled at the sight. Howie Traynor enjoyed a clear view of the women and was hoping Maddy would leave by herself. She barely made it through the door when he slid off the barstool and casually followed her out. Unfortunately, at that exact same moment, at least eight other people left. Howie slipped out as just another person in the crowd.

When she arrived at the bar to set herself up as bait, Maddy deliberately parked her car in a remote lot two blocks away. After leaving the bar when she was approximately half way back to her car, she heard Mitch's voice come through the audio receiver in her ear. He told her about the crowd at the door that left right after her. Unconcerned, Maddy acknowledged the information and kept going.

Howie knew where she was parked and had a different route he could take to get there ahead of her. As soon as he was outside, he began jogging silently down the street to an adjacent alley. He broke into a sprint, got across Charles Avenue and was into the lot before she came into view. Howie ducked down between his car and another and waited for her in the dark, his Taser ready to go.

When Maddy received the news from Mitch Cavanaugh, something in her clicked. Somehow she knew Howie was in that crowd and slipped out unnoticed. Calmly, she opened her purse and put a hand inside it. She removed a small, metal cylinder and held it at her side.

Of course, Madeline knew how dangerous Howie was. She had a pistol in her purse but did not want to use it. Maddy had killed two people, both completely justified, but she was still going through some serious counseling over them. If she didn't have to shoot Howie, she wouldn't. Believing what she held in her hand would be sufficient, she went toward her car.

Strolling through the parking lot, she impressed herself with her lack of fear. Even though he likely left the bar after her, somehow she knew he was waiting for her. Three occupied parking spaces from her car, she sensed rather than heard, a movement coming from behind.

"He's here," she loudly said to be sure the mic she was wired to would pick it up. As she did so, she spun around, let her purse slip to the ground and snapped her right wrist to extend the metal baton she was holding.

Howie lunged at her, holding the Taser out to incapacitate her. Maddy swung the baton at his hand and hit the Taser, smashing it into a dozen pieces. Shocked at her sudden attack, Howie froze for a second, long enough for Maddy to swing again cracking him across the left elbow numbing his left arm.

"Ahhh! Goddamnit..." he yelled.

His left arm hung limply at his side and he swung a poorly aimed right hook at her. Maddy stepped into it, blocked the punch with her left arm and drilled his left knee with the baton. His knee started to collapse, and she hit him two more times across the rib cage, fracturing four or five and across his right wrist. He went down on one knee, puzzled at the ferocity of Maddy's attack while looking into her eyes.

By this time a Ford van was screeching past the parked cars coming straight at them, the lights from the van illuminating the scene.

Howie managed to get up on both feet. His left arm still hung limply, his knee slightly buckled and the pain in his ribs excruciating. The van came to a halt just as Howie said, "Who are you?"

Madeline was standing silhouetted by the lights. Her feet were slightly apart, her right hand holding the baton at her side. She looked and felt absolutely calm and totally unconcerned. The van's doors started to open and Maddy took a half step toward Howie with her left foot, pivoting on it, she spun completely around and drove her right foot into the exposed chest of the helpless Howie Traynor. The kick took him completely off of his feet, flat onto his back and his head banged off the asphalt surface.

Tony Carvelli, Jake Waschke and two other men were out of the van by this time. Maddy stepped over to Howie and straddled his prostate body. She looked down into his barely conscious eyes, snarled and said, "Your worst nightmare. That's who I am, asshole."

The men from the car quickly gagged him, handcuffed his hands and covered Howie's head with a hood. Ignoring his obvious pain, they picked him up and literally tossed him through the side door onto the vehicle's floor.

Carvelli reached Madeline as she was retrieving her purse. "You okay?" he asked with obvious concern.

"Yeah, I'm fine. Now what? What about him?"

"Go home, sweetheart," Tony said and gave her cheek a light kiss. "You've done enough. I'm just glad you're okay."

Maddy looked at Carvelli and said, "So, don't ask questions I don't want to know the answer to, right?"

"Something like that," Carvelli said.

"Tony be careful. I don't want you to get into any trouble."

"Don't worry, I won't. Neither will anyone else. Go home and relax."

SIXTY-SIX

Two nights later, Jake Waschke and three retired cop friends pulled away from a private dock on Mille Lacs Lake. It was after 11:00 p.m. and they had a chore to perform.

Mille Lacs is a two hundred square mile lake located in central Minnesota. It is approximately ninety miles north of the Cities. The short distance makes it one of the most popular resort areas in the state. Normally on a June night, the lake would be semi-busy with fishermen angling for walleyes. Tonight, there were severe storm warnings for the area which cut the boat traffic down to almost nothing. No one wanted to be out on this large body of water with a windy thunderstorm hammering you.

The three ex-cops with Waschke were the same men who helped Carvelli do surveillance on Howie Traynor. Tom Evans was driving the boat, a twenty-three-foot Crestliner with a 200 hp Mercury outboard. The boat's owner, a retired MPD captain, had a half million-dollar summer place on the lake courtesy of his wife's money. The ex-captain and his wife were conveniently away for a few days. Without asking questions, he agreed to the use of the house and boat.

Evans pushed the accelerator down and the big Merc roared to life making the boat jump. The lake was starting to become quite choppy as the wind picked up. Looking west in the direction they headed an ominous dark mass was flashing lightning as it moved toward them. An occasional dull thud of thunder could be heard over the noise of the outboard.

The boat bounced along over the lake's waves, some getting as high as two feet and growing. When they had traveled almost two miles out, Waschke tapped Evans on the shoulder and yelled above the noise, "This should do."

Evans backed the engine down and the boat cruised to a stop. He swiveled around in the captain's chair while his three companions stood up.

Normally this particular boat had six passenger seats. Before setting out, the men had removed two of them to accommodate their cargo.

Steadying themselves on the side of the boat, two of the men, Dan Sorenson and Franklin Washington moved into position. Waschke knelt down on one knee and ripped off the duct tape covering the mouth of Howie Traynor.

"You can't do this!" Traynor immediately whined. "It ain't right. You're cops. You can't do this. Please, I'm begging you, don't…"

350

"Ssssh, ssssh," Waschke quietly whispered and put a finger to Howie's lips. "You should've thought about this a long-time guy, tough guy."

While Waschke taunted Howie Traynor, Sorenson, kneeling at Howie's feet, checked the single chain wrapped around Howie's ankles. Attached to the chain were two forty-pound kettle balls. The chain was also wrapped around Howie's waist and hands and secured with a lock.

"They're good," Sorenson solemnly declared as Tom Evans knelt down next to him.

Waschke looked at the three men while Howie continued to whine and cry. Waschke asked, "Any second thoughts? Now's the time."

"No," each man emphatically said.

"How deep is it here?" Waschke asked Evans.

"The depth gauge had it about twenty-five feet," Evans answered.

"Nice night for a little swim, don't you think?" Waschke said to Howie.

By now, consigned to his fate, Howie had calmed down. Defiantly he said, "I'll see all you sonsabitches in hell."

With that, Waschke replaced the duct tape over his mouth. Sorenson grabbed his feet, Washington took the shoulders, Waschke his mid-section and Evans the two kettle balls.

The four men heaved him up onto the gunwale of the boat. Sorenson edged aside so Evans could toss the kettle balls into the water. At the very last second, before they pushed him in, Waschke said, "Take a real deep breath dickhead. You'll have to hold it for a long time."

Howie held up both hands extended his middle fingers and the ex-cops sent him over the side. The water splashed into the boat and hit all four of them.

Dan Sorenson reached into his shirt pocket and removed a small key. He dropped it into the water where Howie had gone down, laughed and said, "Good luck, shithead."

A few seconds later, the men were back in their seats, Evans had the boat turned around and was heading back to shore.

Howie Traynor sank like a stone. The kettle balls attached to his ankles dragged him to the bottom, through the tall weeds in less than two seconds. Instead of panic or fear, Howie felt at ease, serene even. He always knew his life would end violently and that he was not destined for old age and a peaceful end in a hospital bed. Now that it was here, his mind cleared, and he decided to enjoy the experience.

His feet hit the muddy bottom first and his shoulders a brief moment after. He settled into the weeds and mud to await the end when a tiny object hit him in the face. Reflexively his hands shot up, despite the chain, and he snatched the piece of metal off his right eye.

Remaining calm he held onto it and a couple of seconds later he realized what it was. It was a key that must have been tossed into the water by his would-be executioners.

Had it been mid-day, there would be very little light at this depth. At night, almost midnight, Howie literally could not see his hand in front of his face. The calm Howie felt after accepting and awaiting his fate was instantly replaced with near panic. His conscious brain immediately began to signal his heart and lungs that time was running out. Now that he held the means of escape, a reprieve from his watery grave, his will to survive kicked in.

He found the lock quickly enough and even managed to insert the key without a problem. Howie clicked open the lock and that's when his problems began. The chain was wrapped around his wrist three times and his waist twice. While the clock kept ticking and his oxygen starved brain started to scream, he struggled to uncoil the chain. What seemed like several minutes but was less than thirty seconds, he got his hands free and the chain removed from his body.

While holding his breath, his lungs aching to exhale Howie still had to free his feet. He reached through the weeds and tried to kick his legs free at the same time. The eighty pounds of weights were too much to allow his feet to move. Feeling his way through the mud, weeds and darkness, he found the chain around his ankles. It was wrapped around each one twice and it seemed to take an eternity to get his feet free.

Finally, as his lungs began to involuntarily push the air out in an effort to replace it, Howie began his ascent. On his way up, he removed the tape over his mouth and he could feel his body, deprived of oxygen, literally giving up. He started to lose consciousness, the air in his lungs completely gone and with his final conscious thought he kicked his legs one last time and broke into the night.

Gasping, coughing and spitting up lake water, Howie gulped down the fresh air until his head cleared and his brain went into a mode of relief. For the next minute he tread water ignoring the pain in his ribs, knee, elbow and wrist from the beating he had taken. He finally became calm, relaxed and oriented.

Howie realized he was looking directly at the boat he was thrown from, could see its lights off in the distance a mile or so away. Howie was a strong man and a strong swimmer. It was the one sport he excelled at and enjoyed as a teenager. Despite his injuries, the fractured ribs, elbow and knee, a two-mile swim was easily manageable.

"I once told you I would piss on your grave," he quietly said bobbing in the water and watching the boat head toward shore. "Looks like I'll keep that promise. And I'll have a real good time with that P.I. bitch."

Howie's ears were filled with water and had not popped yet from the pressure of the depth he came from. In addition, the wind had picked up and the waves were getting higher and more frequent. The wind and the waves were hitting him right in the face and he never heard it. Somehow he sensed it, like an unexplained presence and he turned his head a little too late.

A vehicle traveling thirty miles per hour, even a boat through water, will cover approximately twenty-two feet per second. By the time Howie saw the pontoon coming directly at his face, it was barely five feet away. He didn't even have time to blink.

The boat was a sixty thousand-dollar, twenty-eight-foot luxury pontoon with three aluminum pontoon logs. Each pontoon had a metal strap overlapping the prow welded to hold the pontoon closed and water tight. This strap also formed a sharp, hard, metal edge on the point of the pontoon log. The owner's son and his seven friends were hurrying across the big lake in an effort to beat the storm.

The center aluminum log hit Howie squarely in the face. His head was tilted back, the only reflexive action he had time for. The force shattered his chin, dislocated his lower jaw-bone and drove it back under his ears. It smashed most of his teeth, ripped his nose off, fractured his forehead and removed a good-sized piece of the skin of his face.

The force of the blow drove him back underwater, directly beneath the pontoon. Unconscious if not already dead, Howie's back was arched, his head tilted backwards and what remained of his face barely inches below the pontoon. Both arms were extended as if nailed to a cross as the air in his lungs caused his body to rise. Howie's forehead bumped against the back end of the pontoon less than a second after he was initially struck.

The big boat was powered by a 300 hp outboard motor. At thirty miles an hour, the propeller would spin between thirty and thirty-five times per second. If Howie's eyes were able to see, they would have the briefest of moments to register the sight of the whirling four blades an instant before they hit him. With the precision of a razor, the propeller cleanly removed what remained of what had recently been the face of a monster.

"What was that?' one of the girls on the boat asked the driver, the owner's son Colin McIlroy.

"Hit a log," Colin calmly replied. "The motor sounds fine. It didn't hurt anything. We've got to get in."

SIXTY-SEVEN

The three men were in a hurry to get to their favorite early morning spot for walleye fishing. It was before 6 a.m. and last night's big storm would have the fish moving about and biting. Or at least so they believed. Every fisherman had a theory about when and how to fish and every one of them is right. And probably wrong, too.

The lake was calm and the ride smooth as the Alumacraft fishing boat sliced through the water. It was a cool morning and the sun was already appearing over the shoreline trees to their left as they headed north.

Buster, the forty-year-old son of the boat's driver, was seated in the bow. He sipped coffee from a travel mug as he stared out over the lake. A quarter of a mile ahead, slightly to portside, Buster noticed a large object floating on the surface. When they were within a hundred yards, he could see it was human clothing.

"Jesus, Dad, slow down," he yelled back to his father while pointing at the object. "Over there, something in the water. It might be a body."

Mille Lacs County Sheriff Rory Boone was getting ready to leave his house when his cell phone rang. Sitting on the stairs off the living room of his home, one boot on, one boot off, he took the call. Knowing the office would not bother him this early unless it was important, Rory was not surprised at what they had.

He listened carefully, asked a few questions then ended the call. His wife of thirty years, standing in the kitchen doorway wearing a house dress and pink slippers asked, "A floater?"

"Looks like," Rory answered her while forcing on the second boot. He stood and continued by saying, "Over by Isle. Some fishermen found him. The M.E. is on the way. I'll let him fish him out. I'll call you later," he said as he kissed her and gave her a brief hug.

A drowning on Mille Lacs was not an everyday occurrence but was hardly unusual either. The on-duty sheriff's deputies that would be at the scene were both experienced and could handle it. There was no need for the sheriff himself to drive thirty miles to see it.

Ten minutes after settling into his chair at the sheriff's office in Milaca, Sheriff Boone received a phone call from the county coroner, Albert Lindgren. He quickly told the sheriff about what was found in the water and the condition of Howie's face.

"Boat accident?" Boone asked.

"Looks like," Lindgren replied. "Looks like the propeller hit him in the face and shaved it clean off. Teeth, face, everything gone. His mother wouldn't be able to identify him."

"What about fingerprints?"

"He wasn't in the water too long. We should be able to get good prints," Lindgren answered him. "I'm taking him in now. I'll let you know what I find."

"Is Hampton there?" Boone asked referring to one of his deputies.

"Yeah," Lindgren said.

"Have him get fingerprints. We'll run them right away. It's odd because we haven't had anyone call in about anyone missing."

"Will do, Sheriff," Lindgren said. "I'll call you later."

Around 10:30 Charlie Hampton, the deputy who took Howie's fingerprints, rapped on the sheriff's door and went in.

"What do you have, Charlie?" Boone asked.

"You need to take a look at this, Boss," Hampton said handing a document to the sheriff.

Boone, seated at his desk, took it from Hampton, read the name and with a puzzled look said, "Howard Traynor. Why does that sound familiar?"

"Run him on Google," Hampton said.

Two minutes later Boone said to his deputy, "I'll call the state police and they can call Minneapolis. They'll want to know about this ASAP."

At 2:00 p.m. Owen Jefferson and Marcie Sterling pulled into the parking lot of the Fairview Clinic in Milaca, Minnesota, the county seat of Mille Lacs County. Howie's body was taken to the clinic for a preliminary report before being transferred to the coroner's office. Due to the population size of Mille Lacs County, the coroner for the county was in Ramsey, a small city in Anoka County which is part of the Twin Cities Metro Area.

Sheriff Boone, having spoken to Jefferson less than a minute ago, was leaning on his Ford Explorer waiting for them. Jefferson parked and the three of them greeted each other. On their way inside, the sheriff filled them in on what he knew and Howie's condition.

Boone led them to the exam room where Howie, or what was left of him, was being kept. He was lying on a stainless-steel table, naked and covered by a white sheet. Dr. Lindgren was there and warned them about the grisly sight before removing the sheet from Howie's missing face.

Two minutes later, all three of the law enforcement officers were grateful to be back in the parking lot breathing fresh air.

"You ever see that before?" Jefferson asked Boone.

"Yeah, we get car accidents and boat accidents once in a while that can be pretty awful. That's the worst I've seen though," the sheriff said.

"You okay?" Jefferson asked Marcie.

She was leaning against a car and the color in her face was returning. She nodded her head a couple of times then said, "Yeah, I'm okay, I think."

Jefferson turned back to Boone and said, "I've been in homicide for over ten years and I've seen some awful things people do to each other but that..."

"Yeah, I know," Boone said. "Right now, it looks like a boat accident. What do you think?"

Jefferson thought it over for a minute then said, "You're sure about the finger prints?"

"Yeah, we ran them three times. And, the body size fits. What was he doing up here out on the lake?"

"I couldn't tell you," Jefferson said. He paused for a moment then continued by saying, "Well Sheriff, it's your case. I can't tell you what to do. But, my advice is if it looks like a boat accident, if the autopsy confirms that, then close your case. Call his parents. I'll get you their information. If they want the body, okay. If not, dig a hole, put him in it and walk away. No one is very interested in finding out what happened to him. But, you do what you think is best, Sheriff. If you need anything, feel free to call."

At 3:50 that same afternoon, Carolyn buzzed Marc over the office intercom. She told him there was a call from Maddy Rivers for him and Maddy said it was important. Marc, of course, knew that Howie Traynor was back and like everyone else, was on edge about it.

"What's up?" he asked Maddy.

"I just got off the phone with Gabriella. You should turn on your TV set at 4:00 o'clock and catch the *Court Reporter*."

"Melinda Pace is dead. Who's doing the show?"

"I'll talk to you later," Maddy coyly answered him.

At 4:00 o'clock, the entire office was gathered around the television. Marc told everyone about Maddy's call and they were all curious to find out what was up.

"Good afternoon. My name is Gabriella Shriqui, and this is *The Court Reporter*," Gabriella began the show by announcing.

Gabriella went on to explain that the station had decided to honor Melinda Pace by continuing her show. Gabriella was honored, so she said, to be selected to host the show and could only hope to maintain the high standards of journalism that Melinda had established.

She explained that the show was being broadcast live because they had received the news about Howie Traynor moments ago. His shocking death was the lead story and her guest was the lead MPD detective for the Crown of Thornes case, Owen Jefferson.

When the broadcast ended, Marc placed a call to Gabriella and was put right through.

"So, you got the show. Congratulations," he said.

"Thanks. When can I have you on?"

"We'll see. The reason I called was to tell you how impressed I was that you kept a straight face prattling that nonsense about Melinda's journalistic standards. Please tell me you'll do better than that."

Gabriella laughed and said, "I think I can do better than that."

Thank you for your patronage. I hope you enjoyed Certain Justice
Dennis Carstens

Feel free to email me at: dcarstens514@gmail.com

Also Available on Amazon

A Marc Kadella Legal Mystery No. 5

Personal Justice

ONE

Mackenzie Sutherland followed the wheeled aluminum bier down the center aisle of St. Mark's Catholic Church in St. Paul. It carried her husband's coffin toward the church's front entrance on Dayton Avenue. The bier was guided by six young men, all of whom were sons of old friends of her husband.

She walked slowly down the aisle loosely holding the arm of her personal lawyer, Carter Laine. Her face bore an impassive expression; appropriate for a funeral. Anyone looking at her through the black veil attached to her black hat and covering her face would think nothing of the look she wore.

Behind her, having been uncomfortably seated on the same pew with Mackenzie, were her three stepchildren. Robert, the eldest, and his wife, Alison sat with their three unruly children. Then came the youngest, Hailey and her latest *oh so cool, chic and hip bohemian-artist* boyfriend, Chazz. Bringing up the rear of the dysfunctional family was the middle child, another son, thirty-eight-year-old Adam. Of the three of them, Adam was easily the most useless. His problems with drugs and alcohol made gainful employment problematic at best, if he had ever been so inclined toward self sufficiency in the first place.

Mackenzie's husband, William 'Bill' Sutherland, had been a well-known, respected business man for almost forty years. Bill and his first wife, Beth, had worked and sacrificed to build a chain of successful grocery stores. Three months before his death he opened the thirtieth and final store in Eau Claire, Wisconsin. Bill had always treated his employees well, in fact a little too well judging how it was affecting the company's bottom line. However, because of this there was not an empty seat in church.

359

When they exited the church, Carter Laine gently led Mackenzie toward the Cadillac limousine first in line behind the black hearse. While the casket was being loaded into the back of the big vehicle for Bill's last trip, Mackenzie took a moment to look up at the sky.

March in Minnesota can be less than pleasant depending on how long winter decided to linger. The driver of Mackenzie's limo stepped aside to allow Carter to open the door for her. As he did so, a slight involuntary shiver went through Mackenzie.

"Dreary day," she remarked as she entered the car.

She slid across the seat to allow her escort to get in next to her and close the door. While they sat waiting for the other guests to get in line and form the procession, Mackenzie pushed the button to raise the car's privacy glass behind the driver.

"I'll be glad when this is over," she quietly said.

"You're doing fine," Carter said patting her right hand with his left. Mackenzie had placed the hand on the seat between them and Carter held it as if to comfort her.

"Stop," she firmly admonished as she removed his hand and placed hers in her lap. "I don't need consoling, Carter. I need this business to be done."

Despite his marriage, Carter Laine was thoroughly smitten with the very fetching Mackenzie Sutherland. Even dressed in widow black she was still a fine-looking woman. Hiding his disappointment at her admonishment he said "Soon, Mackenzie, just a few more days. Everything is arranged."

"I know," she sighed. "I'm just tired of his damn kids bugging me about money." Mackenzie turned her head to look out the passenger window as the rain began to lightly fall. While watching the rain streak the glass, waiting for the procession to start up to the cemetery, a slight smile curved her mouth upward.

While the two of them were silently chauffeured to the cemetery, Mackenzie retraced the route she traveled to reach this destination. Now, in her early forties her crusade began almost twenty years ago.

Mackenzie Lange, her original maiden name, graduated from the University of Minnesota in her mid-twenties with a marketing degree. A very attractive young woman, borderline beautiful, Mackenzie had little trouble finding employment. She quickly learned she could use her looks, charm and intelligence to excel at sales and she found she liked it. There was something about manipulating people to do what she wanted that gave her a rush.

After a few years, just before turning thirty, Mackenzie moved to St Petersburg, Florida. She had saved enough money, so she could live without a job for at least two years if necessary. Having done her research before leaving to move to Florida, she knew exactly where she would work and in six months the job was hers; new car sales at Bauer Cadillac. It was also the location of the corporate headquarters for Bauer Enterprises, the owner of twelve car dealerships in the Tampa-St. Petersburg metro area.

Mackenzie, using her smooth legs and ample cleavage, shot to the top of the sales board in less than three months. It wasn't long before she caught the attention of the company owner, Joseph Bauer, whose office was in the same building.

Immediately smitten with his beautiful young super saleswoman, within two weeks they were dating. Three months later the angry first Mrs. Bauer was filing for divorce and three days after it was finalized Mackenzie became the second Mrs. Joseph Bauer.

Along with a very profitable business, Mackenzie became a stepmother for the first time. Joseph had two sons, Samuel a mere two months younger than Mackenzie and David, the spoiled Mama's boy of the family.

Everything went exactly as Mackenzie had envisioned it. Having been married to a Jewish Princess for over thirty years, the sexual wild-ride that Mackenzie brought to the conjugal bed turned Joseph into a pliable puppy.

Suddenly, a month after changing his Will, which cut-out both sons, Joseph was found slumped over his desk. At the ripe old age of fifty-five, without any warning, his heart gave out. Three months later the grieving widow sold the business for seventeen million dollars. The amount was probably half what it was worth, but she wanted a quick sale.

The four-million-dollar beach front house was mortgaged to the max. Since her name was not on any of it, Mackenzie did a quick deed in lieu of foreclosure and she was on her way back to the Midwest.

During her marriage to Joseph Bauer, Mackenzie had become acquainted with an old college friend of her late husband. They had socialized several times and Mackenzie had taken every opportunity to flirt and flatter the well-to-do widower. Of course, when Joseph died suddenly this friend, Robert Hays, had flown immediately to Tampa-St. Pete to help the poor widow and console her through her time of grief and help handle the estate proceedings. Although Mackenzie required no help or grief consoling, she was all too happy to let him do it. By the time she cashed out and moved to Milwaukee where he lived Ken Hayes, soon to be husband number two, had been reeled in and landed.

Hays, whose first wife had killed herself while driving drunk several years before, was a partner in a mid-size investment firm. In good times and bad, bull and bear markets and even through recessions, the firm made money. The firm's clients might not have always made money, but commissions were always paid in good times and bad.

Mackenzie had done her due diligence and had a fairly accurate estimate of the man's net worth. Knowing she had him hooked, for appearances, Mackenzie played the part of the grieving widow for almost a year. Unknown to poor Ken Hayes, she even began scouting out the man who would be husband number three.

Almost exactly a year after the death of Joseph Bauer, Mackenzie was the new Mrs. Kenneth Hayes. Along with the ring came a six-bedroom, seven bath home with both an indoor and outdoor pool on the shores of Lake Michigan.

Being married to Joe Bauer had been easy. Bauer had little interest in socializing which left Mackenzie with time to do what she wanted. Ken Hayes was another matter entirely. Being a partner in the firm required a constant stream of entertaining well heeled existing and potential clients. If she wasn't planning an event in the lakeshore home, they were going to one at someone else's. And, as if that wasn't boring enough, Ken was heavily involved in the state Democratic Party. Being apolitical Mackenzie could not have been less interested in any of it. She was also finding out Milwaukee and her husband were about as interesting as warm oatmeal. To top it all off, the cherry on the sundae, were the three dull, useless progeny. The oldest, a married daughter Carol, was a year older than Mackenzie; a son, Kenneth Jr., was a few years younger and the youngest was a spoiled party girl, Faye.

The marriage lasted until at death they did part, not quite eighteen months after the wedding. The Milwaukee police found Ken slumped over the wheel of his Mercedes on the side of the freeway. A quick autopsy revealed a sudden and unexpected heart attack followed by cremation less than forty-eight hours later.

Of course, a few days after the memorial service, when the Will was read, Mackenzie was shocked (she almost fainted) to find Ken had recently changed the Will. He had left fifty thousand dollars to each of his children and the rest to his loving bride, Mackenzie. In addition, there was a three-million-dollar life insurance policy the firm held on each of its partners. The three million was used to buy out the stunned, grieving young widow from any claim in the firm. The final tally was a little over fifteen million, including the house. Shortly after, Mackenzie who was still only thirty-six, moved to Chicago.

Target number three was an old money Chicagoan by the name of Wendell Cartwright. Wendell Cartwright was the great-grandson of a Chicago Robber Baron, Philemon Cartwright. Fortunately for Wendell, Great Granddad had amassed a fortune the old-fashioned way; by ruthlessly crushing any potential competition. At the turn of the twentieth century the old crook was the principal owner of the Chicago Stockyards and almost one-third of the real estate in what would become downtown Chicago.

When he turned twenty-one, Wendell's trust fund became available with almost one-hundred million dollars in it. During the next forty plus years, Wendell had managed to reduce it to approximately forty million by the time he met McKenzie. Wendell had a definite weakness for the ladies and the good life.

Mackenzie would be wife number five. Wendell's four ex-wives were all living quite well on the alimony payments they received each month. In addition, there were two adult children to support. The first child, a forty-year-old woman from his first marriage named Dorothy, was about to divorce husband number three, a twenty-eight-year-old biker who had introduced her to the joy of methamphetamines.

Wendell also had a son; a thirty-three-year-old named Phillip by wife number two. Despite an excellent education provided by Daddy, Phillip was all but totally useless as a human being. Bothering with employment had never been high on Phillip's to do list. Why should it? The example dear old Dad had set for him had done its job. Phillip was following right in Daddy's footsteps and Dad kept the monthly checks rolling.

All of them, four ex-wives, two adult progeny and Wendell's profligate lifestyle were totally dependent upon the trust money. Because of the way the trust was set up, Wendell could not make lump sum payments to everyone and be done with them. Instead, they all would live off of monthly payments until Wendell's death at which time the trust's remaining principal would be paid out to the named beneficiaries.

Within six months of relocating to the north side of Chicago, Wendell Cartwright was wrapped around Mackenzie's little finger. Wendell was absolutely convinced that the over-sexed Mackenzie was his longed-for soulmate. Less than a month after Mackenzie's thirty-eighth birthday, husband number three was discovered in bed dead from a massive heart attack. A perfunctory autopsy, a quick cremation and a shocked young widow was forty million dollars richer.

During her brief marriage Mackenzie had come to know the ex-wives, the two children and the amount each of them were being paid every month. When the Will was read, the exes and the kids discovered that the spigot had been shut off. On the surface Mackenzie appeared shocked and assured them she would do what she could to take care of them. All the while thinking that bankrupting this gang of leeches was the best part of being married to the old fool.

Lawsuits were filed by all of them. Because the divorces were set up with no provision for securing the alimony payments, the lawsuits would be eventually dismissed. Wendell's responsibilities died with him. And to be clear that leaving all of them out of the estate was not an oversight, he made provision in the Will that each were to receive the sum of one hundred dollars.

The local media had a field day with it. The story had everything the public could want, and they ate it up; a young wife, a rich old man, a huge fight over millions of dollars. Unfortunately for Mackenzie, her picture was in the news at least weekly and it was not long before an enterprising reporter tracked her back to Milwaukee. Just about the time the death of her previous husband came to light, the liquidation of the Cartwright estate was finalized. Once that was completed, Mackenzie disappeared to Europe for six months before coming home to St. Paul.

TWO

The drive to the cemetery, even with the motorcycle police escorts, took almost thirty minutes. Mackenzie made a mental note to give the two motorcyclists an extra two hundred dollars each because of the rain. It was a cold, wet, miserable day to be on a motorcycle. The long procession snaked its way through the Catholic cemetery in Mendota Heights. The hearse finally stopped near an open area alongside Augusta Lake. Bill Sutherland had purchased a quarter acre plot overlooking the lake expecting the entire family to eventually be buried there.

A 20 x 20 awning had been set up over the gravesite. A large marble angel resembling the Virgin Mary faced the street in front of the plot. It was set on a concrete base with the name SUTHERLAND prominently displayed.

The chauffer parked and quickly hurried around the limo to open the door for his passengers.

"You okay?" Carter asked Mackenzie.

"Yes, Carter, I'm fine," she quietly answered through the black veil.

The chauffer had a large, black umbrella open and handed it to Carter Laine. He held it over Mackenzie as she exited the car. She took his arm and he guided her to her seat under the awning.

The fifty chairs under the shelter quickly filled up and at least another two hundred people stood in the light rain. The Sutherland children sat in the front next to Mackenzie. She had always been kind to them and they to her; each masking the reality that they despised each other.

Being a Navy veteran, Bill's coffin was draped with an American flag. The casket was centered over a hole next to Bill's first wife, Elisabeth, the mother of his children. Beth, as she was known had died four years ago from cancer. Mackenzie had never met her, and it was obvious the children all resented Mackenzie marrying their Dad.

When the priest had finished, and the service was completed, one of the pall bearers brought the folded flag and handed it to Mackenzie. Holding the flag out she stepped over to the oldest son Bob and held it out to him.

"I think your Dad would want you to have this," Mackenzie said.

Startled by this sudden and unexpected display of empathy, Bob could only mutter his thanks, all the while Mackenzie was thinking, *don't thank me yet, that's all you're going to get.*

Three days later, still clothed in stylish black, Mackenzie took a chair in front of Carter Laine's desk. She was a half-hour early for the appointed time to read the Will of her most recent dearly departed husband.

"It's not necessary for you to be here," Carter reiterated for at least the fourth time. He had taken his chair behind the glass-topped desk and was trying to avoid the sight of Mackenzie's crossed legs.

"I know, Carter," she answered him. "I told you, I want to see their faces."

"Why?"

"That's not your concern," Mackenzie icily told him. "Is everything ready?"

"Yes, including the security guard," Carter replied.

"That won't be necessary..."

"I'm taking the precaution anyway. People can get pretty worked up over these things."

Barely twenty minutes later Carter's secretary buzzed him to let them know the Sutherland's were waiting in the conference room. Carter thanked her and a minute later he opened the conference room door for Mackenzie and the two of them joined the three people already present.

The younger ones, Hailey and Adam, were already seated. Bob was pouring himself a glass of water from a carafe on a credenza. Before the door finished closing behind them, a serious looking man in a dark business suit came into the room. Without a word he sat in one of the chairs along the back wall as if to observe.

Mackenzie smiled slightly at her stepchildren and pleasantly said hello. Carter took the chair at the head of the table, Mackenzie sat in the one to his immediate right. All three of Bill Sutherland's children made a point of ignoring their stepmother as Bob took the first chair to Carter's left.

"We may as well get right at it," Carter began looking at the three children. "Your father came here and secretly changed his Will three months ago, unknown to his wife, Mackenzie."

"I don't believe that," Hailey said glaring at Mackenzie.

Mackenzie leaned forward, her forearms on the table top and her hands folded. She stared right back at Hailey and said, "I knew you wouldn't believe it but it's true. I had no knowledge of it."

"It's true," Carter continued. "He swore me and the senior partner who served him to secrecy."

"We're about to get bent over here, aren't we?" Adam said looking back and forth between Mackenzie and her lawyer.

"Not by me," Mackenzie quietly replied.

"Let's have it," Bob said holding up a hand to cut off his younger brother.

Carter cleared his throat then said, "First of all, you need to know that there is a 'no contest' provision in the Will. What that means is if you contest the Will and lose, you get nothing.

"Your father left each of you the cash gift of one hundred thousand dollars. The residue of the estate, including the house on Crocus Hill and all of the personal property goes to his wife, Mackenzie."

"That's it? A hundred grand each! This is bullshit…" Adam yelled.

"Shut up, dummy," Hailey snapped at Adam. "We still own ten percent of the business. That's worth at least three or four million."

"What you have," Carter continued while Mackenzie sat quietly waiting for the hammer to fall, "is twenty thousand shares which was a gift from your father."

"Yes, we know," Bob said. "We each hold ten percent of the common stock."

"Yes, except, the gift provision provided for the company to repurchase those shares, whenever it wanted to do so and at its sole discretion for par value at any time. Par value was established as one dollar per share," Carter said looking directly at Bob. "Your father never changed this."

"What the hell does that mean?" Adam yelled. "She can buy the goddamn stock back for a buck a share? That's bullshit!"

While Adam said this, his brother and sister stared at Mackenzie who sat with an impassive expression yet thoroughly enjoying the show.

"My parents worked their ass off for forty years growing a chain of grocery stores into a successful business. Then you come along and steal it. You fucking bitch!" Bob said, his voice rising in anger. "First you murder my father then…"

"Stop!" Carter said. "You had better be careful making allegations like that."

While he said this, he noticed out of the corner of his eye the man along the wall stand up and step behind Bob. The man stood there, his hands folded in front of himself.

"Bob, I know you're upset but your father had a heart attack. There was an autopsy…" Mackenzie started to say.

"You bitch," Hailey snarled. "We all know you did it…"

"And if I find out how, I'll get you for it," Bob said as he stood up.

Carter held up his left hand to stop the silent security man from interceding. "That sounds like a threat." Carter said.

"A promise," Bob viciously retorted. Carter Laine stood and faced Bob Sutherland. In his hand he held three envelopes, one for each of the Sutherland children. In each one was a copy of the Will, the stock gift document and a check in the amount of one hundred twenty thousand dollars. He handed them out and without another word, the three of the Sutherland children, obviously steaming, stomped out of the conference room followed by the security guard who escorted them to the elevator.

"That went well," Mackenzie smiled after the room emptied.

"Did you enjoy it?" Carter asked as he was picking up the papers he had placed on the table.

"Not as much as I thought I would, but, enough," she replied. "What about the sale of the company?"

"You just destroyed that family…"

"The sale of the company?" Mackenzie repeated.

"Everything is set. The contract will be sent by messenger to their lawyers this afternoon. The money will be transferred into your account at Ameriprise within forty-eight hours. They're getting a bargain…"

"We've been through this," Mackenzie sternly interrupted her lawyer. "Twenty-seven million is plenty. I told you, I didn't want to drag this out for a year for another five to ten million more. Let me know if you need me for anything else," she continued as the two of them stood to leave. "Oh, and by the way, I didn't do anything to that family. Their father did it." And, she thought, *they didn't get anything they did not deserve.*

Made in the USA
Middletown, DE
05 August 2021